Praise for the Cedar Cove novels of Debbie Macomber

"The Cedar Cove series [is] a delight."
—*RT Book Reviews* on *1105 Yakima Street*

"The characters are well rounded and well thought out, they have issues they work on and change during the telling of their story. Fans of the series will be amply satisfied."
—*RT Book Reviews* on *1022 Evergreen Place*

"Returning to Cedar Cove is always enjoyable. Macomber deftly combines sweet romance and a breath of suspense without losing the homespun charm that's been delighting readers for years."
—*RT Book Reviews* on *92 Pacific Boulevard*

"Macomber does a wonderful job of bringing us up to date on favorite residents, and flawlessly introduces us to new characters. [She leaves] readers anxious for…a return visit to a wonderful town."
—*A Romance Review* on *8 Sandpiper Way*

"[This book's] small-town charm is virtually guaranteed to please."
—*Publishers Weekly* on *74 Seaside Avenue*

"Readers new to Macomber's considerable narrative charms will have no problem picking up the story, while loyal fans are in for a treat."
—*Booklist* on *6 Rainier Drive*

"Debbie Macomber is a skilled storyteller."
—*Publishers Weekly* on *50 Harbor Street*

DEBBIE MACOMBER

1105 Yakima Street

mira

mira

Recycling programs
for this product may
not exist in your area.

ISBN-13: 978-0-7783-0789-1

1105 Yakima Street

For questions and comments about the quality of this book, please contact us at CustomerService@Harlequin.com.

Harlequin.com

Printed in U.S.A.

Also available from Debbie Macomber and MIRA Books

1105 YAKIMA STREET

To my very special cousins
Teresa Seibert
and
Cherie Adler

One

Sunshine splashed into the windows of the Bremerton waterfront café. Rachel Peyton sat in a booth, gazing out at the street and taking occasional sips of the apple juice she'd ordered. It was Friday, late afternoon, and she'd come here after work to meet a friend. She couldn't stop thinking about her marriage to Bruce, wondering how it had disintegrated so fast. They'd gone from an impromptu wedding last December to separation less than ten months later. She turned her head to look in the direction of Cedar Cove. The town was situated on the other side of Sinclair Inlet but might as well have been across the Pacific.

Rachel felt she couldn't go back home to Cedar Cove—to Yakima Street—and yet she had no other viable choice. She'd left after the latest argument with her stepdaughter, Jolene. Although Bruce was aware of the tension between her and Rachel, he'd never adequately addressed it, believing it would eventually resolve itself. Oh, sure, he'd made a halfhearted offer to go to counseling with, or more likely without, Jolene. But that was too little, too late. Nothing had changed, and, as a result, the stress in their home had become intolerable. Now that she was pregnant, Rachel had decided to leave…for the sake of her sanity and for her own health and that of her baby.

She'd lied to Bruce, saying she had a place to stay—with an unidentified friend. Instead, she'd checked into a Bremerton hotel.

The problem was, she needed her job if she was going to support herself, which meant she'd need to find an apartment in Cedar Cove or at least nearby. Everything was complicated by the fact that this hadn't been an easy pregnancy. She had severe morning sickness and her blood pressure was dangerously high. That was understandable, considering the tension in the house. If not for the baby, Rachel might have found the strength to deal with Jolene. She might've been willing to devote all her energy to sorting out the complicated tangle of the girl's emotions, giving her the constant reassurance she seemed to require.

Since Jolene had learned about the baby, the whole situation had become that much more difficult. Not only did her stepdaughter see her as competition for Bruce's affections, but now Rachel had committed an even worse crime by bringing another child into the family, robbing the girl of his undivided attention.

What shocked Rachel was how close she and Jolene had been before she married Bruce. As a motherless child herself, Rachel had taken a special interest in Jolene, part maternal, part friendly. They'd bonded when the girl was just six, a year after Jolene's mother was killed in a car accident. Bruce had brought Jolene into the salon for a haircut and Jolene had sadly told her how much she missed her mommy. Rachel had been drawn to the child because she'd identified with Jolene. She still recalled in vivid detail how she'd felt when her own mother had died and she'd gone to live with her mother's sister, a woman she barely knew.

Through the years, the closeness between Rachel and Jolene had grown—until she'd made the mistake of marrying Jolene's father. To be fair to the teenager, Jolene had wanted Rachel and Bruce to wait until she'd had time to get used to the idea. Bruce, however, wouldn't hear of it. He'd wanted them married. Well, so did Rachel, although she'd asked Bruce to delay the wedding because of Jolene's qualms. But by then…the momentum of their plans had taken over.

In the beginning, after first meeting Bruce, she hadn't considered him anything more than a friend. He was Jolene's dad. He relied on her help with his daughter. For years there hadn't been the slightest indication of romantic interest on either part. Rachel was seeing Nate Olsen, a navy warrant officer she'd met after bidding on him at a fundraiser for the local humane society—the Dog and Bachelor Auction. Shortly after the wedding, Nate was deployed out of state, but now he was back. They'd been in contact recently and, in fact, he was the friend she'd arranged to meet here.

For a while she and Nate had seriously thought about marriage. However, by the time he'd asked her to make a decision, Rachel had come to realize she was in love with Bruce. Surprisingly, miraculously, Bruce loved her, too. From there everything had moved quickly. *Too* quickly…

She had to acknowledge the truth of that old cliché about marrying in haste. Rachel had been all too willing to accept Bruce's assurances that Jolene would adjust. After all, he'd pointed out, it wasn't as though Rachel was a *stranger*.

But Jolene hadn't adjusted. Whatever affection she'd had for Rachel had changed into passive-aggressive behavior and then escalated to open antagonism. Not wanting to distress her husband, Rachel had done her best to deflect Jolene's hostility. The pregnancy was unplanned, and she'd hoped to keep it a secret for a few months, but Bruce insisted it was only right to tell Jolene. That, too, had backfired. And it had led to this.

The café door opened but Rachel didn't look up until Nate Olsen slid into the booth across from her.

"Rachel?"

She glanced up and offered him a weak smile.

Nate's blue eyes narrowed slightly. "You okay?" he asked, sounding concerned.

"You don't have to say it. I look terrible."

"Not terrible," he said. "Just...very pale."

Nate had emailed her when he returned to Bremerton. He felt she should know so that if they inadvertently ran into each other, she'd be prepared. With everything else that was happening, Rachel hadn't paid much attention to his email and hadn't responded. Nate was someone she'd loved in the past. She was a married woman now.

With time on her hands at the hotel, she'd gone to the business center and logged on to her email account. She'd impulsively answered his message, telling him that her marriage was falling apart. After they'd exchanged a few short emails, Nate suggested they meet. She'd accepted his invitation.

"At my last doctor's visit I learned I have an iron deficiency." It didn't help that she hadn't been able to keep down a meal. Her morning sickness lingered for most of the day, making her feel too queasy and uncomfortable to eat. She'd lost weight when she should be gaining.

"I'm glad you got in touch."

"I probably shouldn't have." Only Rachel didn't know who else to contact. She couldn't reach out to her friends; they were the first people Bruce would approach. This separation was difficult enough without dragging her friends into the middle of it.

"I meant what I said," Nate continued. "If you ever need anything, call me. You know I'll do whatever I can."

When the waitress came over to the table with a coffeepot, Nate turned over his ceramic mug and she filled it.

At his words, tears of appreciation sprang to Rachel's eyes. "I know…"

"What can I do?"

She wasn't sure. "Like I said in my email, I… I've left Bruce and Jolene." It went without saying that this fit right into her stepdaughter's plans. Undoubtedly Jolene was ecstatic about having her father to herself again.

"So it's come to that?"

Rachel's dark hair fell forward as she looked down. "I…talked to Teri and she wants me to move in with her."

"Are you going to?"

"I can't. That'll be the first place Bruce goes. I told him I was moving in with a friend… At the time I thought I might take Teri up on her offer, but I can't do that to her. She and Bobby have their hands full with the three babies."

"Three?"

"Teri had triplets."

Nate laughed. That seemed to be a common reaction when people heard about the triplets. "She always does everything in a big way, doesn't she?" he murmured.

He knew Teri, so he also knew that if anyone could handle this, it was her friend. But capable though she was, Teri didn't need a miserable friend to deal with, in addition to caring for three babies.

"So, if you don't move in with Teri, where will you go?"

"I… I don't know." All that mattered was getting out of the house as fast as possible. She got a hotel room, but that was far too expensive to be a permanent solution. At this rate she'd drain her bank account in a week. Besides, it wouldn't take Bruce long to discover where she was, and once he did, he'd do whatever he could to convince her to return home. Rachel couldn't allow that to happen, not while the situation with Jolene was still unsettled.

Nate sipped his coffee in thoughtful silence. Eventually he said, "You could always move in with me."

Rachel's head shot up. That wasn't even a consideration. If Bruce learned she was living with Nate he'd feel blindsided. Besides, it would give Jolene more ammunition to use against her. "I'm grateful for the offer, I really am, but I couldn't possibly do that."

"Why not?"

"Nate, I couldn't… What would Bruce think?"

"Do you need to tell him?"

"I…" She opened her mouth to object, then merely said, "He'd want to know."

"Of course he would, but you don't have to tell him *everything*. The only important thing here is that you're somewhere safe and that you're taking care of yourself."

Rachel stared at him. "Are you suggesting I lie to my husband?"

"Not lie, exactly. I'm saying don't fill in all the blanks. As it happens, the house I'm sharing belongs to a friend of mine. I have a room, but there's a third bedroom available. Unfortunately, Bob's deployed right now, so it would just be the two of us. If you're uncomfortable with that, I understand."

She exhaled, feeling torn. His idea did seem like a good solution, but she could only imagine how Bruce would react if he discovered the truth. For obvious reasons, the two men weren't on the best of terms.

"It might help you decide if I tell you I'm seeing someone."

Actually, that did help. "Is it serious?" Rachel asked.

Nate shrugged. "Serious enough. I'm out with Emily three or four nights a week. You'd have the house to yourself most of the time."

"What kind of rent does Bob charge?"

Nate mentioned an amount that was more than reasonable, then added, "You wouldn't be expected to cook or clean or anything else if that's what you're thinking."

"Oh." She nibbled her lower lip as she considered his suggestion. He'd given her an option she hadn't expected.

"Before you answer, why don't you come over and check out the place."

Still, she hesitated.

"You want to get away for a while, don't you?"

She did, and Nate knew that.

"Someplace where Bruce and his daughter would never think of looking?"

She nodded slowly.

"Don't worry about me," Nate told her once again. "I loved you, Rachel, I really did, but I've moved on. However, I care about you, which is why I brought up this arrangement. If you're concerned about what might result from the two of us being in the same house, then let me assure you right now, nothing's going to happen."

"Okay," she whispered. "I'll go see the place."

"Good." He left money to pay for their drinks, then slid out of the booth.

Rachel stood and immediately felt dizzy. She would have stumbled if Nate hadn't grabbed her elbow.

"When's the last time you ate?"

She closed her eyes and tried to remember. "A while ago. I'm fine."

"No, you aren't. Listen, no arguments. Once you've toured the house, I'm fixing you something to eat."

"You cook?"

"I'm surprised you don't remember that I'm a man of many talents."

His smile was just the salve she needed, his friendship the mainstay that would see her through this upheaval in her life.

She followed Nate to the Bremerton address he gave her. The house was in a nearby neighborhood, convenient to the navy base. The two-story structure, built after the Second World War, had a large front porch and shuttered windows. It was meant for a family.

Unexpected emotion swelled up inside Rachel as

she looked at the house. Her mother had been a single parent and her aunt had never married. All her life Rachel had yearned to be part of a family. When she married Bruce, she'd felt as if she finally belonged. She had a husband and a stepdaughter and they were bonded together by love. It didn't take long for that dream to shatter and now, once more, she was on the outside... The baby stirred, and she pressed her palm against her stomach, hoping her child would one day know the love of a father, a mother and a big sister.

"Would you like to come in?" Nate asked, again clasping her elbow as though he feared she might crumple onto the pavement.

Without answering, she accompanied him up the walkway to the steps.

"I do my best to keep the place neat, but you have to remember I'm a guy and housekeeping is low on my priority list."

"I'll remember," she said, managing a glimmer of a smile.

The house wasn't in bad shape. A few newspapers and magazines were scattered about but the sink was empty of dirty dishes and the living room free of clutter. The furniture, large and dark, wasn't anything she would've purchased, but it would suffice.

"Let me show you the extra bedroom," Nate said, steering her down the long hallway. He chuckled.

"What?" she asked, curious about what he found so amusing.

"I promised there'd be nothing romantic between us, and the first thing I do is take you to the bedroom." He shook his head. "Sorry, the irony was too much for me."

Rachel laughed softly. "I guess it does sound rather… compromising."

The room he showed her was pretty basic. It might have been a hotel room for all the personality it revealed. A bed, a dresser and a nightstand were the only furniture. There wasn't a picture on the wall or any indication that someone else had once occupied the room. The bedspread looked worn and was probably one Bob had purchased years before.

"Like I said, it's nothing fancy."

"Where's your bedroom?" she asked, noting the number of doors leading off the hallway.

"Upstairs. Both of the other bedrooms are."

That meant it wasn't likely they'd run into each other in the middle of the night, which made her feel a little less guilty about the prospect of deceiving her husband.

"So," he said, leaning against the doorjamb with his arms crossed, "what do you think?"

"I…" She paused. Again, she imagined what Bruce would say if he found out where she was living. That would definitely complicate an already complicated situation. But then, as Nate had said, she didn't need to tell Bruce the whole truth—at least, not right away. He only had to be told one thing: that she was safe.

"You really are a good friend, aren't you?" She meant that. She believed in his genuineness, even though he'd been hurt by her choice of Bruce over him.

He grinned. "Anything for you, Rachel, you know that."

"All right, I'll do it. You've got yourself a housemate—but on one condition."

"Sure."

She met his eyes. "You can't tell anyone I'm living here. *No one,* okay?"

Frowning, Nate rubbed his chin. "Since it's Bob's house I can't keep it a secret from him, and I feel I should say something to Emily, but I can ask them not to mention it to anyone else."

"Fine, you can tell Bob and Emily, as long as they're willing to be discreet."

"I'll make that clear. But who do you expect me— or them—to tell?" he asked.

"Your friends. Or their friends. You'd be amazed at how quickly word gets around in Cedar Cove. You might casually mention it to one of your navy buddies and that person might know Bruce and an hour later my husband will show up on the doorstep. Bruce isn't an aggressive or violent man, but he wouldn't take kindly to the two of us sharing a house."

"Okay, deal." Nate extended his hand.

"I'll keep my end of the bargain, as well," she promised, shaking his hand. "I'll do my best to be a good housemate. I'll pay my rent on time and—"

"I wasn't worried about it, Rachel," he broke in. "I guess you can't tell Teri, can you?"

Now, that was going to be painful. Rachel told Teri everything. She was her closest friend and had been for years. But Nate was right; she couldn't leak a word of this to anyone, not even Teri. Bruce would certainly ask her, and Rachel couldn't risk the chance that Teri would accidentally divulge the information. What she didn't know, she couldn't share.

"No, I don't think I will," she said. Hard as that would be, it was necessary.

Two

When the alarm rang at the Cedar Cove firehouse, Mack and his fellow firefighters jumped into action. The address was relayed as he leaped onto the fire truck, and the familiarity of it struck him immediately, although he didn't have time to think about it. Not until the truck, lights flashing and sirens blaring, turned onto Eagle Crest Avenue did he realize the house belonged to Ben and Charlotte Rhodes. Mack had visited there often, taking his daughter, Noelle, to see her grandparents. The smoke billowing out of the house came from the back, where the kitchen was located.

Mack and the two other firefighters pulled out the hose, all of them supporting it, and raced toward the house. The fire engine carried five hundred gallons of water, which enabled them to get water onto the fire without the delay of hooking up to a hydrant. A second truck would arrive within minutes and those firefighters would engage the closest hydrant.

Mack's heart pounded as he ran toward the rear of the house carrying the bulky hose. Already he could hear the second siren in the distance.

Ben and Charlotte, plus several of their neighbors, stood out on the sidewalk staring at the scene. Charlotte wore the horrified look of a woman who couldn't believe what was happening. Ben stood next to her, his arm protectively around her shoulders. He seemed equally shaken.

Because he was busy working on the fire, Mack didn't get a chance to talk to the elderly couple until the blaze was extinguished, which took only minutes. Thankfully the damage seemed to be confined to the kitchen.

The fire squad commander spoke to Ben while Charlotte wrung her hands. She seemed so distraught and anxious that Mack approached, hoping to reassure them all was well.

"Oh, Mack, I'm so grateful you're here," Charlotte said, her eyes brimming with tears, which threatened to spill at any moment.

"Everything's fine," he told her in a soothing voice. "The fire's out."

"This is all my fault," she cried. "I'm sure I must have done something. Oh, why wasn't I more careful? I get so easily distracted these days…"

"The cause of the fire hasn't been determined," Mack said, trying to be diplomatic, although he suspected she was right. "Any number of things could be the cause." With a house of this age, electrical problems weren't uncommon.

"But *I* was the one in the kitchen," Charlotte said in a small voice.

"It could've been an electrical short," Mack said, hoping to calm her. He'd just finished speaking when a car pulled up on the other side of the street and Olivia

Griffin got out. She wore a suit and heels and had obviously just left the courthouse, where she was a judge.

"Mom, Mom!" she called as she dashed across the street, barely watching for oncoming traffic.

Charlotte turned and hurried toward her daughter. They hugged fiercely for a minute, clinging to each other.

"Are you all right?"

"Yes, yes," Charlotte assured her, tears slipping down her pale cheeks.

"What about Harry?"

Mack hadn't seen the family cat and he'd been too busy to remember Charlotte and Ben's pet.

"Ben got him out of the house," Charlotte explained. She glanced around as if unsure where he was currently hiding. "Oh, poor Harry, he must be terrified. He doesn't usually go outside, you know…" Her voice faded.

Mack's experience with the cat was limited. Whenever he, Mary Jo and Noelle visited, Harry made it clear that he was willing to tolerate them, but no more than that. After accepting the respectful greetings he considered his due, he generally ignored them all and retreated to his accustomed place on the back of the sofa. His other favorite perch was the windowsill overlooking the front yard. Harry was probably hiding somewhere, under the porch or maybe in some bushes. If the cat didn't show up soon, he'd help with the search.

The squad commander seemed to be finished speaking to Ben, who now joined the circle. "Mack," the older man said, looking flustered. His white hair, normally carefully groomed, was in disarray, as if he'd rammed his fingers through it repeatedly. "Thank you," he said, his voice husky, "for looking after Charlotte."

Mack didn't feel he'd done anything out of the ordinary.

"Mack, what about the damage to the house?" Olivia asked him.

"That's being assessed," he replied, "but there doesn't appear to be any damage to rooms other than the kitchen."

"I'm so grateful you got here when you did," Charlotte murmured.

"Mom. Ben." Will Jefferson, her son, hoofed it up the last part of the steep street and across the lawn. Apparently he'd run from the Harbor Street Art Gallery, where he lived and worked. It was only a few blocks away, but unfortunately they were all straight uphill.

"Everything's okay," Olivia told him. "Mom, Ben and Harry got out in time."

"Thank God." Will leaned over and placed his hands on his knees, wheezing as he attempted to catch his breath. "I didn't know what to think when you called," he said to Olivia.

"Mrs. Johnson left me a message at the courthouse," Olivia told their mother, "and then I phoned Will."

"I hope I didn't upset you too much," the next-door neighbor said, her brow furrowed. She stood a few feet away. "I saw the fire and phoned it in, but Ben had already taken care of that. Then I thought if it was my house I'd want my children to know what was going on, so I called the courthouse. I do hope that was the right thing to do."

"It certainly was," Olivia said fervently. "Don't ever

hesitate to contact me in regard to Mom and Ben. About *anything,*" she emphasized.

"Me, too," Will chimed in.

"Oh, yes," Charlotte echoed, reaching for her daughter's arm. "I feel much better now that my children are here."

"What happened?" Will asked, still a little breathless. He glanced from Ben to Mack and back to Ben.

"I'm not sure," Ben said, turning to Charlotte.

"I made lunch the way I always do—chicken noodle soup, which was on simmer—and then Ben and I sat down. We were reading when Ben said he smelled smoke."

Ben nodded in agreement.

"I didn't smell anything, so I didn't worry about it. My new cooking magazine arrived today and they had twenty-eight recipes on how to use zucchini and I was absorbed in that. Then all of a sudden Ben threw down his book and let out a yell."

"Yes," Ben said, picking up the tale. "I saw flames."

"Thank goodness Ben can deal with a crisis because I panicked. My first thought was that we needed to put out the fire ourselves, but by then the kitchen drapes were in flames, and it was…just too much."

Mack cringed since trying to handle the fire themselves was one of the biggest mistakes homeowners made.

"One look told me it was already more than either of us could deal with," Ben continued, "so I got Charlotte and Harry out of the house and used my cell phone to call 9-1-1."

Mack was grateful that Ben had remained calm. Too many people stayed inside the home to contact

9-1-1, putting themselves at greater risk. "You did the best possible thing," he said. "The first action to take is *always* to get everyone out of the house, then call the fire department."

"What happens next?" Olivia asked, directing the question to Mack.

"The fire department will investigate the cause," he told them.

"When will the investigator get here?" Ben asked, standing close to Charlotte.

"Usually within a couple of hours," Mack told them.

"What about the Crock-Pot?" Charlotte said suddenly, clutching Ben's arm. "I had tonight's dinner in it. Should we try to find it in this mess?"

"Mom, I think dinner is the least of your problems," Will inserted. "I'd assume the Crock-Pot's a lost cause."

Mack couldn't remember seeing it, but his attention had been focused on putting out the fire.

"What can you tell me about dealing with the insurance people?" Ben asked, looking at Mack. "Will they get in touch with us or will I need to call them?"

"You'll need to notify them."

"The contact information is inside the house," Ben muttered.

"Do you have the same carrier as you do for your car insurance?"

"Yes."

"Then the phone number should be on your insurance card." Washington state law required carrying proof of insurance when driving, so either Ben had the insurance card in his wallet or in the car's glove compartment.

"Of course." Ben grimaced. "I guess I'm more rattled than I thought."

"It's understandable," Mack said. He glanced over his shoulder to be sure he wasn't needed elsewhere and noticed that Andrew McHale, the fire investigator, had arrived. Before he could point him out, Andrew disappeared around the back of the house.

"How long will it be before we can go back in the house?" Charlotte asked. "I do hope everyone will be gone by five—that's when Ben likes to watch *Judge Judy.*"

"Mom," Olivia said, gently patting her mother's hand. "You won't be able to go back in the house. The kitchen's going to need a complete overhaul. It might be several weeks before the house is livable again."

"We can't go back in the house?" she asked in confusion. "For several weeks? Why not?"

Mack realized that Charlotte hadn't taken in what Olivia was saying.

"The kitchen's been destroyed," Will said, speaking slowly and clearly.

"I know that, dear, but the *rest* of the house is fine."

"Still, you can't live there until the damage to the kitchen has been repaired."

"But…" Charlotte turned to Ben as if asking him to plead her case.

Mack understood that she was bewildered and uncertain; she didn't seem to understand the gravity of what had taken place.

"But…where will we go?" Charlotte asked helplessly.

"Depending on the type of insurance coverage you

have, the company might pay for you to stay in a hotel while the repairs are made," Mack explained.

"A *hotel?*" Charlotte shook her head as though the very idea was repugnant to her.

"Mom, you can stay with me," Will said. "I'm close to the house and—"

"Not a good idea, Will," Olivia cut in. "You're living at the art gallery. That's no place for Mom and Ben. They'll stay with Jack and me."

The moment Olivia mentioned her husband's name, he drove up—almost as though he'd been summoned. The town's newspaper editor, Jack Griffin also did reporting duty when required; in this case he would have recognized the address. Accompanied by a cameraman, Jack headed in their direction, his ever-present raincoat billowing out from his sides as he strode across the lawn.

"I suppose you're wondering why I called this meeting," he said, introducing a bit of humor.

Mack smothered a laugh.

"Jack, this is no time to joke," Olivia said, then hugged him. She seemed relieved that he'd come.

"Oh, Jack, they say we can't go back inside," Charlotte wailed. "I'm afraid this is all my fault."

"No one's blaming you," Will said.

"I want Mom and Ben to come home with us until the house is repaired," Olivia insisted.

"By all means." Jack reached for his reporter's pad, a spiral-bound notebook, and had his cameraman get photos of the firefighters as they prepared to leave.

"Jack!" Olivia glared at her husband.

"What?"

"You're not going to interview my mother, are you? Can't you see she's distraught?"

"Ah…" Jack Griffin had the good grace to look sheepishly at his mother-in-law. "I *am* a reporter, Olivia, and this is news."

"I don't mind, dear," Charlotte said, placating her daughter by patting her arm. "Ben was our hero, saving Harry and me and…oh, dear. Where *is* Harry?"

"We'll look for him, Mom." She turned to her husband. "Why don't you talk to Mack," Olivia suggested. "He can explain about the fire."

Mack shook his head. It would be more appropriate if Jack talked to the squad commander. "I'm sure Chief Nelson would be happy to answer your questions." He motioned toward him, and Jack left them, hurrying toward Chief Nelson, pen in hand.

Mack saw Jack scribbling furiously during his conversation with the chief, nodding several times. Once he glanced over his shoulder at his mother-in-law and frowned, which told Mack that the cause of the fire had most likely been attributed to Charlotte—just as he'd guessed. She must have been distracted and left something, maybe the soup she'd mentioned, on the stove. He remembered that she'd talked about reading a magazine.

"You'll be coming home with us," Olivia was saying when Mack returned his attention to Ben and Charlotte.

"But, Olivia…"

"Mom, you can't stay here and you can't stay with Will. Where would you sleep?"

"It would probably be best if you went with Olivia," Will concurred as Ben nodded. "My apartment's pretty small with only the one bedroom. I'd sleep on the sofa if necessary, but frankly, it makes more sense for you to go home with Olivia."

Charlotte nodded. "I'll need to collect a few things. Ben," she said, "will you find Harry?"

"I'll go in with you," Mack offered. "It's better if you don't go anywhere close to the kitchen until after the fire investigator's had a chance to finish his report and the insurance people have come by."

Then Mack joined Ben in looking for the cat. They found him a few minutes later, cowering under the front porch.

"It's all my fault," Charlotte was saying when they returned, shaking her head as if to erase the memory of that afternoon. "Harry!" She held out her arms for the cat. "Oh, my sweetie…" She nuzzled his broad head and then raised her eyes to Olivia. "I'm still not clear on what happened…"

"Don't worry, Mom."

"If Ben and I are going to be with you for several weeks, I'll help you as much as I can," Charlotte promised. "I'll clean and cook and I won't be a bother."

"Mom, you'd never be a bother."

"I'll bake for Jack," she said, her eyes lighting up with anticipation. "You know how he enjoys my baking."

"Jack doesn't need you baking for him, Mom."

"Then I'll cook him a pot roast. Jack's fond of my pot roasts."

"Jack's fond of *food,* Mom," Olivia said. "The fact is, I can't think of a single thing you cook that he doesn't dig into like a starving man."

Charlotte beamed with pride. "Jack's a man of discriminating taste. Haven't I always said so?"

"Indeed." Olivia rolled her eyes. "Come on, Mom, Mack and I'll help you and Ben collect what you need, starting with the cat carrier. Then we'll go to our house."

"You're sure about this?" Charlotte asked.

"Very sure," Olivia said, and slid one arm around her mother's waist.

Ben and Charlotte Rhodes would be fine, Mack mused as he followed them. They had family.

Three

Chad Timmons paced his Tacoma apartment and was so deep in thought, he nearly collided with the wall. That just proved it—the woman drove him to distraction. From the moment he'd met Gloria Ashton, it'd been an on-again, off-again relationship. Like some unpredictable wind, she blew hot and then cold. The worst of it was he'd put up with it. Well, he'd had about all he could take. He refused to play her games anymore—and that was what they were. Games. As far as he could see, there was no way he could win because she kept changing the rules. One day she wanted nothing to do with him. The next, she couldn't keep her hands off him.

Fine. He'd decided he was finished. And he'd stuck to that. Until Roy McAfee had hurtled into his life like a meteorite on its passage to earth. The crater that blast had left was deep enough to bury him.

Gloria was pregnant—with his baby. He was about to become a father.

Talk about changing the rules...

It all added up now. After they'd spent the night together, Chad had felt so sure they could resolve their differences. He was high on love, his head in the clouds, like some sappy walking cliché. The shock of her taking off without a word had made him feel bereft and stupid. Oh, she'd written a note, but that had explained nothing.

So he'd vowed that if this was how she felt, he'd deal with it. He was finished. Chad had resigned from his position at the Cedar Cove Medical Clinic, moved to Tacoma and accepted a job as an emergency room physician. He'd even started dating someone else. Joni Atkins was a lot less volatile and a lot more decisive.

A baby.

Even now, Chad had difficulty coping with Roy's news. If he was shocked, he could imagine Gloria's reaction. Her feelings about him, and about a future with him, seemed tentative, ambivalent at best. She'd moved into the Puget Sound area a few years ago to search for her birth parents. Her adoptive parents had been killed in a small-plane crash and she was virtually without family. Then Gloria discovered something that had completely unsettled her. Her birth parents had eventually married and she had a full sister and brother. She'd told him all that on their first night together—which was also the night they'd met. Their relationship had moved from being strangers to being intimate with reckless speed. That embarrassed Gloria and, frankly, him, too. Chad knew better. So did Gloria. Afterward she'd asked for time to connect with her birth family. She'd done that but nothing had changed. Every advance Chad made was met with stiff resistance. Then it happened again. She'd agreed to a date, and they ended up in bed, which was followed by embarrassment and regret on Gloria's part. Again.

Now Gloria was pregnant.

She hadn't told him, although now he assumed she'd come to break the news the day she'd met him in the hospital parking lot. How was he to know what she'd intended? As far as he was concerned, they were finished. That seemed to be what she'd requested; according to the note she'd left him, she wanted nothing more to do with him. If she'd changed her mind, it was too late, or so he'd felt at the time. He'd moved on and he'd advised her to do the same.

Roy, Gloria's birth father, had taken a tremendous risk by coming to see him. Gloria had asked that Chad be kept in the dark regarding the pregnancy, and Corrie, her birth mother, had agreed. But not Roy.

Years earlier Corrie McAfee had become pregnant while in college. Roy hadn't learned he was a father until after his daughter had been adopted. Apparently it remained a sore point between Gloria's birth parents. Roy wasn't willing to let history repeat itself, although Corrie felt the choice should be Gloria's alone. Going against his wife's and daughter's wishes, Roy made sure Chad knew about the baby.

Chad hadn't decided yet what he should do. He worried that Gloria, who worked as a sheriff's deputy, might undergo too much stress in her normal job; she needed to be on desk duty. He wanted to talk to her, explain how important it was that she look after herself by eating right, taking appropriate prenatal vitamins, seeing her doctor regularly. While rationally he recognized that she was undoubtedly doing all those things, he couldn't help wanting confirmation.

Chad reached for his car keys. It'd been several weeks since his life was turned upside down and, so far, he'd done nothing other than rage about the situation, agonize over it and try to settle on some course of action. The time had come to do *something*.

As he drove into Cedar Cove, Chad stopped at the local bookstore and picked up a baby name book, and a few others he often recommended to his patients. Perhaps that was a waste of money, since Gloria might already own these books, but he didn't care. It made him feel better. Knowing she didn't want to see him, Chad thought he'd ask Roy McAfee to give her the books.

He got the address for the private investigator's office from the business card Roy had left him. Parking on the steep hill, Chad looked down at the waterfront, which bustled with activity on this beautiful September day. Cedar Cove had been his home for five years and he hadn't realized how much he missed it.

The totem pole at the library caught his eye. Its eagle's wings were spread wide as though embracing the entire community. He'd enjoyed spending lunch hours at the waterfront park. Visiting the Saturday market had been another favorite activity; he remembered buying produce so fresh soil still clung to the roots. He saw a couple of kayakers paddling near the marina, their smooth, even strokes sending out ripples behind them. Harbor Street was busy, too, with late-afternoon shoppers and people leaving work.

Chad dragged in a deep breath before he tore his gaze away from the scene below. Shoulders squared, he walked toward Roy's office and stepped inside.

The front desk sat empty. A few chairs were lined

up against the wall in the waiting area and an end table held a number of outdated magazines.

"Mack, is that you?" Roy McAfee called from the inner office.

Chad followed the sound of the other man's voice. "It's Chad Timmons," he said, and let himself into the office. He stood in the doorway, uncertain of his reception.

"Chad." McAfee rose from his chair and extended his hand. "Good to see you. I was wondering how long it would take you to show up."

"Probably longer than it should have," Chad confessed. He sank into the chair across from McAfee and set the bag of books on the carpet. The office was sparsely decorated. A desk, a leather chair and a couple of bookcases. The walls were bare except for a large map of the town.

"I guess my news was a bit jarring."

Chad snorted. "That's putting it mildly." Then, because he had to know, he asked, "How's Gloria feeling?"

"From what Corrie tells me, she's been suffering from morning sickness, but other than that she appears to be doing well." He paused and added, "But then I'm not my wife's favorite person at the moment. She hasn't quite found it in her heart to forgive me for contacting you."

"I'm sorry about that."

"Don't worry. It's not your problem." Roy dismissed Chad's comment with a wave of his hand.

"Does Gloria know that I know about the baby?"

Roy leaned forward, shaking his head. "I haven't said anything and I doubt Corrie has, either."

"In other words, probably not."

Roy nodded. "That would be my take on it."

No surprise there. "I have something I'd like you to give her." He lifted the sack of books.

Roy regarded the bag and then turned his attention back to Chad. "Are you sure you don't want to give those to her yourself?"

Chad wasn't sure of anything. "For now I think it might be best if I stayed in the background. From what Gloria said, she doesn't want anything to do with me. So it makes more sense for you to do it."

Roy didn't respond for several seconds, studying Chad intently. "I don't agree with you," he finally said.

The front door opened. "Dad?"

Roy got to his feet. "In here."

Mack McAfee barged into the office and stopped abruptly when he saw Chad. "Sorry, am I interrupting anything?" he asked, glancing from one to the other.

"Not at all," his father said, reclaiming his seat.

Mack's eyes narrowed. "We've met, right?"

Chad nodded.

Mack took the chair next to him. "Ah, yes, I remember now. You dated my sister Linnette."

"Briefly." That whole scenario had been a disaster, and it had complicated everything else. While Gloria was building a relationship with the sister who didn't know they were even related, Linnette had developed a crush on Chad. Seeing how Linnette felt about him, Gloria had steered clear.

"Chad asked me to deliver some books to Gloria," his father explained.

"Gloria?" Mack swiveled his head to look at Chad. "Why Gloria?"

"Actually, I've…dated her, too."

Mack grinned. "It seems you get around."

Chad responded with a weak smile. "Yeah, I suppose it does."

"I didn't know my sister was big on reading," Mack said, relaxing in his chair, balancing one ankle on the opposite knee. "And if you're dating Gloria, why don't you give her the books yourself?"

"These are a baby name book and a couple on pregnancy," Chad said.

"What?" Mack dropped his leg to the floor. "You and Gloria? Are you telling me you're—this baby is *yours?*"

Chad merely nodded.

For an instant Mack didn't seem to know how to react. Conflicting emotions showed on his face—anger chased by confusion and then indecision.

"Believe me, it came as a shock to me, too," Chad said, sharing a smile with Roy.

"But…but you're a…a physician." Mack stumbled over the words. "If anyone should understand about birth control, it's you!"

"Again, I'm in full agreement," Chad said. "It just happened."

"'It just happened' has got to be the most pathetic excuse in the book. What do you intend to do about this?" Mack demanded.

Mack's anger was justified, and Chad took it to heart. "That depends on Gloria. At this point she isn't aware I know about the baby."

"Why not?"

Mack glared at him and Chad looked over at Roy, hoping he'd supply the answer.

"The thing is, your sister specifically asked that Chad not be told. Your mother agreed to that, but I refused."

"So you went behind Mom's back?" Mack shook his head as if he already knew the answer and disapproved. "*And* Gloria's!"

"I told your mother exactly what I was doing. She wasn't happy about it. In fact, she still isn't." Roy leaned back in his chair, frowning. "I'll take the books to Gloria and explain that I told you about the baby."

Chad scowled. He wasn't ready for Gloria to find that out...

"It's time I told my daughter I went to see you."

"Don't," Chad said bluntly. "Not yet."

Roy blinked at him. "Why not?"

Chad tried to clarify his thoughts. "For one thing, I want Gloria to come to me. At some stage she's going to realize she needs me. If for nothing more than signing the adoption papers. Times have changed, Roy. Fathers have rights, too. Besides, I'm thinking about raising the baby myself." The idea had only occurred to him a few days ago. He wasn't committed to it yet, but the possibility was gaining strength in his mind.

"Wait—Gloria's decided to give the baby up for adoption?" Mack asked. He clenched his fists and stared hard at his father. "You wouldn't let her do that, would you?"

"It isn't our decision," Roy reminded him.

"Yes, but... Okay, fine, whatever, but before that happens Mary Jo and I will raise the baby," Mack said in clipped tones. "If Chad doesn't want to do it." He obviously considered Chad capable of shirking what he himself saw as a duty. "This child is our family's flesh and blood."

"More mine than yours," Chad murmured. But no use debating the issue until they learned Gloria's intentions.

Roy seemed slightly amused by Mack's reaction. "Don't you think you should talk this over with Mary Jo first before you make that kind of offer?"

"She'll agree with me."

"It's a moot point," Chad said. "No one knows what Gloria's going to do. Once she's made her decision, we may need to talk again."

Both men nodded.

"For now, all I ask," Chad said, "is for one of you or even Corrie to see that Gloria gets these books."

"Who should I say gave them to her?" Roy asked.

Chad shrugged. "Let her assume they came from you."

"You're sure about this?" Mack asked.

"Very sure. I want—no, I *need*—Gloria to come to me. She's the one who walked away. Maybe it's just my pride talking, I don't know, but I'd be more comfortable if she made the first move."

Roy allowed Chad's words to hang in the air for a moment before he responded. "I'll hold off a bit longer if that's what you want. However, for the sake of my relationship with my wife, I think it might be a good idea if I confessed sooner rather than later."

Chad understood. "Okay. Go ahead and tell Gloria." He didn't like it but Roy had done him one favor already.

"I'll take the books to her," Mack volunteered. "We've had a couple of good talks recently."

"Oh?" Roy raised his brows in question.

Chad was curious, too, although it wasn't his place to ask.

"Gloria had to tell Sheriff Davis she's pregnant, and as of next week she's going on desk duty." Chad was relieved to hear it. However, Mack looked away as he spoke, which led Chad to believe there was more to this than he was saying.

"Any particular reason?"

"Well, it's standard protocol for pregnant officers." Mack shifted in his seat, clearly uncomfortable with this turn in the conversation. "But, okay, the fact is that Gloria's in her mid-thirties, so the obstetrician is being extra cautious."

"Has she told her mother about this?" Roy asked.

"I believe so."

Roy sighed, and Chad guessed that Corrie hadn't said anything to Roy because she was still upset with him.

"The doctor's scheduled an ultrasound."

"For when?" Chad did his best to hide his own anxiety. He'd dealt with a lot of pregnancies and a lot of babies during his medical career—but none of those babies had been *his*. And although he was well aware that many women had babies later in life, he couldn't help worrying about Gloria.

"I can't tell you that."

"Can't because you don't know? Or because she'd disapprove?" Chad asked sharply.

"Can't because I don't know. It's nothing out of the ordinary," Mack said. "At least as far as I've been given to understand. It's just that when it's someone close to you, I guess you worry more. But at least she'll be sitting safely behind a desk from now on."

Knowing Gloria, she'd hate desk duty. She liked nothing better than being a beat cop, responding to calls and crises, interacting with the people of Cedar Cove. Chad found it interesting that she'd gone into police work, following in the footsteps of the father she never knew.

"Do you want me to call you if she mentions when the ultrasound is?"

Chad nodded.

"Don't worry, son," Roy said, his words and the sound of his voice lending Chad confidence. "Everything will work out. It did for Corrie and me, and I'm convinced it will for you and Gloria, too."

Chad relaxed in his chair. He had to believe Roy was right and there was actually a chance for him and Gloria.

Four

It'd been a week since Rachel had moved out of the house, and Bruce was stunned that she hadn't returned. He'd tried to be patient, giving her the space and time she claimed she needed. But he wanted her back with him and Jolene *now,* back where she belonged. The knot in his stomach hadn't disappeared yet, and it wouldn't, not until she came home.

Bruce still didn't know where she'd gone. He'd talked to her friends. Even Teri seemed bewildered about where she was, and her words rang true. Rachel's best friend was clearly very concerned about her.

"Dad, can you help me with this?" Jolene asked, strolling into the kitchen, a math book clutched to her chest. She'd been lounging in the backyard under a big striped umbrella, talking on her cell phone and pretending to do her homework.

Bruce looked up from the table where he'd been sitting. "You know I'm no good at this." The real problem, however, was his short fuse. He had limited patience when it came to explaining basic math. Computer programs were a different matter. Those he knew his way around; it was the theoretical stuff that stumped him—partly for lack of interest. Things had been a lot better when Rachel was there to step in.

"Dad, this is just review. You helped me last year, remember?" She cocked her head to one side, her dark brown eyes pleading with him. "I passed the test. I never would have if you hadn't helped me."

"That wasn't me," he reminded her. "It was Rachel."

Her smile instantly disappeared. "No, it wasn't. *You* helped me. I wouldn't let Rachel anywhere near my homework."

"Actually, you did," he said a bit more forcefully. He remembered the incident well. Jolene had brought him her algebra homework and he'd tried to work with her. Only when it became apparent that he wasn't particularly clear on the concept himself would his daughter accept Rachel's assistance. What stood out in his mind was how well the evening had gone. The tension between Jolene and his wife had lessened, giving both him and Rachel hope that the girl was finally adjusting to their marriage.

"You could at least try," Jolene snapped.

"Okay, fine, I'll try."

"Thank you, Daddy," she said, all sweetness once again.

The phone rang as Jolene set her textbook on the table and Bruce leaped out of his chair, hoping, praying, it was Rachel. She'd called a couple of times, but their conversations were always short, consisting of her reassurances that she was fine and her avoidance of any real answers. She'd blocked his numbers so he couldn't get in touch with her. If it *was* Rachel, he was willing to promise her anything as long as she came home. He loved her and missed her. He'd agreed earlier to see a counselor but Jolene wouldn't hear of it, and Bruce had foolishly put it off. He was embarrassed by the thought of spilling out their troubles to a stranger. He'd assumed everything would right itself, but he'd been wrong and his gamble had cost him dearly.

"Hello," he said, grabbing the phone, his heart bounding into his throat.

"This is David Miller," intoned the recorded message, "and I'm running for state senator. Are you tired of runaway government spending? If that's the case, I need your vote—"

Bruce disconnected the line before he heard any more. He kept his hand on the receiver and hung his head, fighting back his disappointment.

"Dad," Jolene muttered. "You wanted that call to be Rachel, didn't you?"

"Yes." He wasn't going to deny it.

"We don't need her," Jolene insisted, looking up at him from the kitchen table. "It's been a lot better since she left. I've made dinner all week, haven't I?"

Bruce didn't agree or disagree. Jolene had done her best to fill in, and while the meals weren't always palatable, his daughter had tried.

"I know I overcooked the macaroni and cheese."

"I hardly noticed," he said, and it was true because he'd covered the entire plate with ketchup.

"The meat loaf was good, wasn't it?"

"You did an excellent job." Not exactly, but at least he'd found it edible, again with the addition of ketchup.

Jolene beamed with pride. "Like I said, we don't need Rachel."

It wasn't Rachel's cooking Bruce missed, it was Rachel herself. He missed holding her in his arms and chatting in bed. He missed pressing his hand over her stomach and silently transmitting his love and excitement to their baby. He missed Rachel's smile when he walked into the house at the end of the day and the way she hugged him, welcoming him home. They'd only been married a short while and yet Rachel had filled every nook and cranny of his world. He hadn't realized how alone and lonely he'd been until she'd come into his life. Without her nothing felt right.

"Dad, my homework, remember?"

"Yeah." He'd do his best but he wished Rachel was the one helping Jolene…

It took him nearly an hour. He wasn't a natural teacher and had to grit his teeth several times, but made it through the ordeal without losing his patience. Still, once he'd finished, Bruce was cranky and ready for bed.

Walking into his room, he looked despairingly at the crumpled sheets and the bedspread, which had slipped off and pooled on the carpet. Rachel made the bed every morning before she left for the salon. Apparently the aunt who'd raised her had insisted on it, and the habit had stuck. Then every night Rachel would remove the decorative pillows and neatly fold back the covers. The twisted and disheveled bedding depressed Bruce. He sagged onto the end of the mattress and came to a decision.

He was going to the salon tomorrow, and he'd try his hardest to talk Rachel into giving him a second chance. He had to believe she missed him as much as he missed her. Surely she'd want to come home. That belief was the only thing that got him through the day.

* * *

Friday morning, Bruce woke in good spirits. He had coffee brewing and Jolene's glass of orange juice poured before his daughter even wandered out of her bedroom.

She stared at him a moment before taking her glass off the counter. "You seem to be in a happy mood this morning."

"Do I?" He was seeing Rachel today and he couldn't help feeling a sense of anticipation.

"Dad..." Jolene regarded him skeptically. "You aren't going to see Rachel, are you?"

He didn't answer.

"*She's* the one who left *us,* remember? If she wanted to come back she would have by now, don't you think?"

Bruce ignored his daughter. "Do you have your lunch money?"

"Quit avoiding the subject."

"I have to leave now or I'll be late for my first appointment."

"Dad!"

Bruce wasn't listening. He scooped up his keys and headed out the door, letting Jolene precede him. If he stopped work at four, which he fully intended to do, then he should be at the salon no later than four-thirty. He was his own boss and set his own hours. While he did his utmost to keep his computer clients happy, he had his priorities. Oh, yes, he'd see Rachel, and once she heard how desperately he missed her, how much he needed her, she'd move back home. Bruce couldn't wait. He found himself humming, but stopped when he caught Jolene scowling at him. He didn't care, but he didn't want to set her off, either.

At four o'clock sharp, Bruce was in his car, driving back into Cedar Cove after finishing an on-site call in Gig Harbor.

He parked in the lot outside the shopping mall, and ran his fingers through his hair. He needed a haircut. Rachel had been cutting his hair for the past few years. Jolene's, too. Sooner or later his daughter would realize how much Rachel added to their lives—and it was a lot more than free haircuts! He just hoped Jolene smartened up soon.

He chose the entrance closest to the Get Nailed salon. The salon storefront looked out on the mall and for several minutes Bruce stood there and simply watched Rachel work. His heart felt like it might pound straight out of his chest. He loved his wife.

A moment later, Rachel must have felt his stare because she turned and their eyes met. The brush she held dropped to the floor. She'd lost weight, Bruce noticed, which wasn't good. It told him she wasn't eating enough and that the pregnancy was taking a toll on her health. His first instinct was to chastise her for not looking after herself. She also seemed exceptionally pale. Stephanie, when she was pregnant with Jolene, had suffered from an iron deficiency and Bruce wondered if that was the case with Rachel, too.

While Bruce waited, Rachel finished with her client, then met him just inside the salon doors.

"What are you doing here?" she whispered before he'd had a chance to greet her.

"Shouldn't it be obvious?" he returned, unable to take his eyes off her. "I came to see you."

"You said you wouldn't."

"I did?" Bruce didn't remember that. If so, he'd

agreed under duress and had since changed his mind, although he said none of that. "I miss you," he whispered, and reached for her hand.

Rachel looked down, but not before he saw tears in her eyes. "I miss you, too."

"Come home, Rachel," he pleaded as his thumb stroked the top of her hand. "I'll do whatever you ask. Just come home."

"I wish it was that easy."

"But it is."

"Jolene—"

Rachel had barely begun to speak when his daughter rounded the corner with two of her schoolfriends.

"I thought so!" Jolene yelled, hands on her hips. Bruce recognized the girls, although he couldn't recall their names. "I *knew* you were coming to see Rachel."

Next she glared at Rachel. "I don't care what my dad says, I don't want you in our house ever again."

"Jolene!" Bruce snapped. "You're being rude and your behavior is unacceptable. This is between Rachel and me. Now please leave. We'll talk later," he said in as ominous a tone as he could manage.

"I have as much of a right to be here as anyone." Her eyes sparked with indignation. She was obviously drawing strength from the presence of her friends, who stood with her, forming a silent barrier. Turning to confront Rachel, Jolene continued, "Having you out of the house has been *great* and I don't want you back."

"Jolene, stop right this minute!" Bruce shouted. He lunged and grabbed his daughter by the shoulders. "I told you, this is between Rachel and me!"

"No, it isn't," his daughter insisted. "I live in the

house, too, and it's either me or Rachel because if she comes back, then I'm leaving."

That was an empty threat if there ever was one. "And where exactly would you go?"

"I'll run away."

"Stop it, both of you," Rachel cried, covering her mouth as she struggled to hold back a sob.

Jane, the salon manager, approached them. "I'd appreciate it if the three of you would take this elsewhere. We have customers here, and you're causing a scene."

Until then Bruce hadn't realized that there were two or three ladies in the waiting area a few feet away. His focus had been on Rachel to the exclusion of everyone else—until Jolene arrived.

Taking his wife's hand, Bruce led her out of the salon, although they remained in full view of the customers. In fact, they were attracting a lot of attention—and not just from Get Nailed. Everyone in the mall seemed to be staring at them.

Rachel noticed this, as well. "I think it would be best if you all just left," she said, avoiding eye contact. Then she raised her head to meet Jolene's gaze.

"I can't leave you like this," Bruce muttered. "If anyone needs to go, it's Jolene and her entourage." He looked pointedly at his daughter, demanding that she give him some privacy.

Jolene folded her arms rebelliously and refused to budge. "No way."

"Just go," Rachel pleaded, easing away from Bruce. "Like Jane said, you're causing a scene."

"I don't care." He ignored his daughter and focused on Rachel. He understood now that he hadn't really grasped the extent of Jolene's selfishness. He didn't know how his daughter's dislike of Rachel had reached this point. Nor did he know what had torn the two of them apart in the first place. At one time they'd been so close...

"Don't worry, Jolene," Rachel said. "You can have your father all to yourself."

His daughter's smile could have lit up the entire mall. "Good." To his shock, she and her posse of friends exchanged high fives.

With that, Rachel started to walk away, then apparently had a change of heart because she turned back. "Bruce, it would be better if you didn't come here again."

"I can't promise that."

"If you do show up, I'll get a job somewhere else. This is embarrassing to me and the salon."

Bruce shook his head, unwilling to stay away.

"If anything like this happens again, Jane's going to find an excuse to fire me."

Bruce had trouble believing that. But before he could respond, his daughter grabbed his hand. "Let's go," she said. "We don't need Rachel."

"*I* need Rachel," he countered, pulling his hand free. "And our baby needs his or her father."

"What about *me?*" Jolene demanded. "What about *my* needs?"

Rachel's eyes locked with his. "Don't come back here."

"Okay, fine, but we need to talk."

"No, you don't," Jolene inserted.

"Jolene, leave me and Rachel alone," Bruce said furiously. He refused to have her interfering in his life like this. It was time she recognized her role in the breakup of his marriage. And, he told himself, it was time *he* admitted that he'd allowed her to do the damage she had.

"We need to talk," he said again, wanting Rachel to know how important she was to him. Somehow, some way, they'd find a solution.

"No." Rachel's voice was adamant. "If this...incident today did anything, it solidified my reasons for leaving. I won't go back to a house filled with tension and strife. It isn't good for me or the pregnancy."

"What about—"

Bruce didn't get a chance to finish as Rachel left him standing in the center of the mall with a dozen faces staring at him.

"Come on, Dad," Jolene said, all sweetness now. "Let's go home."

Bruce couldn't bear to even look at his daughter. If he opened his mouth, he was afraid he wouldn't be able to curb his anger. So he simply turned and walked away.

Five

"Mom, you're wearing that goofy look again," Tanni Bliss said as she strolled into the kitchen and selected an apple from the fruit bowl on the table.

"What look?" Shirley asked, although she knew exactly what her daughter meant. She'd just spent nearly two hours on the phone with Larry Knight, a nationally renowned artist—and the man she was now seeing. Although "seeing" wasn't quite the right term, considering how much he traveled. They'd met at the Seattle Art Museum a few months earlier and been in frequent touch ever since.

Larry was a widower of five years' standing, while Shirley had lost her husband to a motorcycle accident the January before last. She'd thought she'd never recover after Jim's death. She'd been convinced that falling in love again was out of the question.

Then she'd met Larry... The problem was that he lived in California and traveled a great deal—with his art exhibits, doing the lecture circuit, taking part in panels and interviews. They spoke every day now and emailed between conversations. They saw each other whenever possible, which wasn't nearly often enough to suit either of them.

"So, where's Larry now?" Tanni asked.

"He's in New Mexico." He might as well be on the moon. Without email and phone calls, she felt she'd slowly go insane. Or maybe *not* so slowly! She'd forgotten what it was like to fall in love. She'd been a college student when she met and married Jim. He'd been in the air force at the time and was about to be discharged. Eager to get on with an airline, Jim had set his sights on living in the Pacific Northwest. Once she'd visited the Seattle area, Shirley had agreed. This would be a lovely place to live and raise their children.

After Jim had been hired by Alaska Airlines, they'd settled in Cedar Cove and turned the basement of their large sprawling home into a studio for Shirley. She would've been content to remain exactly where she was for the rest of her days. Until the accident…

And, even then, she couldn't imagine moving. But she'd met Larry, and that changed everything.

"When are you two getting married?" Tanni asked, breaking into her musings.

"Married!" Shirley gasped. "We hardly know each other."

"Oh, come on, Mom. You haven't been yourself ever since the day you first laid eyes on him."

No use denying the obvious. "I know."

"It's not like I haven't noticed. You're crazy about Larry."

"True."

"So what's holding you back?"

"Well, for one thing, Larry hasn't asked."

"Oh?" Tanni made it sound like she had insider information.

Shirley was tempted to ask if her daughter knew something she didn't. Larry and Tanni chatted frequently, although she assumed her daughter had been looking for information about Shaw, the boy she'd once dated. The boy Larry had assisted in securing a place at the art institute in San Francisco.

"Has…has he mentioned that he's going to ask me to marry him?" Shirley didn't make eye contact. She felt guilty for even asking.

"No."

So much for that.

"But if he did propose, what would you say?" Tanni asked.

Her daughter was teasing her. Playing along, she shrugged as if the question was of no real concern. "I'd probably tell him it was too soon and we should date a year or two first."

Tanni burst out laughing. "You're joking."

She was, but that was irrelevant. Larry hadn't proposed and, even if he did, it would be far too soon to make such a major decision. Besides, it wasn't as if she could just move to California. Tanni had a year of high school left, and Shirley's home and life were here in Cedar Cove.

"I'm not joking," Shirley said. "What are your plans this weekend?" she asked, blatantly changing the subject.

"I thought I'd get together with Kristen and then we might hang with Jeremy."

At one time Kristen had been Tanni's sworn enemy. Shirley hadn't understood her daughter's intense dislike of the other girl. She suspected it was because

Kristen was blonde, beautiful and extremely popular. Boys were drawn to her in a way Tanni seemed to find foreign. Shirley wondered if her daughter resented that she'd only had one boyfriend in her whole life and that relationship was unraveling. Tanni had felt powerless; she hadn't wanted to lose Shaw, although in retrospect it was the best thing for both of them. They were too young and far too emotionally dependant on each other.

"Are you and Jeremy an item now or—"

"Mom," Tanni cut her off. "First of all, *item* is totally dated. Also, we've talked a couple of times and that's it. Don't go making more out of it than there is, okay?" Her voice rang with irritation, a tone that was familiar from the weeks and months following Jim's death.

Shirley instantly backed away from the sensitive topic. "Miranda and I were talking about seeing a movie."

At the mention of Shirley's best friend, Tanni grinned.

"What's so funny?" Shirley asked.

"Miranda."

"What about her?" She and Miranda had been friends for years. Miranda was a widow, too; she'd been married to an artist, which was one reason she understood Shirley's artistic temperament. Shirley had fun with Miranda and appreciated her encouragement, her loyalty and support. Miranda could be opinionated and headstrong, but that didn't bother Shirley. If they didn't agree, Shirley had no problem either arguing with Miranda or ignoring her views.

"I think Miranda likes Will Jefferson," Tanni commented.

Miranda had recently taken a part-ti

Will at the gallery. The fact that she'd even accepted
the position had surprised Shirley, since Will and Miranda seemed to disagree on almost everything—and
not in a friendly way, either.

If what Tanni said was true, and Shirley strongly suspected it was, poor Miranda was setting herself up for
heartache. Shirley had recognized the type of man Will
Jefferson was ten seconds into their first meeting. Will
was all about Will, as Tanni might have put it. Handsome
and charming, he was accustomed to having women fawn
over him. More than that, he'd come to expect it.

Shirley had to admit Miranda didn't possess the
classic beauty that typically appealed to men like Will
Jefferson. Tall and solidly built, Miranda easily stood
five-eleven, and with heels—although she rarely wore
anything but sensible shoes—she was over six feet tall.

Shirley felt that Will's usual preference was an
empty-headed woman so he could be her intellectual
superior. Miranda was his equal in every way. The fact
that Will had made a blatant play for Shirley was—
to her mind—more of an insult than a compliment.

Even Tanni had picked up on Miranda's interest in
him and Shirley worried for her friend. She doubted
that Miranda was prepared for a Will Jefferson or the
effect he might have on her emotions.

"What movie are you going to see?" Tanni asked, un-
aware of the thoughts swirling around in Shirley's head.

"We haven't decided yet."

"I'll be home before ten," Tanni said, reaching for
her car keys. She was out the door, munching on the
apple as she went.

Pouring herself a cup of coffee from the pot she'd
ade earlier, Shirley sat down at the kitchen table,

wondering what to do with this unwelcome information. If she said anything to Miranda, it would only embarrass her friend. And any warning about Will would likely be dismissed out of hand.

Shirley glanced at her watch and, noticing the time, quickly got up from her chair. Taking one last sip, she left the mug in the kitchen sink, hurried to change her clothes and freshen her makeup, then headed out the door. She was supposed to meet Miranda at the Harbor Street Art Gallery at three-thirty.

The drive took less than ten minutes. When she stepped into the gallery, the first thing she heard was Miranda's raised voice. "I'm telling you, the Chandler painting will look better on this wall," she was saying.

"No! It'd be better there," Will Jefferson said, just as heatedly.

"Hello?" Shirley called out.

Miranda responded immediately. "Shirley, come over here. We need your opinion."

Great. Now she was going to be drawn into this argument, too. She walked toward them and glanced at the painting that seemed to be the subject of their disagreement. "Are you ready for the movie, Miranda?" she asked, hoping to avoid taking sides.

"Look at this," Miranda insisted, gesturing at the watercolor.

The piece was stunning, the color choices vibrant and inviting. It portrayed a young girl in a blue cotton summer dress, biking past a white picket fence in a seashore town. A wide variety of flowers bloomed along the fence line. The girl's innocence was in subtle contrast to her unconscious feminine appeal. In style, it was naturalistic but its shimmering colors were influenced by classic Impressionism. "This is a lovely work."

"I agree," Will said, speaking for the first time. "And I want it displayed in the way that will benefit it the most."

"I think it should be on *this* wall and Will says— quite irrationally, I believe—that it should be *there*." Miranda indicated the opposite side of the gallery.

"Irrational," Will repeated from between clenched teeth. "If anyone's irrational, it's you. If we hang the painting on the wall I suggest, it'll be the first thing people see when they enter the gallery."

"*This* wall reveals it in the best light," Miranda countered.

"You both have valid points," Shirley said when they turned to her. "Why don't you compromise?"

"No." Will shook his head. "This is *my* gallery, despite what Miranda seems to think, and we'll do this my way because—" he paused "—I'm the boss." This was said in a challenging voice, as if he expected Miranda to resign. As if he wanted her to.

"Fine. Hang it wherever you like," Miranda said, brushing her hands in exasperation.

"That's exactly what I intend to do."

Miranda sighed and, ignoring Will, said, "Have you ever noticed how important it is to the fragile male ego to have the last word?"

Shirley tried to disguise a smile, but Will obviously wasn't amused.

He bristled. "That is categorically untrue."

Motioning with her head, Miranda seemed to imply that his statement only proved her point.

"Are you ready to go now?" Shirley asked.

"Be right with you." Miranda disappeared around the corner and returned an instant later with her purse and raincoat.

"Which movie are you going to?" Will asked Shirley conversationally.

"Not sure yet."

"Well, have fun."

"We will," Miranda muttered.

He walked them to the door. "I've got you on the schedule for Monday," he said.

"Monday?" Miranda frowned. "I thought I only worked Tuesday, Friday and Saturday."

"Would you mind filling in for me? I'm meeting with the insurance people on behalf of my mother and Ben."

"No, of course I don't mind, but I would've appreciated knowing about it sooner."

"Sorry. I forgot to mention it."

They stared at each other and then Miranda nodded. "I'll be here at ten."

"Thanks."

"No problem," she said brusquely.

As they made their way to her car, Shirley considered Tanni's observation about Miranda's feelings for Will. She also suspected that, despite their bickering, he was actually fond of her—and maybe he respected her more than he let on. He'd certainly come to rely on her.

"Did you choose a movie?" Miranda asked. "What about the latest Matt Damon picture?"

"Sure."

"I have the entertainment section of the paper and—" Miranda paused to look at her watch. "This is perfect. The next show starts in less than thirty minutes, which gives us time to drive there, buy our tickets and get our popcorn."

"Sounds good."

"Did you talk to Larry this afternoon?" Miranda asked as they got into Shirley's car. Her own would stay at the art gallery, and Shirley would drop her off there after the movie.

"For two hours."

"Two hours!"

Shirley laughed. Neither of them had wanted to end the conversation. "Long-distance relationships are difficult," she said. "So, this is how we stay in touch."

"Why don't you just get married? I don't know any two people better suited to each other."

"I wish it was that easy, but I can't uproot Tanni when she still has a year of high school."

"Who said you had to move right away?" Miranda said.

"Well, as I told my daughter, there's one small detail. Larry hasn't asked and at this stage I'd be shocked if he did. I wish everyone would remember we only met a few months ago."

"What was your phone bill last month? And his?"

Shirley rolled her eyes.

"You know what I mean."

"Yeah, I do. Okay, we spend a *lot* of time on the phone. Today wasn't an exception." Whenever he called her, whenever she called him, Shirley felt like a teenager again. Her heart would leap with joy at the sound of his voice.

They'd reached the movie complex, and Shirley parked. They purchased their tickets and popcorn and were about to enter the theater when her cell phone rang.

It was Larry, which struck her as odd, since they'd already talked that day.

"Did I catch you at a bad time?" he asked excitedly.

"No. Miranda and I are just walking into the theater." She was juggling her popcorn, purse, drink and the cell phone, afraid of dropping one, when Miranda helped by taking the large soda out of her hands. "What's up?"

"Are you busy next weekend?"

"Next weekend?" She momentarily closed her eyes, trying to remember if anything was written on the kitchen calendar. "I don't think so... Why?"

"I want you to fly down to California."

"California? Aren't you supposed to be in Nashville next weekend?"

"Yes, but the lecture was postponed."

"I'm sorry."

"I'm not. I want you to meet me at my home in California. I know it's last-minute and I apologize, but I only just heard about this. Tell me you'll be able to come."

"Yes, I think so."

"What about Tanni and Nick?"

"I'm pretty sure they're available. I'll have to check."

"Wonderful. I want all of you to meet my children."

"Your children," she repeated.

"Yes, I feel they should meet the woman I intend to marry."

Shirley froze. The bag of popcorn she held fell from her hand and spilled its contents on the floor.

Six

Linc Wyse stepped outside the Wyse Man Garage and leaned against the building. Staying inside that office a moment longer would've been intolerable. The bills were piling up and he had nothing to pay them with. His bank account, which had been substantial and was supposed to carry him for six months, was nearly empty.

The frustration was killing him. Marrying Lori and keeping it a secret from her family, which hadn't been his choice but hers, had created a fierce enemy in Lori's father. Linc had tried but he'd been unable to convince Leonard Bellamy that he loved Lori, that he hadn't married his daughter for her money. Not that Lori *had* any money now, except what she earned herself. But Linc didn't care; he never had.

Despite that, Bellamy was out to ruin him and he was close to succeeding.

As Linc stared out at the street, a familiar truck passed, slowed down and then came to a stop in front of the garage. His brother-in-law. Linc straightened when Mack McAfee rolled down the driver's window and called out, "Hey, Linc, how's it going?"

Linc managed a grimace that he hoped would pass for a grin. "It's going."

"You don't look that busy. Do you want to join me?"

"Where are you headed?"

"Mary Jo's working late, Noelle's at day care and I just finished helping a friend move. A beer sounds good to me."

"It does to me, too, but I'd better stay here in case a job comes in." The mid-September sunshine made for a warm afternoon, not that Linc noticed the weather much. With no work, he'd sent the men home. No point in paying for idle hands—but it would be just his luck to have two or three people show up and find no one there. That was a chance he couldn't afford to take.

"Tell you what. I'll pick us up a six-pack and be right back."

Mack returned within fifteen minutes, got out of his truck and handed Linc a can. They sat in the office. Leaning back in his chair, Linc pulled the tab off the cold beer and took a long swallow, enjoying the taste. "Thanks," he said to Mack, saluting him with the beer.

Mack nodded. "Haven't seen much of you lately," he commented.

Linc hadn't been getting out. He didn't have the inclination or, these days, the extra cash. But rather than respond, he shrugged.

"You look like a man who's carrying the weight of the world on his shoulders." Mack leaned back, too. "Trouble?"

Once more he answered with a shrug. He was tired of holding everything inside and yet he was used to keeping his own counsel. Fixing his own problems. But this time he couldn't. Bellamy was blackballing him—no other word for it—and the business was sinking fast. Not even Lori knew the extent of what her father had done, nor did she fully understand their financial situation. For that he had only himself to blame. Linc had told her next to nothing about any of this. Lori was angry enough with her father. Foolish and unrealistic though it seemed now, Linc had hoped to bring father and daughter together. It'd never been his intention to drive a wedge into their already strained relationship.

"Everyone's got trouble," Linc replied when he realized Mack was waiting for a response.

"True, but not all trouble is created equal, if you know what I mean."

"Right," Linc agreed.

"I'm here if you want to talk about it."

Linc regarded the man his sister had married. He'd liked Mack from the start, although he'd initially had doubts about their living arrangement. He'd gotten over those doubts pretty fast. A firefighter and paramedic, Mack had helped deliver Noelle, Mary Jo's baby girl. While it had bothered him that Mary Jo didn't live close to her family, he'd felt better knowing Mack was nearby. They'd shared a duplex, he on one side and she on the other. They'd married earlier in the year and Linc was happy for his sister.

"You might have noticed I'm not exactly overwhelmed with work here," Linc began, finally giving in to the relief of divulging his problems to a sympathetic listener. "I'm not inexperienced in this business and I did my homework. By my calculations, I should have more repairs than I can handle."

Mack gestured with his beer can. "Leonard Bellamy?"

Linc nodded. "Well, it's not like you didn't warn me."

Mack sat up straight, his eyes slightly narrowed. "Yeah, but I don't think I knew Bellamy wields *that* much power in Cedar Cove."

"And Bremerton and all the surrounding areas, too, apparently. I couldn't even guess what rumor he's floating about me, but whatever it is, people in this community are buying it."

"I suppose that's causing problems between you and Lori."

Linc glanced away, avoiding his brother-in-law's eyes.

Mack nudged him. "Are you telling me she doesn't *know?*"

"No one does."

"So Lori's in the dark about all this?"

"About almost everything."

Mack stared at him as if he found that hard to believe. "You've got to be kidding, man! This is your *wife.* I know if I held anything back from Mary Jo, she'd be furious. That, in case you're interested, is a lesson I learned the hard way."

Linc gave him a brief smile. Being well-acquainted with his sister's temper, he pitied Mack the wrath of Mary Jo.

"The Bellamys are her family," Linc said, defending his silence. "I'm only trying to protect her."

"Does she want to be protected?"

"Isn't that a husband's responsibility?"

Mack shook his head. "Not if it means keeping her ignorant of things she should know. And," he added, "Bellamy might be her father but you're her husband. You two are in this together—for better or worse. Remember?"

Linc would think about that, but for now he was saying nothing to Lori. They finished their beers, chatting about the football season and the Seahawks' chances. Mack tossed his empty can in the recycling bin, then slapped Linc on the back and strolled out the door.

"Thanks for the beer," Linc said, following him outside.

"My pleasure." He raised his hand in farewell, climbed into the truck cab and was off.

Linc left work early and by the time he arrived home, Lori was already there. Just seeing her warm, loving smile dissolved the tension that had been with him all day—dissolved it for that night at least. Without a word she hurried across the room, slipped her arms around his neck and kissed him with enough enthusiasm to weaken his knees.

"Was that for anything special?" he asked as he spread nibbling kisses down the side of her neck.

"Yup. We're celebrating."

"Hmm...celebrating what?"

"The fact that it's Monday."

Each and every Monday was special when he was with Lori. She'd changed his world, brought him joy, made him laugh. Before he'd met her, Linc had seen life as a series of obligations. He'd run the family auto repair business in Seattle with his two younger brothers. After their parents were killed in a car accident, Linc had assumed responsibility for holding the family together. He'd taken his role as the oldest seriously and was determined to keep his brothers and his sister safe, to maintain a cohesive unit. That hadn't allowed time for anything frivolous like falling in love. Until he actually fell in love—with Lori—and his whole life went through a seismic shift.

"I bought you a present today," she whispered seductively in his ear.

Shivers of awareness raced down his spine. They could barely afford groceries, let alone gifts. "Oh?"

"Do you want to see it?"

He released her and slowly walked away.

"Linc, don't you want to see what I got you?"

"Lori, we're in a bit of a...a financial bind at the moment. It would be best if you didn't buy me anything for a while. I'm sorry, but I'd rather you didn't make any unnecessary purchases. Okay?"

She blinked, then nodded reluctantly. "Of course. I'll take it back. I still have the receipt."

"Thank you." He felt bad asking her to return the item. Whatever it was would be superfluous. He had everything he needed.

"I'd like to show it to you first, though. Okay?"

Linc agreed and sat in the recliner while Lori disappeared into the bedroom. His heart was heavy. He felt her disappointment but they couldn't spend money indiscriminately, especially money they didn't have.

His wife reappeared dressed in a see-through chiffon piece of nothing. Linc's mouth sagged open. "That's...the gift you got me?" Her tempting body was all but revealed, and Linc swallowed hard. "I... I think we might find room in our budget for that." He got the words out, but with some difficulty.

"No, you're right. I should know better than to buy—"

"Lori," he said, closing his eyes. "I'm nearly broke. The business is failing. I don't even know if I'll last the month. I haven't wanted to tell you, but I can't hide it anymore."

She placed her hand over her mouth and stared at him, wide-eyed with shock.

"I realize I was wrong to keep this from you, but I…have my reasons."

Lori continued to stare at him as if she didn't know what to say.

"I'm sorry," he whispered. Leaning forward, he rubbed his hand across his face. "I'm so sorry."

She came to him then, climbing onto his lap and wrapping her arms around him. "I married you because I love you. I don't need anything but you."

Linc buried his face in her neck and pulled her close. She lifted his head and he kissed her. Then she abruptly broke off the kiss, sliding off his lap and standing directly in front of him, her eyes flashing. "Don't you *ever* do that to me again. Do you understand?"

"Kiss you?" he asked in bewilderment.

"Of course not! I'm talking about keeping the truth from me." Whirling around, she went into their bedroom, returning a few minutes later, fully dressed. "Okay. What happened?" Her voice was brisk, all seductiveness gone.

"Happened?"

"To cause this financial shortfall. You're…" She

paused as though everything had started to come together in her mind. "My father." She spoke in a low voice, then repeated the two words more loudly and with more conviction. "My father's done something, hasn't he?"

Linc didn't reply.

"Hasn't he?" she demanded again.

"I...can't say for sure, but it seems that way."

She began to pace, five steps in one direction, five in the other, making quick, precise turns.

Linc found her movements almost hypnotic. "Now, Lori," he began, "there's no need to get upset. I have everything under control."

"That's low, even for him." Either she hadn't heard a word he'd said or she recognized his statement for the lie it was. "This is going to change and it's going to change right now." She reached for her purse and yanked out her cell phone, punching a single button.

"Lori," he asked, "who are you phoning?"

"Who do you think?" she muttered.

Linc stood and circled her waist with his arms. "Lori," he said again, drawing her close. "Tell me what you're doing."

She moved the cell away from her ear. "I'm calling Daddy. And I'm having it out with him."

Linc had seen that look in her eyes only once before and that, too, had been an instance involving her father.

"Hello, Helen, this is Lori Wyse. Is my father still in?"

He started to tell Lori that maybe they should discuss this first, but one sharp glance from his wife told him to forget it. She was furious—and determined.

A minute later Bellamy got on the phone. "Hi, Daddy," she said, all sweetness.

"Hi, baby girl. If you're calling, I figure that means you've come to your senses and dumped that useless husband of yours."

Linc stood close enough to hear Bellamy's half of the conversation. At his father-in-law's comment, his back stiffened. He released Lori, automatically clenching his fists.

"No, Daddy, it's the Bellamys I'm—as you so delicately put it—dumping. For most of my life I've cowered in front of you, caving in to your wishes. No more. You've gone too far this time. You want to hurt the man I love, the man I married. I won't stand for that. I won't! In fact… I never want to hear your name or see you again. You have tried to manipulate me my entire life. Well, I chose to marry Linc. He is my husband and you will stop meddling in our lives. Is that clear?"

Leonard Bellamy seemed amused. "You're talking mighty big for a girl living in an apartment her father owns."

"That's another thing. Linc and I will be out of here just as soon as we can find another place."

For once Bellamy didn't seem quite so sure. "Don't be hasty…"

"No, just the opposite. It's taken me too long. You've done everything you can to ruin my husband, but you don't know what kind of man he is. He's going to make it, regardless of what you say or what you do. And as of this minute I am finished with this family."

"What about your mother?"

"She'll have to make her own decision. I've made mine, and while I hate to exclude *her* from my life, I won't give *you* access to any part of me or my marriage. If that means never seeing Mom again, then so be it."

Bellamy didn't appear to believe her. "Like I said, you're talking big now. But you'll change your mind at the first sign of trouble."

"Will I, Dad? When's the last time I changed my mind about anything? When's the last time you convinced me to back down?"

His hesitation was answer enough.

"Listen, Lori…"

"Goodbye, Daddy," she said softly, and disconnected. With a hiccuping sigh, Lori dropped her cell phone back inside her purse. Then, as if she'd suddenly realized he was right behind her, she walked into Linc's embrace and hugged him hard.

Linc hugged her back. "I wish you'd talked to me before you did that." Linc knew what it was like to be without parents. He didn't fully grasp how important a father and mother could be until he'd lost his own.

"You're the only family I need now."

"Oh, Lori…"

"We have to move," she said. She straightened and rubbed her moist eyes.

"Yes, well, that could be a problem," Linc felt compelled to tell her. He'd known a move was imminent after his last dreadful confrontation with his father-in-law. The problem was, they didn't have enough funds to make a security deposit, plus the first and last month's rent. Even with Lori's salary from a high-end women's clothing store in Silverdale, they didn't have the amount they required. Or anything close to it. Her income covered groceries and daily necessities. And the apartment had been rent-free.

"Where do you suggest we find a new place when our bank account is hovering around zero?"

"What about moving back to Seattle?"

Linc had thought of that earlier but he hated the idea of bringing his wife into the same house as his two younger brothers. He enjoyed his privacy and feared Mel and Ned would see Lori as another Mary Jo, expecting her to take care of the cooking and cleaning the way their sister had. Not that he'd allow it to happen.

"The commute would be difficult for you."

"I'll change jobs," Lori said.

"You love your job," he reminded her.

She nodded. "I'd miss it, but I'll do whatever I have to."

They were both silent for a moment. "No matter what it costs, Linc, we have to leave this apartment."

Lori was right, and he couldn't dispute that. The sooner they found a new place, the better.

Seven

Rachel wasn't sure that seeing Bruce was a good idea. He'd been persistent, however, and after several conversations about it, she'd finally given in. They'd agreed to meet at the Pancake Palace after work. When she arrived, a few minutes late, Bruce's car was already parked out front; he'd probably shown up right at five. She wondered if he'd told Jolene where he was going, and doubted he had. Bruce liked to keep the peace. After all, he'd let his daughter take charge of his life and their marriage. Rachel was astonished that she'd stuck around as long as she had. The situation was emotionally unhealthy for all three of them.

Rachel parked several spots down from his car, hesitated for a moment, half tempted to flee, and then locked up. When she entered the restaurant she saw Bruce immediately. He'd chosen a booth facing the door. He smiled as he stood to greet her. Funny how a simple smile could affect her so strongly. She smiled back, accepted his kiss on the cheek and slid into the booth across from him.

"Hi," he said eagerly, his eyes filled with longing.

He stretched his arms across the table and clasped her hands as if he needed to touch her. "You look fantastic."

"Thanks." She'd taken extra care with her hair and makeup, although she tried not to have high expectations about this meeting.

"You're feeling better?" he asked. "No problems with the pregnancy?"

"None," she assured him.

"Everything okay at work?"

She nodded. The past five days, following the fiasco at the salon, had been relatively calm. Jane hadn't been happy with her afterward, and Rachel couldn't blame her, but fortunately there'd been no further reference to it.

One night recently when she hadn't been able to sleep, Rachel had gotten up for a glass of milk and found Nate in the kitchen. They'd talked for almost an hour. He'd been sympathetic, although never intrusive. During this conversation with Nate, she'd realized with greater clarity than ever why Bruce acted the way he did. He hated confrontation and would do anything to avoid it. He coped by ignoring conflicts and tension, by wishing them away. He didn't want to be caught between his wife and his daughter. She couldn't fault him for preferring to keep the peace, but his approach didn't work.

"You need to look after yourself and the baby," Bruce was saying.

Alicia, the waitress, appeared in her pink uniform with the starched white apron. She automatically poured Bruce a coffee.

"Decaf for me," Rachel told her.

"Coming right up. How about a piece of pie to go with that?"

"None for me," Bruce said.

Alicia scowled at him. "I wasn't asking you. She's the one who could use a little meat on her bones."

"No, thanks," Rachel said, squelching a smile.

Alicia set the coffeepot on the table and started to enumerate the day's selection of pies. "We got apple, blueberry, coconut cream and peach. The apple's my favorite but you choose."

"I…" Rachel looked at Bruce, who was grinning from ear to ear, apparently approving of Alicia's tactics.

"Apple, it is," the waitress announced, picked up the coffeepot and hurried into the kitchen.

"She's almost as bossy as Goldie," Bruce said, chuckling.

Goldie had been at the Pancake Palace forever, while Alicia, who'd started there maybe twenty years ago, was a relative newcomer.

Actually, a piece of apple pie did sound good. With all this stress—the pregnancy, the separation, the emotional upheaval—Rachel had lost weight she could ill afford to lose.

Alicia reappeared with the decaf and a thick slice of apple pie. "Enjoy," she said.

"I will." Rachel reached for her fork but didn't try even a bite. She needed to hear what Bruce had to say, why he'd wanted to meet. Clutching the fork, she waited until Alicia was out of earshot. "You asked to see me."

"Yes. It's time you came home," Bruce said starkly. "You're my wife and I love you. You living somewhere else—it's just plain wrong." His voice fell. "I worry about you and the baby."

She knew he meant every word, but nothing about their situation had improved. Judging by the incident at the mall, Jolene was as angry and caustic as ever. Rachel wasn't wanted nor was she appreciated by her stepdaughter, and her husband wouldn't deal with the girl's hostility. Rachel refused to return to an environment that was unhealthy for her and her unborn child.

"What's changed?" she asked. With great precision, she set the fork aside and studied Bruce.

He cupped his mug with both hands and stared down at it. "I have." He took in a deep breath. "I failed you as a husband by choosing to ignore the obvious. I hoped the two of you would work it out on your own instead of doing what I could to help. If you come back, I promise I won't let Jolene say or do anything disrespectful."

"Bruce, that isn't enough. I'm sorry but this isn't going to be resolved just because you tell Jolene to respect me." Besides, he might be able to control his daughter while he was in the house, although she doubted it, but there were plenty of times when she and Jolene were alone.

His sigh revealed his impatience. "Okay, tell me exactly what you want."

"I want," she said emphatically, "to get to the root of the problem and that means seeing a counselor. A family counselor," she specified. "A professional trained to deal with situations like this."

"Okay." He drew out the word.

His reluctance was evident. He'd said yes to counseling a little while ago but it was obviously the last thing he wanted. Bruce had never been keen on the idea of pouring out their personal troubles to a stranger. For her part, Jolene had been violently opposed from the first. It was one of the factors that had led to Rachel's leaving. "I've heard that before and nothing happened. I'd make an appointment and you'd find a reason to cancel or forget or—"

"I only canceled the one time."

"You said you'd make the next appointment but you didn't."

He glanced down at the table. "I—I'll go. No more excuses. I'll do whatever it takes to bring you home."

Rachel reached across the table and squeezed his hand. "That's a start."

"But I can tell you right now that Jolene won't go," Bruce continued. "And I don't know how to get her to agree."

"Still, a trained professional can teach us how to deal with her."

Bruce frowned. "You really believe that?"

"Of course. Don't you?"

He held her look for a long moment, then shook his head. "I'll go because it's what you want, but I don't hold out a lot of hope that someone neither of us knows is going to help in this situation."

"In other words, you think counseling is a waste of time?" She spoke slowly, letting him know how much his comment discouraged her.

"The thing is, Rachel, if Jolene begs off, which she already said she intends to do, what will we get out of counseling?"

Sometimes Rachel had to wonder which one of those two was the parent. Bruce had more or less told her everything she needed to hear. Without even sipping her coffee or taking a bite of the pie, Rachel slid out of the booth. What *was* a waste of time was meeting Bruce. Despite what he'd said, nothing had changed, nor would it. Bruce just wanted their lives to go back to what he thought of as "normal"—the way they'd been this past year. But Rachel would no longer tolerate Jolene's behavior toward her.

"Where are you going?" Bruce asked, standing, too. He grabbed for her hand as if to stop her.

"All you care about is talking me into moving back home, and you'll say whatever it takes. Sweeping our problems under the carpet isn't going to work."

"I *said* I'd go to counseling," Bruce insisted.

Rachel was sure he'd attend one or two sessions, but then he'd find some excuse to cancel. Jolene would simply refuse to go, and Bruce would be powerless to make her. Rachel wasn't willing to accept half measures. When and if she moved back home, their circumstances had to be completely different.

"Don't leave, Rachel. Please."

"It was pointless for us to talk," she said, tugging her hand free.

"I don't understand what you want. I've offered to go to counseling and that's not good enough. So what *do* you want?" he demanded, irritated now.

"I want my husband to be a man who honors my place in his life. A man who doesn't allow his children to dictate what goes on in his household. A man who'll cherish his role and mine—and frankly, at this moment, you aren't that man. And I don't know if you ever will be."

Bruce blanched. "Don't hold back," he muttered

sarcastically. "See how deep you can cut me. I came here hoping you'd be reasonable, hoping to convince you of my love…"

She rolled her eyes. "You know what, Bruce? I don't think it's a good idea for us to talk again."

"Fine. All I ask is that you let me know when the baby's born."

"Of course I will, but until then I'd appreciate it if you stayed out of my life."

Anger flashed in his eyes. "You don't mean that."

While it was true that she might have a change of heart, right now she was dead serious. "I do mean it."

And with that, Rachel walked out of the restaurant.

She didn't sleep well that night or the next. Thursday afternoon she was with a client when she saw Bruce standing outside the salon. She turned her back, ignoring him.

Jane walked over to her and whispered, "Bruce is here."

"I know."

"He wants to speak to you."

Rachel shook her head. Talking to Bruce wouldn't help either of them. How many times were they supposed to repeat the same argument?

"Rachel, he's only going to show up again and again. This is disruptive to you and to everyone here. I told you I didn't want him back."

"I know. I'm sorry."

"Do you want me to call security?"

Having Bruce escorted from the mall was further than she was willing to go. "No. I'll talk to him." Setting the curling iron aside, and excusing herself to her client, Rachel stepped outside, where Bruce stood waiting.

He'd buried his hands in his pockets and shuffled his feet back and forth like a schoolboy called before the principal. "I didn't feel good about how our conversation ended the other night."

It had bothered Rachel, too, although she had no idea how to change anything.

"Won't you please just come home?"

"No." She hated to be so inflexible, but she didn't have any choice. "I told you before and I meant it—I don't want to talk about this anymore. I don't want to see you, Bruce. It only upsets me."

"I can't stay away, Rachel. I've tried but I can't make myself do it."

"In other words, you're determined to hound me." Thank goodness she'd had the sense not to tell anyone where she was living, not even Teri.

"I want you back."

Apparently he intended to wear down her defenses until he got what he wanted. It sounded as if he planned to wait outside the salon every day until she moved back to Yakima Street. For her, the problem with that was twofold. First, Jane didn't want him hanging around, and second, Rachel feared that in time he *would* wear her down to the point that she'd agree.

"Leave me alone, Bruce."

"I can't," he whispered. "I love you."

She longed to believe they could make their marriage work. For her sake and for the baby's. But every time she felt herself weakening, all she had to do was picture Jolene's face, mocking her with that triumphant smile. The girl had won, and for Rachel there was no going back.

"Don't come here again, Bruce. I'm warning you, if you do Jane will ask security to step in."

"Fine, if that's what it takes to talk to you, then I'll gladly let them arrest me."

Rachel didn't respond to his comment and returned to the salon. She wasn't sure how long Bruce stood there; she did her best not to look in his direction.

At quitting time, Jane asked the security guard to walk Rachel to her car. While she felt a bit ridiculous, she was grateful to be spared the risk of yet another confrontation with Bruce.

Once she got home, to the house she shared with Nate Olsen, she opened a can of tomato soup and had that and a few cheese slices for dinner. She wasn't hungry but she ate because of the baby.

Nate arrived around seven. Rachel was sitting in the recliner with her feet elevated. She had the television on and was reading a magazine at the same time. She needed as many distractions as she could get.

Her housemate took one look at her and frowned. "Bad day?"

"You could say that."

"What happened?"

Unsure how much to tell him, she considered what she should say.

"Wait." Nate held up one hand. He sat on the edge of the sofa. "Bruce showed up at work again."

She nodded, but didn't divulge the details of their conversation. "Jane isn't happy about it, either."

"Did he make another scene?"

"Not really, but he threatened to show up every day until I change my mind."

"That's awkward. It's going to cause problems for you, isn't it?"

She hadn't mentioned this part of the conversation to her boss. Jane was already upset with her over what had happened a week earlier.

"I might have a solution," Nate said slowly.

"What?" At the moment everything felt hopeless.

"A temporary position has been posted at the shipyard," Nate told her. "One of the clerks just had a baby and she'll be out for five months. The job requires basic computer and administrative skills. Do you think you might want to apply?"

Rachel bit her lip. "Would I have any chance of getting the job?"

"As good a chance as anyone else."

"Then why not." Getting on with the shipyard would certainly help her situation. The timing couldn't have been better. And after the baby was born, she'd have to reassess her options, anyway.

"I know someone in HR and I'll drop off a résumé for you."

"Wow, that would be great! Thank you."

Not surprisingly, the next day after work, Bruce showed up at the salon. Rachel ignored him and after several minutes he left.

"Rachel," Jane whispered in warning. "I don't want Bruce hanging around here. Can't you do something?"

"I already have." Booking an extended lunch hour, she'd gone to the shipyard employment office, had an interview and taken a test. She didn't know how well she'd done but it didn't seem that difficult.

Nate was home early that evening, smiling when he walked in the door. "I talked to Becky, my friend in HR," he said. He put his briefcase down, opened the refrigerator and removed a cold soda. "You got the highest possible score."

"I did? Does that mean they might call me in for another interview? Did you tell her that if she hired me I'd give her a free haircut?"

Nate laughed. "No, because that might be construed as bribery."

Rachel smiled, optimistic for the first time in weeks. Months.

"The position will be posted for another couple of days and then Becky will notify the applicant who's been chosen. You'll know one way or the other by the end of the week."

"Thanks again, Nate."

He shrugged off her appreciation. "Anything for a friend."

Rachel had a good feeling about this short-term position. It was perfect for her. The shipyard obviously agreed because a few days later Rachel received word that she had the job.

Eight

"Jack, what's that in your pocket?" Olivia asked, pulling her husband into the hallway that led to their bedroom. He had the grace to look guilty.

"Cookies," he admitted.

"Jack," she moaned. He had to watch his diet carefully, and the cookies and cake Charlotte insisted on baking weren't part of his low-fat eating program. After seeing Jack through one heart attack and bypass surgery, Olivia had been keeping a close eye on his eating habits. He'd been backsliding recently, since temptation, provided by Charlotte, was ever-present these days.

"Your mother baked them especially for me," Jack said. "I couldn't hurt her feelings, could I?"

"Oh, Jack." She sighed, and held out her hand. "At least give one of them to me."

He snorted. "At this rate we'll both weigh three hundred pounds by the time your mother and Ben are back in their own house."

Olivia had already gained a pound and this cookie wasn't helping; still, like Jack, she couldn't resist.

Thrusting one hand in his pocket, he took out the cookies in their paper napkin, and begrudgingly placed two of the four he'd pilfered in her palm.

Olivia finished off her last peanut butter cookie before she went into the kitchen. Her mother was busy with the dishes, quietly singing a hymn as she squirted detergent into the hot water. She put the bottle down by the sink and began a song about Jesus washing all our sins away.

"Mom," Olivia said, coming to stand next to her mother. She reached for a kitchen towel and slung it over her shoulder while she waited for the first clean bowl. "You could always use the dishwasher, you know."

"It only takes a minute to do these few by hand," Charlotte said. "I didn't realize you were back."

She'd arrived home about ten minutes earlier and they'd chatted briefly before she saw Jack slinking away, looking guilty. "We spoke when I came in."

"We did?" Charlotte seemed confused.

"Mom, do you remember baking cookies yesterday?"

"Of course I do. I made Jack's favorites. Snicker-doodles."

"You baked him a pie last night, too."

"Well, yes, the Granny Smith apples are outstanding this year."

Olivia tried to broach the subject carefully. "The thing is, Mom, Jack and I are trying to avoid sweets."

"My heavens, why would you do that?"

"It's a matter of being healthy, eating right, getting in the required number of fruits and vegetables. While it's fine to have dessert once a week or so, every day is simply too much."

Her mother turned to look at her. "But I enjoy baking for you and it makes me feel like I'm doing something to pay for my keep."

"But, Mom, you don't need to do a thing."

"I know that, but I *want* to."

Because Olivia felt guilty she added, "It's not that Jack and I don't appreciate it, because we do. But Jack loves your cookies so much, he can't stop himself from stealing one or two even though he shouldn't."

Her mother beamed with pleasure. "I always did like Jack Griffin. I was so pleased when you decided to marry him."

"I like him myself," Olivia said, smiling as she spoke. "Why don't we compromise? You bake to your heart's content, and we'll freeze the cookies and other goodies."

"Olivia, what a marvelous idea! That'll make everyone happy. No wonder you're such a good judge."

"Thanks, Mom." Olivia dried the clean dishes, put them back in the cupboards, then went to the laundry room. She had a load of whites she wanted to wash. To her surprise, she found them already clean and folded, sitting on top of the washer. Apparently her mother had taken that task upon herself. Unfortunately, she'd added something red—her new towel set? As a result, what had gone in white was now a fetching shade of…pink.

Groaning inwardly Olivia picked up the stack of clothes and carried them into the bedroom.

The phone rang just then, and the readout said Grace's name.

"Griffin residence," Charlotte's voice answered when Olivia picked up.

"Good evening, Charlotte," Grace said.

"I've got it, Mom."

"You two girls go ahead and talk. I'll get dinner on the table."

"I'll be there in a couple of minutes," Olivia told her mother. She heard the phone click as Charlotte hung up.

"So how's it going with your mother and Ben living at the house?" Grace asked.

"Okay, I guess."

"It's not always easy having your mother in your own home, is it?" Grace said sympathetically.

"I'll tell you about it tonight."

"Er, that's what I was calling about."

"You are going to aerobics class, Grace, and I won't accept any excuses." They'd stopped attending their weekly classes during Olivia's cancer treatments, but they'd since resumed. This was *their* time and she wasn't going to be cheated out of it.

"I promised Beth Morehouse I'd stop by her place on Christmas Tree Lane to meet some dogs she wants to bring into the Reading with Rover program." As head librarian, Grace had started the program toward the end of the school year and now it had begun again. Beth, a local dog trainer, had been instrumental in its success. "Have you ever been there?"

"No. You aren't trying to change the subject, are you, Grace?"

"No, I'm serious. She's got quite the operation. Twenty acres of Christmas trees and a full working crew. The house is lovely, too—a big two-story place, charming as can be."

"Grace, you know Wednesday is our exercise night."

"Yes." Olivia heard reluctance in her voice. "But I sort of got out of the habit."

"Then it's more important than ever for us to get back into it."

"You're right," Grace admitted. "I'll be there."

"Good."

"Thanks for the pep talk. I needed it, and to be honest, I wasn't all that excited about driving out to Beth's." She sighed. "I can do it later in the week."

"You're missing Buttercup, aren't you?"

There was a silence, and Olivia realized her friend was fighting back tears over the loss of her beloved dog. "Yeah, I miss her. She was far more than just a pet. She saw me through the darkest days of my life."

Olivia felt her own eyes welling up with tears. She'd loved Buttercup, too. Years before, one of her mother's friends was moving into an assisted living complex; she couldn't take the golden retriever with her and Charlotte had suggested Grace might want the dog. Dan Sherman, Grace's first husband, had disappeared a few months earlier and Grace had been alone for the first time in her life. Those *had* been dark days. It was more than a year before they'd learned of Dan's fate.

"See you at seven," Olivia said once she'd recovered her own voice.

"I'll be there."

Dinner that evening was a four-course meal Charlotte had spent most of the afternoon preparing. Ben had set the table, and Olivia noticed that he'd arranged their cutlery in the wrong order—very unusual for her always impeccable stepfather. They had squash soup, using squash from Charlotte's own small garden. That was followed by a mixed green salad with home-made poppyseed dressing. The main course was meat loaf, mashed potato casserole, fresh green beans, plus homemade pickled asparagus and sweet corn relish. And for dessert, a chocolate zucchini cake.

Olivia would've preferred a light dinner because of her workout, but her mother wouldn't hear of it.

"You're much too thin as it is," Charlotte murmured as she heaped a second spoonful of potato casserole onto Olivia's plate. Olivia forced a smile, took one more bite and then excused herself.

Ten minutes later, Jack joined her in the bedroom. Ten extra minutes during which he was helping him-self to seconds of everything on the table.

Olivia sat on the edge of the bed.

"Sweetheart," Jack said, ever sensitive to her moods. "Are you upset about something?"

"My mother is trying so hard to be helpful and God bless her for it, but I'd rather do my own wash and I'd rather she stopped cooking like it's Thanksgiving every single night."

Jack's face broke into a huge grin. "You don't hear me complaining."

"Wipe that smile off your face, Jack Griffin."

He spread out his hands. "Honey…"

"Don't 'honey' me. Look at this." She flew off the bed to her underwear drawer and yanked it open, then removed the now-pink panties and waved them at him. "Did you see this?"

"Hey, when did you start wearing pink underwear?"

"Apparently today. Mom washed them with the new red towels, which by the way have also turned pink. Oh, and it isn't just *my* underwear that's this lovely color. You'd better hope no one catches a glimpse of you in your pink shorts."

"Ah…"

"Not quite so funny now, is it?"

He frowned and didn't answer.

"That isn't all," Olivia lamented. "Mom cleaned out my sewing room. I asked her to not touch anything in there but either she forgot or she ignored me. Jack, I had all the fabric cut out for my next quilt and Mom decided to put everything away. Except that I don't know where *away* is and obviously it's slipped her mind, as well." A great deal had been slipping her mother's mind these days, and this wasn't the first time she'd noticed. She needed to make Charlotte an appointment with a gerontologist.

"Your mom straightened out my desk, too."

Olivia's eyes went wide. Even she never touched Jack's desk. "She was only trying to help," Olivia explained unnecessarily.

"I know." He sat down beside her and placed his arm around her shoulders.

"I think we need to have Mom tested for Alzheimer's. Or perhaps she has some other form of dementia. But something's wrong and we've got to find out what it is and what we should do."

"Olivia…are you sure? That sounds a bit drastic. She's got a few memory problems, but a lot of people her age do."

"Their house could have burned to the ground!"

"Thankfully it didn't," Jack murmured.

"What about next time? And there *will* be a next time, Jack. Mom's memory is declining and it isn't going to improve."

"Now, Olivia, I agree there's a problem but—"

"Jack, you're a reporter and you've researched stories on this."

"That's true." In fact, not three months ago the *Chronicle* had done a feature on rising rates of dementia, including Alzheimer's, and local resources for families. "I guess I don't like seeing it so close to home."

"You mean *at* home," Olivia said with wry humor.

"Yeah. But your mom and Ben might not be able to go back to their house. Would they continue to live with us?"

"No." That would slowly but surely drive Olivia over the edge of sanity.

"Where would they go, then? A seniors' complex?"

Olivia hadn't given the matter much thought. "I think so."

"There are some pretty good assisted-living places," Jack said. "Remember we profiled a few for that feature in the paper?"

Olivia nodded. "That makes the most sense, doesn't it?"

"Well, yes."

Now that she'd acknowledged the problem, much of what had been happening recently suddenly became clear. The fact that Charlotte had left her knitting in the car at Faith and Troy's wedding, for instance. Her mother was *never* without her knitting. True, it'd been a traumatic day, since Ben had gone to confront his son David.

If it'd been a single incident, Olivia could easily gloss over it, but there'd been countless other ones. Small things such as forgetting where she'd put Olivia's quilt fabric. The problem with the laundry. Then there was the fire...

Olivia stood and walked around to her bedside table, where she reached for the phone.

"Who are you calling?"

"My brother. I need Will's input on this."

Jack's eyes met hers. "Time for a family conference," he said.

Nine

"Oh, what a lovely painting," the older, smartly dressed woman commented as she walked around the Harbor Street Art Gallery. While Will was out running errands, Miranda Sullivan had removed the Chandler painting from the wall where he'd placed it. Then she hung it on the opposite wall, which—in her humble opinion—showed off the watercolor to its best effect. It was all about the light, her husband used to say, and who'd know that better than an artist like Hugh Sullivan? She noticed how quickly this customer was drawn to the painting.

"You have good taste. This is one of our loveliest pieces," Miranda said, walking toward the woman. "Welcome to the Harbor Street Gallery. Are you visiting Cedar Cove? I'm Miranda Sullivan."

"I'm Veronica Vanderhuff. My husband and I recently moved to the area and we're looking for a few pieces by local artists. Your gallery was recommended."

"You've come to the right place. All the art on display is by local talent. The work you're admiring is Beverly Chandler's *Girl in Spring.*"

"It's gorgeous."

"In my view it's the best painting we currently have."

Veronica shrugged her slim, elegant shoulders. "I'm almost afraid to ask the price."

"All our prices are extremely reasonable," Miranda assured her. She'd love to sell this painting before Will returned. Then she could flaunt the fact that it sold only *after* she'd hung it on this other wall.

Veronica checked the price list Miranda handed her and seemed pleasantly surprised. "Oh, this is reasonable. I'll take it."

Miranda wanted to clap and leap up and down. She'd derive real pleasure from rubbing this in Will's stubborn face. Not a very commendable impulse, perhaps, but there it was. In all her life, Miranda had yet to meet a man who irritated and enthralled her in equal measure. She found herself highly attracted to this man she didn't even like. If that wasn't puzzling enough, he was constantly in her thoughts. She knew it was unlikely that Will would ever look on her as anything more than an employee, and yet she couldn't seem to help herself. Frustrating, to say the least.

Miranda finished the credit-card transaction and made arrangements to have the painting delivered. Twenty minutes later, Will came back. He walked into the gallery and didn't bother to greet her, which Miranda considered the height of rudeness. Instead, he went directly to his office, slumping down in his high-backed leather chair.

Miranda followed him, leaning against the doorjamb, crossing her arms. "What's wrong with you?" she asked bluntly.

Will glanced up, frowning. "I need a few minutes alone," he mumbled. He slouched forward as though depressed.

Miranda's sympathies instantly went into action. "Is everything all right with your mother?" She knew Will had been talking with his sister regarding his mother and stepfather. Dealing with the insurance company had demanded a lot of his time and energy. From what Miranda surmised, work in the kitchen was going well, although much more slowly than anyone had expected. But Will shared very little of his personal life with her, so this was based on information she'd managed to pick up from others.

"Mom's doing fine—not great but okay."

Miranda knew she should give Will the privacy he'd requested but felt an almost overwhelming need to comfort him. "Will," she said softly, moving a few feet into his office. "Is there anything I can do?"

He kept his eyes lowered and shook his head. "I have no one to blame but myself."

"Tell me what happened," she urged, wondering why he was so upset if there was no new crisis with his mother. She struggled to hide her feelings for him. Admittedly those feelings alternated between annoyance and attraction, but there were times, such as right now, when she realized how deeply she cared about Will. He was vain, supercilious, pompous and a hundred other adjectives she could think of. On the other hand, he was intelligent and witty, a talented business-man, devoted to his family and kind to animals. Not to mention good-looking in a dignified but still sexy way.

"I ran into Tanni Bliss," Will muttered. "Shirley was in California last weekend."

"So I heard."

Will's head shot up. "You *knew?*"

He asked the question as though she'd personally betrayed him by keeping the information to herself.

"Well, yes. Shirley and I are good friends."

"You might've told me." His eyes snapped with irritation.

Miranda planted one hand on her hip. "And why would I do that?"

"You know how I feel about Shirley."

She looked up at the ceiling and rolled her eyes. "You have got to be kidding me. Shirley is no more interested in you than...than the man in the moon. You're a smart boy. You should've figured that out by now."

"I'm the one who introduced her to Larry Knight." He jammed his index finger against his chest. "I met her first and—"

"Shirley isn't a prize marble," Miranda countered swiftly. "Are you so egotistical that you can't accept the fact that not every woman in the universe is going to fall in love with you?"

He glared at her and said, "Then I guess you'll be happy to know Larry proposed."

As it happened, she was. "Shirley told me. So who told you? Larry?"

"No, Tanni. Like I said," he returned pointedly, "I ran into her at the bank and she said she and her mother had a—" he made quotation marks in the air "—'fabulous time' with Larry and his children. When they got there, Larry asked Tanni and her brother if they had any objections to him as their stepfather. And now… they're engaged."

Miranda smiled delightedly, although she wondered whether Shirley would move to California. She felt a little forlorn at the prospect of not having her best friend close by anymore.

"I feel like I've been kicked in the gut," Will said.

"Oh, for crying out loud, get over it."

Will seemed shocked that anyone would speak to him in such a derogatory tone of voice. "I beg your pardon?"

"You heard me. Get off your pity pot. If you think Shirley was ever interested in you, then you're delusional."

Will got to his feet and placed both hands on the edge of his desk. Leaning forward, he demanded, "And you know this because…"

"Because she told me so herself."

"I don't believe it."

"Believe what you want. You aren't the right man for Shirley. She recognized it from the start. Unfortunately, you didn't."

"Then why did she go out with me?"

That was a no-brainer. "Gratitude. You helped Shaw get into art school and she felt she owed you. That's the *only* reason she agreed to a couple of dates. They didn't mean anything—at least not to her."

"Are you always this…" He seemed to fumble for the right word.

"Correct?" she supplied.

His eyes narrowed and his ears grew red. "I was thinking more along the lines of *smart alec.*"

"Well, *smart* is true enough. I was at the top of my

class," she bragged. "By the way, did you notice the Chandler sold while you were out?"

Will brightened considerably. "Hey, that's great! I didn't even look."

"Yes, to a new customer who recently moved here. Veronica Vanderhuff wants to decorate her home with work by local artists and the first piece in her collection is the watercolor."

Will wore a smug, know-it-all look. "I told you that wall was the perfect place to display it. The Chandler was the first thing she saw when she walked in the door."

"Actually, it wasn't." Miranda could hardly wait to enlighten him. "While you were out, I moved the painting to the opposite wall. She barely glanced at the price before she bought it." Miranda was sure her expression was just as smug as his—but she didn't care. "The morning light on it was perfect."

"You moved the painting?" Will barged out of the office, nearly knocking her over in his eagerness to investigate.

Miranda followed him. The space where she'd hung it was now blank, since she'd brought it to the storeroom for wrapping.

"Who said you could move that painting?" he demanded.

"I knew I was right," she insisted. The painting had sold within thirty minutes, which should tell him her judgment was superior to his. If he wasn't too arrogant to admit the truth...

"You went against my orders," he flared.

"Orders? Did I join a military unit and not realize

it?" she yelled back. "In case you're missing the point here, allow me to remind you. The painting sold."

"It would've sold where I'd hung it."

"I'll concede it might've eventually sold, but we didn't need to wait because once it was effectively displayed, a buyer appeared right away."

"You've overstepped your bounds," Will said. He stalked over to the counter and slapped his hand against it. "I will not have an employee taking matters into her own hands."

"Did I mention we got full price and that Ms. Vanderhuff is interested in more artwork?" Okay, Miranda was willing to agree that she might've been out of line, but she had a point to prove, which she'd done, and very successfully, too. One might think Will would take the fact that she'd sold the artwork—and for top dollar—into consideration.

"You leave me no option," he said. "You're fired."

"You're firing me because I sold the highest-priced item in the entire gallery?" He couldn't possibly be serious.

"I'm firing you because you went against my wishes."

"You're firing me," she repeated tonelessly.

"Yes. Pack your things and go." He gestured to the door as if she needed guidance in finding her way out.

"Okay, but before I go I want you to know I regret one thing."

"Only one?"

"Only one," she echoed. "I deeply regret that I didn't quit weeks ago. You're the worst employer I've ever had."

"Then it's mutual. I want you out of here and you're just as eager to go."

"I couldn't have said it better myself." Miranda marched into the back room and quickly gathered up her things. With her back stiff and her pride intact, she returned to the main part of the gallery. "I'd appreciate it if you'd mail me my final check."

"I'll see to it this afternoon."

"Thank you," she said, and without another word she walked out.

Well, so much for that. Although she pretended otherwise, she was sorry to lose this job. She'd enjoyed it; she knew she was good at it. Although Will Jefferson was as delusional and arrogant as she'd said, she considered him a friend, too. A begrudging friend, but still a friend. That friendship, such as it was, had probably ended now.

The weekend dragged by. Looking back on the incident, Miranda wished she'd handled everything differently. Will had already been upset about learning that Shirley was engaged to Larry Knight. Then she'd heaped hot coals on his bruised ego by boasting about the sale of the painting.

Still, it was for the best that she leave. They bickered constantly and neither one of them was willing to give in. Will was just as stubborn as she was. And then there was this…this useless attraction she felt for him. Yes, it was preferable all around that she seek other employment. Only…she'd really *liked* working at the gallery. She knew many of the local artists and they were familiar with her, too. Her being at the gallery was an asset to Will, but apparently he no longer saw it that way.

Normally Miranda would have confided in Shirley, spilled out her tale of woe. Not this time. But she couldn't explain why she hesitated to tell her closest friend that she'd been fired.

Instead, she hibernated all weekend, not venturing out of her apartment, even for groceries. She used the time to clean her oven, scrub the bathroom walls and sort out the clutter in her kitchen drawers. The tasks suited her mood perfectly. She needed a distraction, something to keep her mind off Will and the blowup they'd had. And this kind of work made her feel more organized, more in control.

When her paycheck wasn't in the mail on Monday, she thought perhaps he'd forgotten. She punched out the phone number for the gallery and waited for him to answer. She couldn't help wondering if he'd already hired her replacement.

"Harbor Street Gallery," Will answered on the third ring, sounding harried.

"It's Miranda. I was looking for my check. It hasn't arrived yet."

"Oh, right. Sorry. I haven't had a chance to write it. I'll do it this afternoon."

"Would you like me to stop by and pick it up?" she asked.

"Sure." He paused. "Would you mind?"

"Not at all."

"When can I expect you?"

Miranda glanced at her watch. "An hour?"

"Perfect."

She replaced the phone and felt better than she had

all weekend. Collecting her purse and sweater, she headed out the door. The early part of the week was generally slow at the gallery. She'd filled in for Will a couple of Mondays that month so he could help his mother and stepfather with the insurance people and the builder remodeling the kitchen.

Will was sitting behind the counter, leafing through a catalog, and stood when she entered the gallery. He didn't smile at first and neither did she. The old wooden floor creaked as she walked across the room, which made her feel even more self-conscious.

"Thanks for stopping by," Will said.

"I have time on my hands, so it's not a problem."

He grinned at her weak joke.

"You have my check?"

"Oh, yes," he said, locating the envelope under the counter. He handed it to her but held on to one end. "The thing is…"

"Yes?" she asked eagerly.

"I believe I might've been a bit hasty in letting you go when I did."

"Really…"

He hedged for a few seconds. "There aren't as many tourists as we usually get this time of year, but…"

"But," she went on, "the gallery has the potential to bring in a large clientele." Miranda had plenty of ideas she wanted to share—like a holiday show, sponsoring an art walk, hosting an event for the chamber of commerce. They could invite local artists, serve wine and cheese, consider ways to work with other businesses.

"I believe there's great potential here, too," Will concurred. "Problem is, I can't do it alone."

"You need an assistant."

"Yes," he agreed, "but I was foolish enough to fire the best one I'm likely to find."

Miranda felt sure she hadn't heard him correctly. "Are you saying you want me to come back?"

"You're cantankerous, insubordinate and a lot of other things I could mention, but two days without you and I was ready to pull my hair out. Pride is a fine thing, but it only carries you so far—and I've reached my limit. I want you back. Would you be willing to let bygones be bygones and start over?"

"I think I could do that," she said, struggling to hide her delight. The knot in her stomach unraveled and the tension eased from her shoulders. "We can talk."

"That sounds like a good idea." Will smiled.

And Miranda smiled back.

Ten

Sitting at her parents' kitchen counter, Gloria Ashton watched her mother move briskly around, assembling a variety of bowls and wooden spoons. Gloria wasn't sure what Corrie was making but it seemed to demand a lot of attention. The cookbook was propped open and a dozen ingredients were lined up on the counter.

Roy was in the living room reading the local paper and that, too, appeared to be completely captivating.

"Would you like more milk?" Corrie asked, nodding at Gloria's half-empty glass.

"No, thanks."

Gloria had first noticed the tension between Roy and Corrie a couple of weeks ago and tried to ignore it. She figured they'd resolve the problem, whatever it was, without interference from her or anyone else. But that didn't seem to be the case.

"Is everything okay between you and Roy?" she finally asked. She'd decided just coming right out with it was better than pretending this uneasiness didn't exist.

Roy rattled his paper and Corrie dropped an egg on the counter, breaking the shell. She tore off a paper towel and used it to shove the raw egg and broken shell directly into the kitchen sink. She turned on the water, ran the garbage disposal, then washed her hands, drying them on her apron.

"What was that, dear?" she asked as if she hadn't heard the question.

"I asked if everything's all right between you and Roy," Gloria repeated.

Corrie stood on the other side of the counter, looking into the living room, where Roy sat with the newspaper hiding his face. "That's something you need to ask your father," she said in a starched voice.

Roy lowered the paper, stared into the kitchen, then resumed reading. He'd been at it a solid hour. Gloria assumed he'd read it from front to back twice over by now. The Tuesday editions were often the skimpiest of the week.

"Roy doesn't seem to be in the mood to talk," Gloria said. The fact that she'd only recently come into their lives had left her with an incomplete picture of Roy and Corrie's relationship. She wasn't sure how they handled disagreements. Her adoptive parents had been both verbal and demonstrative, arguing often and loudly. Roy seemed restrained, which might come from his training as a cop, while Corrie was the more voluble. This was the first serious argument she'd encountered; its duration surprised her.

"I saw Mack a few days ago," Gloria said, making conversation. She hoped to put her mother at ease. If Corrie relaxed, perhaps she'd let down her guard and Gloria could get to the bottom of this.

"You did?"

"Yeah. He dropped off a baby name book and another couple of books on pregnancy. One of them I hadn't heard of. Apparently it's hot off the press."

"Mack brought you books?" Corrie asked, then answered her own question. "Oh, they must be from Mary Jo."

Gloria didn't think so. "These looked brand-new. The spines hadn't even been cracked."

"Have you read them?"

"I've finished with the pregnancy books. Did you know the baby's heart is already beating? Incredible, isn't it?"

"Incredible is right."

"Any news from Linnette?" Gloria knew her sister was overdue by a few days.

"She's ready to have this baby anytime. My suitcase is packed. As soon as we hear from Pete, I'm heading to the airport."

That explained why Corrie was cooking up a storm. She'd be joining her daughter and helping with her grandchild. She probably intended to freeze most of the meals she was preparing.

"Will you…" Gloria wasn't sure she could find the courage to ask.

"Will I what?"

"Help me?"

"Gloria, of course I will!" Corrie said.

"I… I haven't made any final decisions yet," Gloria was quick to add. "I still might give the baby up for adoption. I was adopted into a loving home and I'd want my baby to know the same love I received from my adoptive parents."

"Of course you would."

Roy dropped the paper and let it rest on his lap.

"The laws have changed since you were adopted, Gloria. These days the father has legal rights."

It embarrassed Gloria to think about Chad. She'd rather keep him out of the picture, although that was neither practical nor ethical. Sooner or later she'd have to contact him...

Her father continued to look at her as if anticipating some response. "I don't need to put the father's name on the birth certificate," she eventually said.

"Don't you?" He arched both brows with the question.

"I could say the paternity's unknown."

"Yes, but is that fair to the father *or* your child? What if the baby has a medical issue at some point in his or her life and needs that information? Not only would you have cheated the father but also the baby. It's something to think about."

"Yes, it is," Gloria murmured. And she *had* thought about it. In fact, she'd thought about little else.

Roy's gaze locked with Corrie's.

Corrie whirled around and yanked open the refrigerator door. "You had to bring that up, didn't you? It wasn't enough that you went behind my back but you—" She stopped abruptly.

Roy vaulted out of his chair with a speed that shocked Gloria.

"I'd like to remind you that I *didn't* go behind your back. You, on the other hand," he began, then floundered for words and finished with, "did."

Gloria stared openmouthed at the two of them. "What in the world are you talking about?"

"Nothing." Roy sat back in his recliner and snatched

up the paper. It crackled as he jerked it open to the page he was supposedly reading.

"Not a thing," Corrie told her, resuming her cooking.

Gloria noticed that her mother's hands trembled and she had to pause, drawing in a deep breath.

"Maybe I should go," Gloria said, fearing she was about to get caught in the undertow of whatever was wrong between them. Their disagreement was obviously something neither Roy nor Corrie wanted to discuss in front of her.

"Don't, please," Corrie said, and to Gloria's astonishment, her mother's eyes were bright with unshed tears.

Sliding off the stool, she walked around the counter and hugged her. Corrie felt small and fragile in her arms.

"Your father's never forgiven me for not telling him about you until we were almost married. Unfortunately, it's still a…a problem between us, even after all these years."

"And I refuse to let history repeat itself," Roy said. He tossed the paper aside and returned to the kitchen. "Have you told Chad about the baby?"

Gloria bristled. "No, and I don't intend to…at least, not yet." She felt that when she did tell him, she should know her own intentions. Adoption remained a viable option.

"Even after everything I've said."

Gloria didn't respond. She didn't feel she had to make any decisions right that minute.

"I think you should tell our daughter what you did," Corrie said angrily.

"Fine, I will."

"Tell me what?" Gloria asked, looking from Roy to Corrie and back again.

"Sweetheart," Corrie said, reaching for Gloria's hands. "Chad knows about the baby."

The words went through Gloria with the force of a blow torch.

Gloria jerked her hands free of her mother's. "Who told him?" Although she asked the question, she already knew the answer.

"I did." Roy stepped forward and confronted her face-to-face. "You can hate me if you want, but I wasn't going to let what happened to me happen to another man, especially if that man's the father of my grandchild."

Gloria felt the sudden need to sit down.

"Furthermore…"

"What else is there?" She wondered what other betrayal he was about to hit her with.

"Those books you're reading didn't come from Mack or Mary Jo."

"Chad?"

"Yes," Roy admitted.

"He gave them to you?"

"He asked me to deliver them, but Mack offered and Chad decided that might be best."

She drew in a deep breath. "In other words, he didn't want to give them to me himself."

"Can you blame him?" Roy asked, none too gently. "You've hidden this from him for months. What did you expect?"

"Does he know the doctor wants to do an ultrasound?"

"Yes, Mack mentioned it."

So Chad knew she was pregnant. She'd wanted to tell him, felt he had a right to know—and then she'd learned he was involved with someone else. The situation was complicated enough without adding another person. She'd concluded that it was better to wait until her own plans were clear. Only when she'd made a decision about the baby would she contact him. Telling him now seemed premature.

Her father disagreed with her, and he felt strongly enough to go behind her back.

"Gloria," Corrie whispered. "I'm so sorry. I did everything I could to talk your father out of this."

Gloria looked at Roy, who stared belligerently back at her.

"What…what did Chad say? When you told him, I mean." She could barely get the question out.

"At first he was surprised."

"And later?"

"Angry." Roy didn't try to soften the word. "Who wouldn't be? He has a right to know he's going to be a father."

"Is…is he still seeing…her?" If Gloria had known the other woman's name she'd forgotten it. As it was, she tried not to think about Chad at all, let alone Chad with that lovely blonde.

"You'll have to ask him," Roy said shortly.

The phone rang and for a moment everyone ignored it. Corrie was the first to move. She reached for the receiver while Gloria and Roy looked at each other with no sense of resolution between them.

"A boy…it's a boy!" Corrie cried.

Roy tore his gaze away from Gloria and went to

Corrie's side. He placed his hands on her shoulders while she spoke excitedly into the receiver. "Yes, yes. I'll phone you as soon as I've got the flight numbers and times." Tears welled in her eyes. "Yes, yes, give Linnette my love and tell her how thrilled Roy and I are."

She hung up, then threw her arms around Roy. "We have a grandson," she said in a quavering voice. "Linnette had a boy. They've named him Gregory Paul."

"Gregory Paul," Roy repeated, nodding approvingly. "That's a nice, solid name."

"How's Linnette?" Gloria asked.

"Fabulous. Pete said she was a real trouper. Gregory weighed over eight pounds and is almost twenty inches long."

"He's a big boy," Roy said, smiling proudly. "Corrie, we have our first grandson." His eyes shone with pleasure and they hugged each other tightly.

"That makes me an aunt for the second time," Gloria whispered.

"Oh, my goodness, I've got to get on the internet and book my flight." Corrie raced out of the kitchen.

"I'll call Mack and Mary Jo and tell them," Roy said, heading off in another direction.

"I can help," Gloria offered. She glanced around the kitchen and got to work finishing the casserole Corrie had started. She was about to place it in the freezer when Roy came back.

"Corrie's looking through her suitcase one final time."

"She's arranged her flight then?"

He nodded. "Before we end here, I wanted to be sure everything's square between you and me."

Gloria considered the question. "It's square."

"Good."

That was all he said. Then Roy was back to his paper, looking more at peace than she'd seen him in a long while.

Gloria left about an hour later. She stopped at the grocery store on her way home; as she climbed out of her car she began to cry, standing there in the darkened lot, sobbing.

Gloria wasn't easily given to tears. If anything, she kept her emotions hidden and rarely if ever revealed them to others.

The tears were an obvious reaction to the birth of her sister's son, and to seeing how happy and excited Corrie and Roy were. That had to be it.

Only it was much more. Instinctively Gloria recognized that this went beyond the joy she felt for her sister.

This had to do with Chad.

Eleven

Thursday evening, feeling depressed, Bruce walked into the house and found Jolene working cheerfully in the kitchen.

"I'm making tacos for dinner," she announced. "They're your favorite, right?"

He tossed the mail on the kitchen counter and realized she was waiting for him to comment. "Sure," he said without enthusiasm. His mind wasn't on dinner but on what he'd just learned. He needed time to absorb this latest news about Rachel before he could deal with his daughter's chatter. Until recently, he'd never noticed how much attention Jolene required.

"You're late," she said as she shredded cheese with unnecessary vigor. "I bet you went to the salon to talk to Rachel." She paused and then added, "Again."

He ignored the question in her voice, but that was exactly what he'd done.

"So how is Rachel?" Jolene asked.

Bruce doubted his daughter cared. He shrugged in response. Removing his jacket, he hung it in the closet and started down the hall.

"Dinner will be ready in ten minutes," Jolene called after him.

"Okay."

Bruce washed his hands and by the time he returned to the kitchen, Jolene had set the table and placed the serving dishes in the center.

Bruce pulled out a chair and sat down.

"Aren't you going to say anything?" Jolene asked as if his silence had offended her. Her voice had a singsong quality that reminded him of when she was much younger.

"About what?"

"Dinner! I worked really hard on this and the least you could do is tell me I did a good job."

Bruce looked at the table; it was obvious that she'd put some effort into this meal. "It's very nice, Jolene. Thank you."

Apparently pacified, she pulled out her own chair and sat down. Reaching for the platter of crisp taco shells, she took one and then passed it to him. "I had a good day at school."

He smiled.

"How was work?"

"Okay."

"Lindsey and I are going to a movie on Friday night. That's okay, isn't it?"

"Sure."

"Can you pick us up when it's over?"

He certainly didn't have any plans for the evening. Not without Rachel. "Okay."

"Great," she said, all sunny and happy. "I'll let Lindsey know. You met her mom, remember?"

"I'm afraid I don't."

"Yes, you do," Jolene argued. "She was at the school picnic last year when—" She paused. "Maybe you didn't," she muttered, and paid an inordinate amount of attention to the taco she was busily assembling.

"Rachel went to the school picnic," Bruce told her. He recalled how upset his wife had been afterward. Rachel hadn't said much at the time, but Bruce could tell how miserable she'd felt. Jolene had acted in a rude and insulting manner, and while Rachel had downplayed his daughter's behavior, she'd asked not to attend any more school functions without him. Bruce had agreed.

Every day, it seemed, he was reminded of how badly he'd failed both his wife and his daughter. The situation would never have gotten to this point if he'd realized how bad things were for Rachel and had stepped in earlier.

Father and daughter ate in silence. Bruce made an effort to eat, although he had no appetite. He did manage to force down one taco, but that wasn't enough to satisfy his daughter.

"Have another, Dad," she insisted, handing him the platter of taco shells.

"No, thanks, sweetie," he said, pushing his plate aside. The lettuce had fallen out and spilled salsa ran across the white plate.

"What's wrong with you?" Jolene snapped. "I made your favorite dinner and I tried to have a conversation with you, but you're ignoring me and it isn't fair." Her voice shook slightly and her lower lip protruded.

Bruce rubbed his face with one hand. Now he had both Rachel and Jolene upset with him. It seemed nothing he did was right anymore. If only he knew how to set everything straight…

"I'm sorry, Jolene," he whispered. "I'm pretty depressed at the moment. I went to see Rachel and—"

Jolene leaped on the news, not allowing him to finish. "She's being a witch, isn't she? I bet she wouldn't even talk to you."

"No, that's not—"

"Jane got mad at her the last time you were there, remember?"

What Bruce remembered was the scene Jolene had caused and how it had brought Jane out of the salon to chastise them all. Afterward he'd been asked not to return. He'd honestly tried to abide by the owner's wishes, but he needed to talk to Rachel, to see her.

"Rachel no longer works at the salon," Bruce said.

His announcement was followed by a stunned silence. "Rachel quit?"

"Apparently," Bruce said, hardly able to fathom it. Rachel had worked at the salon for ten years. It was a second home; her clients were her friends, and the other staff members were like family.

Her leaving shocked him. She must've been desperate to get away and the reason, the only reason he could figure, was directly related to him and Jolene. In his eagerness to convince her to come home, he'd sent her fleeing.

"Where'd she go?"

If Bruce had any inkling, this news wouldn't be nearly as devastating. "I don't have a clue."

"Jane wouldn't tell you?"

He shook his head. "Either she genuinely doesn't know or she isn't willing to divulge the information."

"Really?" Jolene's eyes widened.

"I can't believe Rachel would quit without telling me." The fact that she'd left her job was one thing, but not mentioning it to him felt like…like a betrayal. He was afraid he'd lost Rachel entirely and that she never intended to return to their family. He refused to think that was the case.

"I told you she's a witch," Jolene said calmly. She stood and carried the bowls of salsa and sour cream to the kitchen counter. "If Rachel's decided she wants out of our lives, then I say we should let her go." She hummed softly to herself, evidently happy with this turn of events.

Bruce stood so quickly that his chair scraped against the hardwood floor. "How can you say that?"

She spun around to face him. "What?"

"That we should let Rachel go. She's my *wife*."

"You're going to divorce her, aren't you?"

Divorce her? How could Jolene even suggest it? "No!" He nearly shouted the word.

"But we don't need her. I can do the cooking and laundry and cleaning. I made dinner all by myself, didn't I? It's way better when it's just the two of us like before you married her."

Bruce was horrified that his daughter could be so callous. "What about the baby?"

"Well…" Jolene shrugged. "The baby's a small complication, I agree."

"A small complication? A small complication," he repeated. He couldn't get the words out fast enough. "This *small complication* is my son or daughter, your brother or sister."

"I know that."

"In case you haven't noticed, I miss Rachel. I want nothing more than to have her back. It's wonderful that you can make a great taco dinner—don't think I'm unappreciative. But Rachel means more to me than cooking dinner and doing the laundry. She's my wife, my best friend, and I'm miserable without her." He found it unimaginable that his daughter could be so self-centered, that all she thought about were her own interests and desires. She saw this pregnancy as a complication, while he was worried sick about his wife and child.

He sagged back into his chair. "I called Teri Polgar and she doesn't know where Rachel's living, either."

"Rachel doesn't want anyone to know. Not you, not her friends. We should just accept that," Jolene said earnestly.

Bruce looked up. "Have you heard *anything* I said?"

"Yes, but I don't agree. Dad, Rachel wants to get away from us."

Bruce didn't believe that.

"You say you love her and everything, but if she wants to live somewhere else, that's up to her, isn't it?"

Jolene seemed to delight in pointing out that Rachel had left of her own free will. That she was the one who'd chosen to keep her whereabouts a secret.

"Sit down, okay?" Bruce spoke soothingly, gesturing toward the chair.

Sighing, Jolene reclaimed her seat. "What?" she said, folding her arms defiantly.

"Do you remember, after your mother died, how you tried to hold on to your memories of her?" he asked gently.

Jolene nodded.

"Every night when I put you to bed you'd ask me questions about her."

"I liked listening to your stories about Mom," she said. "Sometimes when you talked about her, your voice would go all soft and I could really, really see how much you loved her."

"I did love your mother. I still do and I always will. After we lost her, I didn't think I could ever love another woman as much as I loved Stephanie. Then I—"

"But Rachel ruined everything!"

"No, Jolene. You didn't let me finish. Then I discovered that loving again *was* possible—with Rachel. I want my wife back and I want us all to be a family." Foolishly he'd hoped his daughter would see how sad Rachel's departure had made him.

"Daddy, you and I are a family. Rachel isn't one of us."

"Yes, she is," he told her. "I realize I made a mistake by rushing into this marriage. Rachel and I knew each other for a long time and we were friends before we fell in love. Once we did, we decided to get married, and I felt there was no reason to wait."

Jolene shook her head impatiently but Bruce paid no attention. He had something important to say and he was determined to make her listen.

"What I failed to take into consideration was how you'd feel. For that I'm truly sorry. But it's too late to go back. Rachel and I are husband and wife, and we're going to have a baby."

With her arms still folded and a look of defiance, Jolene muttered, "Don't remind me."

"I *am* reminding you because we have to work this out. Rachel suggested counseling but you refused."

Jolene shook her head again. "That's so lame. No way am I talking to someone I don't know."

"Not even if it helps you understand why you feel so negative about Rachel and our marriage?"

"It wouldn't make any difference," she said angrily. "That's how I feel."

"Please, Jolene."

"I said I won't go and I won't. You can't force me to talk to anyone. If you think it's so awful without Rachel, then you go."

He'd already scheduled his first appointment. "I plan to, but it would mean a lot to me if you'd attend the sessions, too."

"No way." Her mouth thinned in patent disgust.

"Why is it so hard for you to see that I'm concerned about Rachel and the baby? If Rachel's completely on her own, what does the future hold for her and our child?"

Jolene remained stubbornly quiet.

"I remember a time when you begged me for a brother or sister," he said.

"I was only eight and I wasn't smart enough to know that if I had a brother or sister I'd have a witch for a stepmother, too."

"Rachel isn't a witch." He swore if she referred to his wife like that one more time, he was going to lose it.

"Sure, she isn't one to you. The two of you were so lovey-dovey you couldn't see what she's really like."

"What did Rachel do that was so terrible other than marry me?" Unable to stay seated any longer he stood and circled the table, pushing back his hair in frustration. He could imagine how difficult it must've been for Rachel to deal with Jolene. She'd tried everything and, idiot that he was, Bruce hadn't appreciated the self-control it took to put up with his daughter's barbs and insults.

No wonder Rachel had left. Bruce was as much to blame as his daughter. He'd been blind—willfully blind—and oblivious; now he was paying the price. If only he could turn back the clock…

"Dad, be reasonable."

"Me?" he cried. "*I'm* unreasonable?"

"Rachel will tell you when the baby's born. You know she will."

"I want to be more involved in my child's birth than just getting a phone call after the event. My place is with Rachel at the hospital, the way I was there with your mother. My child deserves that and I will not—" He pointed his finger at Jolene. He needed a moment to subdue his irritation before he could continue. "I will *not* let you dictate to me how I should feel about my son or daughter. It's time you grew up and thought of someone other than yourself."

"Me?" Jolene leaped out of her chair, her face reddening. "Me?" she repeated. "The two of you were disgusting, going to bed so early every night. I knew what you were doing. It's repulsive. And then you had to go and do something stupid like not use birth control!"

"You need to snap out of this and accept that Rachel and I belong together." Bruce was shouting now. His voice shook with the effort to control his anger. "This baby, boy or girl, is going to need a father who's present and available in his or her life, just like I was for you."

Jolene wouldn't look at him.

"And he or she is going to need a big sister, too. You've said you see our child as a complication, but this is a sweet, innocent baby who'll love you unconditionally…who'll need your love, too. Are you so biased you can't see that?" he asked. "Are you so coldhearted that you'd reject your own brother or sister because you're jealous of Rachel?"

"I am *not* jealous of Rachel!" Jolene screamed, tears streaming down her face. "I hate her! I hate you!"

"So you hate your brother or sister, too," he said calmly.

Jolene stamped her foot and in a rage swept her arm across the table. Dishes and serving bowls toppled onto the floor, shattering, spilling food in all directions. Then she ran out of the kitchen and down the hall to her bedroom, slamming the door. The sound reverberated through the house.

Bruce sank into the chair and leaned forward, resting his head in his hands. They desperately needed help. This was more than he could deal with, more than he could handle alone. How right Rachel was to insist on a counselor… He should have taken her seriously months ago.

He hoped it wasn't too late.

Twelve

Grace Harding was in her library office reviewing the budget when she heard a knock at her door.

"Come in," she called, expecting her assistant.

Beth Morehouse opened the door and stuck her head inside. "Do you have a minute?"

Grace glanced at the clock and realized it was past closing. She'd been so involved in her review that she hadn't noticed. "Sure, come on in."

Beth walked into the office carrying a picnic basket. Filled with books? Grace wondered but didn't ask. She smiled at this woman who'd become a friend. Beth's love for dogs resonated strongly with her. Not only was she an effective trainer who'd been instrumental in setting up the Reading with Rover program, she rescued stray and abandoned dogs. She found homes for some of them and kept others for the library program. She trained them to sit with children as they read aloud. Being with a dog relaxed children who struggled with reading and were at risk academically. While a volunteer was close at hand, the real focus was on the children and "their" dogs. And on learning to read.

Grace had instigated the program after hearing how it had started in a Seattle bookstore. Because of her own volunteer work at the animal shelter, it had immediately appealed to her. She'd checked with local grade schools and, not surprisingly, the idea had met with enthusiasm.

That was when Grace heard about Beth, who'd moved to Cedar Cove three years earlier. As soon as Grace approached her, Beth had responded with an unqualified yes. Despite the work on her Christmas tree farm, Beth faithfully brought the dogs into the library several times a week. Without her the program wouldn't be possible.

"What's up?" Grace asked, pushing aside her spreadsheets. After hours of staring at numbers, considering proposed budget cuts and trying to do more with less, she welcomed the break. It'd been a draining week and she looked forward to a relaxing weekend with her husband. They planned to go horseback riding along the beach on Saturday, maybe take in a movie Sunday afternoon.

"I need a favor," Beth said, sitting down in the chair opposite Grace's desk. She carefully set her picnic basket on the floor beside her.

"Anything." Grace would never be able to repay Beth. Although the library program hadn't been in operation long, Grace could already see a dramatic difference in the children. At first they'd arrived tense, uneasy about yet another reading exercise, but as soon as they saw the dogs, everything changed. Twice now she'd seen children from the program taking out books. Nothing could've been greater proof of Reading with Rover's success.

"Do you remember the stray dog I found four or five weeks ago?"

Grace recalled that Beth had rescued a golden retriever she'd come across on the side of the road. The poor dog had no identification and she'd apparently been on her own for some time because she was in bad shape.

"Of course."

"She was pregnant."

"Pregnant?" Grace repeated slowly.

"The puppies were born a few days after I brought her home. She had a litter of five. Unfortunately, she didn't make it. She was a lovely, sweet-tempered dog and it breaks my heart to have lost her."

"Five puppies?" The fact that the lost dog had been a golden retriever instantly brought back memories of Grace's beloved Buttercup. Buttercup had been almost twelve when she'd died quietly in her sleep that summer. Grace still couldn't think about her dog without feeling a pang of grief. The golden retriever had loved her life on the ranch and had never seemed happier than when she and Grace took long walks through the property and along the shore. It didn't seem right that Buttercup was gone. Even now when she got home from work, she expected the dog to greet her.

"So if you would, I'd be forever grateful," Beth was saying.

Grace blinked. Caught up in her memories, she'd entirely missed most of Beth's comments.

"If I would do what?" Grace asked.

"Look after one of the puppies for me," Beth said, giving her an odd glance.

"Me? But...how?"

"He needs to be fed every couple of hours. I have a special bottle I'll give you. In addition to the feeding, he'll need lots of attention. This poor baby has lost his mother and he's been separated from his brother and sisters. He's lonely and afraid."

"Beth, I couldn't possibly take on the care of a puppy." It was out of the question. "I have to be at work here in the library. I haven't got the time, and Cliff's constantly busy with the horses..." Her voice drifted off. She didn't add that she was still in mourning for her own dog and couldn't take on another one right now. It was just too hard.

"I can't do it by myself anymore," Beth said. "Not with all the work on the tree farm. We're gearing up for the holidays. We're already getting orders and some trees are being shipped as far away as Hawaii and Japan. I'm overseeing all that, plus I've got the training and the library program, and I can't stop to feed two puppies." She paused. "I can barely handle one."

"I'm sorry..."

Beth ignored her protest. "Suzette has one puppy and Kristen Jamey took another. A third went to a woman at church, and I have one myself, so that only leaves this last little guy. Unfortunately he's the runt of the litter, smaller and more at risk than the others."

"I'm sure you'll find someone...else," Grace said.

Suzette Lambert was an associate librarian, and Grace figured the library was well represented in the puppy-care department.

"I wouldn't bother you if there was anyone else I could ask, and trust me, I've tried. I have nowhere else to turn. It's just for a few weeks," she said, her voice increasingly desperate. "I really need your help, Grace."

Grace started to raise her objections again when Beth bent down to open the basket and lifted out a small puppy. He was so tiny he didn't even look like a golden retriever. His eyes were squeezed shut against the light and he squirmed a little in Beth's grasp.

"Can you tell the breed of the father?" Grace asked as a delaying tactic.

"My guess is that he was probably a mix. Some Lab, some hound and maybe a bit of poodle. It's too early to really tell."

An odd combination, although the puppy was golden like his mother…like Buttercup.

"But I have a lot of responsibilities at the library," Grace said, hoping Beth would accept the excuse.

"Bring him with you. I'm sure he'll be a hit with the children and they'll enjoy seeing him grow week by week."

"Just how long will I—will he need this extra care?"

"A month, six weeks at the most."

"Then you'll be able to adopt him out?"

Beth nodded. "Absolutely."

"Four to six weeks," Grace murmured. She didn't want to do this but didn't feel she could refuse, since Beth had done so much for her and the children. Grace didn't like it, not one bit, but felt she had no other choice.

"Will you do it?" Beth asked again.

Grace sighed loudly. "I guess I have to."

"You won't be sorry," Beth promised. "He really is a sweet little dog."

Beth left as soon as she'd gone through the feeding instructions and other pertinent information. The puppy slept in the basket on the corner of her desk and didn't make a sound the whole time Grace worked on her budget review.

When she'd finished an hour later, she called Cliff at the ranch. There was no answer and she didn't leave a message. Then she stood, retrieving her purse and jacket. "I'll take you home," she informed the puppy, "but don't get too comfortable because you're not staying, understand?"

The puppy slept peacefully on, apparently not distressed by her lack of welcome.

The basket rested on the passenger-side floor during the fifteen-minute drive home. The only sound Grace heard was a weak mewling as she turned into the driveway leading to the house. "Don't worry, you'll get your dinner soon," she said in a grudging voice.

When she pulled into the garage, Cliff left the barn to greet her, as he usually did. Grace climbed out of the car and he kissed her.

"I brought company," she muttered.

"Company?" Cliff looked behind him.

"A puppy," she said. "Beth asked me—no, *begged* me—to take care of him for the next six weeks."

"And you agreed?" He seemed surprised, as well he should be, since Grace had made it clear that she was through with pets.

"I'm not happy about it," she admitted. Walking around to the other side of her car, she removed the basket and handed it to Cliff.

Her husband raised the lid and peered inside. "Oh, he is a tiny thing."

"The runt of the litter." Grace managed to make that sound like an insult.

"Well, we'll just have to fatten him up." Cliff murmured endearments as he took the puppy from the basket and held him against his chest.

"He has to be fed every couple of hours," she told him. "Like either of us has time for that."

Cliff grinned, which irritated Grace even more. "Wipe that smirk off your face, Cliff Harding. I know what you're thinking and you can stop right this minute."

"So you're reading my thoughts now?" Returning the puppy to his basket, he slipped his free arm around her waist as he steered her toward the house.

"You think I'm going to fall for this puppy and we'll want to keep him ourselves. That's not going to happen, so you can put it out of your mind."

"Okay, I will," he said blandly.

He was being far too agreeable, and Grace didn't believe a word of it.

He opened the door to the mudroom off the kitchen and motioned her in ahead of him. The soft mewling continued from inside the basket. Cliff put it down to shuck off his boots.

"Bring the basket into the kitchen where it's warm," he said. "This little guy's hungry."

"Why don't you give him the bottle while I get dinner started," Grace suggested. The less she had to do with the puppy, the better.

"I'll be glad to."

Grace was grateful. She wouldn't allow herself to feel any tenderness for this small animal. She couldn't. Losing Buttercup had broken her heart and she refused to be vulnerable to a pet again. Refused to set herself up for the inevitable grief. As Olivia had pointed out, that was the downside of having pets—their lives were too short. Besides, an additional animal would tie her and Cliff down all the more. As it was, they had the horses. Getting away for even a weekend was difficult and required a lot of advance planning.

Sitting at the kitchen table, her husband cradled the puppy on his lap and gently offered him the tiny bottle of formula. Grace tried not to watch as she peeled potatoes, then bustled about the room, taking the salad fixings out of the refrigerator, washing lettuce, slicing tomatoes and cucumber. She'd put Swiss steak in the Crock-Pot before she'd left for work that morning. All she had to do now was boil the potatoes and finish preparing the salad.

"He needs a name," Cliff said after a few minutes.

"Give him one if you like," she said without any real interest.

"What about Rover after the library reading program?" he asked.

"Sure." A name was just a name and six weeks from now Rover or whatever Cliff chose to call him would be out of her life.

"Nah, Rover doesn't really fit him. Too generic. We need to come up with something else," Cliff said.

"I don't see anything wrong with just calling him Puppy. Or Dog. In six weeks—four weeks if we're lucky—he'll be adopted by a new family and they can name him."

"He needs a name now," Cliff insisted.

"Fine, then you name him."

Although he didn't comment, Cliff's eyebrows shot up.

"What?" she muttered. "I am not going to let that puppy worm his way into my heart. Got it?"

"Loud and clear."

"Do you want a glass of wine with dinner?" she asked, wanting to change the subject before the puppy became an object of contention between them.

"If you do."

"Red or white?"

"Red."

"Okay." She went from the kitchen to the walk-in pantry, where they kept several bottles of wine, and chose a Shiraz. She returned with the wine, used a corkscrew to open it and let it breathe.

"What do you think of Beauregard?" Cliff asked.

"Beauregard who?"

"As a name," he said pointedly.

"Oh, for the puppy. It's fine but a little long, wouldn't you say?" She caught herself, adding, "Not that I care."

"We'd call him Beau for short."

"We?" She placed her hands on her hips and glared at him. "You name him whatever your heart desires but I want nothing to do with it."

Cliff nodded. "Then Beau, it is." He ran his index finger down the puppy's golden back as Beau sucked greedily at the tiny nipple. The bottle looked like something that came with a child's doll.

"Make sure he doesn't do his business in the house," she warned.

"No problem. I'll wait fifteen minutes and take him outside."

Beau was already proving to be a nuisance. "He'll probably interrupt our meal," she complained. "And you know darned well that he'll be awake at all hours of the night. How many years has it been since you've had to deal with a puppy?"

Cliff smiled down at Beau, completely entranced. Her husband was an easy victim to the puppy, but not Grace. She fully intended to keep her distance, emotionally if not physically.

Cliff took Beau outside and returned just as she was mashing the potatoes. He looked in her direction and shook his head.

"No success?" she asked.

"None."

"He's not too bright, is he?"

"Grace," her husband chastised. "He hasn't had a chance to learn what it means to go outside."

She knew that, but was unwilling to admit how critical she was being. She could see how attached Cliff was getting, and the puppy hadn't even been with them an hour.

"Listen, Cliff, we will *not* be keeping this animal, understand?"

He glanced up from where he lay sprawled on the floor, playing with the puppy, and grinned. "Whatever you say."

"I'm not joking, Cliff. I don't want another dog."

"Whatever you want."

Grace narrowed her eyes as she set their dinner on the kitchen table. "Promise?"

"Cross my heart and hope to die."

"Cliff," she groaned, "this is no joking matter. You wait and see, he'll interfere with dinner. It's already begun."

Sure enough, in the middle of dinner, the timer went off.

"What's that for?" she asked, startled.

"Beau. I'm giving him a second chance." Taking his wineglass, Cliff headed outside with the puppy, who'd been curled up on an old towel near the stove.

Grace reached for her own glass and raised it to her lips.

"It's only for six weeks," Cliff reminded her as he opened the door off the kitchen.

Grace had a feeling that these would be the longest six weeks of her life.

Thirteen

Hurrying out of the courthouse, Olivia frowned as she looked at her watch. She'd told her brother she'd meet him at the gallery at four, but a custody hearing had run late. Will had already left one message on her cell phone, although she hadn't taken the time to listen to it.

Thankfully the courthouse was just a few short blocks from the Harbor Street Gallery. It was a crisp October day, so Olivia decided to walk. The trek was downhill, which was something else to be grateful for. And she loved the beauty of the brilliant autumn leaves, which were falling fast and would all be gone in another week.

Olivia walked steadily but she was out of practice and out of breath. She'd be seeing Grace later for their weekly Wednesday-night aerobics class. She was slowly regaining her strength; maybe she'd even catch up to Grace in skill and endurance soon.

Thinking about her friend, Olivia couldn't contain a smile. Grace and Cliff were caring for that puppy of Beth's. Beau had instantly won over Cliff. Not so

Grace, who stubbornly refused to grow attached to him. Olivia wondered just how long Grace would be able to hold out. Her friend had loved Buttercup and she'd love Beau, too, if she'd give him a chance. Still, Grace insisted that in less than six weeks, she'd hand Beau over to Beth Morehouse without a second's hesitation. No matter what, she kept saying, that dog was going back. If Olivia was a betting woman, she'd place her whole retirement income on Grace keeping that puppy.

She arrived at the gallery and entered, accompanied by a blast of wind off the cove. The door banged behind her, rattling the windows.

Will laughed. "That was quite an entrance," he teased as he came toward her. Leaning forward, he kissed her cheek.

"Sorry I'm late."

"Actually, it worked out fine. Miranda," he said, turning to his assistant, "would you take over for me?"

The other woman nodded and smiled at Olivia.

"Shall we go to my office?" Will asked.

"Please."

He followed her inside, closed the door, then took a seat on one of his visitor chairs. Olivia took the other one, perching on the edge with her hands in her lap.

"I understand the repairs on Mom's house are just about finished," Will said, introducing the topic she'd come to discuss.

"That's right. As you can imagine, Mom and Ben are eager to go home." It was all her mother talked about these days—how soon she'd be back in her own kitchen.

"Of course they're eager," Will said. "And I'm

sure you and Jack are, too. Having them live with you couldn't have been easy."

Her brother didn't know the half of it. Olivia and Jack had each gained at least five pounds with all the desserts Charlotte had baked in the past few weeks. Charlotte made it difficult to say no; she was persistent and obviously felt hurt when they tried to decline her cookies, pies and cakes. Olivia's plan to freeze Charlotte's bounty hadn't worked; for one thing, they'd quickly run out of room. As well, the house had been thoroughly cleaned from top to bottom, and nothing was back in its proper place. When asked, Charlotte would gaze blankly at Olivia and assure her she'd put everything exactly where she'd found it. Olivia understood that her mother was only trying to help. She and Ben were considerate, too, giving her and Jack their privacy in the evenings by staying in their own part of the house. And they kept Harry's litter box in their en suite bathroom; most of the time Olivia wasn't even aware of his presence.

"From what I hear, Jack enjoys Mom's cooking." Will didn't attempt to hide his smile.

"We both do and that's another problem. Mom takes great pride in feeding us huge meals. We haven't eaten this well since last Thanksgiving. The problem is, the feast's continued for five solid weeks. Mom's made it her mission to cook all our favorite meals—chicken-fried steak, mashed potatoes, every kind of dessert. I'm just glad we haven't gained *twenty* pounds each."

"Olivia, you shock me. Where's your willpower? I've always thought of you as the one with self-discipline."

"Me? I blame Jack. He keeps saying we should

enjoy this while it lasts. Not only that, I hate to hurt Mom's feelings."

"Well, they'll be going home soon."

"I'm not so sure…" Olivia hesitated. "I know we've already talked about this, but these past few weeks have opened my eyes. It's made me realize that the situation is more urgent than we thought. We'll need to do something sooner rather than later about finding an assisted-living place."

The smile disappeared from her brother's face, and Olivia knew what he was thinking. They'd decided a couple of weeks ago that Charlotte and Ben should go back to the house for the time being, while the two of them investigated other housing options. Will had even added a few extras to the kitchen upgrades as an early Christmas gift.

Olivia and Will hadn't lined up any seniors' residence visits yet, although they had a list of possibilities provided by Jack.

"What happened?" Will asked.

"Well, things appear to be escalating. For example, Mom washed several loads of the same clothes twice. She'd taken them out of the dryer and put them in the laundry basket and then the next morning rewashed the same load."

Will frowned. "She forgot she'd already washed those clothes?"

Olivia nodded.

"That's just a mistake."

"I'd think so, too, but as I said, it happened more than once."

Will leaned back in his chair and laced his fingers together. "Anything else?"

"I didn't keep a list, although now I wish I had. There've been a bunch of little things and some not-so-little things. Here's another example. Grace put aside a mystery at the library Mom said she wanted to read. Then Mom claimed she'd never heard of the book or the author. *Then* she misplaced it two or three times. Jack found it in the refrigerator once and—"

"The *refrigerator?*" Will seemed to find that especially humorous.

"We all got a kick out of it, but when she misplaced it again, Ben found it tucked between the mattress and the box spring."

"Like she was hiding it?"

"Exactly."

Will shook his head.

"It might've gone undetected except that we started getting late notices from the library—and Ben kept complaining that the mattress was hurting his back. So he decided to look and...there it was."

"Did Mom remember putting it there?"

"No. In fact, she forgot she was even reading the book."

Her brother took a moment to mull this over.

"This is more than just a case of forgetfulness," Olivia felt obliged to say. "As we've discussed, Mom is either suffering from dementia or in the beginning stages of Alzheimer's."

"What about the appointment you made for her with the gerontologist?"

She threw back her head, groaning in frustration. "Mom forgot the appointment. Ben was supposed to take her, but either he forgot, too, or he fell asleep. We couldn't reschedule until after the first of the year."

"Oh, no…"

"I reminded her that morning, too. I even put a note on the fridge."

"Next time I'll take her," Will suggested.

"Good idea, but, Will, it isn't just Mom. Obviously Ben hasn't been doing that well, either."

Will brought his hands up to his face. "Okay, he didn't remember the gerontology appointment. What else?"

"All this trouble with his son over Mary Jo and Noelle has taken its toll. Ben tires so easily these days. He takes a nap every afternoon. A *long* nap."

"Well, that explains missing the appointment." He paused. "*Every* afternoon?"

"Yes, and Harry, too. It's the only time I see the cat. He crawls into Ben's lap and the two of them snooze away pretty much the whole afternoon, seven days a week. Ben's mind isn't as sharp as it once was, either. Mom shows more signs of memory loss, but Ben isn't far behind."

Will exhaled slowly. "Are you saying you don't think they should return to the house at all? Not even for the short term?"

Olivia nodded regretfully. "I'm afraid Mom might forget to turn off the stove again and next time we might not be so fortunate."

"Who's going to talk to them about this?" The way he asked implied that he wanted to nominate her.

"I thought we should tell them together."

"Okaaay," he drawled. "Do you have any idea about how to approach them?"

"Not yet. I think it might be wise to know exactly where they should move first, don't you? Or at least have some options to present. We have a list but I haven't got around to doing anything about it yet."

Will sighed, then nodded. "If you want to make us some appointments, we—"

Someone knocked politely at the office door. Will looked mildly surprised. "Yes?" he called out.

Miranda opened the door a few inches. "Excuse me, but Shirley Bliss is here—"

Will was instantly on his feet, his face eager. "Shirley's here?"

"With Larry Knight."

Will's smile faded as quickly as it had come. "She's with Larry," he muttered, as if he found the other man's name distasteful.

"They'd like to speak to you for a moment."

"Sure, send them in," Will said. He remained standing as Miranda ushered Shirley and Larry into the office.

Will made introductions; Shirley smiled and Larry shook hands with Olivia.

"I hope we're not interrupting anything important," Shirley apologized.

"It's fine," Will said. "Olivia and I were discussing a family matter. What can I do for you?"

Larry placed his arm around Shirley's waist. "We wanted to tell you in person that I've asked Shirley to be my wife."

Olivia noticed that Will's smile looked decidedly forced.

"If it wasn't for you, I never would've met Larry." Shirley held out her left hand and displayed a beautiful solitaire diamond ring.

"Have you set the date?" Will asked.

"Not yet," Shirley said.

"But it'll be soon," Larry added. "I've been alone long enough. I want Shirley with me."

"I'm so grateful you asked me to attend that show at the Seattle Art Museum," Shirley said, her expression radiant. "I almost decided not to go and I'm so glad I did."

"Congratulations," Olivia told the happy couple. If Will wasn't going to say it, she would.

"Yes, by all means. Congratulations," Will said.

"We'll be in touch." Shirley started out the door. "Bye, Will, Olivia."

"Thanks again," Larry said, turning to follow her out.

Will closed the door firmly behind them. "Shirley was my date that afternoon and then Larry swooped in on her and—"

"Will," Olivia said. "What's your problem? Anyone with eyes can see how much in love they are."

"I know, I know. But I'd hoped Shirley would fall in love with *me!*"

"And why would she do that?" Olivia asked bluntly.

"Why? Well, because…"

"What do you have in common, other than the fact that you own an art gallery and she's an artist?"

"Isn't that enough?"

"Will, not *every* woman is going to fall at your feet in adoration."

"Jeez, you sound like Miranda! I happen to like Shirley Bliss."

"And you tried to charm her the way you did with practically every woman you've met, whether you were married or not." That last remark was meant to remind him that he hadn't been a good husband. He'd cheated on his wife repeatedly, and Olivia didn't care what his excuses were.

"You could've gone all day without saying that," Will snapped. "Okay, so I wasn't the world's best husband. I admit it. But my ego just took a major hit, and if I want to whine a bit I should be able to."

"Okay, fine. Be a little boy for a couple of minutes and then get over it."

He stood and walked over to the cabinet. "How about a glass of wine? I could use a drink."

"Sure. Shall we invite Miranda to join us?" The gallery was closed by now and she was probably waiting.

Will shrugged. "I suppose."

"Don't sound so enthusiastic."

"We don't get along all that well," he muttered as he took down a bottle of red wine and three glasses. "She's a know-it-all, not to mention contradictory."

"Then why do you keep her on?" Olivia asked, finding his attitude amusing. Her brother's relationship with his assistant fascinated her. They bickered and argued and she couldn't remember a time that Will had anything good to say about Miranda. And yet he continued to employ her.

"I tried to fire her."

"Tried?" Olivia raised one eyebrow.

"Yeah. I was completely overwhelmed without her. Two or three days later, I asked her to reconsider and return to work. I could've hired someone else, but that would mean training that person, which is a lot of time and trouble."

"Miranda came back, though."

He grinned. "She seemed almost glad of it, too.

The truth is, I don't really like her. Miranda's far too bossy. God save me from bossy women."

"Really?"

"Well, not all bossy women," he returned, and broke into a lazy smile. "Not you, my darling sister."

Olivia shook her head and started toward the door. "Before I ask Miranda to join us, are we in agreement that Mom and Ben can't go back to the house?"

"Yes."

"We'll talk to them together about moving into an assisted-living complex as soon as possible," she said, summing up their discussion.

Will exhaled loudly. "Together? Can't you tell them and I'll back you up?" He grinned. "I was hoping we could do this good-cop/bad-cop style and I'd be the good cop."

"No, we'll present a united front and go from there. Okay?"

"Okay, Madame Judge."

Olivia ignored that and opened the door. "Miranda, would you like to have a glass of wine with us? We're celebrating Shirley and Larry's engagement."

Will, who was pouring the wine, nearly toppled a glass. He caught it just in time to prevent it from tumbling onto the beige carpet.

Miranda came into the room. "You're happy about Shirley's news?" she pressed, looking at Will.

Olivia could see that the other woman wasn't easily fooled.

"I can boast that I was the one who introduced them," Will muttered as he passed around the glasses.

"It wasn't going to work out for you, you know."

"Why is it," Will asked sharply, "that everyone enjoys telling me that? You think I haven't figured it out by now? But if Larry hadn't come into the picture, I believe she would've ended up with me."

Miranda exchanged a glance with Olivia that said Will was delusional. Olivia recognized, even if her brother didn't, that he'd never had a chance with Shirley, whether he chose to accept that or not.

"You don't believe me?"

"Will, it isn't that. Let's enjoy our wine and drop the whole Shirley issue, shall we?" Olivia suggested.

It looked for a moment as if he wasn't willing to let it go. "Fine. Whatever."

Miranda raised the wineglass to her lips but not before Olivia noticed that she was humming a song from the 1960s. If memory served her right, the first line was "Goin' to the chapel and we're gonna get married." She burst out laughing.

"What?" Will demanded.

"Nothing," Olivia said, making an effort to keep her composure. She liked Miranda. In fact, Olivia could see that Will's assistant was exactly the woman to rein in her brother's ego and keep him in line.

Poor Will. He didn't have a clue.

Fourteen

Mary Jo McAfee set the large pumpkin on the kitchen counter and found a felt pen in the junk drawer. Since this was Noelle's first Halloween, she was determined to make it special. She already had her daughter's costume picked out. Noelle would be dressed as a ballerina, complete with pink tutu and tights.

Never mind that her baby hadn't yet taken her first step. Noelle was close, so close, but still clung to the coffee table, bending her chubby legs, longing to explore her world and at the same time hesitant to leave the security of something to hold on to.

Mary Jo knew everything would change once Noelle decided she could walk. As it was, her daughter was a champion crawler. The nine-month-old loved to travel on all fours, putting anything and everything in her mouth as she progressed from one side of the room to the other. Mary Jo had to be constantly vigilant.

The front door opened and Mack walked in. Mary Jo smiled and held her arms open to him for a hug and kiss. They'd only been married for two months and still felt the sheer wonder of the intimacy they shared.

As soon as she saw him, Noelle raised her arms, seeking his attention.

"Come to Daddy," Mack urged, getting down on his knees a couple of feet from the coffee table.

Mary Jo held her breath and waited. Noelle glanced at her mother and then at Mack.

"Come on, sweetheart," Mack urged, stretching out his arms.

Noelle took one fledgling step and then another before plopping down on the floor. She let out a wail, more in surprise than pain. Mack scooped her up and swung her around, holding her high above his head.

"That's my girl!"

"She did it! She did it!" Excited, Mary Jo started waving her arms. Noelle was a week and a half from being ten months old and had taken her first step. "That's early for her to be walking."

"Way to go," Mack said as he spread kisses over Noelle's face. Then balancing her on his hip, he turned back to Mary Jo. "Hey—you got a pumpkin!"

"I picked it up on my way home. I thought we'd carve it—actually, I'll leave the carving to you. I'll draw what I want and the rest will be in your capable hands."

"And what do I get out of this?" Mack teased.

"Oh, I'm sure I'll come up with some way of rewarding you."

Mack wore a silly grin. "I'm sure you will, too." Sitting, he bounced Noelle on his knee while Mary Jo continued to draw eyes, a nose and a gap-toothed mouth on the pumpkin. After a few minutes, Noelle squirmed, wanting to be put down. Mack set her on the floor and she immediately took off crawling toward her favorite spot in the house, next to the coffee table. She pulled herself up to a standing position, then twisted around to check on her audience.

"I talked to your brother this afternoon," Mack said conversationally. "We grabbed a coffee after work."

"Oh?" Mary Jo was concerned about Linc. Nothing seemed to be going right for him and Lori. The business was close to failing and he was at odds with his in-laws. The last she'd heard, Lori had disowned her entire family. She wasn't speaking to either her mother or her father.

"Did you know they're looking for a new apartment?"

"No." Mary Jo dropped her pen. She would've thought Linc might mention it to her, but he tended to be private, to keep his problems to himself.

It made sense that her brother and Lori would need a new place. The Bellamys owned the apartment building where they currently lived, and neither Linc nor Lori wanted to be indebted to them. Still, Mary Jo knew that Linc didn't approve of Lori's cutting off her family. He'd tried to talk to her, but Lori was adamant—she wanted nothing more to do with them. Because Linc and Mary Jo had lost their own parents, they had a different view; Mary Jo suspected that Lori wouldn't appreciate how important family was until she was without either parent and there was no opportunity left to reconcile.

"I put out the word to the fire crew and Linc picked up some business this week."

"Great!" She leaned down and kissed him again, letting her mouth linger on his.

"I… I could," Mack said, clearing his throat before he continued, "try to send more business his way."

Laughing softly, Mary Jo patted his back. "You do that."

"Will I get more kisses like that one?"

"Probably."

Mack brightened. "My dad's helping, too."

"Oh?"

"Yeah, he's good friends with the sheriff."

Mary Jo remembered that about Troy Davis and her father-in-law.

"Well, Dad was talking to Sheriff Davis and suggested he might have the city ask your brother to bid on a contract to service police vehicles."

"But, Mack, he has an auto body shop."

"He can manage oil changes, can't he?"

"I'm sure he can."

"And routine maintenance?"

Mary Jo shrugged. "I assume he could."

"Work is work, and your brother is hungry."

Mary Jo was well aware of how hungry her brother was.

"Speaking of hungry, when's dinner?" Mack glanced around the kitchen.

Mary Jo had started on the pumpkin as soon as she got home and hadn't really thought about dinner. "Ah, any chance I could talk you into going out tonight?"

Mack cocked his head. "I could be persuaded," he said, winking at her.

"Very funny," she muttered. "Can we afford to take Linc and Lori? After all, this is a celebration."

"A celebration?"

"Noelle just took her first step."

"Oh, right. Where do you want to go?"

Knowing their own budget was tight, Mary Jo said, "The Pancake Palace. I love their spaghetti and meatballs, and Thursday night is all-you-can-eat spaghetti."

"Sounds good to me."

"I'll call Linc and Lori and see if they can join us," Mary Jo said. "Besides, I have an idea."

"I bet you're thinking the same thing I am."

Half an hour later, when Mack had carved the pumpkin and Mary Jo had fed and changed Noelle, it was time to meet her brother and his wife. They took her car for the short drive down to Harbor Street and the Pancake Palace.

Linc and Lori were waiting for them outside the restaurant, apparently deep in conversation.

"How are you guys?" Mary Jo asked after they'd left the car and unfastened Noelle from her seat.

"Oh, good," Lori said. "Everything's fine."

Mary Jo noticed that her brother didn't echo his wife's sentiment. Lori took Linc's hand, and she was sure that whatever they were discussing concerned their troubles with her family.

They entered the restaurant and were quickly seated, despite the number of families availing themselves of the pasta specials. She recognized Pastor Dave Flemming and his wife, who waved cheerfully. Once the hostess had obtained a high chair for Noelle, Mary Jo gave her daughter a cracker while everyone else looked over the menu. She'd already made her decision—the spaghetti and meatball dinner.

"By the way," Mack said, hidden behind the menu. "This is our treat."

"You don't need to do that," Linc insisted.

"True," Mack said mildly, "but we're celebrating the fact that Noelle took her first step."

"That's early, isn't it?" Lori's eyes widened with surprise.

"Yes, but she's been ready for weeks now," Mary Jo explained. "Only, she was afraid to let go. It took her daddy to get her to leave her comfort zone." Mary Jo knew how hard it was for her staunchly proud brother to allow them to pay for his and Lori's dinner.

Linc lowered his menu. "You've done so much already," he said, sounding almost humble.

This was Linc? Mary Jo looked up. She wanted to ask her big brother if he was okay. Humility was so unlike him.

"What did I do?" Mack asked as he reached for his water glass.

"This is the best week we've had since I opened the shop and practically everyone's made a point of mentioning your name."

"Mine?" Mack feigned astonishment. "All I said was that you do quality work at competitive prices."

"Sheriff Davis stopped by to talk to Linc, too," Lori added. She slipped her arm through Linc's and pressed her head against his shoulder.

Mack raised both hands as though to avert their thanks. "I didn't have anything to do with that."

"No, but your father did. I appreciate everything you've done. If anyone's paying for dinner, it'll be Lori and me."

Mary Jo released a pent-up sigh. That sounded much more like her take-charge brother.

"We'll settle up later," Mack said. "Come on. Let's order."

After they'd finished their meals, they chatted over coffee and dessert. Noelle had eaten at home but Mary Jo spooned some plain spaghetti, cut up and sprinkled with cheese, into her mouth. Soon after, Noelle fell asleep. Mack cradled his daughter in his arms; every now and then he'd bend his head and press his lips against her soft curls.

Mary Jo loved watching Mack with Noelle. He was her father in every way that mattered, every way except the biological. How fortunate she was to have met and married such a decent, honorable man, especially after falling for a jerk like David Rhodes. Thanks to Noelle's grandfather, Ben Rhodes, David was completely out of their lives. She'd never learned precisely what agreement Ben had struck with David, but whatever he'd said or done convinced David to sign the paperwork allowing Mack to legally adopt Noelle. They'd already started the legal procedure.

"I'm going to miss living in Cedar Cove," Lori murmured.

"You're leaving?"

"Looks like it," Linc said without elaborating.

Mary Jo made eye contact with Mack.

"We can't seem to find a place that—" Lori began.

Linc put a restraining hand on her arm.

"Linc," Mary Jo said. "Tell us what's going on."

Her brother remained stubbornly quiet.

"Listen, you two, we're family," Mack told them. "As soon as I heard that you and Lori were looking for a new apartment, I told Mary Jo. We've come up with an idea we wanted to present to you."

Linc and Lori exchanged a puzzled glance.

"Before you say anything," Linc said, holding up

his hand. "Lori and I have decided to move back to Seattle. I don't know how much longer I can hold on to the business. I've had one good week—thanks to you, Mack—but there's no guarantee it'll continue…"

"Why go all the way to Seattle?" Mary Jo asked. "The commute will take hours out of your day."

"We were going to move in with Mel and—"

"No way!" Mary Jo couldn't see that happening in a million years. It was a setup for disaster. Her two brothers, both younger than Linc, were terrible slobs, and Lori would be miserable.

"Mary Jo and I would like to offer a solution," Mack said.

Mary Jo smiled. "We'd like to rent you the other half of the duplex."

Linc stared at them, while Lori's eyes widened.

"But… I thought you'd rented it out?" Linc said after a moment.

"We had a couple who was interested, but it fell through," Mary Jo explained. "They decided to stay in Seattle."

"So, the other half of the duplex is still vacant?"

Mack nodded. "It sure is—vacant and available."

"You could move in anytime," Mary Jo said. "Really. We mean it. We want you to."

Linc slowly shook his head. "I'm honored that you'd offer, but we can't accept." His jaw had that stubborn set Mary Jo knew so well.

"We can't?" Lori looked as if she was about to break into tears.

"We can't," he repeated emphatically. "We'd be trading one charity situation for another."

"Now just a minute," Mack said, raising his voice. "I didn't say we wouldn't be charging rent."

Mary Jo placed her hand on her husband's thigh. Mack had to know that Linc and Lori could barely make it *without* paying rent.

"I'll charge you the same as I did Mary Jo," Mack said. Beneath the table he put his hand over hers.

"How much?" Linc asked.

Mack named the figure he'd first charged Mary Jo, which was a greatly reduced rate. When she'd learned what he'd done, she'd been outraged; it'd been a source of major conflict. Mary Jo was more like her older brother than she'd realized. She hoped he wouldn't object to paying less than market value.

"That's the same amount Mack charged you?" Linc asked, eyeing her closely.

"It is."

"That's incredibly reasonable," Lori told her husband.

"You're sure about this, Mack?" Linc seemed unconvinced.

"Positive."

"We could stay in town, Linc," Lori said, squeezing his arm. "I wouldn't have to quit my job and you'd be able to put all your energy into the business."

"What do you say?" Mack asked.

Linc smiled and thrust his hand across the table. "You've got yourself a deal."

Fifteen

Rachel unlocked the door to the house she shared with Nate Olsen in Bremerton, not far from the naval shipyard. She shed her jacket, set down her purse on the hall table and walked into the living room.

Ever since she'd moved away from Bruce and Jolene, her stress was much lower. Her blood pressure was back in the normal range, she'd started to gain weight and her iron levels had improved. At her routine appointment, she'd heard that Bruce had phoned the doctor's office to check on her and the baby. Their privacy policy wouldn't allow them to divulge any information about her, but they did tell Rachel he'd called. Knowing he was concerned buoyed her spirits.

She'd never questioned his love for her or the baby. What her husband had failed to recognize was Jolene's reaction to having another woman in the house.

Turning on the television, Rachel flipped through the channels until she located a news program. She'd often enjoyed sitting with Bruce after dinner as they savored a cup of freshly brewed coffee and discussed their day while the television played in the background. She missed those evenings.

But she didn't miss Jolene slamming around in the kitchen or bedroom. Her stepdaughter resented every minute Rachel spent with Bruce. There'd been no sign of it before they were married, but once Bruce slipped the wedding band on her finger, it was all-out war. It didn't help that Rachel had tried to bring a bit of badly needed discipline into her stepdaughter's life.

Oh, why was she doing this to herself? Rehashing the past was pointless. Rachel had gone over everything in her mind dozens—no, hundreds—of times. Reviewing the past few months with Jolene and Bruce only upset her. Slumped down in the chair, she was listening to the weather report when the door opened and Nate came in.

"You're here," he said, pausing halfway into the room.

"Are you surprised?"

"Yeah, I guess so. You generally aren't around when I am."

Rachel had purposely stayed out of Nate's way as much as possible. This living arrangement was temporary and she didn't want to burden him by being constantly underfoot. It wasn't uncommon for her to see a late-afternoon movie, go to the Bremerton library or just stroll through the mall to kill an hour or two. She wanted to give Nate a chance to get home and get ready for his date with Emily or his evening with friends—or whatever he had planned.

"I was beginning to wonder if I had a housemate or not," he said, removing his jacket.

"Didn't you have a date tonight?"

"I did, but something came up and Emily had to cancel."

"Would you like me to make dinner?" She'd never enjoyed cooking for one; it always felt like a lot of work for very little return.

"No, thanks. I'm meeting people at Phil's Tavern downtown. I'll pick up something there."

Rachel knew the sports bar was a popular hangout with the military crowd. Monday-night football was a big attraction. "Have a good time."

"I will." Nate disappeared upstairs to his bedroom and Rachel finished watching the news.

She was in the kitchen, searching through her half of the cupboards for inspiration, when Nate left. He waved on his way out the door. When she'd first accepted his invitation Rachel had worried that he might want to rekindle their romance. Fortunately, that hadn't been the case. Rachel had met his girlfriend, Emily, and liked her; she felt that Emily suited him far better than she ever had. The situation was ideal—or as ideal as it could be while Rachel was separated from her husband.

She ate a lonely dinner at the kitchen table while paging through a six-month-old golf magazine. She finished that in short order. Needing something else to occupy her mind, she reached for a pencil and the newspaper to do the crossword puzzle.

That was when she felt it.

At first she wasn't sure—and then it happened again.

The baby moved.

She pressed her hand to her stomach. "Well, hello," she whispered. At her last visit, the doctor had told her she could expect to feel movement at any time. This was so light, like a butterfly landing on her arm, that for an instant she hadn't even thought it *was* the baby.

She wanted to share this joy, but there was no one to tell. Not Bruce. Not Nate. No one.

Before she could talk herself out of it, she got her cell and called her husband.

As she'd feared, Jolene answered. "It's Rachel." Waiting for a sarcastic remark, she closed her eyes.

"Hi," the thirteen-year-old said, sounding almost friendly. That quickly changed and Jolene's voice hardened as she asked, "What do you want?"

It didn't seem possible but for a second or two she wondered if Jolene had softened toward her...

"Could I speak to your father?"

Jolene didn't respond but Rachel heard her set down the phone and call her father. "Dad! It's Rachel."

"Rachel?" Bruce was on the line immediately, firing questions at her. "Where are you? Are you all right? Is anything wrong with the baby?"

"I'm fine," she said, "and so is the baby."

"Why did you block my number so I can't call your cell?"

She didn't want him checking up on her two or three times a day. The scene at the salon had left a bitter taste, and she'd blocked his numbers shortly after that.

"Like I said, I'm fine," she assured him, rather than answer his question.

"The baby?"

"Yes."

"Have you had the ultrasound yet?"

"Yes. A couple of days ago."

"Did you find out what we're having? A boy? A girl? One of each would suit me just fine," he teased.

She didn't even try to keep the smile out of her voice. "I asked the ultrasound technician not to tell me."

"You don't want to know?"

"I'd rather be surprised."

There was a moment's silence.

"I suppose Jane told you I stopped by the salon," he murmured.

Actually, Rachel had been too busy to call her former employer in the past week. "No, she didn't mention it."

"Are you working? Do you need anything? Money? Groceries?"

"I can take care of myself, Bruce, but thank you for asking." He did seem to worry about her, which made Rachel miss him all the more.

"You have another job?"

"I do." She didn't give him any more information, preferring to keep it to herself for fear of another embarrassing encounter at her workplace. She hoped to continue working at the shipyard until the baby was born.

"You have a job at another salon?"

"No." Again, she didn't elaborate.

"You left because of what happened that day with Jolene?"

The answer was obvious, so she didn't reply. "How is Jolene?" she asked, broaching the subject of her stepdaughter cautiously. Rachel hoped that once she was out of the house, their broken relationship could begin to heal. Perhaps that was an unrealistic expectation; Rachel no longer knew.

"Jolene is…adjusting," he said, as though searching for the right word.

"Adjusting," Rachel echoed, trying to determine exactly what he meant.

An awkward silence followed. What he didn't say told her more than what he did. Nothing had really changed. Still, the biting sarcasm was gone when Jolene had initially answered the phone. It might be premature to feel hopeful, but she couldn't resist grabbing hold of that small piece of encouragement.

"The nurse at the obstetrician's said you'd called the office to ask about me and the baby."

"Are you angry?"

"No…no, not at all. I—I was pleased."

"You were?"

"I don't mean to hide from you, Bruce. But…well, it's difficult. For now, I think it's best if we have limited contact."

"I can't accept that," he said swiftly. "It's been over a week since we talked and you kept the conversation so brief I hardly had a chance to find out how you are."

"I kept it brief because you wouldn't stop badgering me about where I'm living and for now that isn't important."

"Why is it such a secret?"

Rachel didn't want this conversation to end on the same negative note as the one week earlier. "You're doing it again." Eventually she'd tell him she was living with Nate but at the moment her roommate was the least of their concerns.

"Okay, sorry. If you want me to pretend I don't care

about you, then I will." He sounded frustrated, and that made her feel guilty.

"Bruce, please—"

"Can I see you?" he cut in. "Or is that asking too much? I *need* to see you, Rachel. At least give me that."

"I…guess we could meet."

"When?"

"Friday night?" she suggested.

"We could go out for Mexican."

Rachel smiled and lifted her hair off her forehead. "I'm afraid Mexican food doesn't agree with me these days." One taste and she had an instant attack of heartburn. She trusted this would pass after the baby was born.

"You choose, then. Any place you want. D.D.'s?"

"Okay, D.D.'s on the Cove, it is."

She could almost feel Bruce's spirits rise.

"I have missed you so much," he said.

"I've missed you, too," she whispered.

"I can't wait to see you."

"I called because—"

"I don't care why, I'm just happy you did," Bruce said.

"I felt the baby move for the first time this evening."

"The baby moved?" he asked excitedly.

"Yes…"

"You're taking good care of yourself?"

"Of course."

"Eating right?"

She laughed. "Yes."

"Friday can't come soon enough for me."

"Me, neither." She wondered if Jolene was listening in, and what her stepdaughter would say when

Bruce hung up the phone. It broke her heart that she and Jolene had lost the closeness they'd once shared. But at this point she didn't know how to regain the girl's trust.

"Before we meet, there's something I want to tell you," Bruce said.

"Okay." He sounded so serious.

"I've seen a family counselor."

This was a huge step for him, and it gave her hope that they could resolve their problems before the baby arrived.

"Did Jolene go with you?"

He didn't respond, but that was answer enough.

"Maybe she will next time," Rachel said, trying to encourage him. "At some point I'm sure the counselor will want to see all three of us."

"Four," Bruce corrected. "You're forgetting the baby."

She smiled. "You're right."

"Will you call again soon?"

"How soon?"

"Fifteen minutes?"

She smiled and leaned against the wall.

"Maybe we should start all over," he said, lowering his voice. "Ease back into a relationship."

Rachel bit her lip, tempted by his suggestion. "Do you think that would help Jolene?"

"I don't know, but it's worth a try, don't you agree?"

"Maybe." She had to be careful. She loved him so much, he could convince her of almost anything. Except coming home...

"What's Jolene doing Friday night?"

"She'll be with a friend. She usually is."

"What friend?"

"Carrie, I think."

"You *think?*" Rachel had been afraid of this. Bruce had ceded all control to Jolene. Rachel had always insisted on knowing where Jolene was going and who she'd be with before she left the house, and Jolene had hated that.

"It's either Carrie or Lucy. Why? What's the big deal?"

"The big deal is that your daughter needs supervision. Jolene is at a vulnerable age. She needs boundaries."

"I told her she had to be home before midnight."

"Midnight?" Rachel thought she was going to be sick. "A thirteen-year-old should be home and in bed long before then. Have you lost your mind?"

"Can we talk about this later?" Bruce said after a strained moment.

"That might be best."

"Shall I meet you at D.D.'s at six?"

"I'll be there." Then, because she felt the urge to talk to Jolene, the urge to try yet again, she asked Bruce to put her stepdaughter on the line.

It was a couple of minutes before Jolene got on the phone. "What?" she demanded.

"I understand you're taking good care of your father," Rachel said, thinking that if she began with a compliment, the conversation might go more smoothly.

"I told you before—we don't need you here."

"And you're right, you don't." That obviously wasn't what Jolene had expected. "Your father and I are going out for dinner on Friday night."

"Great," she muttered sarcastically. "You aren't moving back, though, are you?"

"No."

"Good, because it's been really nice around here without you."

Rachel didn't doubt that was true—in Jolene's mind, if not Bruce's. Rachel responded with silence.

"Dad and I are as close as ever."

Rachel decided to ignore that, too. "I wanted to tell you I felt the baby move today."

For the first time since she'd picked up the phone, Jolene didn't have anything derogatory to say.

Rachel continued. "The doctor says the baby—"

"Do you know yet if it's a boy or girl?"

"Your father asked me the same thing. No, I didn't want to be told. I'd rather be surprised."

"Oh." Jolene seemed disappointed.

"Do you want a baby brother?"

She hesitated. "I guess."

"A sister would be nice, too," Rachel said. "Someone you could be friends with later on. I always wanted a sister."

"I did, too. When I was little."

"Either way, this baby is going to be happy to have a big sister," Rachel said. "It was nice chatting with you, Jolene. Maybe we can do it again, okay?"

"We can talk," Jolene whispered, "as long as you don't move back."

Sixteen

"Oh, Mom," Tanni whispered as she stepped into her mother's bedroom. "You look so beautiful."

Shirley blushed. "Oh, Tanni, do I?" She was about to be married and felt more unsettled than she could ever remember being.

A small wedding was what both she and Larry wanted. Just family and a few friends. Tanni had agreed to be her maid of honor and Miranda would serve as her one and only bridesmaid.

The wedding would take place in the small chapel at the Catholic church, with Father Donahue presiding. Larry and his children had flown in from California early that morning. They either had to get married in this two-day window or wait another three months until he returned from his travels.

To Larry, the three months seemed far too long, since they'd already made up their minds. Shirley had never intended to fall in love again; she'd certainly never expected to. Meeting Larry had overturned all her preconceived ideas about living the rest of her life as a widow.

As Larry said, they were meant to be together. Together.

That was almost worthy of a laugh. With his lecture tour and painting schedule, they'd have this forty-eight-hour period, and then he was off to New York for two weeks, followed by a European tour. Naturally Larry wanted her to go with him, and she would've loved it.

But unfortunately, it wasn't possible. Shirley couldn't pull Tanni out of school or take off for weeks at a time. She wasn't willing to leave her seventeen-year-old daughter to fend for herself. She also had several commissions she was working on and couldn't abandon what she'd been contracted to complete. Above all, she was Tanni's mother and Tanni needed her to be at home.

Losing her father had been a terrible blow to her teenage daughter, and Shirley wasn't going to subject Tanni to another massive change, just when she was starting to cope.

The plan was that they'd have their wedding Friday afternoon, honeymoon for two days and then Larry would be gone for nearly eleven weeks.

The ceremony was lovely, and both families went to dinner afterward. She was relieved to see how well her children and Larry's got along. They joked and teased as if they'd known one another all their lives.

Larry clasped her hand beneath the dinner table. "Are you ready to get out of here?" he said in a low voice.

"Now?" Shirley asked. She was enjoying the families' interactions and hated to have everything end so soon.

"We can stay as long as you like, but we do have a three-hour drive ahead of us."

This was news to Shirley. She'd planned the wedding, but had left the honeymoon to Larry.

"Where are we going?" she asked.

"I have good friends who own a summer home near Leavenworth, which they've lent us."

The Bavarian-style village in the eastern part of the state was one of her favorite places. Since it was an artists' community, she wasn't surprised that Larry had friends living there.

Larry squeezed her fingers. "Let me know when you're ready."

Shirley squeezed back. "We can leave now."

Except that it took at least half an hour to get away, since everyone wanted to wish them well. Still holding hands, Larry led her to the front of the restaurant, where the valet had brought their rental car. Larry helped her in, and with their friends and family gathered around, they drove off to waves and shouts.

"We're on our way," Larry said, glancing at her as he pulled out of the circular drive. "Finally."

Shirley smiled at him.

"You're a beautiful bride," he said.

"And you're an exceptionally handsome groom," she returned. "Are you happy?"

"Very much so—and sad, too."

"Sad? Why?" she asked.

"Because we have so little time."

Shirley didn't want to think about the future, other than this coming weekend. Somehow they'd make it through the next eleven weeks. Then, after Tanni left for college, they could live together in California.

"Have I ever told you how much I enjoy Leaven-worth?" she asked. They often spoke for two and three hours at a time. Shirley supposed she must have mentioned her fondness for the town at some point.

"Not that I recall. I was only there once and liked it tremendously. It's the first place I thought of for a honeymoon."

Shirley nestled in the plush leather seat. She was exhausted and the warm air from the car's heater made her feel sleepy.

"Go ahead and rest," Larry said. "I plan on keeping you up for most of the night."

Shirley sighed contentedly. "Then you should be aware that I plan on wearing you out."

He chuckled. "We'll just have to see about that."

The next morning, Shirley had to admit they were both right. They'd arrived at the cabin around eleven the previous night. While Larry lit a fire and opened a bottle of champagne, she'd unpacked their suitcases and changed into her silk nightgown and robe.

He was a gentle, caring lover. Afterward, they slept for a while and then made love again. In the morning, Shirley woke to sunshine. She sat up and stretched contentedly before she snuggled against Larry's side.

"Mmm." He rolled over, throwing one arm around her. "I like waking up with you beside me."

"Me, too," she whispered. Tossing aside the covers a few minutes later, she shivered in the morning chill and hurriedly reached for her flimsy robe, although it offered little warmth.

The coffee was brewing by the time Larry joined her. He'd dressed and immediately set about building another fire.

Not until she'd poured them each a cup did Shirley look outside. "Larry!" she cried, pulling open the drapes. "It snowed."

"We *are* in the mountains, love."

"Yes, I know, but it's still October, and I wasn't expecting this. It's so beautiful."

"Yes, it is," he said, coming to stand behind her, folding his arms around her. She loved being this close to her husband, loved feeling his embrace. All too soon she'd be back in the real world, alone once again.

They spent one glorious day together, riding snowmobiles, laughing, enjoying each other's company. Larry took her to a wonderful restaurant for dinner and they spent much of that night discovering each other in new and exciting ways. Then, early Sunday morning, Larry drove them back to Cedar Cove.

Since he had to return the rental car to the airport, he took her home first. When they got there, he carried her small suitcase into the house, then held her close. "I don't want to leave you," he whispered.

Shirley didn't want him to go, either. In fact, she felt like weeping.

Larry hid his face in her hair. "The weeks will fly by," he said.

"No, they won't," she protested. "Every minute's going to seem like an hour." She felt his smile against her skin when he kissed her neck.

"I agree," he said. "I'm doing my best to think positive here. How about a little help?"

"I'm positive," she muttered. "Positive I'm going to be lonely and miserable."

He glanced at his watch. "I have to go."

"I know." If he got delayed in traffic or at the rental

return, he'd miss his flight. Shirley dared not keep him there any longer.

They kissed one last time, and she walked him out to the car and waved, forcing herself to smile, refusing to send him off with tears in her eyes. Standing by the fence she waited until the car disappeared from sight.

With a sigh, she went into the house and found Tanni's scribbled note on the kitchen chalkboard. "With Kristen. Home before six."

It was only three now. Her arms around her middle, she sank into a chair, feeling sorry for herself.

"This is ridiculous," she said aloud. She'd met and married a good man—an artist like herself, whose work she admired. Instead of brooding about the empty weeks ahead, she should be counting her blessings.

She picked up the phone and called Miranda. "What are you doing?" she asked.

"Cleaning house," Miranda said. "Somebody stop me."

"Okay, stop. I need your help."

"Larry's gone?"

"Yup. I'm fighting off depression. I can't do it alone. Want to come over and eat ice cream and watch a bunch of romantic movies with me?"

"I'd love to." Her friend didn't hesitate. "Do you have butter pecan or do I need to go to the store on my way?"

"Let me check." Shirley walked to the fridge and opened the freezer section. "I've got vanilla and…" She shuffled aside two frozen halibut filets, a microwave dinner and a box of peas. "Nope, that's it."

"I'll make an ice cream run," Miranda said. "It'll take me…forty minutes. Can you survive that long?"

"Forty I can do. Forty-five would be a stretch."

"I'll tell the grocery clerk this is an emergency and I'll be there as fast as I can."

Before she hung up, Shirley managed a smile. Miranda was a good friend and she was grateful for her willingness to drop everything and come to her rescue.

When Miranda arrived with three flavors of ice cream, Shirley had unpacked her suitcase, started a load of laundry and set out bowls and spoons. A selection of DVDs was stacked and ready. After sorting through her favorite romantic movies, she'd chosen *The African Queen*, *French Kiss*, *Romancing the Stone* and *The Princess Bride*.

Miranda decided they should watch *French Kiss* first. Shirley slipped it into the DVD player while her friend dished up their treats. They both sat on the sofa, eating slowly. "I love this movie," Shirley mumbled through a mouthful of melting ice cream.

"Me, too," Miranda said dreamily.

Given Miranda's often brusque manner, few would guess she was such a romantic. Shirley knew otherwise. The contrast between her no-nonsense exterior and her warm, sensitive heart was one of the interesting things about her.

Shirley didn't know anyone, not even Olivia, who could cut Will Jefferson down to size as effectively as her friend. She'd been observing the bickering and one-upsmanship between the two of them for months. They argued like a long-married couple, and Shirley was convinced they both enjoyed it. That style of interaction wasn't for her, but it worked for some couples.

"Guess what I got in the mail," Shirley said.

"Anything good? A prize from Publishers Clearing House?"

"Better. A card from your employer."

Miranda put her bowl of ice cream on the coffee table, sat up straight and paused the movie. "Will sent you a wedding card?"

"He sure did."

"Will? Will Jefferson? Are you joking?"

"He isn't so bad, you know," Shirley said. "Beneath all that bravado, he's a nice guy."

Miranda frowned, shaking her head. "He's completely wrapped up in himself. His ego is so big I can't imagine how he fits it through the door."

Shirley laughed. "Oh, for heaven's sake. Aren't you exaggerating?"

"You don't work with him. I do. I've seen him at his worst."

"And his best," Shirley added.

Miranda wasn't giving in that easily. "You go ahead and believe what you like, but I know the real Will Jefferson."

Shirley got up from the sofa and retrieved the wedding card, which she handed to her friend.

Miranda read Will's message, then closed the card and looked up at Shirley.

"Well?"

"He's good with words," Miranda reluctantly admitted. "He even sounds gracious."

"Don't act so surprised." The congratulatory note had felt authentic to Shirley. Will had wished her and Larry happiness and claimed he was proud to have played a role in bringing them together.

"He *can* be sincere," Miranda said, still with some reluctance.

Shirley agreed. Despite her initial doubts, she'd

sensed his good qualities—his kindness, his commitment to the artists of Cedar Cove, his generosity. Granted, he'd tried too hard to impress her and had come across as excessively sure of himself. "He's genuinely pleased that Larry and I found happiness together."

"Genuinely?" Miranda snickered.

Shirley studied her friend. "I had no idea you disliked him so much." In reality she knew the opposite was true; Miranda was falling for Will, and fighting it every step of the way.

"I don't dislike him," Miranda said. "In fact…" She closed her eyes.

"What?" Shirley pressed, although she was well aware of what Miranda was about to divulge.

"If you laugh, I swear to you I will get up and walk out of this house and never return."

"I won't laugh," Shirley promised, her expression sober. "Cross my heart."

Miranda frowned at her, as if to gauge the truth of her words. "All right, I'll tell you. I'm afraid…actually, I'm pretty sure I'm in love with him."

"You think I didn't already know that?" Shirley broke into a big grin. Miranda's confession pleased her. Maybe something would finally happen between Will and her friend.

"You knew?"

"Oh, sweetie, we've been friends far too long for me not to see how you feel about Will."

Miranda looked stricken. "Do you think Will knows?" she asked anxiously.

"Will Jefferson?" Shirley asked. "The poor man doesn't have a clue." Although she secretly thought he did…and that he felt exactly the same way.

Seventeen

When Gloria had first discovered she was pregnant with Chad Timmons's baby, it had felt like the end of the world. In the months since, she'd come to think differently. She loved her unborn child with a fierce protectiveness and the kind of intensity she'd never experienced before.

Her obstetrician had ordered a routine ultrasound for Tuesday morning. Sitting on the edge of her bed, Gloria closed her eyes, silently debating what to do. She hadn't seen or heard from Chad since they'd talked in the hospital parking lot, the day he'd been with that other woman.

The blonde had looked beautiful, petite, delicate. Unlike Gloria, who considered herself moderately attractive and took pride in her strength and toughness. As a cop, she *had* to be strong, mentally and physically.

Chad knew about the baby. For reasons of his own, Roy McAfee had told him. She'd been upset that Roy had gone against her express wishes, but she'd forgiven him in time and even found a measure of relief in knowing that this uncomfortable task had been taken from her. After he'd learned the news, though, Chad hadn't made any effort to contact her. That shouldn't surprise her, though. Oh, he'd had Mack deliver those books, which showed he was concerned. But he hadn't reached out to her—nor, for that matter, had she approached him.

It occurred to her that he might want to know about the ultrasound. The nurse who'd scheduled it had told Gloria that she could bring someone with her.

She'd considered asking her birth mother, but Corrie was in North Dakota with Linnette and her new grandson. Otherwise, Corrie would certainly have accompanied her.

But she had to acknowledge that the one person who should be there was Chad. Fingers shaking, she picked up her cell phone and punched the button that would connect her to Chad. A dozen times she'd been tempted to delete his number. She never had. Perhaps she'd secretly wanted to maintain this link.

He answered immediately. "Dr. Timmons."

"It's Gloria." Her throat was so dry, she could barely get her name out.

Silence.

"I understand Roy told you…"

"That you're pregnant," he finished.

"Yes…almost five months."

Silence again, a tense silence that gnawed at her stomach. "I tried to tell you," she blurted out. "That day I showed up at the hospital. But you were with this woman and—"

"I remember," he said, cutting her off.

"How is your…friend?" That was a less than subtle way of asking if he was involved with the other woman.

"That's none of your business."

Gloria clenched her fist. "Right."

"Is everything okay with the baby?" His voice remained cool, detached.

He hadn't inquired about *her*. "Everything is normal so far... I'm having an ultrasound tomorrow at nine."

"And you're telling me this because...?"

"I thought you should know." She regretted calling him. Chad's attitude—indifference verging on hostility—was making this nearly impossible.

"Why?"

"The nurse said I could bring someone," she muttered, feeling foolish.

"You want *me* with you?" His voice softened.

"If possible. I... I realize I didn't give you much notice."

"I work the early shift on Tuesdays."

"Oh." She should've phoned right away...

"I'll do what I can. But I'm not making any promises."

Her heart rate accelerated. Chad was saying he'd join her if he could—that he wanted to be with her.

"Okay," she said, and recited the pertinent information.

"At nine," he repeated.

"Yes, and, Chad, thank you for the books." She wanted him to know that she was aware those had come from him. He might not care about her, but he cared about his baby, and that gave her courage. She wondered if she would've had the nerve to call him if not for that one small sign.

"Mack told you the books were from me?"

"Not at first. I confronted him about it after Roy admitted he'd talked to you." Once she'd found out, her emotions had been chaotic for days afterward.

"I have a right to know I'm about to become a father."

"Yes," she agreed. "You do."

"You should never have hidden it from me." She heard the resentment in his voice; clearly he hadn't yet forgiven her.

"I hope to see you tomorrow," she said, and before their conversation could deteriorate into a verbal battle, she ended the call. She did understand his reaction to her keeping the pregnancy a secret. The ironic thing was, she'd done it for him. Chad was seeing someone else—still might be, for all she knew. At this point their only bond was the baby, and she didn't feel that an unplanned responsibility, one he hadn't asked for, should interfere with his future or his new relationship.

The next morning Gloria arrived at the ultrasound clinic fifteen minutes early. The waiting area held six chairs, four of which were occupied. Gloria took the fifth one, sat down and picked up a magazine. The couple across from her held hands, while the other couple whispered excitedly.

The two holding hands were called in first. Gloria glanced at the wall clock, figuring Chad probably hadn't been able to get the time off.

Ten minutes later, the assistant called her name. Gloria put down the magazine, which she'd hardly looked at, and stood. She followed the woman out of the waiting area and into an examination room. She was on the table, with her pants unzipped and pulled down and her top raised, when there was a knock on the door. The technician was explaining the procedure and what Gloria could expect to see and not see in the ultrasound. She listened intently but found herself distracted by a feeling of aloneness. A feeling of abandonment, of not mattering *enough* to anyone. The lump in her throat seemed about to choke her—and then the assistant opened the door.

"Dr. Chad Timmons is here. Would it be all right if I sent him in?"

"Yes, please," Gloria said. To her embarrassment tears filled her eyes and slid down her face. She desperately wanted to wipe them away but was afraid it would only call attention to the emotion that racked her.

"Come on in," the technician said. She smiled, greeting Chad. "Pull up a chair and sit down. We're about to get started."

Chad arranged his chair so he'd have a full view of the screen. The technician spread a cold gel on Gloria's stomach and placed a wandlike device over the small round protrusion that was her baby.

Gloria stared at the screen. She didn't dare look at Chad.

"Did you want to know the sex?" the technician asked.

"Sure," Gloria answered for them both, then turned to Chad.

"That would be fine," he said.

"Okay, do you see him?"

"Him?" Chad asked.

"Oh, it's definitely a him."

Despite her determination not to look at Chad again,

Gloria shifted her head—and saw his broad smile. He glanced at her and she smiled tentatively.

"A girl would make me just as happy," he murmured.

"Me, too," she whispered.

The technician continued. "We have ten fingers and ten toes."

"You're sure that's not another finger you're seeing?" Chad teased.

"Trust me, Daddy, that's no finger."

Chad laughed, and Gloria relaxed. To her surprise, he reached for her hand in a simple gesture of comfort and sharing. It helped ease the tension between them.

The ultrasound only took a few minutes. The physician would be reviewing it for any abnormalities, but Chad—as a doctor himself—assured Gloria that all looked well.

The technician cleaned the sticky substance off Gloria's abdomen and left the room.

"Have you thought about names?" he asked as she sat up.

"A little… I thought if it was a boy, I'd choose Roy for the middle name."

Chad nodded.

"Do you have a suggestion for a first name?" she asked, adjusting her clothes.

"DiMaggio."

"What?" Gloria asked. She couldn't have heard him correctly.

"DiMaggio. After Joe DiMaggio. I'm a big baseball fan."

"Couldn't we just call him Joe?"

Chad shook his head. "Too boring."

"I am *not* subjecting our son to a name like DiMaggio. He'll grow up hating us for that. What's your dad's name?" It suddenly occurred to her how little she knew of his life before Cedar Cove, his family, his childhood…

"Robert."

"Rob Roy. Oh, no."

"My granddad's name was Simon," Chad said.

"Simon Roy," she repeated. "Well, let's think about it."

"Okay, we'll do that." They walked out of the office together. "I can hardly believe we actually agree on something." Chad smiled. "Or almost agree, anyway."

Chad had good reason to feel that way, and Gloria felt the need to show her appreciation for the fact that he'd come. "I'm glad you were here," she mumbled, looking down at the pavement.

"I am, too."

"I should've mentioned it earlier…"

Chad shrugged. "I traded days with a friend. He owes me."

Neither spoke as he walked her to her car.

"You read the books?" he finally asked, breaking the silence.

"All three, cover to cover." She grinned. "Including the name book, but the only thing I learned from that is how hard it is to make a decision. I found the pregnancy books really useful, though."

"I often recommend them."

"I can see why."

They stood there, facing each other. It seemed that neither was ready to leave.

"I'm on desk duty now," Gloria told him.

"I heard," he murmured. "I bet you hate that."

She motioned with her hands, unsure what to say. When she'd first been assigned to administrative work and the phones, she'd expected to be bored. But that hadn't turned out to be the case. "It's actually okay," she said. "What about you? Do you like being an E.R. doctor?"

He made the same noncommittal hand motion she had. "It's not that different from what I did at the Cedar Cove clinic."

She pushed the button to unlock her door.

"You're feeling good?"

Gloria nodded. "Too good. I've gained five pounds."

"We both want a healthy baby, Gloria. I don't want you to worry about gaining weight."

"I won't," she promised. While she didn't want this conversation to end, she did need to get to work. "I'd better go."

"Me, too."

"Thank you," she whispered, and leaned forward to hug him.

Chad returned her hug. "Gloria?" he said in a low voice.

"Yes?"

"I think you should know I'm still seeing Joni."

Eighteen

Rachel waited inside the Cedar Cove movie theater for Bruce, looking at her watch every few minutes. Their Friday-night dinner date the week before had gone well—almost like the way things had been when they'd first started going out. It felt good to laugh with her husband again.

What hadn't felt good was leaving him at the end of the evening. They'd each driven off in opposite directions. But before they parted, they'd made plans to meet again. Rachel had suggested a movie. She'd already seen this particular romantic comedy on one of her late-afternoon excursions, but she knew Bruce would enjoy it, too. They needed more reasons to laugh together. They hadn't communicated since last Friday and she worried that he might have confused the time or forgotten that they'd agreed to meet.

Just when she was about to give up and go home, Bruce appeared, harried and out of breath.

"I wasn't sure you'd wait," he said. "But I'm glad you did." He took hold of her shoulders and brought her close.

"What happened?" she asked, then realized she knew. "Jolene?"

He nodded.

"I thought she was going to a haunted house with some friends tonight."

"She was…"

"Until she found out you were meeting me."

"She got sick." He rolled his eyes, as though he suspected she was faking.

"But, Bruce, she really could be ill."

"Trust me, I know when Jolene is sick and this was pretty lame. I told her she'd be fine by herself for a few hours and I'd be back soon."

"But…"

"Let's enjoy the movie," he said, steering her toward the ticket counter and then the refreshment stand. They ordered a large bucket of popcorn, a soda and bottled water for Rachel, joking about the fact that their popcorn and drinks cost more than the movie.

Bruce escorted her into the appropriate theater, where the previews had begun. He tilted the popcorn in her direction, then both of them settled in to watch the film.

Not until it ended and the credits were rolling did Rachel have an opportunity to resume their conversation. Jolene had obviously made a fuss about her father's date with Rachel. That was discouraging, especially if Jolene was faking illness in order to keep Bruce from seeing her. She found it hard to believe that her stepdaughter would go to such lengths. The one bright spot was that Bruce had recently had his second appointment with the counselor.

"So, how'd it go with Dr. Jenner?" she asked, once they were outside. It was dark by then and raining.

"Fine. I guess. Do you want to go somewhere and talk for a while?"

She wanted that very much. "Shouldn't you check on Jolene?"

Bruce hesitated. "I asked Anne from next door to look in on her. If there's something wrong, Anne will call me. I'm not letting Jolene force me into giving up this time with you." He grinned and reached for her hand. "Dr. Jenner would be proud of me."

Ten minutes later, they were sitting across from each other in a booth at the Pancake Palace.

Goldie, the long-time waitress, approached their table, coffeepot in hand, menus tucked under her arm. Bruce ordered the club sandwich and Rachel requested a small bowl of seafood chowder. She was full from the popcorn and could've gone without dinner, but Bruce wouldn't hear of it.

"Tell me more about the counselor," she said.

"Well," Bruce began. "So far, I've done most of the talking. He asked about my relationship with Jolene before you and I were married and what it's like now."

"Did Jolene go with you?" Rachel knew it wasn't likely, and she wasn't surprised by his answer.

"No."

That would've been too much to expect, Rachel acknowledged, although she'd hoped Jolene would have a change of heart.

"You started to tell me what happened this afternoon," she said. "What—"

"I don't want to talk about it," he broke in. "You won't tell me where you're living. Fine. You have your secrets and I have mine. Why should I be the one to spill everything when you—"

"It isn't exactly a secret," she protested quickly.

Bruce raised his hand. "You don't want to tell me, fine."

Rachel glared at him. She was perfectly willing to let him know she was sharing a house with Nate—but not when he was in this frame of mind. "If that's the way you want it."

Neither seemed inclined to continue the conversation.

When Goldie delivered their meals, she set the soup in front of Rachel and the club sandwich by Bruce and then retreated one step. "Are you two not getting along?"

"What makes you ask that?" Rachel murmured.

"Both of you have the same sour look. It's not a good idea to eat together while you're arguing. Mel and me have been married for fifty-six years and we never eat or go to bed without resolving our differences." She snorted. "Seems to me you two should do that, too—otherwise, you'll end up with stomachaches and blame the restaurant when it's your own fault."

"You're right, Goldie," Rachel said, without looking the other woman in the eye.

Grumbling under her breath, the opinionated waitress left them, shaking her head as if to say she'd done all she could to help.

Rachel picked up her spoon, although she doubted she'd be able to swallow any of her soup. She took a deep breath and glanced at Bruce.

"I'm sharing a house with a friend in Bremerton," she whispered.

As she said that, Bruce reached across the table to take her hand. "Jolene pulled every trick in the book to keep me home. Pretending she was sick was just one. She wanted you to wait at the theater, not knowing where I was or whether I was even going to show up."

It hurt that her stepdaughter disliked her so much she was willing to miss a night of fun with her friends for the sole purpose of ruining Bruce's plans. This was about keeping him away from *her*. His wife...

"I've let Jolene control my life for far too long. I've set some rules for her. Dr. Jenner calls them boundaries, although they sound like plain old rules to me. Saying Jolene doesn't like it is putting it mildly." He gave a quick shake of his head. "Ever since I've started seeing Dr. Jenner, she's gotten more rebellious."

Rachel didn't know what to say. Depressed, she felt as if they'd never find a solution. The one suggestion she had was that they live apart until Jolene left for college. Then and only then would she and their baby move in with Bruce.

"Let's talk about more pleasant subjects," Bruce said.

"Like what?"

"Christie and James. And their wedding."

Caught up in her own personal crisis, Rachel hadn't thought about her best friend's sister in weeks.

Christie and James, Bobby Polgar's chauffeur and close friend, had gone to Vegas for the ceremony. Bobby and Teri had been married in Vegas, too, Rachel remembered fondly. On the surface those two were an unlikely couple; Teri was practical and emotionally astute, while Bobby, a professional chess player, lived—or used to live—an entirely cerebral life. His approach was logical rather than instinctive. Maybe because of that, they fit together perfectly, each respecting the other's skills and talents. If only her own marriage was as uncomplicated.

"Did you hear about the chess game?" Bruce asked.

"Bobby was in another tournament?"

"No, the video chess game."

"What about it?" The last time she spoke to Teri, her friend had said something about Bobby and James having developed some sort of computer game. It involved chess and a parallel universe. That was all she knew. Teri wasn't sure how it worked so she hadn't explained it too clearly. She was far too busy caring for their triplets to worry about chess or gaming.

Bruce smiled. "They sold it to a major gaming company. The deal's worth a whole lot of money and there's the potential for more games in the future. James has a real talent for this."

"Who would've guessed James had it in him? He's always been so quiet and content to remain in the background."

"Apparently all the paperwork's signed and the game's gone into production. It's going to be the biggest thing since World of Warcraft."

"World of what?"

"Never mind."

"So, how are Christie and James doing?"

His smile widened. "Well…"

"What?" Seeing him so amused made her want to smile, too.

"Christie's decided to fatten him up."

She did smile now. James was tall and rail-thin, always had been as far as she knew. She remembered the first time she'd seen him. He'd come to the salon on an errand for Bobby. He'd looked so uncomfortable and out of place she was torn between sympathy and laughter. "I doubt it'll work. He's got one of those superefficient metabolisms."

"In any case, Christie is cooking day and night. Teri said she's become more domesticated than a house cat. James wanted her to quit her job at Wal-Mart, which she did."

"What about her classes at the community college?" They'd been so important to Christie when she'd enrolled, and Rachel hated the thought of her dropping out.

"She's more determined to finish those than ever."

"Good. She needs to do that for herself."

"Whatever she wants, James is supporting her and eating well at the same time." He paused, grinning. "Even if he stays exactly the same weight."

Clearly Bruce had been to see Teri. "How are the triplets?"

"Growing like grass in August."

"And Teri?"

"Great. The boys are sleeping better now and she looks like she's getting more rest. Bobby, too."

They'd hired a nanny, whom Rachel had met, but Teri kept a close eye on her sons.

"She said you hadn't come over or called her in a while." This sounded a bit accusatory.

Rachel knew that the instant she saw Teri she'd tell her about living with Nate. Teri was her best friend in all the world, but she couldn't keep her mouth shut. The only solution, really, had been to avoid her altogether. Rachel missed her desperately, so she'd give her friend a call or visit soon. She was feeling stronger and it no longer needed to be such a secret that she was living and working in Bremerton.

"James and Christie are happy, then?"

"Sure seem to be."

If he noticed the abrupt change of subject, he didn't comment. Instead, he squeezed her hand and looked directly into her eyes. "Let me come home with you."

"Bruce."

"I won't spend more than a couple of hours."

She knew what her husband wanted and, frankly, she was tempted. *Very* tempted. It was too dangerous, though. She was afraid that they'd walk into the house and Nate would be there. And she wasn't ready for that...

"I can't... I have a roommate, don't forget." That probably wouldn't matter to Bruce, so she decided to elaborate on the truth. Okay, she'd lie. "My roommate's having a big party tonight..."

"Oh."

"So let me go home with you," she said quickly.

Bruce hesitated.

"I won't stay longer than...necessary," she said, and then because it sounded so calculating, she started to giggle.

"What's so funny?"

"Us. We're married and we can't find a place to be alone. This is ridiculous."

"Jolene's still at the house," Bruce said.

"Oh, right. That won't work, then."

"It's *my* house. I don't care what my daughter thinks. You're my wife."

"Let's not pick a fight with her now, especially if she isn't feeling well."

Neither said anything for several seconds.

"We could always get a hotel room," Bruce said under his breath.

"You've got to be kidding."

He grinned sheepishly. "I'm not."

"But…"

"Do you have a better idea?"

Rachel didn't.

Bruce rubbed his thumb over the top of her hand. "I've missed you."

"Me, too," she said breathlessly. "Are you sure about this?"

He grinned. "Why not? I want to be with you, and if that means paying for a room, then so be it." He was already halfway out of the booth.

"Bruce," she whispered. "We don't have the bill."

"Don't worry, Goldie will get it to us." He peeled off a five-dollar bill, dropping it on the table for a tip, then extended his hand to Rachel.

She stood and Bruce bent to kiss the side of her neck.

Sure enough, Goldie appeared with their bill mere seconds later. "Anything wrong with the food?" she asked.

Their meals were almost untouched.

"Everything was fine," Rachel said.

"Do you want a take-out bag?"

"No, thanks." Bruce placed his hand on the small of Rachel's back, not hiding his eagerness to be on their way.

"You two still fighting?" Goldie demanded.

"Not anymore," Rachel told her.

"We're about to kiss and make up," Bruce added.

"That's what I like to hear. Good for you!"

"Yup, good for us." Bruce grabbed Rachel's hand. They paused only long enough to pay for their meal.

By the time they were in the parking lot, Rachel felt almost giddy. Bruce backed her against the side of his car and kissed her with a hunger that assured her she'd been greatly missed.

Wrapping her arms around her husband's neck, she returned every kiss in full measure. "Bruce…"

"Hmm?"

"If we get a hotel room…"

"If?"

She ignored that. "I think you should check on Jolene first."

"No way. Like I said, I'm not giving her any reason to bring me home earlier than I want to be." Bruce was far more interested in unlocking his car door while still kissing her.

"Wait," she murmured, dragging her lips from his.

"Wait?" he asked as he straightened. "For what?"

"I drove my own car here."

"Oh, yeah." He stepped back—and just then, his cell phone rang. Rachel froze.

So did Bruce. He pulled out his cell and his shoulders tensed with what could only be dread.

"Go ahead and answer it," she whispered.

Reluctantly Bruce did. "What?" he snapped. His eyes locked with Rachel's. "Sorry. Yes, of course. I'll be right home."

This was obviously serious. "What's wrong?" she asked even before he could disconnect.

"It's Anne from next door."

"And?"

"Jolene called her over. She's been throwing up all night. Anne said she hasn't been able to keep anything down. She's afraid there might be something really wrong. She thinks it's a good idea to take her to the E.R."

"Then you should go," Rachel said.

Bruce reached for her. "I'm sorry."

"I know. I'm sorry, too."

And she was, far more than she dared admit.

Nineteen

Shortly after nine on Thursday morning Miranda Sullivan was getting into her car to run errands when her cell phone chirped. Digging in her purse, she retrieved it, all the while wondering who'd be calling this early. Caller ID identified Will Jefferson. He'd given her the day off and she planned on putting it to good use.

"Hello?"

"Where are you?" he asked.

"On my way to the grocery store. I'm picking up treats for the goblins who'll be coming by tonight."

"Oh, right, it's Halloween. Aren't you doing this a little last-minute?"

"Maybe, but if I buy candy too early I tend to eat it myself."

"No willpower?"

Miranda frowned and refused to take the bait. He knew exactly which buttons to push with her. "Is there a reason you called?" she asked.

"Actually, speaking of last-minute, I was hoping you'd be able to work this afternoon."

"I thought you said you didn't need me."

"I didn't then, but I do now. My sister wants me to come with her to check something out…"

"What?" She'd counted on a free afternoon and wasn't giving it up without a good reason.

"Okay, if you must know…" He sighed. "Olivia and I have appointments at a couple of assisted-living complexes in the area."

Miranda did sympathize but she had her own appointment at Get Nailed. "I have plans this afternoon," she said.

"Oh." He sounded somewhat morose. "So you can't come in for a few hours? Well, I could close the gallery, I suppose. It probably wouldn't hurt for one afternoon. Only I hate the idea of doing that…"

"Oh, all right," Miranda said, capitulating far too easily. She could phone the salon and reschedule for later in the week.

"That's great." He leaped at her offer without any hesitation. "Can you be here around two?"

"I'll be there."

"Thanks, Miranda. I really appreciate it."

"Bye." She called the salon to cancel her appointment, then shut her cell and put it back inside her oversize purse. So much for shopping, hair and fun. She quickly revised her plans.

First things first. She ran errands, going to Safeway for the candy she needed. In addition, she bought an extra bag of miniature chocolate bars and a plastic pumpkin for the gallery. Then she picked up her dry cleaning. Shirley met her for an early lunch, and when they'd finished, she dropped off some books at the library. From there Miranda got to the art gallery with fifteen minutes to spare.

Will was with a customer when she arrived. He raised his hand briefly but otherwise didn't acknowledge her. Miranda hung her coat in the back room and stashed her purse in a safe place. Then she opened the candy, dumped the small chocolate bars in the pumpkin and set it on the counter near the cash register for customers to help themselves.

Will was at the door saying goodbye to his customer when she returned.

"What's that?" he asked, nodding toward the plastic pumpkin.

"What does it look like?"

"You brought candy in here?"

"Yes." The answer should be obvious.

"You don't need it and neither do I. Whenever possible I avoid sweets."

"Then don't indulge. I thought you were the one with *willpower*," she said sarcastically. When he started to respond, she said, "It isn't for you, anyway." Was he so self-absorbed that he assumed she'd purchased the bag for him?

"Then who's it for?"

"Customers," she said irritably. "Is that a problem?" She'd done him a favor and Will acted as if she'd brought poison into his precious gallery.

"We don't get that many children—"

"Isn't it time you met your sister?" she asked, interrupting him.

Will gave her a startled look. "Right. I shouldn't be longer than a couple of hours. Three at the most."

"If you aren't back by five, I'll close for the night and head home."

"I'll be back by then."

"So he says," Miranda muttered under her breath. If Will heard her, he pretended he didn't.

The rest of the afternoon was busy, much busier than she would've expected. She sold another Beverly Chandler painting, a sculpture and a quilt. Will should be pleased, but knowing him, he'd invent reasons to find fault. She just hoped he realized that if she hadn't given up most of her afternoon, they wouldn't have made three rather large sales. If he'd placed a closed sign on the door, he might never have known what he'd missed. After all, there was no guarantee those customers would've come back.

A little after five, as she was putting the cash from the till into the bank deposit bag, Will walked into the gallery, looking completely worn out.

"We had a great afternoon," she said, eager to share her news.

He nodded absently. "Olivia and I are shocked. You wouldn't believe the monthly fees these adult residences charge."

"I sold the quilt," Miranda bragged. It'd been in the gallery for three months and she'd almost lost hope that it would sell.

Will still wasn't listening. "Of course, when you take into account that the fees include meals and utilities, I don't suppose it's *so* bad."

"Another Beverly Chandler painting, too." If nothing else, this should get his attention.

"They have a lot of programs for the elderly," he continued. "They do everything they can to keep the residents physically fit. The social activities sound great. Both Olivia and I think this mental stimulation is exactly what Mom needs. Ben, too." He shook his head. "Still, we'll have to talk to Ben's son—and I don't mean David—"

"Have you heard a single word I said?" Miranda asked.

Will glanced up. "What?"

"Never mind." She tossed the deposit bag on the counter and went into the back room for her coat and purse.

He followed her. "Why are you in such a state?"

"Because of you."

"That figures. Apparently everything I do annoys you."

"You have no idea how true that is. And you seem to be just as annoyed by me. I'm not even sure why you keep me on."

"I'm wondering that myself," he murmured. "Furthermore I doubt *you* heard a single word *I* said."

"Yes, of course I did." She marched into the outer room and grabbed the plastic pumpkin.

"Where are you going with that?"

"Home. You don't appreciate it, so I'm taking it with me."

"I didn't say I didn't appreciate it. Anyway, I didn't have a chance to pick up any treats, so I was going to use it tonight in case any of the neighborhood kids stop by."

"That's unlikely."

"Okay, fine. Whatever." He glared at her.

Miranda glared back.

"Why are you like this?" he demanded.

"Like what?"

"So…so moody. You jump all over me every chance you get. I don't understand what your problem is."

Miranda took offense at that. "I am the most even-tempered woman you're likely to meet. Ask anyone."

"You fly off the handle over nothing."

"That is not true."

He gestured toward her. "Just listen to how defensive you are. Can't we have a civil conversation without you making all kinds of false assumptions?"

"I... I—" Perhaps she *was* being defensive. Okay, true, she was, but she had no choice. It was either that or own up to how attractive she found him...

"What are you thinking?" he asked, frowning slightly. He didn't seem to know how he should react when she didn't have an immediate comeback.

"I... I—" she started again, and then, without considering her actions, she stepped forward and kissed him.

For an instant they were both too shocked to do anything but stare at each other. Then Will reached out and caught her by the shoulders as if to shove her away. Instead, he brought her close, kissing her deeply, passionately.

They both seemed to realize what was happening at the same time. Breaking apart, they retreated, gazing at each other in shock.

Miranda could feel her face heating up with acute embarrassment. In all her life, she'd never been the one to take the initiative and kiss a man. Well, not the first time they kissed, at any rate. This was completely out of character.

"What was that about?" Will asked, frowning.

Miranda could play this one of two ways, she decided. She could be nonchalant about the whole thing and dismiss it as unimportant. Irrelevant. Or she could simply say he'd made her so angry that it was either kiss him or slap him across the face. And that being the case, she'd opted for the lesser of two evils.

Before she could choose which approach to take, Will raised one hand to his face and narrowed his eyes. "You just kissed me."

"No one's ever kissed you before?" she asked flippantly.

"Not like that."

"What's *that* supposed to mean?"

Not answering, he turned away and then abruptly turned back. "Do you do that often?"

"Do what?" she said, playing stupid. Because that was how she felt. Stupid.

"Walk up to a man and kiss him," he said. His voice seemed to echo around the gallery. Thankfully they were closed; otherwise, some unsuspecting customer might breeze in. But maybe that wouldn't be so bad because she'd be able to escape.

"No, I don't usually go around kissing men," she admitted. "It seems to me you enjoyed it, though."

"I most certainly did not."

"Oh, please!" She laughed outright.

"What's so funny?"

"You. Come on, Will. I don't understand why you're so thrown by a little kiss."

"Why'd you do it?"

There wasn't going to be an easy way to extricate herself from this awkward situation. She could confess that she was strongly attracted to him. No, that would be totally the wrong move. It would give him the upper hand, always dangerous with a man like

Will. Acting defensive and ill-tempered protected her, although she'd rather burn at the stake than admit it.

"Explain," he insisted.

"Ah..." She'd really done it this time. "It was a mistake."

"Yes, it *was* a mistake. A big one."

"Whatever."

"As your employer, I'm finding this all rather... amusing."

"You *would* find it amusing." Leave it to Will to use this to embarrass her even further—although a moment ago, his reaction had been quite different.

"I prefer to kiss rather than be kissed."

"Oh, you have rules for such things," she murmured, not pointing out that he'd done his share of the kissing. This entire conversation was ridiculous. She yanked her raincoat from its hook and thrust her arms into the sleeves.

"Everyone has rules about kissing," he said.

"Like I told you, it was a mistake. An accident..."

"An accident," he repeated. "You're joking. That kiss was probably the most deliberate action you've taken since the moment I hired you."

"I moved the first Chandler painting," she was quick to remind him, "the one that sold a month ago."

He ignored that. "When I kiss a woman, I prefer she not be a big-boned, opinionated windbag."

So now he was going to insult her. Miranda didn't need to hang around for that. Grabbing her purse, she stomped out of the gallery.

"Where are you going?" he asked, following her.

"Why do you care?"

"I don't. I'm just...curious."

She was at the door, which stubbornly refused to open. She twisted the handle several times, but couldn't budge it. So much for making a grand exit.

Will reached over and flipped the lock so that when she tried again she stumbled backward and almost fell into his arms. He clutched at her shoulders to steady her. It didn't take much effort to shake herself free.

As soon as the door opened, she hurried around to the rear of the building where she'd parked. Again, Will followed her.

"What are you doing?" she asked sharply.

He didn't answer, and it occurred to her that he was as bemused as she'd been. He didn't know what he was doing or why. That was comforting—at least a little.

Before she could open the car door, Will planted his hand on the side window and turned, leaning against the vehicle so she couldn't leave.

"What?" she said heatedly.

Then Will hauled her into his arms and kissed her full on the mouth. When he released her, she faltered for a second or two.

He looked as shocked as she'd felt when she'd kissed him.

"Where are you going?" he asked again, his voice faint.

"Home." He wasn't the only one with voice problems. Her own sounded as if a mouse had gotten control of her voice box; her words came out like a high-pitched squeak.

"Will you be back in the morning?" He seemed anxious, as though concerned that she might resign her position.

"Yes, why wouldn't I be?"

"I didn't want a little thing like a kiss to stand between us," he said with a frown.

"You kissed me."

"Yes, I know."

"And I kissed you…first. Okay, I'll admit it."

"Do you plan on doing it again?"

"Why are you asking?" After all, he was the one who claimed she was a big-boned, opinionated windbag. "Do *you* want to kiss *me* again?"

His head shot up. "Let's just call this whole episode a slip in judgment."

"On both our parts," she added.

He offered her a tentative smile. "On both our parts," he agreed.

Twenty

The puppy's soft mewling cry woke Grace from a sound sleep. Cliff had been feeding Beau in the middle of the night, and usually seemed to hear the puppy before Grace did. Often she got up, too, but there really wasn't much she could do. So, after a few minutes she simply returned to bed.

"Okay, okay, I hear you," she muttered as she threw aside the covers. Cliff continued to sleep peacefully, which told her he was especially tired. It was her turn to get up with the puppy.

Beau slept in a cardboard box in the corner of their bedroom. She didn't like it, but there wasn't anyplace else they could keep him where he could be heard at night. Unfortunately, he still needed to be fed every few hours.

Reaching for her fleece housecoat at the end of the bed, Grace slipped it on and tucked her feet into the warm, fuzzy pink slippers that had been a gift from her daughter Maryellen last Christmas.

Cliff had the puppy formula ready, so she got it out of the kitchen and carried Beau into the living room.

As she set him in her lap, he latched on to the small rubber nipple and sucked greedily.

"You're not as cute as you think you are," she felt obliged to inform the puppy. "Buttercup was a great-looking dog," she said aloud. Sighing, she realized she actually wanted this small, runt-of-the-litter dog to feel jealous. Beau wouldn't grow up to be half the dog Buttercup was. Nope. Not in a million years.

"I hope you're happy," she said. Beau might think he'd finally got her where he wanted her, but he was dead wrong. Grace had no intention of letting this puppy, or any other dog, capture her affections. The *only* reason she'd agreed to take him was as a favor to Beth. Even now she was sorry she'd allowed herself to be talked into this.

Grace had managed to steel herself against the puppy—so far. In fact, she went out of her way not to pay attention to Beau. During the day Cliff looked after him, which helped. Unfortunately, he had a meeting with fellow horse-breeders the next day and wouldn't be able to bring Beau with him. That meant she'd have to take the puppy to work for the first time—something she'd rather not do.

Holding the baby bottle, she focused her gaze on the opposite wall. "Buttercup would've looked after you," she said. It was still difficult not to tear up when she thought of her beloved golden retriever. Not a day passed that she didn't think of Buttercup. Her dog had always greeted her when she returned from work, and in the evenings Buttercup would lie at Grace's feet while she read or watched television.

"You could pet him, you know." Cliff's voice startled her. Grace looked up to see her husband leaning against the archway that led into the living room.

"What time is it?" he asked.

"I didn't see. Early. Too early for either of us to be up. This dog isn't worth losing sleep over," she grumbled.

"Sure he is," Cliff said, crossing his arms. "Just look at him, cuddled up on your lap. Pet him, Grace. He needs affection."

"He's not getting it from me."

Cliff shook his head. "You're a hard woman."

She ignored that. "You think I don't know what you're doing?"

"Which is what?"

"You're trying to coax me to be friends with Beau. Well, it isn't going to happen."

"You bought him the chew toy."

She had, but that was for self-preservation. "I didn't want him cutting his teeth on my shoes." Because she was often on her feet for long periods of time, Grace purchased high-end pumps that were both attractive and designed for comfort. The last thing she wanted was for Beau to make a meal out of one of those.

"I have that meeting at ten," Cliff reminded her.

"I know." She wasn't happy about it, but she had little cause for complaint, since Cliff had been so accommodating toward the puppy.

"He'll sleep all morning."

"We can only hope." She worried about what would happen if the puppy got away from her at the library. If he got lost...

"He's a good-natured little guy."

"Maybe someone will steal him," she joked. Well… sort of joked.

"Grace!"

His disapproval annoyed her. "If you're up, you might as well feed him."

"I'd rather watch you."

Grace frowned. "You don't seriously want this dog, do you?" She didn't give him a chance to respond. "Puppies are a nuisance." The fact that Cliff had disregarded her wishes concerning this dog didn't sit well with her. It hadn't taken him more than a day to fall under Beau's spell.

"If anyone had asked me," Cliff said, "I would've agreed with you. We don't need a puppy."

"Thank goodness," she murmured.

"Then Beau arrived on our doorstep…"

"He was foisted on me by a woman with a conniving mind," Grace said irritably.

"He's a good puppy."

"He's a nuisance."

"To you, maybe, but he's grown on me."

"Cliff," she wailed. "I can't believe you're saying this. Do you think it was any accident that Beth placed this puppy with us? You're falling right in with her schemes."

"Is that so bad? All Beth wants is a good home for these puppies."

"But I don't *want* a puppy," Grace said, glaring across the room at her husband. "Or any other dog for that matter. Buttercup is gone, and that's the end of any pets for us. Agreed?" she asked pointedly.

Maybe Cliff thought he could convince her to

change her mind; in that case, she wanted it understood *right now* that wasn't going to happen.

"Whatever you say, Grace. This is totally up to you."

"Good, because my decision's already made." She heard a sucking noise and realized the bottle was empty. Gently she withdrew the nipple from Beau's mouth.

"It wouldn't hurt you to give him a bit of affection."

Grace ran her index finger down the puppy's back. He was so small and skinny she could feel the ridges of his spine. Poor thing really was undernourished. To Cliff's credit, Beau looked healthier than when he'd first arrived, but that wasn't saying much.

Beau's deep brown eyes seemed to plead with her. Well, if he was hoping to steal her heart, he could look elsewhere.

"Should I give him a second bottle?" she asked.

"No. It's not good to feed him too much at once. Better to let him eat smaller meals but more often."

That made sense.

"I don't need to burp him, do I? Like a baby?"

"No. He'll be asleep in a few minutes."

Sure enough, Beau settled contentedly onto her lap and quickly went back to sleep. Grace wished it was as easy for her. When she returned Beau to his box and got into bed, she tossed and turned, unable to sleep. Cliff, on the other hand, obviously had no problem. Within minutes—no, *seconds,* she thought enviously—he was deep in dreamland.

Lying on her back, staring up at the ceiling, Grace recalled the day Charlotte Rhodes had brought Buttercup to the house. Except that Charlotte had been Charlotte Jefferson then.

That was such a dark time in Grace's life. Dan had gone missing and, to all appearances, seemed to have run off with another woman. She remembered the day someone had reported seeing him in town, driving a pickup truck. Later, her husband had been spotted just down the street from the library. Grace had run out, coatless, chasing after him in such a frantic hurry that she'd stumbled, fallen and skinned her knee.

It wasn't Dan that day. It couldn't have been. Almost a year passed before she learned that her husband wasn't with another woman. He'd killed himself, unable to let go of a crime he'd committed as a young man serving in Vietnam.

For years after the war he'd periodically sink into black moods, during which he'd lash out at those around him, at those who loved him. Any effort to question or comfort him was met with fierce, uncontrollable anger. After a while, Grace stopped trying. His mood would reverse itself after a few days or weeks and it would be as if nothing had happened. For their entire married life, she'd loved a man who had what was essentially a split personality.

Grace must have fallen asleep because the alarm startled her awake. Her eyes flew open and she sat up and switched it off. Cliff rolled over, pulling the blanket over his shoulder. Leaning down, she kissed his ear. "I'll start the coffee," she said.

"Thanks," he mumbled.

She climbed out of bed and grabbed her housecoat. Shrugging into it as she walked to the kitchen, Grace paused at the cardboard box to discover Beau tightly curled up in the receiving blanket Cliff had found for him. "I see the alarm didn't bother *you* any," she whispered.

She waited until there was enough coffee in the pot to fill two mugs, then carried them into the bedroom. Cliff was up and in the shower.

Drinking her coffee as she dressed, she slipped into a long-sleeved polo shirt and a jumper. She wore something similar most days; it was almost a uniform. Cliff took his coffee from the dresser as he strolled out of the bathroom with a towel around his waist. The radio was reporting on weather and traffic in the Seattle area. Half listening, she plugged in her curling iron and applied moisturizer to her face.

When Grace had finished putting on makeup and fixing her hair, she saw that Cliff had removed Beau from his box. The puppy had made his way over to one of her fluffy slippers, snuggled inside and gone right back to sleep.

"You have to admit that's cute," Cliff said, coming to stand behind her.

"No, I do not. I don't want that dog in my shoe."

"Come on, Grace. Hallmark would print a card with a picture like that. Or…how about if I put him on You-Tube? He'd be a star. Just look at him."

"You can look all you want but I have to get to work."

Cliff shook his head and bent to take Beau from her slipper.

Grace hated to be so coldhearted but she couldn't lower her guard, not even a little. The instant she did, Beau would wriggle his way into her affections, which was exactly what Cliff and Beth hoped would happen. Grace was determined it wouldn't.

Half an hour later, after a second cup of coffee and a toasted English muffin, Grace drove to the library with Beau in the box beside her. She had several small bottles of formula, which she'd have to feed him during the day.

Cliff said that if the meetings ended early, he'd come and pick up Beau, but he wasn't making any promises. She figured she'd be stuck with the puppy all day.

Naturally Beau had everyone on the library staff wrapped around his tiny paw the moment she carried him into the building.

"Anyone want to feed him?" she asked. If she could arrange for someone else to do it, all the better.

Every single employee volunteered. She let them work out a schedule as she retreated to her office and assumed her tasks for the day. Writing the email newsletter that went out to patrons every Monday morning was at the top of her list.

Beth phoned shortly after the library opened. "How's it going?" she asked.

"It's going. Cliff named him Beau."

"I heard."

So Beth had been in contact with Cliff. If Grace was a paranoid kind of person, she'd wonder if those two were teaming up against her. More than likely Beth had phoned the house and Cliff had answered, then simply forgotten to mention the call.

"Have you weighed Beau lately?"

"Not me. Cliff did, though."

"Do you remember his weight?"

"Sorry, no."

Beth asked a few additional questions, but Grace was no more helpful with those than she'd been with the first one. Cliff had taken on nearly all Beau-related duties and that was how Grace intended to keep it.

Once she was off the phone, she went to check with the children's librarian regarding story hour that Friday afternoon. She needed the information for her newsletter.

As she walked toward the children's section, she noticed several people smiling in her direction. She didn't think anything of it until she looked back. Beau was trotting after her as if he were her shadow.

Grace stopped and so did Beau. He sat on his haunches and stared up at her, his tail wagging. Ignoring him, she moved forward purposely. Beau ran after her, his small legs hardly able to keep up.

Finally she couldn't stand it a minute longer. Crouching down, she picked him up and cradled him in her arms. He licked her hand, then reached for her face.

She raised her chin out of his range. "I am not going to love you, no matter what you do," she insisted. "Don't even try, okay?"

Beau whimpered as if to disagree.

"We're going to find you a good home," she said, stroking his soft fur. "A family with lots of children for you to play with. That's what you need—a family with children. You don't want to live with Cliff and me. We won't feel like playing chase or throwing a Frisbee or doing any of the other things you'd love. It's for your own good. Do you understand?"

Apparently Beau didn't, because he licked her hand again.

Twenty-One

Teri Polgar was enjoying her first peaceful moment of the day. She sat in the most comfortable chair in the family room, rested her feet on the matching ottoman, leaned back and closed her eyes.

The triplets were all asleep and, after the morning she'd had, Teri was ready for a nap herself. Friends and family claimed that if anyone could handle a multiple birth, she could. It was a nice compliment, and she took it as such, although she was beginning to doubt the high opinion they had of her abilities.

Bobby and James were off for the next few days meeting with the video game people in L.A. Bobby was a huge help with their sons, and of course Gabrielle, their nanny, was, too. Still, the major part of the triplets' care fell to her. Other than quick trips to buy groceries, Teri couldn't even remember when she'd last ventured out of the house. As for "girl time"—it'd been practically nonexistent. Her hair needed to be cut and her fingernails were a mess.

She missed Rachel, although they'd talked a few days ago—for the first time in ages. Rachel had described her situation—her housemate and the temporary position she'd taken with the shipyard. That girl must like living on the edge because she was definitely *not* in her right mind to be living with Nate Olsen. Teri could only imagine what Bruce would say once he found out. Well, she wasn't going to be the one to tell him.

Bruce Peyton. Teri felt like slapping him silly. Honestly—letting a thirteen-year-old dictate his life. How crazy was that? Teri knew what poor Rachel had endured in the months that led up to her moving out. She certainly didn't blame her. In Teri's opinion, Rachel deserved a medal for putting up with that spoiled brat.

Then, last week, just when things seemed promising—because Bruce was seeing a counselor and Jolene appeared to be softening—everything had blown up in Rachel's face. Jolene had gotten sick and Bruce had to hurry home. But Bruce soon discovered that this so-called illness had been self-inflicted. He found an empty bottle of ipecac in the garbage and confronted his daughter. He'd emailed Rachel, and Rachel had subsequently told Teri. This marriage wasn't looking good. Not good at all.

The doorbell chimed and Teri bounded to her feet with more energy than she'd realized she had. If whoever it was woke any of the triplets…

Bruce stood on the porch.

"Bruce?" She was too surprised to say any more. Then she added, "What are you doing here?"

"I came to talk to you about Rachel."

Teri shook her head, unwilling to let him in. This was Rachel's worst fear, that Bruce would ask Teri for information. "I don't think I should," she said bluntly.

She'd vowed she wouldn't supply Bruce with any of the details Rachel had so recently and reluctantly shared. Not until Rachel had the chance to tell him herself, which she'd fully intended to do until she'd heard about this latest trick of Jolene's.

"I have something I want you to give Rachel," he pleaded, still on the porch.

His sad eyes did her in. Teri had always been a sucker for sad eyes. She'd learned more quickly than her sister had, however. Christie's heart had been broken more times than a carton of eggs, usually over some down-on-his-luck loser. Christie did eventually learn; it just took her longer.

"All right, you can come in," she said, not very graciously. Stepping aside, she gestured into the house, then led him into the family room. It was far enough away that they wouldn't disturb the triplets, but at the same time she could hear them if they cried. That was especially important, since Gabrielle had the night off.

She motioned toward the sofa, which Bruce sank into.

"What can I do for you?" she asked, not bothering with small talk.

"I need help," Bruce admitted.

"I'll say you do." However, Bruce needed more help than she could give him. She hoped he was continuing to see the counselor.

He sighed. "I really blew it with Rachel, didn't I?"

No point in answering *that*. Bruce already knew he was in trouble with his wife.

"Did you hear what happened last Saturday?" he asked.

"I did."

He exhaled slowly. "I was beginning to think Rachel might be willing to move back home. Then the three of us could all go to the counselor together. We need to work on being a family, and Rachel living somewhere else complicates everything."

Teri couldn't even manage an encouraging smile for fear she'd blurt out her opinion, which she was sure Bruce wouldn't appreciate. As far as she was concerned, Jolene should be grounded until she turned thirty or wised up, whichever came first. Teri felt the girl would see the light far more quickly that way.

Bruce apparently thought the best approach was to attempt reason. What a joke! Reason with a teenager? No wonder their marriage was falling apart.

"Have you talked to Rachel in the past week?" Bruce asked with wide-eyed hopefulness.

"Yeah." Teri mentally zipped her mouth shut. She refused to divulge a single detail of their conversation. Not one.

"How is she?"

Now, that was tricky. "All right… I guess."

Bruce leaned forward. "We had dinner two weeks ago and everything went so well that we started talking on the phone."

Teri knew that, too, but didn't respond. Rachel would never forgive her, and this was her closest, dearest friend in the world. Well, other than her sister. Rachel had entrusted her with this secret, which Teri vowed she would keep to herself. Not even Bobby knew.

"But after last weekend, she won't answer my calls anymore," Bruce concluded.

She'd missed a whole section of what he'd been saying, which was just fine. The less she heard, the better.

"I'm worried about her."

She clamped her teeth tightly together. If Bruce was worried, he didn't have anyone to blame but himself. How he could've been so oblivious to Jolene's manipulations for so long would forever remain a mystery.

"Like I said, I want you to give Rachel something for me."

"What is it?"

He stood and took a wad of bills out of his pocket.

"You want to give her *money?*" He thought that was how he'd win back his wife? Even Bobby, with his chess brain, wouldn't dream of doing anything so... so dumb. And he'd had some prize ideas in his time, adorable though he was.

"She must be low on cash," Bruce explained. "So, would you give this to her for me?"

"What makes you think she's low on cash?"

His gaze held hers, and Teri quickly looked away, afraid he'd read something in her expression that she didn't intend to tell him. "I know she's working but she's also paying rent," he said, "and there have to be additional expenses. I just feel I should be helping her financially."

"You should talk to her about this, not me."

"Yes, but she refuses to discuss money with me— or anything else."

She murmured a few noncommittal words.

"I do know she's working," he went on, "but not where. I called every salon in the Kitsap area looking for her."

Teri gave him high grades for trying. She still hadn't

taken the money, although he continued to extend it to her.

"I want to be sure she has vitamins, good food—stuff like that. She might not want to talk to me, but I'd feel better if I knew she had the things she needs."

"Well…"

"I understand why she's upset, but I feel responsible for her and the baby."

"You should," Teri said without censure.

"So, would you give this to Rachel for me? Please?"

Reluctantly Teri accepted the cash. She was about to suggest he buy something for the baby, which would go a long way toward convincing his wife that he was serious. Again, she managed to suppress any comment. She had to carefully weigh every word she spoke. No offers of help. No advice. No information.

"When you talk to her," Bruce said, "would you mention how much I love her? Tell her I'm still going to the counselor and that Jolene has agreed to meet him."

Now this was promising news. "I'll tell her."

"Thanks, Teri." That was all he said, but the gratitude in his eyes, the hope and longing, almost made her cry.

After Bruce left, Teri stood by the window and watched him pull away. As soon as his car was out of sight, she rushed to the phone and called Rachel's cell, which went straight to voice mail.

"Rach, it's Teri. Call me ASAP. Bruce just stopped by the house."

Five minutes later, the return call came. Her friend didn't even say hello. "Did you let him in?"

"Of course I did," Teri said. "It would've been rude to slam the door in his face."

"What did he want? You didn't tell him anything?"

The worry in her voice made Teri regret that she hadn't immediately set Rachel at ease. "No, nothing. I swear he doesn't know a thing."

"Thank you," she said in relief.

"Can you come by this afternoon? Bobby's away and I could use the company."

Rachel hesitated.

"Besides, Bruce gave me something for you."

"He did?" Rachel's curiosity was piqued.

"Yup, but I'm not saying what it is. You'll have to come over here."

A half hour later, Rachel did.

Teri hugged her and practically dragged her into the foyer. "Gabrielle's out and we only have about thirty minutes before the boys wake up." The triplets had started to teethe and Teri's life wasn't her own anymore.

Rachel followed her into the kitchen and Teri began preparing a cheese and cracker plate with apple slices and grapes. She could use a snack herself, and this was a good excuse to feed her friend. She'd forced herself not to tell Bruce that she was worried Rachel wasn't getting enough fruit and vegetables or high-quality protein. From the tidbits Rachel had dropped, Teri surmised that she dined out alone two or three nights a week, which probably meant fast food. That couldn't be the best thing for Rachel or the pregnancy.

"You said Bruce left something for me," Rachel began.

She sat on the bar stool and propped her elbows on

the counter. Teri had washed the grapes and sliced two apples; now she was cubing the cheese and arranging it on the platter. Only about half the cheddar found its way to the plate. The other half seemed to automatically end up in her mouth.

"Here," she said, offering the plate to Rachel, who reached for a piece of apple and speared some cheese.

"Bruce?" she prompted before taking a bite.

"Oh, yeah, Bruce." Teri dug in the hip pocket of her jeans and brought out the wad of cash.

"Money?"

"He wants to contribute to your care and the baby's. He loves you. He's feeling guilty and miserable and lost."

"You didn't…"

Teri pantomimed locking her lips. "I swear I didn't say a word. I told you I wouldn't and I didn't." She paused. "You should take the money," Teri urged. She set it on the counter, then crossed her arms. "He looked pretty broken, Rach."

Rachel didn't say anything at first. "Did he talk about what happened last Saturday?" she finally asked.

"A little. But he also said he's been seeing the counselor—and Jolene agreed to go."

Rachel's head jerked up. "She did?"

"Well…for one time, anyway."

Rachel nodded, but she didn't seem too encouraged. "I wonder what Bruce had to promise to get her to do that."

"He didn't promise her anything." He hadn't really said, but Teri got the impression that Jolene hadn't been given a choice.

"Trust me, Bruce must have bribed her."

"Don't be so sure."

A baby's cry came from down the hall, soon followed by a second and a third. Teri sighed.

"Where's Christie?" Rachel asked.

Now that James and Christie were married, her sister lived in the apartment above the garage with her husband.

"She's with James. You remember how it is when you're first married. They're constantly together."

"I do remember," Rachel whispered. "Unfortunately, the honeymoon for Bruce and me didn't last nearly long enough."

Rachel counted the money. Five crisp one-hundred-dollar bills. She put them back on the counter. "Please return it to him for me. Okay?"

"You don't need it?"

She shook her head and Teri knew instinctively that she was lying.

"Rachel, don't be unnecessarily stubborn. Bruce wants you to have this."

"No," she insisted. "Tell him to spend it on the counselor for him and Jolene."

Twenty-Two

"You can put that box in the master bedroom," Lori Wyse told her brother-in-law, pointing the way, which was silly. Mack owned the duplex and knew exactly where the master bedroom was.

He disappeared down the hallway as she started to unpack the dishes, setting them in a cupboard in the compact kitchen. The duplex was smaller than their apartment had been. Nevertheless, it would serve their needs nicely.

"I think that's it," Mack said, hands in his back hip pockets.

"Can you go with me to turn in the rental truck?" Linc asked.

"Sure thing."

Linc kissed Lori on the cheek as he walked out the door. "I shouldn't be long. Don't work too hard."

"I won't," she promised, although she was determined to get as much unpacked as she could.

"Need any help?" Mary Jo asked, joining her, the baby in her arms. She set Noelle on the kitchen floor, where she was content to play with a large toy rabbit.

"That would be great." Lori wasn't about to decline such a generous offer. She dragged over the box of pots and pans and showed her sister-in-law where she wanted them placed.

They worked in silence for a while, with the radio playing softly in the background. "Linc and I are so grateful to get out from under my father's thumb," Lori said. "I don't know what we would've done if it wasn't for you and Mack." Moving to Seattle was one of their few options, and they were both grateful not to be living in Linc's family home with his two younger brothers.

"This helps me and Mack, too."

Lori didn't know Mary Jo well yet, but she felt they'd already become friends. Mary Jo sat on the kitchen floor and reached for a second box. "Do you want these bowls down here or in the cupboard above the dishwasher?"

"Above the dishwasher," Lori told her.

Noelle threw her rabbit aside and yawned loudly.

"Looks like it's nap time," Lori said. Come to think of it, she was tired, too. Linc had left the apartment to pick up the truck before six that morning. But they'd been awake since four, finishing the last of the packing and cleaning.

"Come on, baby girl," Mary Jo said, scooping up the toy, then bending to retrieve her daughter. "Let me change your diaper and put you down for a couple of hours."

"She sleeps that long?"

"Almost every afternoon. She still takes a morning nap, too, but she'll outgrow those pretty soon."

Lori knew she had a lot to learn about babies. She

and Linc had talked about starting a family and had decided to wait a couple of years. As newlyweds, they were still getting used to living with each other and to the demands and compromises of married life. They'd weathered a couple of challenges in the past year, thanks largely to her father. Leonard Bellamy refused to give Linc the opportunity to prove himself and had gone out of his way to sabotage every effort Linc made.

His attitude infuriated Lori. Linc was a decent, honest, hardworking man. Her father should thank God that she'd married a man as wonderful as Lincoln Wyse. Leonard was determined to control her life and she wouldn't let him. Because of that he was punishing Linc and, through Linc, her.

When she'd phoned home and severed her relationship with her family, Linc felt she'd overreacted. It was true that she'd acted on impulse, but she'd meant every word.

Linc arrived home just as she finished sorting out the silverware. "Looks like you're making good progress," he said.

"What amazes me is how much stuff I've accumulated."

"Pretty shocking, isn't it?" Linc slipped his arms around her from behind and buried his face in her neck. "Do you think we could initiate our new home tonight?" he whispered.

"That's a distinct possibility," Lori whispered back, her hands covering his.

There was a polite knock at the open front door.

Instantly Linc dropped his arms. They both turned

to find Kate Bellamy standing on the other side with a small gift bag in her hand.

"Mom," Lori said, forgetting for the moment that she was no longer speaking to her family.

"I stopped by the apartment and the neighbor told me where you'd moved," Kate said. "I brought you a small housewarming gift."

She seemed to be waiting for an invitation to step inside. Lori was too stunned to react.

"Mrs. Bellamy," Linc said, taking charge. "Come in, please." He pushed aside a series of empty boxes, clearing a path for Kate. She made her way to the small table in the breakfast nook, where he pulled out a chair for her.

Lori was uncertain of what to say. She'd stood up to her family, and pride wouldn't allow her to back down. Still, this was her mother; she couldn't very well ask her to leave. Especially since her real problem was with her father...

"Would you like some coffee or tea?" Linc asked.

"So you've unpacked the kitchen?" Kate asked, eyeing the cardboard boxes stacked against a wall.

"I know where the tea bags are and I can boil water," Lori said. Mary Jo had unboxed the pots and pans, so she knew exactly where to find one.

Her mother grinned. "I taught you well," she said in a joking voice.

"As a matter of fact you did," Linc said smoothly. "Lori obviously picked up her cooking skills from you."

"Oh, honestly, Linc, you'd been eating your brothers' cooking. Anything was an improvement over that."

"Mary Jo cooked, too," he was quick to tell her.

Ignoring him, Lori said to her mother, "Actually, I could stir fry crabgrass and Linc wouldn't complain."

"I remember when your father and I were first married," Kate said with a wistful look. "I was a terrible cook. I ruined almost every meal and yet he ate all those atrocious, burned dinners and said they were delicious. That's what love will do for you."

Lori set the kettle on to boil and found three mugs. A canister in the cupboard held the tea bags.

"Open your gift," her mother said, handing her the package.

"You didn't need to do this," she said as she took the bag. The pink tissue paper inside was folded into peaks. Her mother had always been a stylish woman whose sense of elegance and beauty transformed everything around her. Since those early days of her marriage, Kate had learned how to cook, and every meal was as lovely to look at as it was to eat. *Beauty* had become her watchword in all things. Even now, dressed in slacks and a sweater with a rain jacket, Kate resembled a model. She was tall and slim and Lori had rarely seen her without perfect hair and makeup.

Lori wished she could be more like her mother, although she believed she'd inherited her interest in fashion from Kate.

"It's just something small," Kate murmured.

Lori pulled out the paper and discovered a hand-held blender. She didn't have one. "Oh, Mom, this is great. Thank you so much."

"I love mine, and I hoped you hadn't bought one yet."

"No, I haven't. You're always so thoughtful." She

knew her father wouldn't have approved of this. "Does Dad know you bought a gift for us?"

Her mother's silence told her what she'd already figured out.

After an awkward moment, Kate raised her chin and announced, "Your father and I are no longer speaking."

Lori sat down on one of the kitchen chairs. "You and Dad aren't talking?" The kettle whistled and Linc removed it from the burner.

He went to stand behind Lori and placed his hands on her shoulders. "Does this have anything to do with Lori and me?" he asked.

Her mother looked at them, then nodded. "We all know your father is a stubborn man."

Lori snickered. "That's putting it mildly."

"Once he gets an idea in his head, no one can convince him he's wrong. No one."

Lori studied her mother closely. Kate wasn't an emotional woman but tears filled her eyes. She blinked them away.

"What happened, Mom?"

"When you phoned last month and told your father you were finished with the family…well, as you might assume, I got upset. I wasn't about to lose my daughter."

"Oh, Mom, I was just angry. I probably shouldn't have said anything until I'd calmed down." She did regret distressing her mother, who was invariably loving and supportive. Not only that, Kate had accepted Linc, despite Leonard's decrees.

"Your father refuses to be reasonable. It makes no sense. He wasn't a rich man when we met—he had to prove himself to my father and he did. Yet he won't give Linc the same chance my family gave *him*."

"It doesn't surprise me that Dad's being so unreasonable. He thinks he knows what's best for me, but he doesn't. I made a wise choice in my husband, and nothing Dad says or does is going to change my mind." Lori reached up and pressed her hand on Linc's.

Kate lowered her gaze. "After your call, your father said good riddance and he was cutting you out of the will."

Lori laughed. This was a threat he'd made more than once through the years. She was tired of him holding that over her head, trying to manipulate her. "If that's what he wants, Mom, I don't care. I have everything I'll ever need or want right here with Linc."

Her husband bent forward and kissed the top of her head.

"I told your father he was being ridiculous and that if he cut you out of the will, I was leaving." She paused and inhaled deeply. "Unfortunately, he didn't believe me."

"Mom?" Lori wasn't sure what her mother was saying. "Are you telling me—"

Her mother cut her off. "Your father called our attorney and, while he was talking to Matt, I packed my bag. He thought I was just making a point and that I'd be back the next morning."

"You're not with Dad?" If she hadn't already been sitting, Lori would have collapsed into a chair from shock.

"Like I said, your father and I are no longer talking. Or…living together."

"Where *are* you living?" Linc asked.

"With my sister."

"Aunt Hilary?" Lori asked.

Kate nodded. "My sister's a widow," she explained to Linc, "and the two of us have been enjoying ourselves."

"What about Dad?" Lori asked. Her father relied on Kate for everything. Lori couldn't imagine him surviving one day on his own, let alone weeks.

"I wouldn't know," Kate said, her back straight and her chin raised. "That's his concern."

"You haven't had any contact with him?"

"None."

Undoubtedly her father blamed Linc for this, too, along with everything else. "Is there anything I can do for you, Mom?" Lori asked. She felt dreadful that things had deteriorated this far.

"For me?" Kate repeated. "Good grief, no. As I said, your father is being completely unreasonable. I've stood by him all these years, backed him even when I disagreed, but this time he went too far."

"Oh, Mom, I feel awful."

"Why should you? Anyone who spends half an hour with Linc knows he's everything you said. Even more apparent is how much he loves you. While your father might not like Linc because he isn't some high-priced attorney or bank president, he should be grateful our daughter's found a man who loves her and makes her happy."

Lori couldn't have put it any better herself. "I *am* happy married to Linc. Happier than I ever imagined."

"I'm sorry our marriage has caused such a problem in your family," Linc said.

Kate dismissed that. "It hasn't been a problem for anyone other than Leonard."

Linc nodded slowly. "What would it take for you to move back home?"

"What would it take?" Kate asked. "Well, first Leonard would have to apologize to you for everything he's done to undermine your business. Then he'd have to apologize to our daughter for his high-handed behavior. And last…last, he'd have to apologize to me."

Lori knew it would be difficult to get one apology out of her father, never mind three. None of this was likely to happen.

"Oh, Mom."

"Actually, Hilary and I get along just fine."

"Mom!" Her mother could be just as stubborn as her father. This was a formula for disaster. She was afraid one of them would do something stupid—like file for divorce. Lori didn't know if she could live with herself if that happened, regardless of the fact that Leonard brought it on himself… Maybe she should've given him a chance to meet Linc again, more time to get used to the idea of her marriage. And yet, she reminded herself, she was an adult with the right to make her own decisions.

Her mother left shortly afterward, making Lori and Linc promise not to mention her visit to anyone in the family.

Lori sank into her chair again after walking Kate to her car. "I can't believe this. I have to do something," she told Linc frantically.

"What can you do?"

"I… I'm not sure."

"Do you think your brother and sister know that your mother's moved out?" Linc asked.

"I doubt it. They would've told me."

Frowning, Linc nodded.

"I'm going to phone my father and try to reason with him. All these weeks without Mom… He must be going nuts."

"Do you think that's wise?" he asked.

"I have to try."

Linc seemed to agree with her. He dragged his chair close to hers and held her free hand while Lori called the family home. To her surprise, her father answered.

"Where's Lou Lou?" she asked, shocked that the woman who'd been their housekeeper for more than twenty years didn't pick up.

"She no longer works here."

"Lou Lou quit?"

Her father ignored the question. "Who is this?"

"Come on, Dad, you know who this is. Lori."

"Lori who?"

"Lori, your *daughter*," she said, struggling to hold on to her temper.

"Unfortunately, I don't have a daughter named Lori."

His words felt like a slap in the face. "Okay, Daddy, if that's the way you want it." She clicked off the phone and hid her face in Linc's chest.

His arms came immediately around her. "I'm so sorry, honey," he whispered, kissing her hair.

"Me, too," she murmured tearfully. "Me, too."

Twenty-Three

"Can you meet me at the gallery a little after five?" Miranda asked Shirley, keeping an eye on the clock. She needed to leave for work soon.

"The gallery?" Shirley repeated. "You don't work on Thursdays, do you?"

"Today I do. Will asked me to come in."

"Again?"

"He's got something he has to do." He'd mentioned that he and his sister were going to revisit two of the assisted-living complexes they'd recently toured. Miranda assumed that was scheduled for this afternoon, although why he couldn't have told her earlier…

"It seems to me that Will Jefferson takes a lot for granted as far as you're concerned."

Miranda agreed, but now wasn't the time to discuss it. They could do that over dinner. "So, can you stop by around five?"

"Sure."

"I'll see you then." Disconnecting, she tossed her phone in her purse and headed out the door. If there was one thing she hated, it was being late.

When she arrived at the gallery, she found Will sitting in the showroom, working on his laptop. Their relationship had been a bit uncomfortable ever since they'd kissed. Now they were both making an effort to pretend nothing had happened.

Only it had. And ignoring the events of that afternoon—it'd been Halloween afternoon—wasn't working.

Part of the problem was that Miranda wasn't doing a good job of hiding her feelings for Will. She wasn't usually shy; she preferred to discuss differences, talk things over and avoid miscommunication. With Will, she hadn't done that, but couldn't explain why. She was just being silly, she told herself. He was a sophisticated man and this would hardly be the first time a woman had fallen for him. Really, what did she have to fear? Well, other than the fact that she'd look like an idiot. He'd probably find her attraction to him highly amusing. Judging by his infatuation with petite, charming Shirley, Miranda clearly wasn't his type. She wondered about his marriage—and his divorce—but he'd never spoken about his ex-wife and she'd never asked.

Will smiled when he saw her. "I can't tell you how much I appreciate this," he said.

Miranda deposited her coat and purse in the back room. "Well, don't get used to it. I've got more to do than be at your beck and call."

His eyebrows shot up. "My, my, aren't we testy."

"I have plans this evening," she said, without enlightening him that those plans involved Shirley Knight. She figured they'd have left by the time he returned from his appointment. Anyway, it was none of his business, although she'd rather let him think she had a date. "I had to cancel my hair appointment."

"You could always have said no, but I'm grateful you didn't."

"I'm not doing this for you," she said curtly. "It's for Charlotte and Ben."

"For my mother and stepfather?" he asked, crossing his arms. "Why?"

"You said something about going back to a couple of the assisted-living places," she reminded him.

"Perhaps I did. But—"

"Yes, you most certainly did." Miranda wasn't pleased. "What's going on? Why else would you drag me here on my day off?"

"Maybe I wanted the pleasure of your company." He grinned. His sexy smile never failed to lower her guard. Unable to meet his eyes without butterflies swarming in her stomach, Miranda looked away.

"You should've told me about your hair appointment. Go ahead and keep it. I'll change my plans."

"A little late now." She snorted. A customer walked in the door and Will gestured for her to do the talking. Matt Langley, a local attorney, wanted a birthday gift for his wife, telling Miranda that Olivia Griffin had recommended her brother's gallery. Miranda sold him a painting, the most expensive one they currently had.

"Damn, you're good," Will said admiringly after Matt left.

Miranda didn't respond. She'd already started to make arrangements to have the painting delivered to the attorney's home Saturday afternoon.

"Can't you take a compliment?" Will asked with a slight edge.

"Yes, of course I can. It just depends on who's giving it."

Will grumbled under his breath.

"Did you say something?" she asked in a sharp voice.

"Yes, as a matter of fact, I did."

"And what was it?" she challenged.

"I wondered why you find it so difficult to simply say thank you. That's what most people do when they receive a compliment. But not you. Oh, no, that would be far too conciliatory. Why are you constantly fighting with me, Miranda? Am I really such a terrible employer?"

"No," she admitted with some reluctance.

"You don't sound like you mean it. Listen, it was a mistake to call you in on your day off. Go. I'll be fine. I can rearrange my dentist appointment and my—"

"A dentist appointment! You called me in because you have a dentist appointment?" He knew which days she had off and obviously he'd scheduled this one knowing full well she'd have to come in.

He turned his back on her and walked into his office. "It's at three—after Olivia and I see the people at Stanford Suites."

So he *did* have an appointment at the assisted-living place. Why hadn't he just said so? she thought irritably. What kind of game was he playing?

Miranda followed him into the other room. "I'm here now. You might as well go."

"Don't worry about it. I'll reschedule with Olivia and the dentist."

"I said I'd stay."

He kept his hand on the phone. "Like I said, you could've told me no."

"I could have," she agreed.

"Then why didn't you?"

"And why do *you* leave everything to the last possible minute, as if I don't have any plans or responsibilities?"

"Guilty as charged. You're right. I should've asked you sooner. But the appointment at Stanford Suites was on fairly short notice. And the dentist had a cancellation. Still, I apologize." He seemed to think he could charm his way back into her good graces.

Miranda reviewed their short conversation earlier that afternoon. Will had called her at home around noon and, despite everything, she'd been excited to hear from him. He'd asked if it was possible to work on her day off for a few hours. She'd said yes and even been eager to do so. She'd overreacted just now because…because she needed to keep her distance, emotionally and otherwise.

"You aren't going to tell me off?" he asked, sounding half amused and half surprised.

"No, I guess not."

"You're not coming down with a fever, are you?"

"No," she replied tersely. "Like you'd care."

He immediately sighed. "Oh, good. You're back to normal."

He was right; snapping at him was her normal reaction—especially since their kiss…or rather, kisses. Until that very moment, she hadn't really understood what she was doing or why. She wondered if Will had reached the same conclusion. Probably not. After the incident on Halloween she'd redoubled her efforts to hide her attraction, from him if not herself.

"Keep your appointments," she insisted. "I've already rearranged my schedule to accommodate yours, so there's no need to cancel now." She hurried out of his office and avoided him until he left. They exchanged a curt goodbye and that was it.

Will was away from the gallery for two and a half hours, arriving back at quarter to four, but he might as well have been invisible. He went directly into his office and shut himself in. After closing the gallery a few minutes early, she knocked at his door, hoping to at least clear the air before their next encounter.

"Come in," Will called.

"I'm getting ready to go." She wanted to escape as soon as Shirley arrived, sparing them both an awkward moment. Maybe they should just have met at the restaurant…

He glanced at his watch, apparently surprised at the time, then nodded. "Thank you for coming in this afternoon," he said formally.

She hesitated. "I, uh, wanted to be sure everything is okay between us."

"Why shouldn't it be?" Will asked in congenial tones.

"No reason, I guess."

He stood, leveled another of those killer smiles directly at her and held out his hand.

"What's that for?" she asked, leaning forward to extend her own.

Will's handshake was firm and solid. His smile didn't waver as his eyes connected with hers. "Friends?"

"Friends," she echoed, but her voice sounded odd.

"I promise not to call you into work on your days off. I apologize again. I should've talked to you much earlier. I don't know what I was thinking."

Miranda knew very well what he was thinking. Will was thinking of himself, the same way he had most of his adult life. No, she admitted to herself, that wasn't entirely true. He was capable of very generous behavior. Only it was dangerous—to her sanity and well-being—to view Will as anything but self-centered and self-absorbed. Somehow she managed to nod and smile.

Before she could leave his office and shut the door, Shirley arrived at the gallery. Will brightened the instant he saw her, becoming animated and happy. "Shirley, it's good to see you." He clasped her hand in both of his and couldn't seem to take his eyes off her.

Miranda had to look away for fear he'd notice her reaction.

"I'm here for Miranda," Shirley said as she withdrew her hand.

"Where's Larry?" Will asked, ignoring the comment.

"London."

"Without you?" The sympathy in his voice made Miranda grit her teeth.

"Tanni's still in high school," Shirley reminded him. "And I have work to complete here."

Will nodded with that same unctuous sympathy.

"Larry often travels to England. Hopefully I'll be able to join him next time," Shirley went on to say.

"I thought we could walk down to D.D.'s on the Cove for dinner," Miranda suggested, purposely turning the subject away from Larry's absence. "It's close, and that way we won't need to worry about finding a parking spot."

"Sounds good."

"You're going for dinner?" Will asked, arching his eyebrows slightly. He seemed to be expecting an invitation. He moved away from Shirley to stand beside Miranda.

"We are," she said. "Just the *two* of us."

"Girls' night out?"

Shirley nodded.

Changing tactics, Will rested one hand on Miranda's shoulder. "Well, then, have fun, you two."

Miranda shrugged off his hand and glared at Will. Whatever he thought he was doing, she refused to be part of it.

Shirley started out the door.

"I'll be there in a minute," Miranda told her. She waited until the gallery door was completely closed before she whirled around.

"What?" Will asked with a look of innocence.

"Why did you put your hand on my shoulder?" she demanded.

"I don't know what you're so upset about. It didn't mean anything."

"You were trying to make Shirley jealous, which is *ridiculous*. In case you've forgotten, she's married to Larry Knight and has no feelings for you whatsoever. I realize it's difficult for your fragile ego to accept that any woman would choose a man other than you, but—"

"*You'd* choose me," Will said, cutting her off.

"That's…not true." She could feel a hot blush crawling up her face.

"Is it so strange that you're attracted to me?" he asked.

"I will not acknowledge anything so asinine," she said, turning away from him. This was one of the few times in her life when she couldn't be truthful, didn't even want to be. The sooner she made her escape, the better. She hoped the November air would cool the embarrassed color heating her face.

"Miranda." He whispered her name.

"What?" she barked, refusing to turn around.

"We need to talk about the day you kissed me."

"No, we don't," she said, not adding that he'd kissed her, too. She kept her back to him, her hand on the doorknob, eager to get outside where Shirley was waiting.

"I've done a lot of thinking about it."

"Sure you have," she muttered sarcastically. And, no doubt, laughing his head off, too.

"I have," he said, his voice low and seductive. He placed his hand on her shoulder again, stroking it gently. "We do need to talk about this."

"Everything's already been said. It's a dead subject."

"For you, maybe, but not me."

That did it. She whirled back toward him. "Don't play with me, Will. You need me because your ego's taken a hit. What better way to prove to Shirley that you're over her. An affair with her best friend would tell her that, wouldn't it?"

He frowned but didn't contradict her.

"You obviously assume I'm an easy target…that I'm so starved for affection I'd willingly fall into bed with you, even though you'd break my heart without a second thought. But you're wrong, Will. I'm not interested."

"Your kiss said otherwise."

"Sorry, but you've misread the situation. I don't know why I kissed you." A blatant lie. "But trust me, it was one of the biggest mistakes I've ever made."

"I don't think of it that way."

"Stop!" she shouted, clenching her fists. Much more of this and she'd end up taking a swing at him. "Do you honestly believe you're going to persuade me with... with lies? If you say anything else, I swear I will walk out this door and never return. That isn't an empty threat, Will. I mean it."

A pained look came over him and he nodded. Then, to Miranda's astonishment, he stepped closer, held her face between his hands and kissed her.

When he broke it off, she nearly stumbled backward in both shock and wonder.

"I—I quit," she stammered.

"No, you don't. I expect you here by ten tomorrow morning."

Twenty-Four

The Pot Belly Deli was decorated for Thanksgiving. Gloria glanced around at the dried cornstalk and gourd arrangements, nervously sipping her juice as she waited for Chad. He'd asked for this meeting, and she'd agreed, but she still wasn't sure it was a good idea.

Since the ultrasound, there'd been no direct contact between them, although they'd exchanged a number of emails over the past few weeks. These were generally short messages in which she answered his questions about the pregnancy and her health.

Gloria resisted the urge to ask him about Joni. Every time she thought about the two of them together, her stomach twisted. But *she* was the one who'd rejected *him,* so she couldn't blame him for dating someone else. Sometimes she didn't understand her own actions and could only regret what she'd done. It was because of her shame and uncertainty that she'd run out of his bedroom last summer, after spending the night with him. Then, when she'd gone to tell him about the baby—and perhaps even try to reconcile—it was too late.

The door opened and Chad came inside. He looked around until he saw Gloria, smiling tentatively when he did.

"Hi," he said as he approached her.

"Hi." She didn't meet his eyes but gestured for him to take a seat.

The waitress stepped up to the table with a coffee-pot and he righted his mug. "Would you like a menu?" she asked.

"No, thanks, just coffee."

She nodded and left them alone.

Now that they were together, Gloria's nervousness grew more intense. Nausea attacked her stomach, and her hands shook.

"You look great," Chad said.

He wasn't the only one to say so. Roy had said that pregnant women really did have a glow about them, adding that she was more beautiful every time he saw her. Her biological father didn't hand out compliments casually and his comment had taken her aback. She hardly knew how to respond to Chad's words any more than she had Roy's.

Finally she managed to say, "Thanks." And left it at that.

"Would you mind standing?" he asked.

"Ah, sure." She pushed back her chair and stood.

His eyes rested on her stomach, and a slow smile spread across his face. A warm, wholehearted smile that said Chad was going to love this baby. Seeing his reaction nearly brought her to tears.

"May I?" he asked, extending his hand toward her.

Gloria came closer and he pressed his palm against the small bump.

"Do you feel him moving yet?"

She smiled. "All the time."

"Good."

She sat back down and reached for her drink to hide how moved she was by what he'd done. She noticed that his hand shook as he picked up his coffee.

"So," he said after a moment. "Have you given any more thought to the name?"

"A little. Have you?"

"Actually, I've been thinking about it a lot."

When he didn't immediately make any suggestions or comment on other names he liked, she asked, "Do you want to share your thoughts?"

"No... I feel it would be best to wait until you make up your mind."

"About?"

"About giving the baby up for adoption. Have you decided?"

Gloria held her arms protectively around her stomach. "I think adoption is a viable choice. I was adopted into a loving home with parents who badly wanted a child."

Chad lowered his eyes, as if he couldn't tolerate the idea, but didn't want to argue with her.

"My mother gave me up because she was still a teenager with several years of school ahead of her. Roy didn't even know she was pregnant."

"I'm aware of that. But thanks to your father, I know about this baby." Chad stiffened, apparently unable to keep quiet any longer. "And I'm entitled to a say in what happens to *my child*." He emphasized the last two words. "If you decide you don't want him—"

"Do you think that's what adoption is?" Gloria

asked. "Do you really believe a mother who gives her child to another family acts out of selfishness? Do you think that's what Corrie did with me?"

"I...no."

"She loved me enough to offer me a better life with two parents who yearned for a child of their own."

"Our baby has two parents."

"Every baby has two parents, Chad," she said, hoping he'd see the humor in his statement.

"True. Every child has two parents, biologically speaking. What I meant is that times are different from when you were born. A father has legal rights and I intend to pursue mine. If you prefer to give the baby up for adoption, then I think it's only fair to tell you that I'd take him myself."

"As a single father?"

"Yes."

"What about your hours at the hospital? Who'd look after him while you're working? You make it sound easy. It isn't."

"And you know this how?"

"Because I'm a woman."

"And I'm a doctor. I can pretty well guarantee I've handled more babies than you have."

"You do have an advantage over most men," she had to agree. "But you don't know what it'll be like to spend sleepless nights if the baby's colicky—"

"Hey, I was an intern and a medical resident. I know about sleepless nights."

"But..."

"I want our baby, Gloria."

"The thing is," she said, gazing down at her hands. "I do, too. I've decided to raise him myself."

"I see." Chad sounded disappointed and that disturbed her even more.

"You wanted him all to yourself, didn't you?"

"Just like you did." He nodded. "Okay, we'll need to work out a parenting plan. My son *will* know his father."

"Are you still dating Joni?" she blurted out, unable to resist.

His eyes locked with hers. "That has nothing to do with you."

"You're right. Forgive me for being so blunt but what will *our* son call Joni?"

"Does it matter? We'll figure that out when the time comes."

Gloria didn't like it, but she couldn't say so without sounding churlish. Finally she conceded, "Fair enough."

He sipped his coffee.

She sipped her juice.

When she couldn't stand the silence anymore, she said, "You asked to see me. Was there anything else?"

"Why are you so eager to get away? Are you meeting someone?"

"That's *my* business."

"You're dating someone?" He frowned, as if the possibility hadn't occurred to him until now.

"Like I said…"

"That's your business," he finished for her.

Clearly the thought unsettled him. Well, good. She hoped it did. Chad didn't like the idea of her seeing someone else any more than she enjoyed the knowledge that he was dating another woman.

"Well, hello." Roy stood in front of their table, shocking Gloria. She hadn't seen him arrive.

"Nice to see you both," he continued.

Gloria wasn't sure how to respond. "Uh, hi," she muttered.

"Hello, Roy." Chad stood and the two men shook hands.

"What are you doing here?" Gloria asked.

"Troy Davis and I come here for coffee once a week. I certainly didn't expect to find the two of you."

Gloria knew the sheriff and her father were good friends, but she hadn't realized they routinely met at this restaurant. Although she worked in the sheriff's office, she wasn't privy to Troy Davis's schedule.

"Do you mind if I join you for a few minutes?" Roy asked.

Without waiting for an invitation, he pulled out a chair and sat down. "I'm glad to see you together." He looked from one to the other, as though assuming they'd enlighten him.

"We don't do this often," Chad explained.

"In fact, this is the first time we've met since the ultrasound," Gloria added.

Roy shook his head. "I'm sorry to hear that."

"Roy, please. This is difficult enough." Her father was making it more so by interfering with their conversation.

"I don't mean to be rude or obnoxious, but can one of you tell me what went wrong with your relationship?"

"We don't get along," Gloria said, giving him the easy answer.

"It seems to me you get along just fine," Roy murmured, "or at least you did."

"This is between Gloria and me," Chad said. "Discussing it with you isn't going to solve anything."

"In other words, you want me to butt out?"

"Something like that," Gloria said.

"Okay, message received." Roy stood, smiled down at them and turned away. He took a couple of steps, then turned back. "The thing is, that boy deserves a family. A mother and a father who'll love him and raise him to be a fine young man. And…he deserves his grandparents, his aunts and uncles and cousins."

"Yes, Roy," Gloria said.

"Message received," Chad said, echoing Roy's earlier statement.

Gloria felt she needed to apologize. As soon as Roy was seated at another table, she whispered, "I'm sorry about that."

"Not your fault. But it might be a good idea if we went somewhere else."

Gloria nodded. "Any suggestions?" she asked.

"The Wok and Roll is down the street."

She remembered that Chad liked Chinese food. The scent of fried food made Gloria feel queasy but she should be fine; she hadn't thrown up in several weeks. "Sure, let's go."

They paid and waved an obligatory goodbye to Roy. Then, with his hand under her elbow, Chad escorted her to the Wok and Roll. The moment they walked in the door, Gloria was assaulted by the aroma of spices and frying meat, and her stomach instantly revolted. Taking a deep breath, she grabbed a corner of the front desk.

"Gloria?" Chad asked. "What's wrong?"

She closed her eyes, trying not to vomit. This shouldn't be happening anymore, but because of the meeting with Chad, she'd been tense all day. As a result she hadn't eaten much, which was probably a good thing.

"You're pale. Do you want to sit down?"

"No." She dashed to the women's restroom. Pushing open the stall door, she barely made it inside. Bent over the toilet, she lost the juice she'd managed to drink.

When she finished, she turned to discover Chad waiting for her by the sink, holding a wet paper towel. "Are you okay now?"

"Yes, sorry. I didn't expect that. I should've known." She wiped her mouth and then smiled. "Do you make a habit of walking into women's restrooms?"

"Only when—" He stopped short. "No," he said, amending whatever he'd been about to say. "Let me get you home."

She obediently followed him out of the restaurant. Her apartment was close to the library and near the waterfront. Chad had been there often enough not to need directions.

"I won't stay long," he said when she'd unlocked the door.

After she'd rinsed out her mouth again they sat on the sofa, he at one end and she at the other.

"Does that happen often?" he asked.

"Not anymore… It was just nerves, I guess." She didn't explain what she'd been nervous about, but he obviously understood.

"I haven't slept well for several nights either," Chad confessed.

"We're a sad case, aren't we?" she whispered. It seemed the only place they'd ever been able to communicate was in bed.

"Are you working today?" Chad asked.

"No. I took personal leave. What about you?"

"I have Thursdays off."

That made sense, since he'd requested the meeting for this afternoon.

She tried to hide a yawn. She didn't succeed and he responded with a yawn of his own. They looked at each other and smiled.

Chad stood. "I'll leave and you can nap."

Suddenly she didn't want him to go. But she knew instinctively that if she asked him to stay, he wouldn't. Instead, she got up, too, and reached for his hand. He frowned as she led him toward the hallway, hesitating when he saw her bedroom.

"Gloria, where are you taking me?" Then he answered his own question. "Your bed?" He inhaled sharply and said, "I hope you remember that's what got us into this mess."

"It isn't what you think."

"What, then?"

"A nap. All I want you to do is hold me, feel our baby move. Nothing more. We're both tired and stressed. I want us to sleep. Once we do, we'll be able to talk and make the decisions we need to make."

He stood next to her bed. "You're sure this is what you want?"

"Sleep, Chad. That's all. Understand?"

"No," he muttered. "But then I've never been able to understand you."

"Do you want to leave?"

"No," he said. "In fact, I'm finding it downright impossible to walk away."

"Good." She folded back the covers, removed her shoes and slid beneath the blankets. Rolling onto her side, she turned her back to him and closed her eyes. It took Chad several minutes to join her. He climbed into the bed, fully dressed, and cuddled her spoon fashion. After a moment, he slipped his hand over her side, pressing it against her stomach.

"The baby just moved."

Gloria smiled sleepily. "I know."

"I felt him."

"He's going to play soccer, I think."

"And baseball."

"We'll see. Now close your eyes and nap."

It wasn't long before she heard the deep, even rumble of his breathing, which told her he was asleep. Tired though she was, Gloria stayed awake.

She'd acknowledged it herself—they'd only ever been able to communicate in bed. Now that they had decisions to make, this seemed the best place for that to happen.

Twenty-Five

"Olivia, I can't tell you how excited I am to be in my own home," Charlotte said as Ben unlocked the front door of 15 Eagle Crest Avenue. The kitchen had been completely remodeled.

Olivia exchanged a look with her brother. She had reservations about her mother and Ben returning here, but when she'd broached the subject of moving into assisted living, Charlotte had instantly rejected the idea. Ben hadn't been keen on it, either, automatically dismissing it as "too expensive."

So far, none of the places she and Will had checked out had any apartments available, but they'd put their name on a couple of waiting lists. Maybe, when something appropriate came up, Charlotte and Ben would be ready to consider it. Like it or not, eventually they'd have to leave this house. Probably before another year was up.

"I want to see my new kitchen," Charlotte said, walking into the house and heading straight to the remodeled room. "Oh, my." She brought her hands to her cheeks. "Everything is so…new."

"We decided to replace the cupboards," Olivia reminded her, coming to stand beside her mother.

"We did?" Charlotte looked to Ben for confirmation.

"We picked out the white oak together," Ben said.

"Of course. I remember now." Charlotte pulled open a couple of drawers, which then slowly glided shut. This was a new feature; unless the drawer was pulled out completely, it would automatically return to the closed position once it was released.

"Everything's back exactly the way you left it," Olivia reassured her. She'd taken great pains to make sure of that. She'd replaced the ruined pots and pans with new ones that were as similar as possible. Charlotte frowned as if she didn't believe that. "Is everything all right, Mom?" Olivia asked.

"It just looks so different…"

"There's a new stove, too," Will said, opening the oven door to display the large baking area.

Slowly, deliberately, Charlotte examined the knobs and studied the burners. "It looks complicated."

"I'll read over the instruction manual and we'll learn about it together," Ben said.

"That would help." Every word and movement revealed her hesitation. "I'm afraid I'm so accustomed to my old stove and this one…well, it looks far too modern for me."

"It'll be fine," Ben told her. He placed his hand on her shoulder.

"Is there anything else I should know about?" Charlotte asked Olivia.

"You have a new refrigerator," Will said, and gestured proudly toward it.

"But why? The old one was working fine and it wasn't damaged in the fire, was it?"

Will answered. "We figured you'd want a new one, since all the other appliances are new," he said. "It's an early Christmas gift. I thought you'd be pleased."

"I am, I am," Charlotte was quick to tell him. "I'm just used to seeing the old one here. What did you do with it?"

"It's on the back porch, Mom," Olivia said. "For extra things." Seeing her mother's puzzled expression, Olivia added, "Cold sodas and beer, stuff like that."

"Oh."

"We can take the new fridge back if you don't like it," Will offered.

"No, it was so thoughtful of you… Of course we'll keep your gift, Will. I wouldn't dream of sending it back."

"Is there anything else I can do for you, Mom?" Olivia asked. She and Jack would be meeting Grace and Cliff for dinner, but that wasn't for hours yet.

"No, dear, everything is fine. It's so good to be home again." She rubbed her palms together as her eyes darted about the kitchen. Charlotte had visited the house frequently since the fire, but this was the first time she'd seen everything in place and complete. She walked over to the apple-shaped cookie jar and rested her hand on it. That, at least, was familiar. It'd been around for as long as Olivia could remember. Countless times through the years that jar had held her mother's home-baked cookies. Luckily it had survived the fire.

On her way out, Olivia hugged her mother and Ben, and so did Will. Brother and sister left together.

As soon as the front door closed, Will asked, "So what do you think?"

They'd gone over their plan of action repeatedly. They'd let Ben and Charlotte move back into the house for a while and then bring up the idea of assisted living again. It seemed only fair, despite their fears, to give their mother and Ben an opportunity to adjust to their new surroundings, see how things worked out. Olivia hoped that once they were ready to move, there'd be an opening at one of the better facilities.

"This is exactly what I was afraid would happen," Olivia said. They reached their cars, which were parked at the curb.

"What's that?"

"Mom. The new kitchen's overwhelmed her."

"Are you afraid she'll leave a burner on again?"

"No, actually, I don't think Mom will turn on any of the burners unless it's absolutely necessary. She won't want to cook because she's unfamiliar with the stove."

"Mom not cook?"

"I know. That was one of her main objections to moving into assisted living. She still enjoys working in the kitchen." She'd rejected the idea out of hand and *then* listed a number of excuses, that being the first.

"But she can still cook," Will said, showing his frustration. "There's a huge kitchen at Stanford Suites for anyone who wants to bake or prepare a meal."

Olivia nodded. "I know." But the person they needed to convince was their mother.

"It's a shared kitchen," she pointed out. "Mom's used to her own pots and pans and, well, her own kitchen."

"That kitchen is gone," Will said.

He was right. The fire had destroyed more than a few cupboards, the walls and flooring. What had once been the heart of their childhood home had become a pile of ashes. In its stead was a sterile room that lacked the familiarity, the memories, of the past sixty years. In many respects Olivia felt the same disappointment her mother did. She wanted everything to go back to the way it was, although that was obviously impossible.

"What do you suggest we do now?" Will asked.

"I… I don't know." Olivia didn't expect it would be easy for Charlotte to make the transition, leaving the only home she'd known all her adult life. "Do you have any suggestions?"

Will shook his head. He shoved his hands in his pants pockets and shrugged. "This is hard."

"You're telling me?"

"I hoped Ben would see the wisdom of moving and smooth the way."

"It's as unsettling for him as it is for Mom," Olivia commented.

"After all the moves he's made in his navy career, one would think it'd be old hat."

"One would think," Olivia murmured. "The thing is, I don't want Mom to feel we're kicking her out of her own home. We can't force her to leave, nor should we. She has to accept this and she hasn't. Not yet."

"Part of the problem," Will said, "is that she's afraid of what'll happen to the house if she isn't there."

It was a point worth considering. "She loves this house."

"The first question she asked was if we'd sell it," Will reminded her, frowning. "Eventually we'd have to do that, and I get the feeling that upsets her more than the need to move."

Olivia sighed. "We wouldn't have any option. Renting it out could be a nightmare," she said half to herself, remembering the troubles Grace had encountered when she rented out her house on Rosewood Lane. Olivia hated the thought of anyone vandalizing her family home, which was exactly what had happened to Grace's house. No, renting wasn't an option she wanted to consider.

"Ben might be more amenable to the idea than he's led us to believe."

"Really?" Olivia could only hope her brother was right. "Did he say anything to you?"

"Not directly, but I could tell how concerned he was when Mom first saw the new stove. He loves Mom, and realized right away how flustered and unsure she is with all these changes."

Olivia nodded; she'd seen the same doubt and hesitation in her mother's eyes and it had shaken her. Charlotte seemed almost childlike in her reaction to the changes taking place around her.

"If you have any ideas, let me know," Will said. He reached for his car keys.

"Any plans tomorrow?" Olivia asked.

"Not really. What have you got in mind?"

"Jack wants to watch the Seahawks game on TV and you'd be welcome to join us."

"One o'clock?" he asked.

"Perfect. See you then."

Olivia hoped she and Will could continue their conversation the next day. Surely they could come up with a solution. The problem had seemed less immediate while Charlotte and Ben were living with them, since both Olivia and Jack were able to help. Despite various incidents with the laundry and so forth, Olivia had grown accustomed to having her mother close. It was comforting to find Charlotte waiting for her at the end of the day with a cup of tea and one of her many baked treats. Necessary as Olivia knew the transition to an assisted-living environment was, she found it painful. The loss of Charlotte and Ben's independence, the loss of their familiar surroundings and, most of all, the loss of the person her mother had been… Olivia hated it. And yet she had to be practical and protect their safety and well-being above all else.

A moment after Olivia got home, Jack pulled into the driveway behind her. He'd been to an AA meeting and, as was his habit afterward, had gone for coffee with his friend and sponsor, Bob Beldon.

"How was the meeting?" she asked, walking back to join him.

"Good." Jack wrapped his arm around her waist and kissed her. "How'd everything go with your mother and Ben?"

She blinked back tears, and Jack leaned forward to get a better look at her. "Liv?"

"Not good…"

"Come inside and tell me about it."

The early evening was dreary and overcast, and it reflected how Olivia felt. With his arm around her waist, Jack led her into the house through the back door.

While he removed his coat, Olivia put on the kettle for tea. This was something her mother had done all her life. Whenever it was time to have a serious discussion, Charlotte would reach for the teakettle and her favorite ceramic teapot with the butterflies painted on it.

Olivia remembered the day she'd come over to tell her mother that she and Stan were separating. Olivia had been emotional and weepy. That had been the most horrible year of her life, and her mother, teapot in hand, had been a constant source of love and support.

In a one-year span, Olivia's oldest son had drowned and her marriage had fallen apart. She didn't know what she would've done if not for her mother and, of course, Grace.

"Olivia?" Jack asked gently. "You've been standing in front of the stove for five minutes."

"I have?" Embarrassed, she brushed the tears from her cheeks. "I was just remembering all the talks I had with my mother over tea," she whispered.

Jack guided her toward a chair, then set out two mugs. At the moment Olivia felt incapable of performing even that simple task. Reaching across the table she grabbed a tissue and blew her nose. "I'm sorry. I'm being ridiculous."

"No, you aren't," Jack said.

"I was thinking about the day Mom made me tea when Stan and I decided we couldn't stay married."

"What brought that up?"

"I… I don't know exactly. It's just that she was so wonderful, so reassuring and supportive. That wasn't the only time, either. I could always count on her to see me through whatever crisis I faced."

"And you can't now?"

She shook her head. "Everything's reversed—I'm the one taking care of Mom. She needs me more than

I need her. So does Ben." She held the tissue to her mouth and swallowed a sob.

Jack stood behind her and rubbed her shoulders. "You have me and your brother and your kids."

"Yes, I know. But this is…different."

The kettle whistled and Jack returned to the stove. He poured the water into the pot and carried it to the table.

"This is all because of taking your mother and Ben to the house?"

"Oh, Jack, it's so hard for me to watch my mother grow old… She's trying to pretend everything's the same, but it isn't. Today it was even more obvious that she and Ben can't stay in the house much longer."

"Do you want me to talk to them?" he asked after a short pause. "My parents both died years ago, so I haven't been through this, but…"

"No. I appreciate the offer, but this has to come from Will and me. I can't blame Mom. I wouldn't want to leave my home, either. And then there's the problem of what to do with the house itself."

When they'd visited the assisted-living complexes, both Olivia and Will had felt encouraged and excited. It'd all sounded so positive, with a variety of programs that would keep her mother and Ben entertained and involved in life. She could visualize her mother leading the knitting group and Ben playing pinochle.

The facilities had exercise and physical therapy programs, musical evenings, reading and craft circles, excursions and more. At each place she must have counted at least five different activities for every day. The meals were well-planned and the menus were nutritious and appealing. Olivia wouldn't mind eating there herself.

But convincing her mother of the benefits of making that move seemed beyond her.

The phone rang and Jack answered, glancing at caller ID. "It's Ben or your mother," he said to Olivia.

"Hello, Charlotte." Almost immediately his gaze went to her. "Charlotte, of course. Now don't worry, we'll be right there."

Olivia nearly leaped out of her chair. "What happened?" she asked in a panic.

"Everything's fine," Jack said calmly. "Apparently Ben fell. He can't get up and Charlotte can't help him."

"Everything's not fine!" She took a deep breath. "Why didn't you tell her to call 9-1-1? Is Ben hurt? He might've broken his hip… Oh, my goodness, Jack, this is serious."

"Ben isn't hurt. But your mother's been trying to get him up, and she can't do it. They're both exhausted."

"How could this have happened?" She ran for her jacket, then grabbed her purse and headed for the door.

"She said Ben slipped on the rug in the kitchen."

Will had purchased the small rug and placed it in front of the new refrigerator, but it had a rubber backing and shouldn't have slid.

"He didn't remember it was there," Jack continued as if reading her mind, "and he stumbled over it."

"They should call 9-1-1," Olivia cried. Jack put on his coat and followed her out of the house.

"Ben is embarrassed enough as it is," Jack said. "And Charlotte told me he's not hurt."

"We don't know that."

"No, but we'll find out soon enough." They hurried to Jack's car and were off, not even bothering to lock up.

Charlotte met them at the front door, pale and shaken.

Jack walked straight past her and into the kitchen, where Ben sat on the floor, knees bent and head down. "I feel like an old fool," he muttered.

"It was an accident," Jack said. "We'll have you up in a second."

With his hands under the older man's arms, he hauled Ben to his feet, hardly exerting himself.

"Are you okay?" Olivia asked.

"Yes. Except for my pride, which has taken quite a beating."

Charlotte pulled out a chair and collapsed into it. "I just didn't know what to do," she said, her voice trembling. "Oh, thank goodness you were able to come."

Olivia crouched beside Charlotte and hugged her, whispering reassurances. It was just as she'd told Jack. Just as she'd known for a while. She was the parent now. She'd become her mother's mother.

Twenty-Six

Monday afternoon, Rachel left work early. She went to the Cedar Cove library, where she sat in one of the big overstuffed chairs and awaited her stepdaughter's arrival. She'd called Jolene's cell to make this appointment; the girl had agreed to meet her but Rachel had no idea what to expect. Jolene had attended a counseling session, and it had been a complete waste of time, according to Bruce. She'd been sullen and silent through the entire session, refusing to participate in the conversation. The longer Rachel stayed away from her husband and stepdaughter, the more obvious it became that she wouldn't ever be able to return. It was time to make other arrangements, permanent ones.

Rachel wondered if Jolene would stand her up and was somewhat surprised when the library door swung open and the girl stepped inside. She came alone, which was also rather unexpected, since Jolene usually traveled with a pack of friends.

She stood in the foyer and scanned the library until her gaze fell on Rachel. As soon as she saw her, Jolene's eyes narrowed. Walking across the library, she carelessly dropped her backpack on the floor and sat in the chair next to Rachel's.

"You wanted to talk to me?" she said without any greeting. Her voice was devoid of warmth.

"Yes, thank you for coming," Rachel replied pleasantly, choosing to ignore her stepdaughter's attitude.

"Why did you ask me to come here?"

"Actually, I have several reasons."

Jolene looked conspicuously at her watch. "How long is this supposed to take?"

"Not long," Rachel promised. So far, the meeting was going exactly as she'd feared. The girl's hostility was undisguised. The battle lines were drawn and swords ready. Except that Rachel was about to hand over her weapon. She was finished.

Inhaling deeply, she came directly to the point. "Mainly, I wanted to tell you I've decided to leave the area."

Jolene's eyes flew to hers. "Does my dad know?"

"Not yet." She would tell Bruce later.

"Why are you telling me?"

"Well," Rachel said, "I thought you'd want to celebrate. You've beaten me, Jolene. You win. You can have your father all to yourself. I won't be in touch."

"What about the baby?" she demanded. "You can't do that to my brother or sister."

Rachel shook her head. "I grew up without a family. My aunt tried but she didn't have a warm bone in her body. She was raised in an era when children didn't speak unless spoken to. Her mantra was that cleanliness was next to godliness, so what she held most important was a spotless house. There was very little fun in my life and—"

"You told me all this before," Jolene said, defiantly crossing her arms.

"You're right. Sorry, no need to repeat myself, is there? All I meant was that my aunt taught me what *not* to do, what not to be."

"What'll happen with the baby?" Jolene sounded like an attorney representing her father's interests.

"Happen?" Rachel shrugged. "Well, I'll raise this child and love him or her to the very best of my ability."

"What about my dad?"

"What about him?"

Jolene glared at her. "He has a right to the baby, too."

"I'm not preventing your father from having contact with the child, Jolene, I'm protecting him or her."

"Protecting him or her from *what?*"

Rachel hardly felt a reply was necessary. The answer should be obvious, even to Jolene. If Jolene hated Rachel this much, then she couldn't trust her to feel any differently toward her child.

When Rachel didn't immediately reply Jolene's eyes widened as realization dawned on her. "I would never hurt a baby," she insisted as though highly insulted.

"Perhaps not physically," Rachel agreed, "but there are other ways of inflicting damage. I can't risk that."

Jolene's gaze moved past her and she swallowed visibly. "Where will you go?"

She hadn't decided. "I'm thinking of Portland."

"Oregon?"

Rachel nodded.

"Why there?"

"It's close but not too close, and far enough away

that your father won't be tempted to…" She let the rest fade.

"Dad's been seeing a counselor."

"Yes, I know."

"I went, too."

"So I heard."

Jolene looked away, apparently embarrassed by her behavior at the counseling session.

Rachel hadn't expected changes overnight, but there had to be *some* effort and Jolene seemed unwilling to bend at all.

"You need to talk to Dad."

"I will." Rachel hadn't spoken to Bruce during the past three weeks. They'd exchanged a few emails, in which they'd kept each other up to date. After Jolene's stunt—making herself ill—and then the wasted counseling session, Rachel felt convinced the situation was hopeless. If Jolene would rather throw up than let her father see his wife—well, what more was there to say?

"The counselor has Dad *setting boundaries* with me." She said the words sarcastically. "It's stupid."

"Uh-huh."

Jolene looked down at her feet. "You gave Dad back the money, too, didn't you?"

Rachel was surprised the girl knew anything about that. "Your father told you?"

"No, Teri Polgar did. She came to the house and made a big stink about it."

Rachel could well imagine that scene. Teri wasn't one to hold back her opinions. No doubt she'd told both Bruce and Jolene what she thought of them, whether they wanted to hear it or not.

"Dad was pretty upset about it. You not taking the money, I mean."

"Tell him—that is, if you want to say anything about our meeting—tell him the baby and I are doing well. I don't need money. I can care for the baby on my own." She didn't want a thing from him. Eventually her pride would give way and she'd need to ask, but until then she was content to manage on her own without any help, financial or otherwise, from Bruce or Jolene. They'd both done quite enough.

"My dad loves you."

The lump was back in her throat. "Yes, I know."

"If you loved him you wouldn't be doing this," Jolene accused her. "You wouldn't be keeping the baby away from him."

Rachel wasn't willing to be attacked for the difficult choices she'd had to make. But rather than defend herself, she disregarded the girl's comment. Standing, she placed one hand over her stomach. "I appreciate you meeting me this one last time," she said in a low voice. "Goodbye, Jolene." She started to walk away.

"Wait," Jolene cried.

"Wait?" Rachel echoed. "For what?"

"I…have something for you."

Rachel wondered if Jolene was telling the truth.

"I told my dad you called and wanted to meet. He wrote you a letter. I wasn't going to give it to you, but… I think maybe I should." The girl reached for her backpack, unzipped it and dug around inside. After a moment she pulled out an envelope, then handed it to Rachel. "Go ahead and read it," she said.

"Have you?" Silly question. Of course she had.

Jolene's eyes dropped so quickly, that was answer enough. "Just read what Dad wrote."

Rachel opened the blank envelope, which either hadn't been sealed or had been replaced.

Dear Rachel,
I don't know how to start this. I've tried writing this twenty times and gave up every time. When I realized you'd blocked me from calling you, I was angry at first. I'd hoped we could reconcile. Then I understood why you did it and I have to say I probably would've done the same thing. Nothing changed, despite all our efforts. It was the same problem over and over again, only worse.
I apologize that I didn't step in earlier to help you with my daughter. Jolene has major issues, and I should have recognized them earlier. I've made some changes here at home and attended several counseling sessions now. You were right about that, too. I should've agreed to talk to someone *much* sooner… If I had, it might have prevented this. Jolene went, too, not voluntarily, but at least she's had to listen. It's helping, I think, but I'll be the first to admit we have a long way to go.
Teri Polgar returned the money.
I'll abide by any decision you make.
Oh, Rachel, I can't stop thinking about you and the baby. I've never felt such sadness. When Stephanie died, it was like someone had ripped off both my arms. This is different but just as painful. I've failed you and failed our child.
I don't think there's anything more I can say,

other than to tell you again how much I love
you. Although Jolene would never admit it, she
needs you, too.

Ending this letter is impossible. Words are impossible. I know I've lost you but I can't say
goodbye.

Bruce

The last two lines blurred as tears filled Rachel's
eyes. She swallowed, blinking hard, so Jolene wouldn't
know how emotional the letter had made her.

"Thank you for giving this to me." Her hand trembled as she folded the paper and slid it back inside the
envelope.

"Dad's right," Jolene whispered.

Rachel looked up and saw that Jolene's head was
bent. A tear splashed on her backpack and she jerked
her hand across her face.

"Your father is right?" Rachel repeated softly.
"About what?"

Jolene shook her head, refusing to answer.

"If you ever need me, all you have to do is check
in with Teri Polgar. She'll get in touch with me and
I'll give you a call."

"You'd do that?" Jolene asked.

"Yes."

"After everything I've done?"

"Yes," she returned without hesitation.

"Why?"

"First, you're my stepdaughter, and second, you and
I used to be close." That felt like a long time ago, but
Rachel could look back through the years and hold on

to the good memories without allowing the more recent ones to taint her perspective.

"The baby…" Jolene began, and then paused. "You've got a tummy."

"I see you noticed."

"How could I not?" she said, and almost smiled.

The door of the head librarian's office opened and Grace Harding came out. Behind her a puppy scampered, running across the library and directly toward Jolene.

Bending down, Jolene scooped the small dog into her arms. The puppy started to lick her chin. Squinting, Jolene laughed and held him away from her face.

"Beau," Grace called out as she hurried toward them. "I'm sorry."

"It's okay," Jolene said. "He's just so cute."

"He's a darn nuisance. I keep forgetting to close the office door behind me. This is the second time today." She reached for Beau, but Jolene continued to hold him.

"Would it be all right if I petted him for a while?" she asked, looking up at the librarian.

Grace glanced at Rachel as though to get her permission.

"Fine with me," Rachel said.

Grace lingered a moment. "When are you coming back to the salon, Rachel?" she asked. "With both you and Teri gone, I've had a heck of a time finding someone to cut my hair the way I like."

"I…won't be coming back."

"That's a shame." She paused. "And I bet that's how all your clients feel."

She didn't know what to say. Rachel had heard via

Jane that a number of her clients were looking for her. She hated to disappoint anyone but she seriously doubted they'd follow her to Portland or wherever she landed.

"Bring Beau back to me when you're tired of playing with him," Grace said.

"Okay." Beau had settled down in Jolene's lap and chewed on her finger until she moved her hand just out of his range.

Rachel enjoyed watching Jolene with the puppy. Several minutes later, she stood to leave but Jolene asked, "Could you stay a little longer?"

"Okay." She waited, unsure if Jolene had something else to say. She leaned down and petted the puppy, who immediately tried to chew on her finger, too.

"Be careful, he's got sharp little teeth."

Rachel had discovered that. "Ouch." She jerked her hand away and examined her finger to see if he'd drawn blood. Thankfully he hadn't.

"I never had a dog," Jolene said. "I wanted one but Dad said we'd have to leave him alone all day, and that didn't seem right."

"I never had one, either." Her aunt hadn't been keen on pets, although Rachel had longed for a dog.

"Too messy?" Jolene guessed.

"Too messy," she confirmed, and offered her stepdaughter a tentative smile.

Jolene cuddled the small dog as though that required her undivided attention.

"Rachel," she whispered after several minutes. "Don't move to Portland."

"You want me to go someplace else?" She frowned, a little confused.

"No."

"Another town farther away?"

"No," Jolene repeated emphatically. "I don't want you to move at all."

Rachel didn't say anything, afraid she might be reading more into this than warranted. "Are you asking me to stay in Cedar Cove?"

"I… I don't know."

That wasn't the answer she'd hoped to hear.

"All I can say is I don't know what my dad will do when he finds out you're leaving the area."

Rachel realized her decision would be hard on Bruce, but she didn't feel she had any choice.

"I…don't want you to go, either," Jolene said.

Perhaps that was a start.

Twenty-Seven

Is Thursday still your day off? Gloria texted Chad. It was less intimidating than phoning.

She didn't have long to wait for a reply. Yes.

She bit her lip and texted back. Could you come over?

Now?

Anytime.

His reply was almost instantaneous. On my way.

Gloria hoped, prayed, she was doing the right thing.

Forty minutes later her doorbell chimed. Nervously wiping her palms on her maternity-front pants, she opened the door.

"Everything okay?" Chad immediately asked.

"Yes."

"You wanted to see me?"

She nodded, realizing she'd left him standing outside, and let him into her apartment.

Chad walked in and looked around as if this was the first time he'd ever been there. "What's up?"

"I need some help," she said.

"Okay."

Gloria had gotten in touch with him on impulse. She *did* need help, which she knew Mack or Roy would've been happy to provide. But she couldn't resist asking Chad, although she was afraid it might be too late for them.

"What do you need?"

"I...purchased a crib."

His gaze met hers. "So did I."

"Oh." That shouldn't have surprised her. They'd more or less agreed to share custody of the baby. Returning to the matter at hand, she continued. "Have you assembled yours yet?"

"No. Have you?"

"Well, I tried, and frankly, I found it rather confusing. I was wondering if you'd mind helping." It was an excuse to see him again, to end this tension between them. If they were going to share custody, then they needed to feel comfortable with each other. Adversity and mistrust weren't in the baby's best interests. Or theirs...

"*That's* why you asked me over?"

She nodded. Yes, it was an excuse but she'd wanted to see him again.

Everything had changed after their...nap. That was a week ago. Nothing had happened that afternoon, nothing physical, and yet it had made a difference, at least for Gloria. Now, whenever she crawled into bed and closed her eyes, she could feel Chad lying beside her and it comforted her, calmed her. She wanted that closeness again, that feeling of being protected and cherished. Everything before had been about the powerful physical attraction between them. But they'd experienced something else that afternoon—tenderness toward each other and love for their unborn child. Gloria had felt a bond with Chad, a feeling of wholeness that she'd lost with the death of her parents. She had a blood relationship with the McAfees and they'd welcomed her into their lives. What she didn't have were the memories, the shared times, the laughter and private moments that connected the members of a family.

"Where's the crib?" he asked, giving her an odd look.

Caught up in her thoughts, she'd been staring off into space. Startled, she led him down the hall and escorted him into the second bedroom, which she planned to turn into the nursery.

He paused halfway into the room. "You've bought quite a lot of stuff already."

Gloria rested her hand on the changing table. "Corrie saw this on sale and phoned me from the store. I bought it sight unseen, and then Mack and his brother-in-law picked it up for me and brought it to the apartment." The change table was white wood with six drawers, three on each side. There was a brightly colored pad on top.

"I want to paint the room a light shade of blue." Mack had volunteered to do that for her. She'd thanked him and declined. She wanted Chad to offer.

He didn't.

Chad looked at the two ends of the crib that leaned against the outside wall. She'd taken everything out of the cardboard packaging, which she'd put in the recycling bin.

"The assembly directions are in several different languages," she said, handing him the printed sheets.

"I suspect the English version might be a bit difficult to follow."

"In other words, English isn't their first language."

"Exactly."

"Hmm." Chad studied the directions, then flipped through several pages. "The pictures will help."

Gloria had made that assumption herself, only to give up in frustration. "I have all the tools we'll need."

"Good. I didn't think to bring anything with me."

"Why would you?" He didn't know until he arrived why she'd contacted him.

They sat down on the floor together and Gloria marveled at how thorough Chad was. He read the entire booklet before he even reached for the screwdriver.

"We shouldn't have a problem."

An hour later, Gloria had to get up off the floor. Everything ached. "How about a cup of coffee?" she asked.

"I'm more in the mood for a shot of whiskey. Has anyone ever successfully assembled one of these cribs?"

"I… I don't know. Sorry, I don't have anything stronger than wine."

"What time is it?" he asked.

"After six." She hadn't even thought to look until he asked. It was already dark.

"Six?" he repeated, and in one fluid motion he was on his feet. He grabbed his cell and rushed out of the room.

"Do you need to be someplace else?" she asked, and assumed he was meeting Joni. Her chest tightened as she held her breath.

Talking on his cell phone, Chad stepped outside the

apartment onto the second-story walkway. He paced back and forth, intent on his conversation. Several minutes passed before he returned.

"Do you need to leave?" she asked, hoping she'd be able to hide her disappointment if he did.

"No. I'll stay."

"I apologize… I should've realized you might have made other plans."

"Don't worry about it. I'll finish up here."

"No, it's all right, really," she insisted. "It isn't like I'm due next week or anything. We have plenty of time."

"I said I'd stay."

She swallowed hard and nodded. "Thanks."

Chad went back to the baby's room and she went into the kitchen. The cupboard above the refrigerator held a bottle of merlot. Gloria couldn't remember how long it'd been there—well over a year, anyway. But aging red wine was supposed to improve the flavor. Opening the bottle proved to be a challenge but she managed. She poured Chad a glass and carried it into the bedroom.

"Here, this might help," she said, handing him the wineglass.

"Thanks."

"I wish I could join you…"

"Another time, perhaps. After the baby's born." He sent her a warm smile, which she immediately fell victim to; he'd had that effect on her from the beginning.

"I also bought a mobile." The words tumbled out in her effort to break the spell he had over her.

"Does it need assembly?"

"No."

"That's a relief," he teased, laughing.

She laughed, too.

He had one side of the crib attached when her stomach growled, reminding her that it'd been a long time since lunch. If she was hungry, Chad likely was, too.

"I'll fix us some dinner," she suggested, eager to do something useful. She wasn't much help with the crib, other than to reread the instructions aloud. Every once in a while he'd ask her to repeat a step and she'd struggle with the poor syntax and confused vocabulary. At one point Chad muttered that English must be the author's fourth or fifth language. Smiling, Gloria agreed.

"Don't go to any trouble," Chad said.

"I won't."

Not until she was in her kitchen did she realize this was the first time she'd ever cooked for him. She'd soon be giving birth to his son and yet they'd never once shared a home-cooked meal. She had to wonder if Joni ever cooked for him and decided she probably did.

Gloria didn't have a large repertoire of recipes. One of her favorites was a seafood pasta dish. Corrie had given her the recipe, which she, in turn, had received from Peggy Beldon. Setting a pot of water on to boil, she got the shrimp and scallops from the freezer and canned clams from the cupboard.

She'd chopped the onions and fresh parsley when Chad appeared. "I need a break," he said, holding his half-full wineglass.

"I hope you aren't allergic to seafood?" she asked, suddenly worried.

"Nope. Love it."

"Oh, good." What a sad commentary that she should know so little about him.

Chad leaned against the counter and she wondered if he had any idea how sexy he looked.

The phone rang and she answered it without checking caller ID. It was her brother.

"Just calling to make sure you don't need any help putting that crib together," Mack said.

"I've got it under control. Thanks, though."

"No problem. Linc said he could help, too, if you want."

"Thank you both. I appreciate it."

"Okay, well, give me a call if you need anything."

"I will."

When Gloria replaced the receiver, she saw Chad frowning into his wine. He obviously thought her conversation had been with someone she was dating. Remembering how wretched she'd felt when he was on the phone with Joni, she didn't explain. Let him think what he would. He didn't ask and she didn't enlighten him.

Chad finished his glass of wine and replenished it.

"Would you like me to turn on the radio?" she asked.

He shrugged. "Sure."

Soon soft rock filled the kitchen, followed by radio personality Delilah's soothing voice.

While the fettuccine boiled, Gloria set the table, adding a bowl of freshly grated Parmesan cheese. She placed two candles in the center, as well.

"It looks like you've created this intimate little scene before," he commented as she stirred the pasta.

"With the hours I work?" While she was on patrol duty, she'd rotated between swing shift and graveyard. Her nights and days were often reversed. Chad knew that.

Her answer seemed to please him. When the timer went off, he took the kettle from the stove and emptied the pasta into the strainer. Then he transferred the hot noodles to a ceramic dish she'd set on the counter. She poured the seafood sauce in its olive oil and fresh herb base over top.

Chad carried the serving bowl to the table. "This smells fabulous."

"It's a family favorite," she said. "Corrie served it several months ago and everyone raved about it."

Chad pulled out her chair. "You know, that's the first time I've heard you refer to Corrie and Roy as family."

"It is?" That was how she thought of them now, especially since she'd discovered she was pregnant. While Gloria hadn't been happy when she learned that her father had told Chad about the baby, in retrospect she was glad of it.

Chad took the chair across from her. "You seem more comfortable with who you are," he said thoughtfully.

Gloria wrapped the noodles around her fork, savoring the scent of basil and oregano. "Yes, I suppose I am."

"Any particular reason?"

She didn't need to think about her answer. "The baby. Roy and Corrie have been wonderful and Mack, too." Then, feeling mildly guilty, she added, "That was him on the phone earlier."

"Your brother?"

She took her first taste of the pasta and nodded.

Chad tried it, too. "Hey, this is good."

"Don't act so surprised. I *can* cook."

"Clearly." He beamed her another of his irresistible smiles.

Gloria needed every ounce of self-control she possessed to pull her gaze away from him.

"More wine?" she asked when she noticed his empty glass.

"No, thanks. I'm driving."

They finished their dinner and carried their plates to the sink.

"Thank you," Chad said as he set down his plate. "That was great."

"Well, you've heard the old saying," she joked. "The way to a man's heart is through his stomach."

He shocked her by taking her hand and raising it to his lips. "You already know the way to my heart, Gloria. You always have."

She could hardly breathe as his eyes held hers. Gloria felt as if her legs were about to collapse. She swayed toward him and his arms went around her, drawing her into his embrace.

Their kiss was magical. Exquisite. Powerful.

When the baby kicked, Gloria broke off the kiss and hid her face in his shoulder. "Did you feel that?"

"I did." He sounded amused.

"I think he likes it when we're together."

"I know I like it." Chad's arms tightened briefly. "But… I need to go."

Looking up, she did her utmost to send him off with a smile. "That's okay." She dropped her arms, then retreated a step. "Thank you. For everything."

He pressed his hand against her face. "I'll be back to finish the crib next week."

"Sure, anytime."

"Wednesday night?"

"That's perfect. I'll cook, okay?" He backed away a couple of steps, then rushed forward and kissed her again. By the time he left she was breathless and shaking.

And happier than she'd been in months.

Twenty-Eight

"Oh, this is so much fun," Charlotte said as she linked her arm through Olivia's. It was a rainy Saturday afternoon and they were visiting local craft fairs.

Olivia carefully set her pace to match her mother's.

The biggest fair was at Cedar Cove High School. "Don't you just admire how clever people are?" Charlotte asked.

"I certainly do," Olivia said. She pulled up the hood of her raincoat to protect her hair from the drizzle. Still, no weather could have kept her away from the Christmas bazaars. They'd seen a range of crafts and artwork, from quilts and sewing to original paintings, blown glass and jewelry.

"I've been looking forward to this afternoon."

"Me, too, Mom." With equal parts anticipation and dread. Will would be joining them later, and together brother and sister would once again bring up the subject of their mother and Ben moving into an assisted-living complex.

"I used to enjoy knitting for the charity bazaars," Charlotte was saying as they moved across the crowded high school parking lot. "I haven't donated anything in the past few years. I'm not sure why. Time just seems to get away from me."

"It does with all of us," Olivia said as they walked. They'd both made several purchases, which she carried in a plastic bag draped over her free arm.

"Where to next?" Charlotte asked.

"Stanford Suites," Olivia said, trying to sound casual.

"Oh? That's where Bess lives now. She moved there…a little while ago."

Olivia hadn't heard that, but found the news encouraging. Charlotte had obviously forgotten exactly when Bess Ferryman went to Stanford Suites; however, it must have been recent. "They're having an early Christmas bazaar, too," she said. "Some of the seniors have craft items for sale."

"How nice."

"When's the last time you saw Bess?"

"Monday. Bess is still part of the regular knitting group at the Senior Center."

Olivia stopped just short of pointing out that Bess could visit the others whenever she wished, even if she did reside at the retirement complex. She was afraid that if she said too much about it, Charlotte would become suspicious. Olivia had worried about this ever since they'd made the arrangements. All she could hope was that her mother and Ben would be more receptive than they'd been earlier.

The parking lot at Stanford Suites was nearly full.

"Look how busy they are," Charlotte said as they pulled in.

"Would you rather skip this and go directly to

lunch?" They'd decided to eat at a Mexican place. Her mother was obviously tiring, and so was Olivia. It was only months since she'd finished her chemotherapy and radiation treatments, and fatigue hit her sooner than it used to. And, she had to admit, she was quailing at the prospect of the conversation ahead.

"I wouldn't mind going in," Charlotte said, "if that's all right with you."

"I'll do whatever you want, Mom."

"Then let's go inside. It'll be fun to see what kinds of crafts they have for sale. I've been looking for a special gift for Ben. He's so hard to buy for, you know."

That wasn't the case with Jack. Books, music, DVDs—he loved them all; she just needed to keep track of what he already had. She'd also taken over purchasing his clothes and even he agreed that was a good thing. Except for his raincoat. She hadn't been able to convince him to give up that shabby old coat of his. She'd bought a new one, which hung unused in their closet. He said it felt too stiff and insisted there was nothing wrong with his old coat. She knew that eventually he'd start wearing it, but all the hints and suggestions she made were pointless until Jack was ready to switch, and he'd decide that for himself.

Funny how thinking about his raincoat made her realize that same approach might work with her mother and Ben, too. In other words, all she should do was mention Stanford Suites, ensure that Ben and Charlotte were aware of the place and its advantages. Pressuring them would only cause resentment and, if anything, make them more resistant.

She drove slowly around the lot. Luck was with her; a car parked close to the front left just as she drew near. Right away Olivia grabbed the empty space. She hurried around to help her mother out of the passenger side, afraid Charlotte might slip on the sidewalk. Ben's fall had emphasized how vulnerable both of them were.

"My, the grounds are nice here," Charlotte said, glancing at the flower beds. "You know, I feel so bad about neglecting my garden. Ben and I were in the backyard earlier this week. There's so much we need to do…"

"Jack and I can come over and—"

"No, no," Charlotte said, immediately dismissing the offer even before Olivia could make it. "Ben and I are thinking about hiring a yard service. But I have to tell you, Olivia, the price for goods and services is so high these days."

"Jack and I have a yard service." In Olivia's opinion, it was worth every cent. She enjoyed working outdoors, but her spare time was limited. While on medical leave she'd spent hours in her garden, especially after she'd started feeling better and regained some of her strength. Until then, Olivia had forgotten how much pleasure she got from her garden. Jack had helped, too, but it wasn't something he did for the joy of it. Not like her. He had an ulterior motive. Pulling weeds and preparing the earth, he'd watched her constantly. He'd been terrified that she'd become dizzy or faint or, worse, that she'd collapse.

When Olivia was diagnosed with breast cancer, Jack had hardly let her out of his sight. If Olivia had ever doubted her husband's love—and she hadn't— he'd proved himself a thousand times over while she underwent cancer treatments. And, as a bonus, their garden had benefitted, too.

A youngster held the door open as Olivia and Charlotte entered the complex.

"Merry Christmas," he said with a toothless grin.

"It's not even Thanksgiving until next week," Charlotte said.

"But it's Christmas here," the young man told them earnestly. "My great-grandma said so."

"Then who are we to argue?" Olivia said as they walked in. The large open room was filled with tables placed in a U-shape for easy access. Bess sat at the second table, her baked goods and knitted items on display.

"Charlotte!" she cried. She put down her knitting needles to lean over the table and give her friend a hug. "I'm so glad you came. When I mentioned the bazaar last Monday, you didn't think you'd be able to stop by."

Her mother hadn't said anything about the craft show and Olivia assumed Charlotte had simply forgotten, or—another possibility—she hadn't wanted to give Will and Olivia an opportunity to promote the idea of assisted living.

"I'd like to introduce you to my friends," Bess said, and animatedly waved her arm in the direction of several other women. "This is Eileen, and over here is Rosemary and that's Eve." She pointed to the other ladies, who had their own booths. They raised their hands and waved. "I see you met my great-grandson."

"That's Billy?" Charlotte asked.

"He's eight now. Unbelievable, isn't it?"

"I helped Bess with a sweater pattern when he was

two. It had a dinosaur on the front," Charlotte explained to Olivia.

Interesting how her mother would remember that and not a conversation she'd had just a few days ago.

"Bess talks about you all the time," Eileen said.

"What are you selling?" Charlotte asked as she moved closer to Eileen's table.

"Oh, I make polished wood pens. My husband used to love writing with a wooden pen, but they aren't available the way they once were. One year, I decided they couldn't be that difficult to make, so I attended a woodworking class at the community college and made him several for Christmas. He used them until his dying day."

"A wooden pen," Charlotte repeated. "Why, Ben would love that." She looked at Olivia. "You know how he likes to do the crossword puzzle every morning? Well, he does it in ink."

Olivia nodded. "Getting him one of these pens is a great idea. Very classy."

Charlotte purchased a pen and so did Olivia. Every booth sold something wonderful, and Olivia ended up spending more money at the retirement complex bazaar than the three other craft fairs combined.

They left loaded down with gifts, plus baked goods, homemade candy and watermelon pickles to serve with Thanksgiving dinner. Olivia knew Ben would enjoy the peanut brittle Charlotte had bought, as well.

Over cheese enchiladas, Olivia and Charlotte reviewed their Thanksgiving menu. Little had changed through the years. They'd have turkey, of course, and two kinds of stuffing. The traditional inside-the-bird bread stuffing and a much-loved family recipe for rice stuffing, too. Old-fashioned homemade gravy. The salads and vegetable selections hadn't altered much from the time Olivia was a child. Potatoes, mashed and sweet. And at least three choices of pie for dessert.

"Justine's bringing the appetizers," Olivia reminded her mother.

"Oh, yes." Charlotte frowned. "We're having dinner at your house, right?"

"Yes, Mom." The entire family had celebrated the holidays at Olivia and Jack's place for a number of years. Her home was larger than anyone else's and the kitchen was bigger. "Would you rather have it at your home, Mom, with your new kitchen and all?"

"No. No." She shook her head adamantly. "I just wanted to be sure everything's set for your place."

"It is, so there's nothing to worry about."

"Of course, I'll be helping with the dinner."

"Of course," Olivia echoed. "I wouldn't dream of making Thanksgiving dinner without you."

They finished their lunch and headed back to Charlotte and Ben's.

"Did you two have a good time?" Ben asked when they went inside. A blast of wind nearly slammed the door behind them. The weather remained dark, wet and dreary. Not that Harry, her mother's cat, seemed to notice. He sat contentedly in his usual position on the back of Ben's chair, his long furry tail draped over the cushion.

"We had the loveliest time," Charlotte cooed.

Olivia's cell phone chirped, and as she took it out of her purse, she saw that the call was from her brother. "Hello," she said, looking at her watch. He was supposed to "drop by" in about half an hour.

"Hi. Listen, something's come up and I won't be able to make it."

"At all?" So her brother was leaving this in her hands. Her warm feelings for him and the help he'd given her recently dipped by several degrees.

"I can probably stop by but not at the time we agreed."

"When can you?" she asked, struggling to hide her irritation.

"Ah, I'm not sure. I have to see someone and—"

Someone? Olivia was not amused. "Male or female?"

"Does it matter?"

"It might."

"Fine. Male. The guy's an artist I've been wooing. A painter from Bellevue. I want him to bring his work to my gallery. Miranda's the one who got him to talk to me."

"Is she with you?"

"Miranda? Not right this minute, but she will be. Actually, we decided to double-team him, convince him to sell his art on this side of Puget Sound. Are you going to get all huffy about it?"

Olivia sighed. "No." In fact, she had to acknowledge that Will's excuse was legitimate and she hoped his overtures to this artist paid off.

"Can you handle things without me or would you rather put it off?"

"No. The sooner we settle this, the better."

"I think so, too. Good luck. I'll talk to you later."

"Thanks." She snapped her phone shut and put it back in her purse.

"Who was that, dear?" Charlotte asked.

"Will."

"Oh. I'm so happy about the way the two of you have reconnected since he's moved back to town. It does my heart good to see you getting along so well."

That was true. Will and Olivia *had* reconnected. They were closer now than at any other time in their lives. It was a gift she hadn't expected, and she was grateful for it.

"I was just telling Ben about our bazaar shopping," Charlotte continued. "We had such a good day, didn't we?"

"We did," she said.

"And, Ben, the very best place wasn't the big craft bazaar that they hold at the high school. Remember, I mentioned it earlier?"

"That's the one you were looking forward to."

"It was—until we got to Stanford Suites. Oh, my, you wouldn't believe what I found there."

"Show me."

"I can't, because almost everything I bought is for you for Christmas."

"At that assisted-living complex?" he asked incredulously.

"Yes. Bess lives there, you know, and she told me how much she loves it. Her great-grandson was the greeter. Oh, and they had the most beautiful decorated sugar cookies I've ever seen."

"Did you buy any?"

"Sure did. The ladies' group baked them. They have Bible study on Tuesday mornings and a bridge club and a knitting circle and art lessons…"

"At the assisted-living complex?" Ben repeated with a frown. "I had no idea they offered all that."

"Me, neither."

Olivia refrained from pointing out that she and Will had described all the amenities and programs to them—more than once. "Mom, before I go," she said. "Jack wanted me to ask what you're making for tonight's dinner."

Ben and Charlotte exchanged a glance.

Olivia had asked because she suspected her mother hadn't even tried the new stove.

"We had cornflakes last night," Ben admitted.

"Cornflakes?" This was worse than she'd thought. "Oh, Mom, I was afraid this would happen."

"Microwave popcorn the night before," Charlotte murmured, shamefaced. "The microwave is easy to work. You just press the button that says *popcorn*."

"It's my fault," Ben said. "I started to read the instruction manual, but the stove's got all these bells and whistles and, to tell you the truth, I just sort of gave up."

Olivia wasn't surprised. The owner's manual was a good hundred pages thick. She'd read shorter novels.

"The grounds at the complex were so lovely, too." Charlotte turned the conversation away from the stove and back to the retirement complex.

"Mom, are you talking about Stanford Suites again?" Not that Olivia was complaining...

Charlotte nodded and looked at Ben. "They have a container garden there. Bess told me. The zucchini for the zucchini bread she sold me came from the garden. And the green tomatoes for the mincemeat, as well."

"Really?" Ben raised his eyebrows.

Olivia reached for her car keys. It no longer seemed

necessary to say anything. Her mother was doing all the talking.

"So you liked Stanford Suites?" Ben asked Charlotte.

"Yes… I did."

Ben caught Olivia's eye. "Charlotte, do you feel we should live there? I thought you were dead set against it."

"Well, I was, but after being there today and meeting Bess's friends, I think I might like it. I never believed I would, but I can see the advantages to us. And really, Ben, nothing will change other than our address." She paused. "Bess said they have two openings coming up."

Ben didn't look nearly as convinced. "What about the house?"

Charlotte grew quiet. "I forgot about that."

"Will and I may have a solution," Olivia said, trying not to reveal how eager she was to tell them. She and Will had been talking about this all week.

Her mother and Ben turned to her. "You do?" her mother asked.

"Will wants to buy it from you." This was the news her brother was supposed to be there to impart. Well, she'd have to do it for him.

"Will wants to move into this old house?"

"You can discuss the details with him. We planned to talk to you this afternoon, until he got called away," she said.

"What about the apartment he fixed up at the gallery? Surely he doesn't want to just abandon it after all the work he's done there."

"It won't go to waste. In fact, he's already got a potential renter."

"Who?"

"Miranda Sullivan. She works at the gallery nearly full-time now, and she said she'd be happy to rent the space, which would be ideal." This possibility had evolved during the past few days. Olivia was pleased by the growing closeness—professional and, she guessed, personal—between Miranda and her brother.

"It'd be a good solution for us," Ben said thoughtfully.

"I know I'd feel much better about leaving the house if Will would buy it." She chuckled. "You tell him, though, that he'll have to get me another Christmas present—otherwise, I'm taking that new refrigerator."

Twenty-Nine

"Come on, Dad, it's Thanksgiving," Jolene said. "You're being a real drag."

Bruce forced a smile. There'd been plenty of Thanksgivings with just him and his daughter before, but this year, without Rachel, was different. He'd picked up a precooked turkey with fixings at the grocery store, and everything was in the oven heating up. This wasn't the kind of meal he wanted, but unfortunately it was the best he could do.

Jolene had set the table. She'd brought home a decorative papier-mâché pumpkin she'd made in art class, which served as the centerpiece. Using a white linen tablecloth and their good dishes, his daughter had gone to some trouble to make this a special event. He tried to show his appreciation, but his attempt had fallen decidedly short.

Jolene threw herself down on the sofa next to him and sighed. "It doesn't feel right without Rachel, does it?"

He was shocked that his daughter was willing to admit it. "No. I wish she was here." Despite Jolene's unexpected concession, he braced himself for her backlash. But he didn't really care; he was tired of pretending, of putting on a brave front. Every day was an effort without Rachel.

"Can we call her?" Jolene asked, shocking him again.

Bruce shook his head "She blocked all my numbers."

"She didn't block mine."

Bruce stared at his daughter. "How do you know that?"

"She said I could phone her anytime."

He exhaled slowly. He wished she'd told him sooner. "Have you called her?"

Jolene's long hair fell forward as she hung her head. "No. I was going to a couple of times, but I didn't. She…she wants to move."

Bruce leaped off the sofa. His daughter was only *now* telling him this? Jolene had seen Rachel a week ago last Monday. He'd hoped to pry information out of her, but Jolene had remained stubbornly tight-lipped. Eventually he'd given up. All he'd been able to learn was that Rachel had read his letter.

"Moving? Where?"

"She mentioned Portland."

"When?"

Jolene shrugged. "I… I don't know. I asked her not to leave."

"What did she say?" He found it difficult enough with Rachel living in Bremerton, which was just across the cove but felt like it was on the other side of the world. Portland would be so much harder.

"Nothing. She didn't tell me when she plans to go."

"You don't have any idea?"

"I asked her to stay," Jolene reiterated.

"Thank you," he whispered.

Jolene refused to meet his look. "But I'd rather she went to Portland."

"Jolene!" Bruce couldn't help it; he exploded. Pacing the room, he tore at his hair like a crazy man, tempted to slam his fist against the wall.

"If you felt that way, why did you even ask her to stay?" he demanded.

Jolene didn't immediately answer. "You," she said in a small voice.

"If you're so concerned about me, then Rachel would be back in this house where she belongs." He jabbed his index finger at the floor.

"You don't want me here anymore, do you?" she shouted, hiding her face in her hands.

"Don't be ridiculous! Of course I want you here. You're my daughter—I love you."

"But you love Rachel more."

"I don't love her *more*. I love her, *too*. She's my wife and she's carrying my child." His pacing continued. "A child I might never get to know because of this whole mess." Unable to bear it, he stormed out. With nowhere else to go, he went into his room, closing the door, and sat on the edge of his bed. He felt like crying but was too numb, too drained by his anger.

He had no idea how long he'd been there when he heard a knock on the door.

"What?" he snapped.

Jolene opened the door and stood framed in the hallway light, holding her cell. "Rachel is on the phone. Do you want to talk to her?"

"You called her?"

"Yeah. You shouldn't be moping around on Thanksgiving. I knew you'd want to talk to her. You do, don't you?"

Bruce swallowed painfully and nodded. "Very much." The words were thick with emotion.

Jolene handed him the phone and then left, closing the door quietly behind her.

Bruce waited until the door had clicked shut. "Happy Thanksgiving," he said, doing his utmost to sound upbeat and positive.

"Same to you. Jolene said the two of you are about ready to eat."

Eat? Bruce had no appetite. He'd be lucky to manage a roll, let alone an entire meal. "I bought us one of those prepared turkey dinners from Albertson's. They're supposed to be halfway decent." But nothing compared to the home-cooked meal they would've enjoyed if Rachel was with them.

"So I've heard."

"What about you?" he asked, wondering if she'd be joining Teri Polgar or one of her other friends.

She hesitated. "I'm cooking today."

"Turkey and all the fixings?"

"Yes…for my roommate and some friends."

"That's nice," he said dully.

"They're away from home and family, so we pooled our resources and decided to have our own Thanksgiving celebration."

"So you're living with a female navy—what?—officer?" Bremerton was filled with navy personnel.

"Not exactly."

"Navy, though, right?" He didn't mean to turn this call into an inquisition, but he couldn't help being curious. Rachel had told him so little about her living arrangements.

"Yes, navy."

"A man?" he pressed, and could tell right away that she didn't appreciate his questioning her.

"It doesn't really matter, does it, Bruce?"

"No, I suppose not." He did his best to pretend it didn't. Then he suddenly realized where she was staying and it nearly destroyed him. His hand almost crushed his daughter's cell phone. "You're living with Nate Olsen, aren't you?" he asked starkly.

"I thought you said it didn't matter."

"It matters if it's Nate." He clenched his jaw.

Rachel was completely silent.

"Rachel?"

More silence.

He inhaled and slowly released his breath. "Either I trust you or I don't. I choose to trust you. If you'd wanted to marry Nate, you could have. He wanted you and so did I. You chose me. Whether that was the right decision or not, you're my wife…"

"Yes, I am. I trust you, Bruce, and I expect you to trust me."

"I do."

"Good." A moment later, she added, "He's been a friend to me. That's all. A friend."

It wasn't easy, but he had to believe she was telling him the truth.

"You talked to Jolene?" he asked.

"Yes, when she called me just now. I told her when we met at the library that she could phone me anytime, day or night."

"Were you surprised she called you today?"

"A little, but she didn't call me for her sake. She did it because of you."

"It's a start."

"A small one."

Bruce couldn't disagree. "Can I see you again?"

"I don't know if that's a good idea."

He could argue, but decided against it. "Jolene said you're thinking of moving to Portland."

"I'm considering it." She didn't add any further information.

"Wherever you are, I'd like to be with you when the baby's born." That shouldn't be asking too much. As the baby's father, he had the right. All he could do was hope she agreed.

"We can talk about that later, okay?"

"Okay." But he wasn't willing to drop it.

Bruce could tell she wanted to end the conversation. "It's Thanksgiving, Rachel, and before we hang up I want you to know that, despite everything, I'm grateful you're in my life. I will always love you."

"Thank you, Bruce."

"Goodbye."

"Bye."

He noticed she hadn't told him she loved him. Not that he'd blame her if she'd given up on their marriage...

He walked back into the living room, where Jolene sat in front of the television. He handed her the cell phone. "Thanks."

She looked up at him. "I've been kind of a brat, haven't I?"

At least she recognized her role in all this.

"Something like that."

The timer on the stove indicated that the turkey was done. "Are you ready for dinner?" he asked.

She regarded him skeptically. "Are you?"

"Sure." He'd make an effort; Jolene deserved that much. "After dinner, do you want to work on a jigsaw puzzle? Or we can play Yahtzee if you prefer."

"Let's do a puzzle. The one with the dogs playing poker."

"Why not?" They'd worked on a different puzzle last Thanksgiving. Rachel had been with them then, and it was the best Thanksgiving in recent memory. Jolene and Rachel had cooked the meal together.

Bruce and Jolene sat at the table with their purchased meal. Neither of them ate much, although they made a pretense of being happy. They'd just finished putting the leftovers in the refrigerator when the house phone rang.

"I'll get it," Jolene said, leaping on the one in the kitchen as if she thought it might jump up and run away.

Bruce smiled, observing that his daughter was almost back to the way she'd been a year earlier, before he'd married Rachel.

Rachel. His heart sank. He could pretend all he wanted, but he missed his wife.

"Dad," Jolene said, holding the phone against her shoulder. Her dark brown eyes seemed twice their normal size. "It's... Rachel. She wants to know if it would be all right if she came over for a little while."

His heart rate automatically doubled. "Of course it would be all right. She doesn't need to ask."

"She's asking me. She tried my cell, but I left it in my bedroom and didn't hear it ring."

"If she's asking you, then you need to answer." He gripped the back of his chair, waiting to see how his daughter responded.

"What if I say no?"

He closed his eyes. "I don't know."

She studied him, then returned the phone to her ear. "Dad and I were just about to start a jigsaw puzzle."

He nearly grabbed the phone away from her, wanting to tell Rachel that this was *her* home and she could come anytime she wanted, no matter what he and Jolene were doing.

"We did one together last Thanksgiving, remember?" Jolene went on.

Rachel must have said something, because his daughter was silent for a moment.

"No, not yet. Dad got a pumpkin pie with the turkey." A short silence and then, "It was all right, I guess, for turkey, but last year's was way better. The stuffing was pretty bland. I like yours a lot more."

Bruce relaxed. They were having a normal conversation. "I like pecan pie and so does Dad," she said next. "Sure. I'll tell him. Bye."

She replaced the phone. "That was Rachel," she said, as if he didn't already know.

"So, is she coming by?" He tried to sound casual. Nonchalant.

"Yeah, in about an hour. She said we should get started on the puzzle and get all the border pieces in and then she'd help us with the rest. Oh, and she's bringing a pecan pie. We have whipped topping, don't we? Because I told her we did."

"I think so. If not, there's ice cream."

"Dad," his daughter said in an exasperated voice. "We have *strawberry* ice cream. That would be awful with pecan pie."

"Hey, don't knock it until you've tried it."

Jolene rolled her eyes, but she was smiling and so was he. Really smiling for the first time that day, and it felt darn good.

Thirty

"It's so good to get back into our regular schedule," Grace said as she slid into the booth at the Pancake Palace. She and Olivia had finished their aerobic workout—a Wednesday-night tradition for years—and stopped for coffee and coconut cream pie. Another tradition.

Their schedule had been disrupted for months after Olivia's surgery for breast cancer and the chemotherapy and radiation treatments that followed. She'd lost weight and grown so weak that for a time Grace had feared her best friend might not survive. If there were lessons to be learned from this experience—and there were—one of the most profound was how dear Olivia was to her. How important their friendship was. Grace treasured her and their special times together. Every week they made a point of catching up with each other. They'd shared so much through the years. Grace relied on Olivia to sympathize when necessary, to tell her the truth and to laugh with her. And Olivia expected the same from Grace. They'd seen each other through births and deaths, marriage and divorce, triumphs and disappointments.

"Coffee, girls?" Goldie asked as she sidled up to the booth.

"Tea for me," Olivia said, surprising both Grace and Goldie.

"Tea?" Goldie echoed. "When did this happen?"

Olivia shrugged. "Coffee leaves a bitter taste in my mouth these days. I don't know if it's because of the prescriptions I'm taking or what, but I prefer tea now."

Goldie snorted, shook her head and, after pouring Grace's coffee, returned to the kitchen.

"You usually order tea when there's something on your mind," Grace said, studying Olivia. Her friend had been unusually quiet all evening.

"I guess so, but I really have gone off coffee."

"You're the one who told me you've had the most important conversations of your life over tea, remember?"

"Yes, I suppose I have. Most of them in the kitchen. My mother's or mine." She thought for a moment. "Conversations with my mother. With Stan. With Justine." She smiled. "Jack and I have had some of the most intimate discussions of our marriage in the kitchen. Funny, isn't it, that the kitchen and a cup of tea would play such a major role in my life?"

"Maybe because it's such a comfortable setting. So personal," Grace said. "Anyway, what's on your mind tonight?" She couldn't see any reason not to be direct.

Olivia leaned forward to reply, but didn't have a chance before Goldie came back with a small white ceramic teapot and a tea bag on the side. "I thought

I'd better ask if you're ordering coconut cream pie or if that's changed, too."

"I'll have coconut cream pie," Grace said. This was her one indulgence of the week and she wasn't about to give it up.

"What other kinds do you have?" Olivia asked.

Grace had to bite her lip to keep from giggling at Goldie's horrified reaction. "You've got to be kidding me," she burst out. "Now you're quitting coconut cream pie, too? What are those drugs doing to you?"

"I also like pumpkin pie," Olivia said evenly, "and I think it would be a better choice health-wise."

"You're not a pumpkin pie kind of woman," Goldie argued. "If you order pumpkin, I swear you'll have to get some other waitress to serve it. Fact is, I'm wondering what those doctors did to the Olivia I used to know."

"I'm right here. Okay, you win, I'll have a piece of coconut cream pie."

Goldie's face broke into a wide smile. "You were just playing with me, weren't you?" Not waiting for a response, she turned sharply and marched back to the kitchen.

"Okay," Grace said. "*Now* you can tell me what's on your mind."

Olivia reached for her fork and stared at it. "It's because of Mom moving and everything else—things I never thought would affect me."

Grace knew that Olivia and Will had been concerned about Charlotte and Ben for some time.

"Your mother's memory problems are getting worse?" Grace asked, testing the waters.

"No…actually, I think she's a little better now that

she's back on familiar ground. Although…who can tell how long that'll last? But since she and Ben decided to move into Stanford Suites, Mom's been cleaning out the basement. She's like a woman on a mission. You know my mother. Once she's made a decision, there's no stopping her. Ever since Thanksgiving she's been sorting through sixty years of accumulated stuff. I know it's necessary but I didn't realize how hard it would be for me."

"Why? What kind of stuff?" Grace had been in that basement herself and tried to remember what was stored there.

"A lot of it is unimportant—canning jars, old clothes and things Mom kept for one reason or another," Olivia said. "But some of that stuff is part of my childhood. I know there's no real reason to hang on to a perfect spelling test I did in the second grade. Mom kept it, she said, because she was so proud I could spell *Mississippi*."

"You got an A on *every* spelling test," Grace reminded her. "So you could see this one as representative," she said, pleased with her explanation.

Olivia laughed. "I guess what I'm saying is that when Mom and Ben agreed to move into assisted living, I was so relieved I didn't think about how all of this would affect me—about how it would *feel*."

Grace considered that for a moment. "You mean you'd be losing some of your personal history, as well."

Nodding, Olivia said, "Naturally Mom wants me to take all the files she's saved. She held on to so much and it's so neatly organized. On the one hand, I'm tempted. On the other…what use is it? It's just a bunch of childhood memories."

"Happy memories," Grace murmured.

"Yes, but it's ridiculous to save all this stuff."

"Then pass it on to your children and grandchildren."

Olivia appeared to be mulling over that thought as she stirred her tea. "I could, I suppose, but what good is an old spelling test to my family?"

"I don't know. You'll have to ask Justine and James."

"No need," she said briskly. "I'm going to throw out most of those old files. My kids have their own clutter—they don't need mine. But I have to tell you, Grace, it's hard letting go of all that…evidence. Those tests and drawings and Valentine cards bring back so much of my childhood."

"What about Will?"

Olivia raised her eyebrows. "Will? He tossed everything without a qualm. All of it went right in the garbage. He didn't even have to think about it."

"I bet Cliff would do the same thing," Grace said. "Men. I swear there isn't a sentimental bone in their bodies."

"Some men," Olivia agreed and then added, "Jack can be shockingly romantic at times."

"Yes, but you have to admit he's the exception."

"Well, maybe. The problem is, most men don't want us to know how sentimental they can be."

Goldie appeared with their coconut cream pie. "Enjoy," she said, and it sounded like an order.

"Yes, ma'am." Olivia saluted smartly and exchanged a smile with Grace.

After a sip of coffee, Grace picked up her fork. She'd looked forward to this all week. The library had been hectic, what with putting up Christmas decorations, creating displays of Christmas books, planning programs and events.

"Your turn," Olivia said, after taking her first bite. "What's happening in your world?"

Grace hardly knew where to start. "Well, I heard from Ian and Cecilia Randall. Remember them? Ian's still in the navy. They have two kids now and Ian's been transferred back to the Bremerton base."

"Of course I remember the Randalls. It'll be good to see them again."

"They asked about the house on Rosewood Lane and my current renters are moving out this month. It was a short-term rental after Faith Beckwith—I mean, Davis—left."

"That should work out well, then."

"Yeah. I like them."

"Me, too," Olivia said. Slicing off another bite of pie, she casually asked, "How's Beau?"

Grace frowned. The dog was the least welcome subject. "That puppy is a nuisance."

"Grace, he's adorable!"

"Sure, he's cute but he's a pain. I'm not keeping him."

"Really?"

"Really," Grace insisted. Everyone, right down to her two daughters and their kids, refused to believe her. But she *wasn't* keeping him. She wasn't! It was out of the question. Grace didn't have the time or inclination for training a puppy. The fact that Beau followed her around like a pesky little shadow didn't influence her one bit.

"Does Beth have a home for him?"

"Yes. Mine. She thinks she's so clever," Grace said,

growing more animated as she spoke. "She came to me with this song and dance about being so busy shipping Christmas trees to Japan and Hawaii and wherever that she hasn't had time to look for another home and could I just hang on to him. She assumed that because I agreed to help her with this puppy I'd want to keep him myself. Well, she's wrong."

"What does Cliff say?"

Grace narrowed her eyes as she stared intently across the table. "Olivia?" she murmured, her heart sinking. "Not you, too."

"Not me, what?"

"You think I should keep Beau."

"Only if you love him."

"I don't. He needs a good home and it isn't with me. I refuse to become attached to that dog. Besides, he's nothing but trouble. Did I tell you I found him chewing my new shoes the other day?"

"I believe you might have mentioned that once or twice."

"My point exactly." The more she thought about Beau, the more convinced she became that she didn't want him.

"Do you realize you talk about Beau quite a lot?"

That was an exaggeration, but Grace was determined not to argue. "Mark my words, Olivia, I am *not* keeping that dog. If anything, I'll give him to Maryellen and Jon for the kids. If they'll agree... Katie and Drake are at the age where they'll love having a puppy. Beau will be happy with them."

Before her friend could pursue the subject further, Grace changed it. "How are things going for Will?"

"So far, so good."

•

"Buying your mother's old house is a brilliant solution. Who came up with that idea? You or Will?"

"Will. It's a tremendous help to Mom and Ben," Olivia said. "Everything's working out beautifully. Will is moving into Mom and Ben's place, and Miranda will take over his apartment at the art gallery right after New Year's."

A smile quivered at the edges of Olivia's mouth. "I'm pretty sure my brother's attracted to Miranda. She isn't the type who'd normally interest him. She's not petite or demure. But she *is* his equal and isn't afraid to stand up to him. He's falling for her, and I can tell he isn't all that happy about it."

A smile became impossible to hold back. "I had a feeling something was going on between those two. Who would've believed it?"

"Oh, Grace, she's just perfect for him."

Grace settled back and giggled like a schoolgirl.

"She doesn't let him get away with anything," Olivia went on. "She sees right through him and calls his bluff. I don't think a woman's ever spoken to him the way Miranda does. Including his wife… In the beginning, I thought Will would lose it. I'm pretty sure he fired her at least once, and I know for a fact that she walked out on him one day."

"That must really have set him off."

"It did."

"But it wasn't long before Will realized what an asset she is, so he had to humble himself and ask her to return."

"Will? Humble? Those are two words that don't mix."

"No, they don't, which is why Mom and I think the world of Miranda."

Oh, Miranda was going to be so good for Will. Because he was attractive and successful and sophisticated, Olivia's brother took pride in getting women to fall for him. His ego seemed to need it. She also wondered if he was one of those people who loved being in love, who was addicted to the excitement and unpredictability, the chase and the challenge. She'd actually fallen for him herself after her first husband's death. Will had almost ruined her subsequent relationship with Cliff. Fortunately, she'd broken off with Will, which he'd made even more difficult by insisting he loved her. In retrospect Grace saw that he hadn't really loved her at all. Yes, he was fond of her but what he really enjoyed was being in control.

Miranda wouldn't be so easily manipulated and that would frustrate Will no end. But it was the best thing that could've happened to him.

"I do have to say Will's attitude has changed since he came back to Cedar Cove. That's been a surprise," Olivia said.

"Oh?"

"You know better than anyone that my brother and I have had our differences over the years. I disapproved of some of the things he's done, but it's his life." Olivia raised one shoulder in a shrug. "I didn't know if I could trust him after he moved back here."

Grace knew exactly what her friend meant…

"But he's made an effort to get involved in the community. And I can't tell you how grateful I am that I don't need to deal with everything concerning Mom by myself."

Grace agreed. "He's been wonderful with your mother and Ben."

"I've come to appreciate my brother."

"I'm glad."

Goldie returned to their table with a coffeepot in one hand and a pot of hot water in the other. "You two ready for a refill?" she asked.

Grace looked at her friend. "None for me. What about you?"

Olivia shook her head. "I'm pretty full, too."

Glancing down at the half-consumed slice of pie, Goldie asked, "You want me to wrap that up for you?"

"No, thanks."

Goldie gave a disgusted snort. "Okay, well, see you girls next week."

Next week. Same time. Same place. Grace would meet with Olivia, who'd always been with her. Who shared her burdens and doubled her joys. Her friend for life.

Thirty-One

Linc stepped into his office and smiled at the stack of work orders on his desk. Sheriff Troy Davis had helped him immeasurably by sending business his way. The sheriff was active in a number of service organizations, such as Rotary Club and Lions, where he'd made a point of spreading the word. At first, business had trickled in slowly, but as the weeks progressed, the auto body shop drew more and more work. As it stood now, Linc had all his employees working a forty-hour week.

The business wasn't the only thing going well in Linc's life. He was delighted with the duplex and his growing friendship with Mack. Most of all, he deeply loved Lori and looked forward to every minute he spent with her. If he'd known marriage could be this satisfying, he would've tried it a lot sooner, he'd joked to Lori. Laughing, she'd informed him that he never would've found anyone who suited him nearly as well—and she was right.

Thinking about Lori, he felt a twinge of sadness as he thought about the situation with her family. The conflict between him and his father-in-law remained unresolved. The fact that Leonard and Kate had separated over Leonard's reaction to their daughter's marriage was an additional burden.

Lori was in close contact with her mother once again. They talked nearly every day, but although Kate put a good face on it, Linc could tell how hurt and disappointed she was that Leonard had made no effort to get in touch with her.

Sitting down at his desk, Linc reached for the telephone directory and flipped through the pages. He quickly located the listing for Bellamy Enterprises in Bremerton.

A woman answered in a crisp professional voice. "How may I direct your call?"

"I'd like to speak to Leonard Bellamy's assistant," he responded in the same businesslike tones.

"One moment, please."

"This is Helen," another woman said an instant later.

Linc drew in a breath. "Helen, this is Lincoln Wyse." He paused, waiting for a reaction. When none came, he continued. "Would it be possible to schedule an appointment with Mr. Bellamy?"

"Let me check his schedule."

Linc was put on hold for several minutes before the woman came back. "Mr. Bellamy said he's available in half an hour."

"Mr. Bellamy," Linc murmured. He hadn't counted on the assistant speaking directly with her employer. Glancing at his watch, he asked, "Four?"

"Yes, four."

"I'll be there." It was already three-thirty. Linc realized that if he didn't leave right away, he'd be late. No doubt Bellamy would add that to his list of crimes.

Linc washed up, then drove the entire distance above the speed limit, risking a ticket. He found a convenient parking spot, then ran to the downtown office complex. He'd only been here once before, and an unpleasant scene between him and Bellamy had resulted.

Linc hadn't had enough time to consider what he wanted to say to Bellamy. All he could do was be as forthright and honest as possible.

He dashed up the steps to the building and caught an open elevator. Getting off on the top-floor lobby, he checked his watch and heaved a sigh of relief. Right on schedule.

A middle-aged woman sitting at the front desk glanced up as he approached. She had short salt-and-pepper hair and looked every inch the professional assistant she was. Her nameplate identified her as Ms. Helen McDonald.

"Lincoln Wyse," he said.

"I'll let Mr. Bellamy know you're here." Helen picked up her phone and curtly announced his name. When she'd finished, she gestured toward a chair. "Please have a seat."

Linc did. Five minutes passed and then ten. So this was the game his father-in-law had chosen to play. Apparently Bellamy assumed Linc would lose patience and walk out. The fact was, Linc could be just as obstinate, just as unyielding. They had more in common than Leonard Bellamy realized.

A full hour went by before the phone buzzed. Helen answered and nodded in Linc's direction. "Mr. Bellamy will see you now."

Linc stood. "Thank you."

She led him to the private office and opened the door. Linc walked inside, gazing at the bookcases, the upholstered guest chairs, the desk of dark polished wood. Bellamy sat there, head bowed as he wrote. He didn't acknowledge Linc or give any indication that he knew Linc had entered the room.

Linc waited in front of the desk. He occupied himself by examining the family photographs, which stood in a row on the credenza behind his father-in-law.

"I'm surprised you're still here," Bellamy said, not bothering to look up. He set down his pen and leaned back, a frown creasing his brow.

Linc wished now that he'd taken the time to go home and change out of his work clothes, although he hadn't had the opportunity. Getting here by four meant jumping right in his truck. No doubt if he'd been a minute late, Bellamy would have refused to see him. Score one point for his father-in-law, making Linc cool his heels like that, and another for catching him in greasy coveralls.

"So," Bellamy said. "What do you have to say for yourself?"

"What do you want to hear?"

"You're the one who asked for the appointment, not me," Bellamy muttered.

"Yes, I did." Linc tried to corral his thoughts. "Mostly I came because I need to know what you find so objectionable about me being married to your daughter."

Bellamy laughed. "The fact that you have to ask tells me everything."

"Maybe I could understand it if I hadn't learned

about your own background," Linc said. He sat down and crossed his legs, hoping to create the impression of being at ease.

"What do you mean?" Bellamy asked sharply.

"I have no idea why you took such an instant dislike to me. I'll admit the circumstances leading up to Lori's and my wedding left a lot to be desired. We were foolish to rush into marriage..."

"Foolish doesn't even begin to describe what you did."

"If I could, I'd go back and meet both you and your wife and ask your blessing before I married Lori."

"I'd never have given it." Bellamy seemed to take grim pleasure in informing him of that.

"Possibly not, but I hope you will now."

Bellamy glared at him across the desk. "Are you out of your mind? What would ever make you think I'd give you and Lori my blessing? Especially now that Kate—" He stopped abruptly, his lips pinched, as though he regretted mentioning his wife's name.

"I hope I've proved myself to you," Linc said. "You threw a number of roadblocks in my way when I tried to establish my business in Cedar Cove." He took a deep breath. "Nevertheless I'm making a go of it."

Bellamy didn't deny it, which only went to show what Linc already knew. His father-in-law had done everything he could to sabotage his auto body shop and had nearly succeeded. If not for his brother-in-law and Sheriff Davis, Bellamy *would* have succeeded.

"What puzzles me most is why you object to me when the two of us are so much alike."

"I sincerely doubt it," Bellamy snapped.

"From what I gather, your own father worked as a welder."

Bellamy stiffened. "That means nothing."

"It means you came from a family with a strong work ethic, which is the same ethic my father taught me. As it happens, I followed in my father's footsteps. I might have chosen my own path, but that option was taken away from me when both my parents were killed and—"

"And you saw a faster way of getting what you wanted by marrying my daughter," Bellamy interrupted.

Linc inhaled slowly in an effort to hold on to his temper. "You might find this hard to believe, but when I married Lori I didn't have a clue that she was from a wealthy family."

"You're wrong, I don't find that hard to believe. I find it *impossible* to believe."

Rather than argue, Linc said, "My point is this. Like you, I'm willing to work hard. I'm ambitious—"

"Of course you're ambitious. That's the reason you married Lori."

"I married your daughter because I'm in love with her. Lori is the best thing that's ever happened to me."

Bellamy snickered loudly.

"All you have against me is that we didn't wait to get your approval before we married. By your own admission, it's unlikely you would've given it, anyway, so it's a moot point, right?"

"As a matter of fact, it isn't," he countered. "And my situation was completely unlike yours. I fell in love with Kate the minute I set eyes on her. When I learned she was from one of the richest families in the state, my heart sank. I was afraid she'd never go out with me."

"But she did." Now it was Linc's turn to interrupt and show his father-in-law that he wasn't completely in the dark. Thanks to Kate, he knew the family history now and had a better grasp of Bellamy's feelings toward him.

"Yes, Kate did accept when I asked her to a school dance."

"You were college juniors."

Bellamy stopped and glared at him. Linc might have squirmed under such scrutiny, but instead he smiled pleasantly and waited for Bellamy to continue.

"I know darn well when we met," he said irritably.

"How long did you date?"

"Five years," Leonard said, and grew wistful. "I worked three jobs and saved every penny I could."

"And Kate's father? How did he take to his daughter dating the son of a welder?"

"Ambrose and I were…friendly." He didn't elaborate beyond that.

"In the end, perhaps, but that's not the way I heard it. Kate said that when you first started seeing each other, her father objected."

"I proved myself to Ambrose and to Kate's mother, as well."

"So she told me."

He ignored the reference to Kate.

"Five years I waited," he said, growing morose. "Five torturous years. By the time I married Kate, I'd purchased my first business complex and was saving for a second."

"I'm hoping for the opportunity to prove myself

to you," Linc said. "The way you proved yourself to Kate's family." He paused for a moment. "Unfortunately, we started off on the wrong foot, but I'm willing to let bygones be bygones if you are."

Bellamy laughed but there was little amusement. "I'll wait five years to make my decision about you, the same way Ambrose did with me. Five years before he gave me permission to marry Kate."

"Fair enough, although I should tell you that Lori and I plan to have a family by then."

He ignored the comment.

"Kate wanted us to elope," Leonard murmured. "But I wouldn't hear of it. I had something to prove to her father first."

"Which you did in spades."

"Don't try to flatter me, young man."

Linc raised both hands. "No flattery intended."

Bellamy relaxed in his chair, hands folded across his middle. "Before he died, Ambrose claimed he couldn't have chosen a better husband for his daughter."

Linc carefully considered his response. "My hope is that one day you'll say the same thing about me."

Leonard scowled. "I doubt that will happen."

Again, Linc didn't feel it was necessary to argue.

Shifting in his chair, Bellamy avoided eye contact. "I take it you've been talking with Kate."

"Not me so much as Lori."

He cleared his throat. "How is she?"

"Lori or Kate?"

"Kate, of course!" he snapped.

Linc enjoyed seeing the other man uncomfortable. "Fine, as far as I can tell."

"I see."

"Have you spoken to her lately?" Linc asked, knowing Bellamy hadn't.

"That's none of your damned business."

"Right." Feeling that the conversation had reached a natural end, Linc stood. "I appreciate your taking the time to meet with me, Mr. Bellamy. I trust we understand each other now."

Bellamy stood, too. "You still have to prove yourself to me, young man."

"I consider that a personal challenge."

"Good, and if you happen to see... Kate in the next while, would you give her my best?"

Linc hesitated on his way out the door. "Doubt me if you will, Mr. Bellamy, but one fact you'll never be able to dispute is that I love your daughter."

"That remains to be seen, doesn't it?" He accompanied Linc to the door and opened it for him.

"I can tell you right now that if Lori and I had a disagreement that caused her to leave me, I would move heaven and earth to get her back."

"Lori isn't nearly as stubborn as her mother," Bellamy barked.

"No, I'd say she's far more like her father in that regard." With those words, Linc walked out of the office.

Thirty-Two

Dad and I painted the baby's bedroom. The text came on Rachel's cell phone.

Rachel texted back. What color?

Yellow.

Nice. Her connection with Jolene was still tenuous, although it had vastly improved in the past month. The process of rethinking their relationship was a slow one, but Rachel remained hopeful. So hopeful that she wanted to go home by the new year. January 1 was a symbolic time to start fresh. She hadn't believed it would happen but now...it seemed possible.

Jolene continued to see the counselor and seemed to be opening up more to Dr. Jenner. When they'd last spoken, Bruce had said it wouldn't be long before the three of them could meet as a family. The fact that Jolene was texting her was a good sign.

No sooner had she pushed the send button than her phone rang. Caller ID identified Jolene.

Rachel answered right away. "Hello, Jolene."

"It's Bruce."

"Hello, Bruce," she amended.

"Can I see you tonight? Are you busy?"

Rachel had just gotten home from work and done little more than hang up her coat. "I don't have anything planned."

"How about dinner?"

"That would be fine." She couldn't think of any reason to refuse; even if she had, she would've accepted his invitation. "Will Jolene be there?"

"No."

Rachel hesitated. "How does she feel about that?"

"I don't know and I don't care. This is about *us,* you and me."

No, it was about Jolene, too. "Let me talk to her, okay?"

"She's in her room."

Why would he try to keep her from speaking to his daughter? "Please put her on the phone."

A few anxious minutes passed before Jolene spoke. "You wanted to talk to me?" Her voice was low.

"Yeah. Your dad asked me to meet him for dinner."

"I know."

"What are you doing?"

"Lindsey and I are going to a movie later. That's what we usually do on Friday nights."

Rachel could hear Bruce in the background. "What if you and I went out instead?" Rachel suggested. The two of them needed to work on their relationship, re-build the trust that had vanished.

"Dad wouldn't like that."

"Probably not," she agreed. "But I think it's more important for you and me to spend time together than for your father and me to have a night out."

Rachel heard Jolene's sigh. "Dad wants to talk to you, though."

"I'll see him after I drop you off at the theater." If he was disappointed about losing out on dinner, she'd bring him something to eat.

"Where do you want to go?" Jolene asked, displaying more enthusiasm now.

"How about Mexican?" Rachel suggested, knowing that was Jolene's favorite, too. She couldn't tolerate spicy food herself at the moment, but she'd order something fairly mild.

"Great!"

For a couple of minutes they chatted about what they'd have. "Could you give the phone back to your father?" Rachel asked when they'd finished.

"Okay."

A moment later Bruce was on the line. "You're having dinner with Jolene and not me?" he demanded.

"I'll drop her off at the movies after dinner and then drive over to the house."

"If that's what you want," he said, but he didn't sound pleased by this unexpected turn of events.

"If it'll put you in a better mood, I'll bring you takeout."

"I doubt anything's going to put me in a good mood," he muttered.

This didn't bode well. "What's the problem?"

He sighed. "More of the same. We'll talk when you're here."

Dinner with Jolene had been an inspiration, Rachel decided a little while later. There was a new level of honesty on the girl's part and traces of the easy affection that used to exist between them. Her stepdaughter talked about seeing the counselor and admitted she'd been jealous of Rachel's relationship with Bruce. Jolene's willingness to acknowledge her role in the separation was a huge step forward.

Jolene looked down at her plate. "Dad wants you to move back home," she said.

"I know." Rachel pushed aside her own half-eaten bowl of tortilla soup.

"Are you going to do it?"

"Probably. I hope so. But not yet."

"Dad wants you home before Christmas, so we can be like a real family."

Rachel didn't comment one way or the other.

"I'm glad you're not moving to Portland, Rachel," Jolene told her.

Rachel, who'd been fishing inside her purse for her wallet, paused and looked up.

"If you left, that would be really hard on Dad…and I would've missed you, too."

This was welcome news. "Do you miss me now?"

Jolene hung her head. "I didn't think I would, but I do. Before you and Dad got married, it was just him and me. But you were always there whenever I wanted to talk or do stuff. Everything changed after the wedding. I didn't like having to share you with him, or share my dad with you. And…well, I felt like the two of you were pushing me aside because all you needed was each other." She gulped noisily. "I… I hated seeing the two of you all lovey-dovey."

Rachel understood why Jolene had reacted the way she had. They'd all contributed to this situation. "Your father wants us to be a family, and I want that, too."

"I know, and now the baby changes everything all

over again. The counselor and I talked about that. It helps that he listens and doesn't tell me I'm bad for feeling like I do."

Rachel nodded. "You have to understand your feelings before you can modify them."

"You sound just like him," Jolene said with a quick grin. Then she grew serious again. "I know that once the baby's born I'm going to love him or her a lot, but right now I don't feel anything except...afraid."

"Afraid of what?"

"Of the baby getting all the attention," she blurted.

"We'll do our very best to see that doesn't happen." Rachel wasn't sure how else to respond. "Before I drive you to the movies, I want you to know I'm grateful you helped your father paint the nursery," she added.

"It was sort of fun."

Smiling, Rachel checked her watch and realized that if they didn't leave within the next few minutes, Jolene would be late meeting Lindsey. She paid their bill and they hurried over to her car.

Jolene was quiet on the drive to the theater. When Rachel pulled up in front of the movie complex, Jolene reached for the door handle. "I'm glad it was just you and me for dinner," she murmured.

"I am, too. I'm also glad you're being honest with me," she said. "The truth can be painful, but I'd rather know exactly what's going on with you."

Jolene opened the car door and stepped outside, then leaned down, saying, "It *is* hard, and Dad doesn't like me telling him how I feel."

"He has to hear it, though, and so do I." She waited

until she saw Jolene connect with her friend before driving off.

Bruce stood by the living room window watching for her when Rachel parked in the driveway. He had the front door open by the time she was out of the car.

As soon as she was inside, Bruce drew her into his arms and simply held her. He didn't speak or make any effort to kiss her; all he did was hold her close. Finally he stepped back and brushed the hair from her face as if to get a better look at her.

"I have missed you so much," he whispered.

Sliding her arms around his waist, Rachel pressed her head against him. His heartbeat pulsed in her ear. How long they stood in the small entry like this was lost on her. It felt so good to be in her husband's arms.

Reluctantly Bruce let her go. "How was dinner with Jolene?"

"We had a nice time."

He frowned slightly as he took her hand and led her into the living room. They sat on the sofa beside each other, still holding hands.

"She didn't say anything to upset you, did she?" Bruce asked.

"No," Rachel reassured him. "Jolene was open and honest, and I appreciated that."

"Did she tell you she wants you to move back home?"

Rachel was uncertain how much of their conversation she should repeat. "She told me she was grateful I'm not moving to Oregon."

His frown darkened. "That's not the same thing."

"No," she said, "but it's progress."

"I want you back here with us. Nothing feels right without you."

"In time," she promised.

He studied her intently. "In time?" he echoed. "How much time?"

Rachel gestured vaguely. In her own mind, she'd set January 1, but that date wasn't firm. Not until she was convinced they were ready would she come back home.

"Before Christmas?"

Unable to respond, she exhaled slowly.

Bruce released her hand and stood, then walked around the coffee table, apparently composing his thoughts. "When will you know?" he asked after a moment.

"Bruce, I can't answer that."

He stared at her long and hard. "Do you *want* to move back here?"

"Of course I do!"

"It doesn't seem like that to me. In fact, I'm beginning to think you and Nate—"

"Don't!" She pointed her index finger at him. "Don't even suggest such a thing. Nate was a good friend when I needed one and I won't have you insinuating there was anything more between us."

"I wouldn't know, would I?"

Bruce's sudden jealousy was ridiculous. Hadn't he said he trusted her? "Look at me, Bruce. Really look at me. I'm married to you and pregnant with your child. Why would Nate be interested in me…especially now?"

"Because you're beautiful and…and wonderful. He was in love with you at one time, and those feelings don't entirely go away. They just don't. Once you commit your heart to someone, it's forever."

"For you it is," she said, knowing that Bruce didn't give his heart easily. He loved deeply, completely, with his whole being. She'd realized that if she married Bruce, it would be a lifetime commitment for both of them.

He shook his head as though he didn't understand what she'd said.

"You commit yourself completely, but not everyone does."

His face fell. "Is this a way of telling me you don't love me anymore?"

"Bruce, how could you even ask a question like that?"

"You said—"

"I said *some* people don't feel as strongly as you do, and Nate is one of them. I wasn't just the woman he wanted to marry—I was the means to an end for him. His father is in politics and Nate is thinking along those lines himself. So he wanted a wife he felt ordinary voters—" she said this a bit sarcastically "—could relate to."

"Okay, fine, but what does that have to do with you moving back home?"

"Absolutely nothing." She could see that this conversation wasn't improving matters. Standing, she reached for her purse. "I think it would be best if I left."

Bruce took her hand again. "Don't, please." He breathed slowly, eyes closed. "Rachel, I'm sorry. What I said about Nate was out of line." Then he opened his eyes, meeting hers, and tugged gently at her hand.

"Let me show you the bedroom Jolene and I painted for the baby."

Rachel went with him to the third bedroom. When Bruce turned on the light, Rachel gasped in surprise. The baby's nursery was totally furnished.

"Jolene helped me pick out the crib and dresser and changing table."

"This is…perfect. All of it."

He walked over to the dresser, opened one of the drawers and pulled out a tiny T-shirt. "Who would've thought anyone could possibly be this small?"

Rachel smiled. Bruce and Jolene had seen to everything.

"When Jolene said you might be leaving the state, I had to do something. Otherwise, I would've gone crazy. So I focused all my energy on preparing for the baby."

Rachel stood in the middle of the bedroom on the round white rug and looked steadily at her husband. "I know this is hard."

"Hard?" he repeated. "You have no idea."

"You're wrong, Bruce. Do you think I wanted to leave you? Do you think it was easy to pack my suitcase and walk out that door? I can assure you, it wasn't. It nearly killed me to walk away from you and Jolene, but I had to because Jolene—"

"She's doing better now. She's been to the counselor and—"

"And she's come a long way," Rachel finished for him. "But she isn't quite ready and if we rush things now, like we did with the wedding last Christmas, we could be making another mistake. I'd rather play it safe and wait."

"We can't cater to Jolene's whims," he insisted. "This is where you belong. You and the baby."

"And this is where I want to be. But I don't feel that giving Jolene time to understand that she has to share you with me and the baby is catering to her."

Shaking his head, Bruce walked out of the bedroom. She knew that wasn't what he'd wanted to hear, but he had no choice other than to accept her decision.

Rachel found him standing in front of the fireplace with one hand braced against the mantel and his back to her. She stood behind him. "I'm sorry, Bruce, but we really can't rush this."

"I thought you'd only be gone a week or two, and *that* seemed unbearable. Now it's three months and you're still saying the time isn't right. I'm afraid it'll never be right again. I feel like I've lost you."

"You haven't," she whispered, placing her hand on his back. "I'm not going anywhere. More than anything I want to be with you and Jolene. I want our baby to be part of our family."

Bruce turned and studied her for a long time before he held out his arms to her. She slipped into his embrace.

"Will you come back and visit again...soon?" he asked.

"Okay. When?"

"Next weekend. Jolene and I are putting up our Christmas tree and I'd like you to be here."

Rachel nodded. That would be especially revealing. She'd be intruding on Christmas traditions that had always been reserved for Jolene and her father. If they could make it through that without Jolene getting upset and territorial, then maybe, just maybe, she could move back before Christmas.

Thirty-Three

Feeling good, Gloria climbed the steps to her second-floor apartment. She'd had lunch out with her mother, who'd recently returned from North Dakota. They'd chatted about Christmas and a couple of family events planned for the season. Gloria loved being included. She felt more like family than at any other time since she'd come into their lives.

As she inserted her key into the lock, Gloria noticed a woman getting out of a car in the parking lot below. She didn't think too much of it, although the blonde looked somewhat familiar.

She was inside and had just hung up her coat when there was a knock at her door. Checking the peephole, Gloria recognized the woman she'd seen in the parking lot.

Seeing her up close Gloria realized why the blonde woman seemed familiar. This was Joni, the woman she'd seen Chad kissing that day at the hospital in Tacoma. The woman he was dating.

Bracing herself for…she didn't know what, Gloria squared her shoulders and opened the door.

The two women stared at each other before Joni's eyes fell to Gloria's midsection.

Gloria didn't feel like uttering a bunch of meaningless niceties. "Would you like to come in and talk?" she asked, getting straight to the point. She wondered how Joni knew her name, how she'd found her address. She decided not to ask. Chad could have told her. Or Joni could have followed him. She could have seen Gloria's name on his cell phone and looked up her address on the internet.

Ultimately it didn't matter.

Joni hesitated briefly before she responded. "Yes, please."

Gloria stepped aside and held the door so the other woman could enter.

Joni looked out at the cove from Gloria's living room window, her hands deep in her coat pockets. "That's a lovely view."

"I think so." She folded her arms, not knowing what to expect. "Would you like something to drink?" She didn't want to be impolite, although she had the distinct feeling this wasn't a social call.

"Just water."

Gloria went into her kitchen, filled a glass and brought it to the living room. Joni had taken a seat on her sofa. When she handed her the tumbler, she saw that the other woman's hand shook visibly.

Joni took a small sip and then wrapped both hands around the glass. "Chad doesn't know I'm here."

Gloria would have been surprised if he had.

"He told me he was stopping by later today. His shift doesn't end until five, so he won't be here until almost six and I thought… I hoped maybe the two of us could talk before he arrived."

"Okay." Gloria tried to look relaxed, but the tension between her shoulders held her rigid.

"I understand Chad told you about us?"

"He did." Gloria didn't elaborate.

"He told me about you, too."

Gloria nodded.

"And about the baby," Joni added.

"He's going to be a good father," Gloria said. He'd been so caring and thoughtful, and made it clear how much he already loved their baby.

"I think so, too." Leaning forward, Joni put her glass on the coffee table, taking a moment to position a coaster first. Now that her hands were free she didn't seem to know what to do with them. She clasped them in her lap and stared down at the carpet.

"Do you love him?" Gloria asked. She wanted to know where the other woman stood before they continued this awkward discussion.

Joni looked up and her eyes filled with tears. "I'm afraid so."

Gloria felt like crying herself, but struggled to maintain her poise. "I'm afraid I do, too," she admitted. Funny that she was so willing to tell the other woman how she felt about Chad, but couldn't tell him. It'd taken her a long time to recognize the depth of her feelings. Now it might be too late.

"You've hurt him badly."

"I wasn't in a good state of mind… I regret what happened."

"The baby, too?" Joni asked.

"No," Gloria answered. "I'll never regret the baby."

Her answer made Joni frown. If anything, it appeared to affect her even more strongly. "I... Chad loves the baby. That's all he talks about when we're together, and I suspect he loves you. No, I don't suspect. I *know* he does."

Gloria wasn't sure how to respond. "Chad and I met when I was at a low point in my life," Gloria began, feeling she needed to explain. "I'd just lost my adoptive parents. I was an only child and they were both only children, so I had no one. No aunts, no uncles, no cousins. No family. We... Chad and I felt an immediate physical attraction and, well..."

Joni looked away and seemed to be studying the view outside the window. The Bremerton shipyard showed clearly in the distance, with the mothballed aircraft carriers and submarines against the backdrop of a metallic gray sky.

Gloria found her own attention wandering and forced herself to focus on her guest. "I'm not sure why you're here," she said.

"I came because I need to know how you feel about Chad."

"Does it matter?"

"Yes, it matters a great deal." Joni picked up the water glass and took one long swallow. "I know what I have to do now." She set the tumbler down in a decisive movement.

"And that is?"

Joni wiped the tears from her cheeks. "I'm ending my relationship with Chad."

"Ending it," Gloria repeated. "But...you just finished telling me that you're in love with him."

"I am...but I know the odds and they aren't in my

favor. Chad loves you and pretty soon you'll give birth to his son. I care enough about him to bow out now."

Gloria had trouble believing the other woman was sincere, but the tears streaking Joni's cheeks told her she meant every word.

"The only thing I need from you," Joni said, then paused to gather her composure. "All I ask is that you love Chad. He's a good man, and a caring physician. I just hope you appreciate what you've got. If you don't, trust me, some other woman's going to do her best to steal him away and that…that other woman might well be me."

Gloria flattened her hand over her heart. "I don't know what to say."

"Then don't say anything. Remember what I told you. If you hurt Chad again, you can't claim I didn't give you fair warning." Reaching for her purse she walked to the door.

Gloria followed her. "You really love him, don't you." It was a statement rather than a question.

"More than either of you will ever realize. It's only because I love him that I'm willing to give him up. Don't think I'm doing this for you or the baby. I'm doing this for Chad. Just make him happy."

"I…will."

The apartment seemed to vibrate with the shock of Joni's declaration. Gloria stood by the door, hardly able to absorb what had happened. Chad loved her. She'd sensed that he did, even though he'd kept his distance, emotional and otherwise, since their last breakup.

Chad showed up at the apartment three hours later. Thankfully that meant she'd had time to think about Joni's visit and analyze her own feelings.

"Hi," he said as he came in. He appeared ill at ease, not quite himself.

"Hi," she returned. They'd planned to go Christmas-tree shopping. Chad didn't want her hauling in a tree and decorating it while she was pregnant. She guessed that his offer was really an excuse to see her again. Not that she was complaining; she welcomed any and every opportunity to be with him.

"Do you mind if we don't go shopping for a tree today?" he asked. "I'm not in the mood."

"That's fine. We can do it another time."

He walked over to the window and stood there, gazing into the night. Lights blinked out at sea.

"Is everything okay?" she asked, wondering if he'd lost a patient. He took any death personally, especially a child's.

"I had a visitor this afternoon," he said.

Gloria walked toward him until they were only a foot or so apart, both staring into the darkness. "Interesting, because I did, too."

"Anyone I know?"

"Joni."

Chad nearly dislocated his neck as he jerked toward her. "*Joni* came to see you?"

Gloria clenched her hands and nodded. "She needed the answer to an important question."

He waited for her to continue.

It took Gloria a moment to find the courage to explain. "She came to ask me if I was in love with you."

"How did you answer her?"

"I told her what happened when I first moved to Cedar Cove—and why."

"I take it you left out the part about falling into bed together a few hours after we met."

"Yes."

His expression grim, he started for the door.

"Where are you going?" she asked.

"I think I've heard everything I need."

"Don't you want to hear my answer?"

"I already have. You gave her an excuse for your behavior and left it at that."

"As a matter of fact, I didn't leave it at that. I answered her question."

"And?" he asked, sounding bored with the entire conversation. He seemed almost eager to escape.

"I told her I'm in love with you." She held herself straight, fearing his reaction. He might laugh in her face and say he didn't believe her. Certainly she hadn't done anything to reveal how she felt about him. On the contrary, she'd tried over and over to prove that she had no affection for him whatsoever.

He said nothing. But he turned around, obviously studying her to see if she was telling the truth.

Gloria met his gaze boldly.

"Joni came to see me, too," he said after a moment.

"I figured she might." The other woman had said she'd be seeing Chad, although Gloria hadn't expected it to be this soon.

"She broke off our relationship."

Gloria felt almost sick to her stomach. "I'm sorry."

"She knew it was over. It was from the minute I learned about the baby. The problem was, I didn't realize it myself, not until recently. I never stopped loving you, Gloria. I tried to get you out of my mind and my heart, but it didn't work. At night you haunted my dreams. During the day I imagined you around every corner. You've had a grip on me from the night we met."

Gloria's experience had been the same, only she hadn't been willing to admit it. "I'm so sorry, Chad," she whispered. She stepped closer and he did, too. "I can't seem to do anything right when it comes to you."

He broke into a smile. "I disagree. You're giving me a son."

"I'm giving you my heart, too."

He opened his arms and she walked into them. He held her tight against him and whispered into her hair, "It took you long enough."

"I don't understand why I fought you so hard."

"I don't, either." He kissed the top of her head and moved down the side of her face, finally reaching her lips.

When Chad pulled away minutes later, Gloria felt weak and breathless. She thought about taking him to her bedroom, which was how these sessions usually ended. But she wouldn't allow that to happen this time. They couldn't let sex confuse the issue or distract them from what they needed to work out.

"Why do you make me feel like this?" She'd never reacted physically to any man the way she did to Chad.

"I don't know. I don't care. Just don't change."

She clung to him, kissing him with tears running down her cheeks.

"I want us to get married," he said.

"Okay." It wasn't the romantic proposal she'd always dreamed of, but it was good enough.

"Soon."

"Okay."

"Before Christmas."

"Christmas?" That was three weeks away!

"You'll move in with me."

All these commands were given between lengthy, heated kisses. "With you…"

"Yes, move in with me," he said again.

"Can't you move here?"

"No."

"My family's here. My job…"

"You have a new family now. You, me and the baby. And there are jobs in Tacoma, too."

"Yes. Maybe, later on, I can join their police force."

He nodded. "Besides, it's not like you'd be that far from Cedar Cove and the McAfees."

"True."

Another kiss, this one even more potent and powerful. "Chad," she whispered, gasping for breath. "I do love you."

"I know. I've always known."

"You did?"

"Yes."

"Oh."

"You talk too much."

"Sorry."

He laughed. "Don't apologize."

"About Joni…"

He kissed her again. "She'll be fine. Another doctor is crazy about her."

He said more things, but everything else was lost on Gloria. All she knew was how happy she felt.

Thirty-Four

Sunday afternoon, Grace and Cliff Harding were stringing Christmas lights around the roofline of the house. Cliff stood on the ladder while Grace held the lights and kept a careful eye on her husband. Beau was on his leash, which was tied to the porch railing.

A car appeared at the head of the long driveway between the two fenced pastures. Cliff's horses, lazily chewing grass, looked up at the vehicle.

"You expecting anyone?" Cliff called down to Grace.

"No." It wasn't unusual for one of her daughters to stop by without phoning first, but neither of them drove an SUV. "It's Beth Morehouse's car," she told him a moment later.

"Has she come for Beau?"

Grace had been adamant from day one that she wouldn't keep the puppy. He gnawed on her shoes and hid Cliff's socks and he was constantly underfoot. Besides, he insisted on following her everywhere she went.

"Grace?" Cliff called again.

"I don't know," she said. They hadn't actually set a date for Beth to pick up the puppy. If she'd found a good home for Beau then…great.

Beth parked in front of the barn, got out and walked over to them.

Cliff climbed down the ladder and placed his arm around Grace's shoulders, as Beau whimpered and barked excitedly.

"Hi, Beth," Grace said. She bent down and scooped up Beau, who'd been busily digging in her flower beds. His paws and face were smeared with dirt.

"How about a glass of eggnog?" Cliff suggested. "Grace and I are ready for a break."

"Thank you. I'd enjoy that, but I can't stay long. I need to get back to the farm. I've got a full crew working. I had a couple of errands not far from here, so I thought I'd see if you were home."

"We're here," Grace said unnecessarily as she led the way into the house. She stopped in the mudroom off the kitchen, washing Beau's face and paws and then her own hands, while Cliff took Beth into the kitchen and pulled out a chair.

"I'll get the eggnog," Cliff said, taking three glasses from the cupboard. "This is Grace's family recipe."

"You make your own?" Beth asked, turning to look at Grace, who came into the room drying her hands.

"It's pretty simple. I'll be happy to pass along the recipe if you'd like."

"Yes, I'd love to have it."

As Cliff carried the filled glasses to the table, Grace brought a plate of sugar cookies she'd baked with her grandchildren the day before.

"I take it you've come for Beau?" Cliff asked.

On hearing his name the puppy raced over to Grace, stretched up on his hind legs and set his front paws on her knees. He stared at her with such love and warmth that she was forced to look away. Almost against her will she petted his head, and when he whined she couldn't resist lifting him onto her lap. He licked her hand, then curled up tightly and went immediately to sleep.

"Well…actually—"

"Do you have a good home for him?" Cliff broke in.

"Not exactly."

"Do you have a home for him, period?" Grace pressed. This was her big fear—that Beth had come to depend on her keeping the puppy. Well, that wasn't going to happen.

"The truth is, no. I don't have a home for Beau."

"No?" Grace cried.

"No," Beth repeated, "and now I have another problem."

Grace and Cliff exchanged a glance. "Concerning Beau?"

"No… Well, yes. Indirectly. As you know, I've rescued a few dogs and done some training, which I enjoy and seem to have a knack for."

That was a real understatement. Not only had Beth been her partner in the library reading program, she'd started training dogs to visit with the sick and elderly.

"Apparently word's gotten around that I take in strays. Several people have brought me animals they've found or can't keep and I do what I can to get them good homes but it's…it's become overwhelming." Her voice cracked.

"What do you mean? Has something happened?"

Grace asked, feeling anxious about Beth's obvious distress.

"Yes. Two totally unrelated and unexpected things. I'm trying to figure out how to handle them. I'm sorry to inflict this on you. It's just that…it's all too much."

"Tell us what's going on," Grace said gently. She'd never seen her friend so disconcerted.

"Well, first, it seems my ex-husband is coming here for Christmas. The girls will be home from college and he asked *them* if it's okay to visit and they really want him to." She sighed. "I could turn him down but not them. Anyway, I talked to the Beldons, and they told me Kent has a reservation at their bed-and-breakfast."

Grace was aware that Beth was divorced but knew nothing of the circumstances.

Cliff sipped his eggnog, leaving the questions to her.

"Is that a problem?" Grace asked.

"Yes," Beth said bluntly. "Kent and I haven't spoken in three years—well, except when it has to do with the girls. Bailey and Sophie are both away at school, so there hasn't been much need for us to communicate."

This was the most personal Beth had ever been, the most she'd revealed about her divorce. Although Grace regarded her as a friend, Beth had never divulged many details about her life prior to Cedar Cove. Grace knew she spent her time with the dogs and running her farm. Her place was one of several in the area that sold live trees. In fact, the address—1225 Christmas Tree Lane—couldn't have been more appropriate.

Cliff finally spoke up. "Why did your daughters arrange this?" he asked her.

"I'm not sure… Kent and I have always been civil.

It wasn't a bitter divorce or anything. We just…grew apart. And like I said, we've had very little to do with each other since."

"I wonder if the girls have some hope of a reconciliation," Grace mused, and didn't realize she'd spoken out loud until she noticed both Cliff and Beth looking at her.

"I think it's a good idea for Kent to stay at the Thyme and Tide," Beth said, not responding to Grace's comment. "Really, I couldn't have him at the house. It…it would be too uncomfortable."

"Yes, I imagine it would."

"When does he arrive?" Grace asked.

"The twenty-third… This is all so unexpected— and then there's Ted."

The only Ted she knew was the local vet. Considering how often Beth visited him, it made sense that they might have struck up a friendship. She gathered that Ted donated some of his services, since Beth was essentially running a charity.

"The vet," she said, confirming Grace's assumption. Beth nervously rubbed her hands together. "We've sort of been…seeing each other. Nothing serious, though."

Grace couldn't keep from smiling. She'd hoped for something like this. Ted Reynolds was about Beth's age, attractive and unfailingly good-humored. Grace and Olivia had half-jokingly commented that Ted's single status was a waste. There weren't *that* many eligible, good-looking men around.

"Then this morning…" Beth stared down at the floor. "Remember how I said people have been bringing me dogs?" She drew in a deep breath. "Well, this morning I got a big surprise on my front porch." She let out her breath. "A basket full of puppies. A *large* basket."

Grace could feel her pulse accelerate. If Beth had to find homes for a whole litter of puppies, then she wouldn't be keen to take Beau.

"How many puppies?" Cliff asked. "And what breed?"

"Ten. And they seem to be black Labs. Or part Lab, anyway."

"*Ten* puppies?"

Beth nodded. "They're adorable, but ten? How am I ever going to find homes for ten puppies?"

"Actually, make that eleven," Grace murmured.

"Eleven?"

"Don't forget, Beau needs a home, too."

"Beau?" Beth's eyes flew to Cliff.

Cliff responded with a shrug.

"Beau," Grace repeated. For some time she'd suspected that Beth and Cliff had joined forces against her, and this proved it. Well, they could scheme all they wanted, but they wouldn't change her mind. The puppy had to go.

"But…but didn't you say something about asking Maryellen and Jon to take Beau?" Beth looked at her with desperate eyes.

"I decided against it," Grace said stiffly.

"The thing is," Cliff explained, "Grace wants Beau to be adopted into a good family. But she doesn't want him going to one of our children for fear she'll see him on a regular basis. Because, unwilling though she is to admit it, she loves that dog."

"That is *not* true," Grace insisted, but her argument

fell on deaf ears. It was all too obvious that neither one believed her.

Even Beau's soft snore sounded more like a snort of disbelief. Seeing him curled up so contentedly on her lap made her realize how far she'd lowered her guard when it came to this puppy.

"Fine. I'll call Maryellen and ask if she'll take Beau for the kids," she said, hoping to dispel their skepticism. "Maybe she'll want him as a Christmas gift."

"Thank you," Beth said gratefully. She finished her eggnog and brought the empty glass to the sink. "And thanks for the drink. I'll wait to hear from you about Beau. I apologize if I vented. It's just that everything seems to be coming down on me at once."

"We completely understand," Cliff assured her.

Beth left a few minutes later and, the second the door closed, Cliff presented Grace with the phone.

"What's that for?"

"Aren't you going to call Maryellen and Jon?" he asked, arching his brows. "The kids are old enough for a puppy. And Jon's certainly expressed an interest in getting a dog."

"I'll do it later," she told him, not ready to make the call. She couldn't understand why it had to be done right away. "In fact, I think it might be better if we waited until just before Christmas."

"I thought you wanted him to go to his new home as soon as possible."

"Maryellen's busy," she said, knowing her daughter's hectic schedule. "I'll call her next week."

"Why wait?" Cliff continued to hold out the phone, which only irritated her.

"Okay, fine, since it's so important to you." She

grabbed the receiver and hit speed dial for her oldest daughter.

Maryellen answered on the first ring. "Hi, Mom."

"Hi." She swallowed hard.

"What's up?"

Grace's hand rested on Beau's head. "Cliff and I have a question for you about the kids' Christmas gift."

"They're each making a detailed list of toys they want Grandma and Grandpa Claus to buy them."

"I'm sure they are." Grace liked nothing better than spoiling her grandchildren. While they were baking cookies yesterday, Katie and Drake had made a point of telling her which toys they were interested in for Christmas.

"What would you think if Cliff and I got them a dog?" There, it was out. Cliff didn't believe she'd do it, but she had and it wasn't nearly as difficult as she'd expected. Beau would love the children and they'd love him just as much. Watching them play with him on Saturday had told her that.

"A dog, Mom, or a puppy?"

"A puppy," she clarified. "I was thinking of letting them have Beau."

"Beau?" Maryellen sounded shocked. "You'd give up Beau?"

"Of course. I never intended to keep him. You knew that." Grace had certainly made her intentions clear to any and all who'd listen.

"Well, yes, but, Mom, he's your dog. He follows you everywhere. He's obviously decided you're his owner."

"He'll adjust," Grace said, refusing to let her resolve waver.

"I suppose he will, but I'm not so sure about you."

"You're being ridiculous." Grace didn't want to argue but found it annoying in the extreme that everyone insisted she wouldn't be able to give up Beau when the time came. They were wrong. Each and every one of them. "Now, do you want him or not? Because if you don't, then…then Cliff and I will take him back to Beth Morehouse."

"In that case, sure, we'll take Beau."

The lump in Grace's throat thickened. "Good. We'll deliver him on Christmas Eve."

Cliff raised his hand, indicating that he wanted to say something.

"Hold on a minute," Grace said, covering the mouthpiece.

"Why wait until Christmas Eve?" he asked. "Tell Maryellen we'll bring him over this afternoon. We're headed that way later, and it would be convenient to drop him off."

"No need to rush, is there?" Grace muttered. "He's a Christmas gift."

"Mom?"

Grace returned the phone to her ear. "Yes?"

"I heard what Cliff just said. It'd be great if you brought him today. He'll distract the kids from all the Christmas madness and keep them occupied."

"Today," Grace repeated slowly. "All right… Why not? We'll stop by this afternoon with Beau and all his paraphernalia." She was astonished by how much stuff they'd managed to accumulate for one small puppy.

"Wonderful. Come anytime."

"Okay. See you later." Grace clicked off the phone and handed it back to Cliff. "I hope you're happy," she lashed out.

He smiled, ignoring her waspish tone.

"Wipe that grin off your face. You think I won't be able to give up Beau? Well, you're in for a surprise, Cliff Harding. Let's go right this minute. The sooner this dog is out of my life, the better." She carefully set Beau on the floor, then hurried from room to room, shoving his chew toys and stuffed animals into a big plastic bag.

Cliff didn't help, which infuriated her. This was *his* brilliant idea, so the least he could do was gather up Beau's food.

"You ready?" she snapped when she'd finished. She had his toys and his bed, plus the new bag of dry puppy food she'd picked up the day before. "Oh, I don't want to forget his vaccination records," she said, retrieving them at the last minute.

Beau climbed obediently into his carrying case. She'd taken him to the library with her a number of times now. The moment he saw the carrier, he knew it meant a trip, and he loved being with Grace no matter where she was going.

Grace zipped up the carrier, and Beau lay down, resting his chin on his paws, perfectly content and trusting.

"We're taking you to a new home," she told him. "A home with children who'll run and play with you. Remember Katie and Drake? They already love you and you can play with them and…and—"

"Okay, let's go." Cliff said, coat on and car keys in hand.

Grace stood there, immobilized.

He waited at the door. "You coming?"

"Yes." She forced herself to take one step and then

another. Each step required effort and determination. The carrier was still on the floor. She'd have to reach down and pick it up...

"Are you coming or not?" Cliff asked.

"I said I was." Bending down, looking at Beau, with his dark eyes focused directly on her, she tried to reassure him and herself that this was for the best. "Katie and Drake are going to love you so much."

Unblinking, Beau stared up at her.

"Grace." Cliff's voice was gentle. "Are you sure this is what you want to do?"

She started to assure him it was and then realized she couldn't. "No," she whispered. "This isn't what I want at all." Just saying the words seemed to free her. "I do love Beau."

"I know. You couldn't help yourself any more than I could." Cliff came over and put his arms around her, hugging her. "Does that mean we can keep him?"

"He isn't Buttercup."

"No, he's not. He's Beau. Our Beau."

"Our Beau," she agreed. She knelt down, opening the zipper to his carrier.

Beau leaped right into her arms.

Thirty-Five

"**I** don't know about this," Lori told Linc as she set a tray of decorated sugar cookies on the coffee table. She rubbed her hands nervously together.

Linc had his own reservations, but was unwilling to say so. "It'll be fine," he said confidently. "Don't worry."

Lori looked unconvinced. "If this is a disaster, then…"

"I'll accept full responsibility."

"No, you won't," she said, coming to stand at his side. "I went along with this idea of yours. So if everything goes down in flames, I'm going down with you."

His wife didn't seem to hold out much hope. Linc, on the other hand, believed there was at least a chance this would all work out.

"Dad might not even come," Lori said, which was one objection she'd raised when Linc had first suggested setting up a meeting between her parents. Kate didn't know her husband would be there, otherwise she'd never have agreed to visit.

"He'll be here."

"But you only talked to him that once. You said it hadn't gone well."

"Your father and I still have some ground to cover, but one thing came through loud and clear. He loves your mother."

"But Mom's already filed for divorce."

"I'm fairly sure your father's heard about that." Linc's biggest concern was that Kate would be upset with Lori. Still, they'd deal with that if they had to.

"Is the coffee ready?" Lori asked, glancing into the kitchen.

"It's finished brewing." So far they hadn't done much entertaining, not counting Mary Jo, Mack and Noelle. They were family, though... Well, so were Kate and Leonard, but that was different. They were *estranged* family, which made everything a lot more tense.

Lori had cleaned the duplex until Linc thought she'd scrub the paint off the walls. The kitchen floor shone so brightly he could almost see his reflection, and the furniture had been polished until it gleamed. They'd put up their small Christmas tree the day before and Lori had spent hours decorating it. She'd done a lovely job, too. Linc had tried to help but Lori wanted to do it her way and he was just as glad to let her.

At precisely two o'clock the doorbell chimed. Lori jumped as though it had caught her completely off guard. She grabbed Linc's forearm. "You answer that, okay?"

He kissed her cheek. "Relax," he whispered.

"Easy for you to say," she muttered back.

Linc went to the door. Leonard stood on the other

side, a frown darkening his face. "What's all this about?"

Linc didn't reply as he opened the screen door. "I see you're right on time."

"I didn't get where I am in the world by showing up late."

"Hi, Daddy." Lori stood in the middle of the room, clenching her hands. "Welcome to our home."

Leonard looked around and whether he approved or disapproved he didn't say.

"Would you care to have a seat?" Linc asked.

"No. You said Kate would be here."

"She will be…" Lori told him. "Unless she recognizes your car and decides to leave."

Bellamy's gaze shot directly to Linc. "She doesn't know I'm coming?"

Linc shook his head. "We figured it would be best not to tell her."

Leonard walked over to the window and gazed out. "She had divorce papers served to me on Friday."

"I know," Lori said.

"She refuses to talk to me and then she has the gall to send a clerk from some Seattle law office to serve me with papers."

"Aren't you grateful for the chance to talk to Mom?"

"Damn straight I am. I'll give her a piece of my mind. We've been married all these years and she can't talk to me? Her own husband?"

"Daddy," Lori interjected sweetly. "I don't think it'll do much good to yell at Mom."

"I'm not yelling," he shouted.

Lori winced and Linc moved to her side. He'd learned a valuable lesson about his father-in-law this past week. Bellamy barked loudly but rarely bit. However, when he did bite, he bit hard. Linc had the teeth marks to prove it.

"Mom doesn't like it when you yell."

"Apparently your mother finds more than the tone of my voice objectionable," Leonard said, lowering his voice.

"Can I get you a cup of coffee?" Linc asked.

"You don't have anything stronger?"

"No, Daddy, we don't, especially this early in the afternoon."

"Then I'll take the coffee." He sat down on the sofa and let his hands fall between his parted knees. "When should we expect your mother?" He glanced at his watch as he asked.

"Any minute," Linc said from the kitchen. Ever the optimist he poured four cups. No sooner had he finished than the doorbell rang again.

Lori answered it this time. Linc remained in the kitchen and watched as Bellamy got to his feet.

Kate stepped inside, stopping abruptly when she saw her husband. "I didn't realize there'd be other guests," she said coldly. She stiffened as if to prepare for a confrontation. "I wondered if that was your car out there, but I didn't think it could be. I can't believe my own daughter would set me up like this."

Lori looked anxious but Leonard ignored the comment. "Hello, Kate."

Linc sighed with relief. At least Leonard wasn't yelling.

She gave a curt nod. "Lenny."

Linc suspected Kate was the only woman in the world who could address Bellamy as "Lenny." He carried the coffee into the living room and handed Leonard and Kate each a mug before returning for the other two. Both declined cream or sugar.

Earlier he'd brought two kitchen chairs into the small living room so there'd be four places to sit. Linc and Lori sat down on the chairs, leaving Kate and Leonard no choice but to take the sofa. They sat as far away from each other as possible.

"Would anyone like a cookie?" Lori asked, hopping to her feet a moment later and picking up the plate.

Kate shook her head.

"None for me." Leonard held up his hand, palm out.

Lori sat down as though disappointed. She turned to Linc, her eyes pleading with him to say or do something to ease the tension in the room.

"I'd like to propose a toast," Linc said.

The two older people regarded him skeptically.

"To marriage." Linc didn't wait for anyone to chime in, but raised the mug to his lips.

They each took a small sip. Linc noticed that Kate clung tightly to the mug handle and focused all her attention on her coffee. Leonard, on the other hand, kept staring at his wife as if he couldn't stop himself.

"I didn't know if you were aware of the fact that I went to see Leonard this week," Linc said to his mother-in-law.

"No," Kate told him. "Lori didn't say anything about it."

"I would have, Mom, but anytime I mentioned Dad you said you didn't want to hear his name again."

"I didn't and I don't," she snapped.

Rather than allow the two women to get sidetracked, Linc continued. "We had a nice, long chat. Isn't that right, Leonard?"

"We, uh, did," Bellamy said.

"What I found interesting was the story of your courtship." Linc paused and waited for some reaction. "Kate had talked about a few things, but Leonard filled in the blanks."

"That was a long time ago," Kate said, then added pointedly, "When I was young and foolish and didn't know any better."

"We were both young and foolish." Leonard took another sip of coffee and set the mug aside.

For just an instant, Linc feared the other man was about to walk out. Fortunately, though, Leonard sat back, crossing his arms over his chest.

"That conversation made me understand why Leonard and I started off on the wrong foot." Linc reached between the two chairs to link hands with Lori. "Leonard worked hard to prove himself to your family, didn't he, Kate?"

"He did," she agreed begrudgingly.

"How many years did it take?"

"A few... I've forgotten now."

Linc would bet that Kate knew, right down to the day.

"Five," Bellamy supplied. "Five long years."

"Lori and I didn't wait," Linc said. "We each saw what we wanted and went for it. That was a mistake, and one I've regretted ever since."

"You regret marrying me?" Lori asked, wide-eyed with shock.

Linc squeezed her hand. "Not for one second."

"Give yourself time," her mother interjected. "The regrets will come."

"Kate," Leonard said in a sharp voice. "Can't you see how much in love these two are? Don't disillusion them."

"What I regret, Lori," Linc said to clarify his statement, "is that I didn't go to your parents and give them an opportunity to meet me first."

"I didn't want you to meet them," Lori insisted.

"I know," Linc said, "but I shouldn't have listened. I should've followed my instincts."

"You didn't want him to meet us?" Kate asked, staring at her daughter, her expression aghast.

"No, I didn't," Lori said again. "I was afraid you'd tell me what bad judgment I'd shown with Geoff and that you couldn't trust me to find a good man and… and I didn't want you to try to talk me out of marrying Linc."

"In other words, you didn't care what we thought," Leonard said. His arms remained crossed.

"I did but…" Lori didn't finish.

"None of that's important now," Linc continued. "Lori and I are married, and while Leonard and I still have some way to go in building a relationship, I believe we've come to terms."

"Have we, now?" Bellamy arched his brows.

"I believe we have," Linc returned calmly. "We just got off to a rocky start."

"You mean you're willing to forgive and forget everything my husband—my soon-to-be-*ex*-husband—did to sabotage you and your business?" Kate asked aggressively.

Linc met his father-in-law's look head-on. "I'm willing to forget it because when I stopped to analyze Leonard's reasoning I could see his point."

Leonard uncrossed his arms and leaned forward.

"This was a man who loved his daughter enough to put an upstart like me to the test. Hopefully I passed."

"Frankly, I don't see why he felt it was necessary to test you at all," Kate said. "All he had to do was read the investigator's report to know you're a good man. But he wouldn't believe that. Oh, no, he was prepared to risk our relationship with our daughter just to prove he was right. He was absolutely convinced you'd turn out to be underhanded."

"*What* investigator's report?" Lori blurted.

Leonard ignored her question. "That was before—"

"Before the two of us talked this week," Linc finished for him.

Leonard nodded.

"Now, while I was talking to Leonard in his office, there was something else I learned. Something that struck me as profound."

Leonard leaned forward again. Kate, too, seemed interested.

"I discovered how much Leonard loves his wife and family. He's an example of the kind of husband and father I want to be to Lori and our children." While that was a stretch, it was close enough to the truth. The essential part of his remark was genuine. Leonard might be arrogant and controlling but at heart he wanted the best for his family. His intense desire to protect them sometimes made him oblivious to *their* desires and to their ability to make independent decisions about their own lives.

Kate glanced at her husband and Leonard met her

eyes. "It's true," he whispered. "I love my wife and my children." As though he couldn't stay seated any longer, he jumped to his feet and began to pace. "I suppose that's why what happened on Friday came as such a shock. I never thought my wife would stop loving me."

"How can you say that?" Kate retorted. "I've loved you all these years, haven't I?"

"A woman who serves her husband with divorce papers brings that into question."

"I hope you got the message."

Leonard turned to face her. "I got it all right, loud and clear. You want to end our marriage and—"

"Mom," Lori said, cutting off her father. "Do you still love Dad?"

"Of course I do. That's a ridiculous question."

"Will you still love me if we're divorced?" Leonard asked.

"Yes, but I'd learn not to."

"Which you seem quite willing to do."

"It'll be difficult, but I'll manage."

"Difficult and completely unnecessary," Linc inserted. He gestured toward Leonard. "When I went to his office, I found a man who's lost and broken without his wife."

Leonard opened his mouth to contradict Linc, but apparently changed his mind.

Kate shook her head. "One thing Lenny's never been is lost or broken. His pride would carry him for the rest of his life before he'd admit he was wrong."

"Is that so?" Leonard challenged, glaring at her.

Kate glared right back at him. "Can you admit you

made a mistake? And that you regret the way you've treated our daughter and her husband?" she demanded.

Leonard looked from his wife to Linc and Lori. "I... might've been a bit hasty in judging Linc's motives for marrying Lori."

"See what I mean?" Kate muttered. "He's still not convinced." She stood and carried her mug into the kitchen. "He hasn't been able to admit he's wrong in over thirty years."

"I...may have jumped to conclusions on occasion," Leonard said in a loud voice.

"There's no need to yell, Lenny. My hearing is perfectly good." She left the kitchen and strode to the front door. "He simply can't acknowledge when he's made a mistake."

Linc frowned at his father-in-law. If Leonard didn't stop Kate now, there was nothing more Linc could do.

Kate was opening the door when Leonard shouted, "Okay! Okay. Fine, if it's so important for me to say the words, then I will. I was wrong about Linc and Lori. There. Are you satisfied?"

Kate froze, one foot inside and the other out the door.

"Did you hear me?" Leonard asked.

Slowly she turned toward her husband, her head held high. "Can you apologize?"

Leonard hesitated and his jaw tightened.

"See what I mean?" Kate murmured.

"All right, all right. Linc, I apologize."

"All is forgotten," Linc said, and they exchanged a handshake.

"Satisfied *now?*" Leonard asked Kate.

Instead of answering, Kate looked at Lori.

Leonard sighed. "Lori, you, too."

"You, too, what?" Kate said.

"I apologize."

"Thank you, Daddy." Lori walked over and gave her father a hug. He returned her hug and held his daughter close.

"Anyone else?" he asked Kate.

She offered him a smile. "That wasn't so difficult, was it?"

Leonard shrugged. "Actually, it was, but now that I've done it, I feel a lot better." He reached out and squeezed Lori's hand. "I love you, you know."

"Yes, Daddy, I know." She leaned forward and kissed his cheek.

"I love your mother, too," he said. "If she leaves me, I—"

"I could be talked into reconsidering," Kate broke in. "Under certain conditions, of course."

Leonard's features softened. "Would it be possible to talk right now, just the two of us?"

Kate smiled and then nodded. "I think that would be very nice."

A few minutes later, they left together, in their own cars. Linc didn't hear where they planned to go but it wouldn't surprise him if it was the family home, where they both belonged.

"Oh, Linc," Lori said, slipping her arms around his waist. "That went so well."

"I knew it would." His in-laws would be fine, and so would he and Lori. Next year and thirty years down the road, he would love Lori as much as Leonard loved Kate.

Thirty-Six

Late on Wednesday afternoon, Will Jefferson and his sister met in the foyer at Stanford Suites. Luckily a unit had become available, and over the weekend they'd moved Charlotte and Ben into their new apartment. The most difficult aspect of the move was deciding which furniture to take. So many pieces were part of their family history.

"Mom," Will had said, "you've got to do something with all this dead relatives' furniture. I have my own stuff—I don't need it."

"I can't just get rid of it," Charlotte had moaned.

In the end, they fit what they could into the small apartment and what didn't fit was doled out to him, Olivia and Justine, with a few pieces held back for James. That appeared to satisfy Charlotte. All she wanted was to know that those antique sofas and chairs and cabinets would be loved and treasured the way they'd once been. They wouldn't have the same sentimental value for him or Olivia, but he wouldn't sell them on eBay, either.

A good portion of what hadn't been allocated was

stored in his basement. It could stay there indefinitely as far as Will was concerned. Being single and without children, he hadn't accumulated a lot of possessions, other than basic furniture, a TV and so on.

"You talked to Mom?" Will asked his sister.

"I did. She's doing all right so far."

"And Ben?"

"Him, too."

The transfer of the house on Eagle Crest was a simple matter of a few signatures and a check. The house was in good shape, especially with the new kitchen. Will was happy to return to his childhood home, and even happier to be helping his mother and Ben. He'd come full circle, he mused. He'd lived in this old house during his childhood, and now he was back. With this move came a sense of rightness, of completion. He'd been away from Cedar Cove for most of his adult life, had faltered and failed. He'd disappointed himself. Moving home had given him a fresh start, a new perspective, a chance to become the man he'd always wanted to be.

Miranda's decision to rent his small apartment might not be the best plan, he thought. Will frowned slightly. He had a real love-hate relationship with his assistant. She was an asset to the gallery and he'd come to rely on her knowledge of art and of the community. Half the time he was convinced she couldn't stand the sight of him. Then she'd do something to throw him off balance—like kissing him. If that wasn't shocking enough, he'd kissed her, too. And enjoyed it.

Miranda Sullivan wasn't like any of the women he'd been attracted to in the past. Including Shirley… In fact, she was their opposite. That confused him, although he tried not to think about it. Sometimes he and Miranda laughed at the same things; sometimes they had lively discussions. Since they were together practically every day, it was understandable that they'd grown comfortable with each other. They'd developed a mutual respect—and maybe even a fondness.

"You're frowning," Olivia commented. "Are you worried about Mom?"

"No... I was thinking about Miranda."

"She's still taking the apartment, isn't she?"

"So she said."

Her sister eyed him warily. "Then why the frown?"

"No real reason," he said, dismissing the question. Actually, he'd prefer not to discuss Miranda. It was hard enough to analyze his own feelings about her, let alone explain them to anyone else.

As soon as Charlotte and Ben walked out of the elevator, their mother broke into a huge grin. "I'm so glad you're both here."

"We arranged this earlier, Mom," Olivia reminded her as she kissed their mother's cheek. She caught Will's eye. Charlotte would continue to suffer memory lapses. The appointment with the gerontologist was in January. Then they'd know the extent of her memory loss and what, if anything, could be done.

"But I was talking about the singing. There'll be home-baked cookies and old-fashioned wassail."

"We have the papers for you to sign, too," Olivia said. "For the sale of the house."

"Yes, yes, I know, but does that need to be done right away?"

"I'd like to get everything in order. It won't take long, I promise." Olivia had her briefcase; fortunately, as a lawyer, she was qualified to handle the paperwork.

Charlotte looked at Ben. "I don't want to be late for the singing."

"Your mother has a lovely voice," Ben told them, as if they weren't aware of their mother's talent.

His mother had often sung him to sleep, and it was a memory Will would always hold dear.

"The choral group's asked me to join them," Charlotte said, obviously pleased by the invitation. "We sing at special events, like this Christmas gathering. We also sing at church services every week right here in the complex."

As promised, it took only a few minutes to sign the necessary papers, which they did in Charlotte and Ben's apartment. When they'd finished, Olivia handed him the house keys.

"So when's moving day for you?" she asked on their way out the door an hour later. They'd stayed for cookies and part of the singing but left during the break. Olivia needed to get home, because she and Jack had a social engagement that evening. And Will was eager to start shifting some of his things over to the house. He wasn't especially happy to be moving in December, but there was no avoiding that. He'd be out of the apartment in time for Miranda to move in January 2.

The gallery was officially closed when Will returned, although Miranda was in the office, going through some invoices.

"How did everything go with Charlotte and Ben?" she asked, looking up from the desk.

"Great. I even got a few cookies out of the deal and listened to some Christmas songs."

She grinned. "Lucky you."

"How was the afternoon?"

"Pretty good. Better than we expected."

"Excellent." Then, before he could change his mind, he asked, "Would you like to go to dinner?"

She scowled at the question. "You…and me?"

"Why not? I just bought a house. I'm in the mood to celebrate."

"And Shirley's married."

At her comment and its implication, Will shook his head. "What does Shirley have to do with anything?"

"Nothing, I suppose, except she's the one you were hot to trot with, not me."

Will couldn't remember the last time he'd heard that expression and it made him laugh.

"You find that amusing?"

"Frankly, yes. *Hot to trot?* Give me a break." As her eyes narrowed, he quickly added, "Don't worry, I'm not looking at you as her replacement."

"I should hope not."

"The dinner invitation wasn't meant as an insult, Miranda. However, considering your reaction, I withdraw the offer."

"That's just fine."

"Good." The woman continually sent him mixed messages. He feared he was guilty of sending a few of those himself.

"I'll be leaving, then."

"Yes. Thanks for staying." He turned his back on her and hung his coat on a peg by the office door. "See you in the morning."

"Right." She reached for her coat and purse and was gone.

"Well, so much for that," Will muttered. It was probably better not to waste time dining out, but he wasn't looking forward to dragging boxes from one residence to another.

Once he'd loaded up his car and driven it over to the house, he spent the next half hour unloading. The house had been professionally cleaned and smelled of pine-scented cleanser. His sister had arranged this on his behalf and Will was grateful.

Standing in the middle of the living room, hands on his hips, he surveyed the home that was so familiar to him. He'd make it his own, he decided, turn it into a place that suited his adult personality.

Walking into the master bedroom that had once belonged to his parents, he had to smile. As a kid a trip into this room usually meant he was due for a walloping by his father. He'd gotten his share of those growing up. Olivia, too, although his father was always much gentler with her than with Will.

He relived other memories as he walked from room to room, feeling a mix of nostalgia and melancholy. This house had been a place of happiness much of the time. His parents had high expectations of him and his sister, but nothing was more important than family. He—

The doorbell chimed, surprising him. He suspected it might be one of the neighbors, coming to check in. No doubt his mother had told everyone in the vicinity that he'd be taking up residence.

He discovered Miranda Sullivan on the porch. She held a bucket of fried chicken in her hand and looked more than a little uncomfortable. "I brought you dinner," she said, shoving the bucket at him.

"You didn't need to do that." Her thoughtfulness caught him unawares.

"I know."

She was about to leave when Will stopped her. "Would you care to join me?"

She hesitated and then nodded. "Sure."

"I'm afraid I don't have much furniture in the house yet."

She didn't appear to mind. "I've eaten sitting on the ground more than once in my life."

"Me, too." Although Will couldn't remember the last time. A picnic, probably, and that would've been years ago. He didn't have much interest in that sort of thing.

They sat in front of the gas fireplace. Will turned it on with the flick of a switch. That was a good thing because he doubted he was capable of building a fire. A lot of years had passed since he was a Boy Scout.

The chicken was delicious. Will didn't make a habit of eating fried foods so this was a rare treat. The biscuits were good, too, especially drizzled with honey.

"What prompted this?" he asked, setting a leg bone aside and reaching for a second piece.

"I don't know… I was halfway home and trying to figure out what I should do for dinner when—"

"When you realized how foolish you'd been to turn down an invitation for a meal with me," Will finished for her.

"No. I thought about you hauling those boxes to the house by yourself and…" She paused and shook her head. "I probably shouldn't have come."

"I'm glad you did." And to his astonishment he meant it. Until the doorbell rang, Will had been wrapped up in memories of his childhood and starkly aware that he was alone. His mother had Ben, plus him and his sister. Olivia had Jack, her two children and a handful of grandkids. The reminder that he was by himself, in his sixties and without a family of his own, had left a hollow ache in the pit of his stomach.

Miranda polished off a piece of chicken and wiped the grease from her hands with a paper napkin.

"I should be completely moved within the next week," Will said, making small talk.

"So you'll be settled before Christmas."

"That's the idea. You can start bringing your stuff over to the apartment anytime after that."

She nodded.

"What about Christmas?" he asked, knowing she didn't have children.

"What about it?"

"What are your plans?"

"I… I'm not sure yet. Shirley and her kids are going to California to be with Larry." She seemed to be watching him for a reaction.

"That'll be nice for them," he said carefully. "It'll be their first Christmas together."

"It will, and I'm pleased for Shirley, really pleased. She found the right man for her and…"

He'd be alone at Christmas. Olivia's family would include him, but much as he loved his sister and Justine and everyone, he couldn't help feeling like an obligatory guest. Uncle Will, who had nowhere else to go.

"And," Miranda said, interrupting his thoughts, "well, this is totally selfish of me to admit."

"Oh, go ahead," Will urged. He'd begun to feel that this impromptu dinner was a turning point in his relationship with Miranda.

"Well, Shirley almost always had me over for Christmas."

"So you'll be alone this year."

"I have other friends," she said defensively.

"Of course you do. But as it happens, I'll be alone, as well."

"You?" Miranda seemed stunned at the prospect. "What about Olivia?"

"She'll invite me for dinner," he said. "But I feel like I'm intruding on her family time." They'd all make an effort to involve him in their activities. Yet it wasn't the same as having a family of his own, *belonging* to someone. Even during the worst years of his marriage, he'd felt as though he belonged.

"I know what you mean," Miranda said in a low voice.

She glanced down at the carpet, and Will realized she wasn't just saying that, she really *did* understand how he felt, because she'd experienced the same feeling herself.

"I don't suppose," he began. "No, never mind."

"Suppose what?" Miranda asked.

"You're alone. I'm alone." He paused, waiting for a sharp retort, a negative comment. When he saw none, Will continued. "Would you like to get together here at the house, make dinner together, share Christmas Day?"

"The two of us?" she asked, as if she couldn't quite believe it.

"Well, yes. If you're game, I am, too."

"Turkey, stuffing, the whole nine yards?"

"Whatever you want." He'd never been much good in the kitchen but he was willing to give it a try.

She seemed to be mulling over the idea. "I think we could do that," she finally said.

"Then it's a date. You and me and Christmas."

"You and me and Christmas," Miranda said with a smile.

Thirty-Seven

"Remember, Dad, when we used to string popcorn and put it around the Christmas tree?" Jolene asked, her voice elevated with excitement as she climbed into the front seat of the car.

"I remember that you ate a lot more popcorn than you managed to thread." Smiling, Bruce slid into the driver's seat and turned on the ignition.

Jolene giggled. "Where are we going to buy the tree?"

"Where else? On Christmas Tree Lane." That was their tradition. "But first, we're meeting Rachel."

"We are?" Jolene instantly sobered.

"We invited her, remember?"

"Yeah, sort of. To decorate. But it's always just been the two of us when we went to get the tree."

Bruce did his best not to show how disappointed he was in her response. "I want her to come with us. Can you deal with that?"

"I guess." But she let it be known that she wasn't completely happy.

It was times like these that made Bruce want to groan with frustration. Just when it seemed they were making progress, something would happen to remind him how far they still had to go.

He drove to the terminal, where the foot ferry from Bremerton docked. Rachel had texted him earlier to say she was taking the eleven o'clock ferry. He'd texted back that he'd be there, with Jolene, to pick her up. Then they'd drive to the Christmas tree farm and select their tree. Once they got home, they'd set it up; after that, they'd spend the rest of the afternoon decorating it. As a family.

Jolene had received a special ornament every year since her birth. Stephanie had started that tradition, and he'd continued it. Each year it was those ornaments that Bruce brought up from the basement first. With great ceremony Jolene would place them on the tree.

As soon as he'd mentioned that Rachel would be with them, Jolene had grabbed her cell phone and started texting.

"Who're you texting?" he asked, glancing over at her in the passenger seat.

"Carrie."

"Do I know Carrie?"

"Dad, she was over yesterday."

"She was?" Bruce didn't remember seeing anyone at the house.

"Well, she might've left before you got home from work."

"Oh." Bruce wasn't keen on his thirteen-year-old daughter coming home to an empty house. He'd felt much better about it when Rachel lived with them. For one thing, Rachel had a day off during the week; for another, she was diligent about keeping in touch with Jolene after school. But there was no alternative as long as Rachel lived in Bremerton.

She was standing by the totem pole when Bruce pulled up. He waited for Jolene to get out of the front seat and go to the back. Instead, she stayed where she was.

"Jolene," he said impatiently. "Give Rachel that seat."

Rachel had already opened the rear door and slipped inside. "It's okay," she murmured.

She didn't sound like herself but before Bruce could say anything, Jolene said, "Rachel doesn't care."

Bruce's happy mood was quickly whirling downward, but he had to choose his battles carefully and there were bigger ones to wage. So he dropped the issue.

He turned on the radio, which played Christmas music, and soon both he and Jolene were humming along. Rachel didn't join in. He glanced into the backseat and she offered him a tentative smile, which he returned. Still, he sensed that something wasn't right.

When they arrived at Beth Morehouse's farm on Christmas Tree Lane, Jolene was the first one out of the car. Beth served hot cocoa while her crew directed customers to various areas, depending on the type and size of Christmas tree they wanted. His daughter got in line for her cup of cocoa.

When Bruce came around to open Rachel's door, she had her hands over her stomach and was deathly pale.

"Are you okay?" he asked anxiously.

She gave him the same tentative smile she had earlier. "I think so. I had a bad night, but I'm a little better this morning."

"What's wrong?" He was growing concerned.

"Nothing... I'm just under the weather."

"You should've stayed home," he said, crouching beside the car.

"Is everything all right, Dad?" Jolene raised a cup of hot cocoa at him.

"I wanted to be with you and Jolene," Rachel said. "I've been looking forward to this all week. I've never cut my own tree before. It sounds like fun."

"Dad!" Jolene again.

Bruce glanced over his shoulder.

"You go ahead," Rachel said. "I'll stay in the car."

Reluctantly he stood. He didn't feel good about leaving her alone, especially if she was ill. The farm took up quite a few acres and he could be away as long as an hour, searching for the perfect tree.

Jolene joined him and looked anxiously at Rachel. "You okay?"

"I'll be fine in a little while. You two go on."

"You sure?" Jolene asked. "You can come, really. I don't mind."

Rachel smiled. "I appreciate it, but I'm just not feeling that well."

"I don't think we should leave you," Bruce said.

"I'll be fine," Rachel insisted again. "I'll be here when you get back. Now go."

Still, Bruce hesitated, worried about her pale, clammy skin and obvious discomfort. In the end he and Jolene went in search of a tree, only his heart wasn't in it. Halfway up the hill, he stopped.

"Dad?"

"I'm going back."

"Do we have to?" Jolene asked, clearly disappointed.

"Rachel is my wife," he told his daughter. "There's something wrong. I can feel it. You can go on by yourself if you want to. I'm taking Rachel to the doctor or the hospital or whatever she needs. I'm sorry our day got ruined, but Rachel's more important than a Christmas tree."

Jolene nodded, biting her bottom lip.

"Do you want to come with me?"

"I don't know yet." She turned back and walked over to another tree.

Bruce wasn't waiting. He headed toward the road, moving quickly. The scent of cut evergreens mingled with the soft mist falling, but he barely noticed. By the time he reached the parking lot he was running. At some point he'd realized that Jolene was right behind him.

Once he was at the car, he jerked open the back door to find Rachel curled up in the backseat. She looked at him and sobbed. "I think you'd better get me to the hospital."

"Is it the baby?" Jolene asked over his shoulder, her voice frightened.

Rachel didn't answer, and Bruce saw tears streaking her face. A sense of urgency filled him as he raced around the car and jumped into the front seat. Jolene threw herself in beside him and slammed the door.

"Hurry, Dad!" she cried. "Please hurry."

How they made it to the Bremerton hospital without causing an accident or getting a ticket, Bruce didn't know. He roared to a stop at the emergency entrance and dashed inside.

"My wife is pregnant and needs help!"

A minute later, Rachel was whisked onto a stretcher and into an exam room, where she was seen by a physician.

"Is the baby going to be okay?" Jolene asked him, sounding as worried as Bruce.

He paced the waiting area restlessly, wondering how long this would take. "I don't know. I just don't know."

"Oh, Daddy, I'm so scared."

He was, too, but for his daughter's sake tried to act confident and composed.

An eternity passed before the doctor came into the waiting room and called for Bruce. Jolene went with him.

"Your wife has food poisoning," the doctor explained. "As far as we can tell, it was something she ate yesterday afternoon. It isn't serious but she's badly dehydrated. We'd like to keep her overnight."

"And the baby?"

"Your child appears to be fine."

"Thank God." Bruce closed his eyes, so grateful for his wife's health and his child's that it felt as if his knees might go out from under him. He slumped into a chair.

Jolene sat down next to him. "Why did Rachel come with us if she was sick?" she asked.

Bruce placed his arm around his daughter's shoulders. "Because she wanted to be with us—to do something together as a family. Rachel never had this opportunity as a child. Her aunt didn't ever buy a tree. At Christmas she gave Rachel money and had her buy her own gift."

Jolene dropped her head. "I'm sorry, Dad."

"I know."

"Can I get Rachel some flowers and apologize?"

Bruce squeezed her shoulders. "Flowers are a nice idea, but what's more important to Rachel, and to me, is bringing her and the baby into our family. That's where they belong."

Jolene considered this over for a moment and then nodded. "At first, when I was afraid Rachel was in labor, I thought she might lose the baby. I'm looking forward to when the baby comes and I felt sick inside because I know it's too early."

"We could have lost more than the baby," he said, pressing his cheek against Jolene's hair. "We could have lost Rachel."

She covered her face with both hands and started to weep. Her shoulders heaved convulsively as she buried her face in Bruce's side and gave way to her tears. "I'm so sorry," she gulped. "So sorry."

He patted her back and whispered soothing words. He'd give anything to make things right between his wife and his daughter. Counseling had helped a little, but for every step forward they seemed to take two back.

After several minutes of comforting Jolene, Bruce stood and approached the nurses' station. "Can I see my wife?" he asked.

"Yes, I'll take you and your daughter back. We're getting her a bed right now. It shouldn't be long."

"Thank you." Bruce and Jolene followed the woman to a cubicle, where Rachel lay on a gurney. She was on her side, doubled up in almost the same position as she'd been in the backseat of the car. An IV bottle was attached to her arm.

"Rachel," Jolene whispered, touching her hand.

Rachel's eyes fluttered open. "Hi," she whispered back, and attempted a smile.

"The doc says they want to keep you overnight," Bruce said, putting his hand on her forehead, needing to touch her, needing reassurance that she was going to be all right. Rachel and their baby.

"I'm sorry I ruined your Christmas tree outing."

"We'll go again when you're not so sick, okay?" Jolene said as if talking to a child.

Rachel smiled again. "I'll help decorate the tree, too."

"If you want, you can put up my special ornaments with me. I want to get one for the baby next year. One that says Baby's First Christmas—just like the ornament my mom got for me."

"That can be your Christmas gift for your little sister."

"I'm getting a sister!" Jolene grinned at Bruce. "I was hoping for a sister!"

"A girl?" Bruce said. This was news to him. "I thought you wanted to be surprised."

"I thought I did, too, but I asked at my last ultrasound. I was saving the news until Christmas. This is close enough."

"A girl," Bruce repeated in awe. "Rachel, junior."

"Rachel, junior," Jolene muttered, shaking her head. "No way are you going to stick my sister with a name like Junior."

"What do you suggest?" Rachel asked.

"Madison," Jolene said without a pause.

"Not *my* daughter," Bruce said just as quickly.

"I've always liked the name Corinne," Rachel told them both.

"Corinne Rachel," Bruce mused. "That's a name I could live with."

"Can you come home for Christmas?" Jolene asked. "You need someone to look after you."

"Do I?" Rachel murmured.

Bruce noticed the way they locked eyes, reading each other.

"Yes, and I want to do it, too. Dad needs you, and so does Baby Corinne."

"What about you?" Rachel asked.

Tears formed in Jolene's eyes and ran down her face. She nodded. "I need you most of all."

Rachel held open her arms and Jolene went into them, sliding her own around Rachel's neck and sobbing loudly. "I've missed you so much."

"I've missed you, too," Rachel whispered.

The nurse came into the cubicle. "Hey, what's going on here? Is everyone okay?"

"Never better." Bruce smiled. And once they brought Rachel home, it would be a hundred percent true.

"We can take your wife to her room now," the nurse said.

Jolene released Rachel and held on to her hand as they wheeled the gurney out of the cubicle and down the hospital corridor. As they rounded the corner, Rachel's eyes met Bruce's.

Christmas was two weeks away. They would be together as a family. And when Rachel was out of the hospital, when she'd regained her strength, they'd return to Christmas Tree Lane and cut down that evergreen and have a real family Christmas. He and Rachel, Jolene and…and their daughter-to-be.

* * * * *

Don't miss the final story in the Cedar Cove series,
1225 Christmas Tree Lane.

Join the people of your favorite small town to
find out who'll be getting Beth's rescued puppies,
and discover how things go with her
ex-husband—and Ted the vet.

1225 Christmas Tree Lane
by Debbie Macomber
Available now from MIRA Books.

"Next time is my treat," Melissa said.

"I'll look forward to it," he answered. Eli's words had
a ring of sincerity that again warmed her far more than it
should.

They walked outside into a lovely April night, rich
with the scent of the ocean, with flowers, with new life.

She could hear the low murmur of the waves along
with the constant coastal wind that rustled the new leaves
of the trees next to the restaurant.

Oh, she had missed it here. She had lived in many
beautiful, exotic places since she'd left Cannon Beach,
but none of them had been the same. She had lived
here longer than anywhere, from the age of thirteen to
eighteen. It was home to her.

"That was lovely," he said when they reached
their respective vehicles in the parking lot. "The most

enjoyable meal I've had in a long time. Thank you for inviting me."

"You're welcome. Thank you for insisting on paying for it."

"Yeah. Thanks," Skye said cheerfully. "It was fun."

Melissa couldn't make a habit of it. She was far too drawn to him.

"Have a good evening, Eli."

Their gazes met, and those shadows prompted her to do something completely uncharacteristic. She stood on tiptoe and kissed his cheek, intending it only as a warm, friendly, welcome-home kind of gesture.

He smelled delicious, of soap and male skin, and it was all she could do not to stand there and inhale.

She forced herself to ease away, regretting the impulse with every passing moment.

"Good night, Melissa. Skye, it was a pleasure. Persuade your mom to take you to my dad's place sometime soon so you can practice your pool game."

"I will! Thanks."

"See you Monday," she said.

"Put some ice on that wrist," he answered, his voice gruff.

She nodded and ushered her daughter to her vehicle. Though her wrist still ached, the injury seemed a lifetime ago.

Don't miss
A Soldier's Return *by RaeAnne Thayne,*
available February 2019 wherever
Harlequin® Special Edition books and ebooks are sold.

www.Harlequin.com

#1 *New York Times* Bestselling Author
DEBBIE MACOMBER

"Dear Reader,
Guess what? I'm falling in love!
With Mack McAfee..."

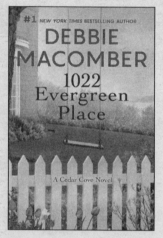

My baby daughter, Noelle, and I have been living next door to Mack since the spring. I'm still a little wary about our relationship, because I haven't always made good decisions when it comes to men. My baby's father, David Rhodes, is a testament to that. I'm so worried he might sue for custody.

In the meantime, the World War II letters I found are a wonderful distraction. Both Mack and I are trying to learn what happened to the soldier who wrote them and the woman he loved.

Come by sometime for a glass of iced tea and I'll show you the letters. Plus I'll tell you the latest about Grace and Olivia, my brother Linc and his wife, Lori, and all our other mutual friends!

Available now wherever books are sold!

DEBBIE MACOMBER

33019	ALASKA HOME	___	$7.99 U.S.	___	$9.99 CAN.
32918	AN ENGAGEMENT IN SEATTLE	___	$7.99 U.S.	___	$9.99 CAN.
32798	ORCHARD VALLEY GROOMS	___	$7.99 U.S.	___	$9.99 CAN.
31894	ALWAYS DAKOTA	___	$7.99 U.S.	___	$9.99 CAN.
31888	DAKOTA HOME	___	$7.99 U.S.	___	$9.99 CAN.
31883	DAKOTA BORN	___	$7.99 U.S.	___	$9.99 CAN.
31868	COUNTRY BRIDE	___	$7.99 U.S.	___	$9.99 CAN.
31864	THE MANNING GROOMS	___	$7.99 U.S.	___	$9.99 CAN.
31860	THE MANNING BRIDES	___	$7.99 U.S.	___	$9.99 CAN.
31829	TRADING CHRISTMAS	___	$7.99 U.S.	___	$9.99 CAN.
31580	MARRIAGE BETWEEN FRIENDS	___	$7.99 U.S.	___	$8.99 CAN.
31551	A REAL PRINCE	___	$7.99 U.S.	___	$8.99 CAN.
31441	HEART OF TEXAS VOLUME 2	___	$7.99 U.S.	___	$8.99 CAN.
31413	LOVE IN PLAIN SIGHT	___	$7.99 U.S.	___	$9.99 CAN.
31341	THE UNEXPECTED HUSBAND	___	$7.99 U.S.	___	$9.99 CAN.
31325	A TURN IN THE ROAD	___	$7.99 U.S.	___	$9.99 CAN.
31917	BECAUSE IT'S CHRISTMAS	___	$7.99 U.S.	___	$9.99 CAN.
31535	PROMISE TEXAS	___	$7.99 U.S.	___	$8.99 CAN.
33018	ALASKA NIGHTS	___	$7.99 U.S.	___	$9.99 CAN.
31624	ON A CLEAR DAY	___	$7.99 U.S.	___	$8.99 CAN.
31903	WEDDING DREAMS	___	$7.99 U.S.	___	$9.99 CAN.
31907	THE KNITTING DIARIES	___	$7.99 U.S.	___	$9.99 CAN.
31926	THE SOONER THE BETTER	___	$7.99 U.S.	___	$9.99 CAN

(limited quantities available)

TOTAL AMOUNT	$ _____
POSTAGE & HANDLING	$ _____
($1.00 for 1 book, 50¢ for each additional)	
APPLICABLE TAXES*	$ _____
TOTAL PAYABLE	$ _____

(check or money order—please do not send cash)

To order, complete this form and send it, along with a check or money order for the total above, payable to MIRA Books, to: **In the U.S.:** 3010 Walden Avenue, P.O. Box 9077, Buffalo, NY 14269-9077; **In Canada:** P.O. Box 636, Fort Erie, Ontario, L2A 5X3.

Name: _____

Address: _____ City: _____

State/Prov.: _____ Zip/Postal Code: _____

Account Number (if applicable): _____
075 CSAS

*New York residents remit applicable sales taxes.
*Canadian residents remit applicable GST and provincial taxes.

Harlequin.com

MDM1217BL